Subtraction

By

Sheila Deeth

An Ink-Filled Stories Publication

First published 2017 by Indigo Sea Press

First IFS print edition 2018
First IFS ebook edition 2018

Cover design by Sheila Deeth

Dedication

With special thanks to my special critiquers, Amelia, Beki, Judy and Karin, who did their level best to keep my writing American and sane. Any insanity, inconsistency, or excessive Englishness is entirely my own fault. Many thanks also to all my friends at the Writers' Mill, whose group critiques are always invaluable, and to my Coffee Break friends for their enthusiastic prayers and encouragement. I especially want to thank my mum who becomes a member of both Coffee Break and the Writers' Mill whenever she visits from England. But most of all I thank God for reminding me there will always be good in the world, in people, and in merciful forgiveness.

OTHER TITLES BY SHEILA DEETH
IN THE MATHEMAFICTION SERIES

- **Divide by Zero**—*a community divided by tragedy*
- **Infinite Sum**—*a woman close to breaking point*
- **Subtraction**—*the man who wasn't there to help*

ABOUT THE AUTHOR

Sheila Deeth is an English American, Catholic Protestant, mathematician writer, with a math degree from Cambridge University England and a life-long love of words. Her works include the Mathemafiction series of contemporary novels, science fiction and fantasy novellas, picture books, animal stories, and the Five-Minute Bible-Story Series. Connect with her online at www.sheiladeeth.com

SUBTRACTION

Readers say:

"Mystical and lyrical, Sheila Deeth's latest novel offers redemption, forgiveness, love and more than a dash of suspense. It is a worthy read that will both move and sustain you." *~G. Davies Jandrey*

"A powerful, mystical story of renewal and redemption." *~Donna Fletcher Crow*

"This mixed-genre 'mathemafiction' novel kept me up past midnight to finish and find out how the story ends." *~Jean Harkin*

If only the world weren't such a cruel place. If only the small town of Paradise hadn't allowed so cruel a crime. But if onlys are just a door to more pain. How do you forgive the world, and how do you move on?

Andrew Callaghan suspects his student Amy, who has gone missing, may have been murdered. With the help of Stella DeMaris, the school's new art instructor, he sets off on a road trip to find what happened to her. Tortured by memories of his own dead daughter, Andrew sees Amy's body in every passing shadow, while Stella, ever hopeful, sees cats. But where will the cats lead them, and will Amy be dead or alive at the end of the trail?

Subtraction

Part 1

~1~

A ndrew marched to the front of the classroom, ready for the afternoon's lesson. Same kids. New year. Same topic. New hope for success. He coughed lightly in the back of his throat. "Now children." Coughed again to strengthen his voice. "Today I will teach you to subtract." Then he pondered whether addressing a middle-grade, special-needs audience as *children* might be deemed insulting. But his mind seemed devoid of alternative words, so he let himself sink into more familiar mathematical terms. "Subtract," he repeated, with coughing confidence and a frowning hint at certainty… *To subtract, take away, abuse, discard, destroy…*

Youthful faces, ranging from blandly accusing to accusingly bland, stared back at him. They clearly couldn't care less if Andrew frowned or cried. Faint groans arose, inspiring that familiar tightness in his chest. But these students, subtracted from their regular classes, weren't rejects he reminded himself. Not yet. Andrew wasn't going to fail them if he could help it.

"Sub-trac-tion." He spoke the syllables carefully now, and wrote the word with a purple flourish on the whiteboard. The pen squeaked louder than the nervous quiver of his throat while he half-turned to check the students were still seated, and to see who was laughing.

Class Clown Zeke bounced on his chair in the middle of the room. "Is that like action that's not acting right?" Beetled eyebrows wiggled, mimicking the rolling motion of the tall boy's limbs.

"Nah," groaned the one known as Jonah the Whale, squashed like a deflated football in his seat near the door. The force of Jonah's voice blew strands of sandy hair up like a helmet as he clawed his armpits with stubby fists. "*Sub*-track. It's like acting subhuman, like what *you* do." He pointed to the clown.

Andrew rapped a ruler on the desk. "No teasing in class," he insisted. Then he repeated, slowly, solemnly—fiercely driving down the whimper of his new-year apprehension— "We're studying subtraction."

For a moment the deep, cultured, teacherly tone of his voice distracted him. *Who am I?* Andrew wondered, and *who am I to teach them?* But he couldn't pause to evaluate the answer. "Subtraction is sometimes called *taking away.*" *And what has been taken from me?*

Andrew's gaze took in his students' shapes, positions, posture, provocation and more. Meanwhile he pondered what these middle-school rejects might make of the phrase, *taken away*—they who'd never been given enough in the first place? He coughed at an awkward inhalation of dry-erase solvent then began to walk around the room.

Fair-haired Amy sat near clownish Zeke. She wrapped thin, freckled arms around the treasures on her desk. Her lips were parted as she muttered under her breath, "Not take away. Not take away." The delicate voice reminded Andrew of the tick from an antique clock, from an antique home, from a life long lost and gone. He leaned forward to offer comfort to the child. Doll-eyes blinked, but she didn't look at him. Her gaze was fixed on some curious infinity. Her face, pink-cheeked and porcelain smooth, bore only the tiniest hint of unlikely concern, as if she were looking through a window at someone else's lesson.

Tick. The classroom clock counted seconds, minutes and hours but showed, as ever, a slightly skewed rendition of the time.

Andrew sighed. "Ah, Amy. Nobody's going to take your treasures away."

Three safety pins from a diaper set were arrayed in the middle of her desk. Buttons in multiple colors formed jagged hills beside them. A pencil, with rainbow-colored point, was neatly positioned with a pad of rainbow notelets between Amy's musically drumming fingers.

"First we add things," Andrew said, raising his voice as he marched toward the front of the room again. "Then we have a collection"—*a collection of buttons perhaps,* and did Amy know how many were lying there?—"and then we…"

"Takeaway! Like burgers!" brayed Julie's rusty voice of triumph behind him.

Andrew turned. "Well, not quite, Julie." The classroom's focus splintered.

"I want my takeaway. I want." Loud thumps on a desk accompanied Tom's voice. Angry Tom, he was in his fourth special school for misbehavior and might soon be dropped entirely unless teachers like Andrew could win him over. But chaos rumbled over other desks as well.

Andrew tensed, needing a clearer answer before things fell apart. Then a bubble of inspiration twisted his frown to a smile. This was why he did this job. This was why he loved it.

"Yes. Yes. And yes." Andrew stood behind his desk and faced the class with triumph, pumping his arm like a teenager. His tones turned increasingly valiant as his gaze slid across the sea of puzzled faces. "You're right." He pointed to Julie. "Tom's right… And you… and you… Let's order some takeaway, just as soon as we've got this done." Then he started to count, pointing to each student in turn. "Let's order… seven, eight, nine burgers."

"I want nuggets!"

"Nine orders of food." Andrew corrected himself. "And I'll be in charge of passing them around."

He had their attention now, or burgers and fries did anyway.

"I'll set the box of nine meals down on my desk, right here. And when I've handed one meal to Jonah… you tell me… how many more will be in the box?"

"Me first," shouted Tom, ignoring the question. But others students waved fingers to count and tried to work it out.

Shy Amy's head hung down as she continued to play with the buttons on her desk. Her fingers wove a hypnotically distracting pattern. *Don't look at her. Don't watch. You'll make her mad.* But blue eyes focused suddenly on Andrew, cold as winter, distant as spring. Red-button lips pursed into words, spoken out in a quietly determined, uninflected voice. "Eight."

"Very good, Amy. So then I give one meal to Amy." Andrew waved a hand with the imaginary parcel. "Just wait a minute, Tom. And how many are left?"

Middle-grade minds needed a pause before answering, "Seven?"

"Then to Tom... "

"Hurray!"

"Six... five... four..."

The students completed the sequence at last, and Andrew announced in triumph, "That's subtraction, class. When we take something out of the box, we've subtracted it."

Faces shone back at him in that pause within the triangle of trouble, food and learning. Then Jonah the Whale bounced his chair, legs creaking scarily. "So, when can we eat?"

Whispers rustled while Tom's bleak voice rang out, combining threat and doubt. "Order it! I'm hungry."

Andrew took out his phone. "What's the number? Anyone know?"

Then food's calm promise brought peace, giving Andrew a chance to spend more time in *quiet* discussion with Tom. He said all the right words, warning of all the right consequences, taking into account the rightness of Tom's desire for burgers, and adding a reminder that the whole class needed to learn. *Subtract a little bad behavior here and there, don't shout too loud, look like you're taking notice, and all will be well.*

Meanwhile Shy Amy drew with her rainbow pencil, plus and minus signs intertwined with whispering shades and colors on the rainbow page. *Take away her autism, and who might Amy be then?*

Take away Amelia's *autism...?*

Voices from the past ushered a host of memories in Andrew's mind. Amelia was the girl long gone, child of a house whose antique, ticking clock kept perfect time. Amelia was lost under green of trees and the pricking of tangled branches in a place called Paradise—Amelia, Andrew's parents, Carl… all subtracted like numbers from Andrew's page. He let his gaze drift to the window, hoping the sky's bright tones would wash his palette clean again. But *who-am-I* doubts combined with the whispering of leaves and chatter of children. He couldn't forget. That long slow walk between Tom's desk and the classroom door could take a lifetime, waiting for delivery's knock.

*****

Her neighbors' cat died when she was twelve. It was called Coal, a beautiful thing. Her mother told her not to look, but Evie peeked anyway, through fingers laced over her eyes. She saw black and red stripes on the road. Then the neighbors moved away. Meanwhile a ginger tom adopted Evie, lived with the family for a year, and died the same way. Cars and cats don't mix.

Evie told her husband all this while they were courting. Really, he should have known it anyway; they'd grown up on the same street with the same neighbors and cats. Now their daughter was dead.

Crowds had gathered, blown in by ashen winds around the gravesite. Fall's dankness spread its pall over the ground, shimmering like mist so gravestones seemed unanchored, floating on air. Scant trees shook miserably and distant buildings stared.

Evie, standing in an empty space by the grave, wore that same lost frown from the time the two cats died. Wind brushed stray hairs against her face, and she ignored them. Cold air clasped her knees under the thick gray skirt and held her upright. She'd pushed the sleeve up on her coat. Now her bared arm was held over her chest in self-defense, her ungloved hand cupping its elbow. Fingers rubbed against that muddled round

7

of roughened, half-stretched skin. Her eyes were clear, focused on the gray fall sky while, all around her, neighbors looked down at the ground. A broken heart-beat rang in her ears, the world's only sound.

It wasn't Amelia's heart-beat though, nor Amelia's fingers testing Evie's skin. Amelia's confusing words didn't drift on the air, demanding to be answered when they couldn't be heard.

Ancient forests surrounded the cemetery, providing cover for ghosts and mystery. The dead girl had loved trees; had danced like a wraith among them in the park. She'd have liked this place; might even have liked the displaced silence of its people. But she wasn't here, and the trees watched, mourning her.

Something stirred. A bird flew into the clouds with an angry cry then circled warily, but too high. No one was looking. Nobody let it distract them from listening to prayers, sharing memories, staring at damp earth and a hole waiting to be filled. If anyone had cared to turn, they might have seen the cause of the bird's sharp rise; a figure stepping forward from the edge of the trees, a ghost perhaps, come to welcome another of its own.

The stranger's shoulders were hunched, as if to disguise his height. They shook as he shuddered in the buzz of a leaf-blown breeze. His straggly beard blew wide, and he patted it down with lank fingers streaked black and brown, combing through dirty gray. Then he turned his attention to the halo of hair now blowing over his head. He could have been a ghost, but he probably wasn't.

A white cat spotted the stranger. Stepping slowly away from the crowd, back arched, paws treading high over mulch and pine, it made its shadowed way toward the tree line. No one saw it leave the grave party. No one saw it curl around the stranger's feet, pale fur shining starkly against the washed-blue, gray, and brown of worn-out jeans. Its tail swung high and tapped the visitor's knees.

Someone sobbed by the grave. Not Evie though. And no one heard the stranger's sneeze, his grunt of dismay, or the yowl of the cat as he bent a leg and aimed to kick it away. Small furry legs ran free, unwounded and brave. Small clods of earth fell down and crumbled on a small child's grave. Small Evie whispered, "I wish I could cry." And the priest intoned his prayer.

"Ashes to ashes. Dust to dust." *Leaves to leaves*, perhaps.

Amelia was gone. So was the shadow under the trees.

*****

Loud banging on the classroom door brought Andrew quickly back to the present day. The children shouted with glee. They tried to storm the doorway, but Andrew waved his arm to silence them, and pointed back at their seats. "Don't want the principal coming in, do we?" he threatened. They laughed and obeyed, noses lifted in the air to smell their promised treat.

As soon as the door was closed, the students thronged the aisles again. "Sir, Sir. Where's my food?" He had to plough through rippling bodies as he carried the box to his desk. Then he pointed to their chairs again.

"Subtraction!" The sudden sharpness in Andrew's voice drew a prompt response of silence. "Remember, we're studying subtraction. Now, everyone sit down."

For a moment Andrew wasn't sure it would work, but he smiled anyway at the rising scents of food—ten meals, not nine, since he'd decided he'd need some sustenance of his own. "Sit down. Sit down." It wasn't so hard to lighten his voice, a happier mood rising over dark memories which he buried again in their woods. *Dust to dust*, and burgers to kids. These were good kids really. "Now, let's start counting."

Neat paper parcels were tugged from their box to a chorus of shouts. "Me first. Me first." Angry Tom leapt to the front.

"We're counting, Tom. Remember. Subtraction first."

So they counted out ten meals aloud, and Andrew took one away. "How many are left?"

"Me first."

Andrew held the package high over his head. "Who knows how many are left?" And silence reigned.

Shy Amy must know the answer, but the clamor had frozen her. She was counting buttons again, or shuffling buttons, or dreaming buttons and more. But Andrew didn't mind. It gave the other kids a chance to learn.

Tom's patience failed and he rushed to the desk, stopping to count the parcels steaming there. "One, two three... There's nine left, Sir." Then he snatched his reward from Andrew's hand.

"And now?" Andrew asked, while Angry Tom ate. He raised another parcel in the air, double nuggets this time, ordered especially for Jonah's delight. "Jonah? Do you know?"

"Eight, Sir?"

"Good job."

Then seven, then six, then five... Andrew placed the last two parcels together on Amy's desk. He asked which she wanted but she couldn't decide, so he asked her how many buttons she had today.

"Seventy-five."

"That's a lot of buttons. Do you want some lunch?"

"It's not lunchtime."

"No, it's afternoon. But this is a treat. My treat." He opened the wrapper and watched Amy's hand drawn forward in spite of herself. Then he left one parcel on her desk and walked to the front with a burger all his own. Time to eat in peace while the children subtracted multiple bites of their treats until nothing was left...

While time subtracted multiple bites from the past?

Who am I? Andrew pondered again, his mood dripping red as the sauce. Andrew Callaghan. Teacher to the lost, the subtracted. Would he ever find himself?

*****

The crowd split in two directions when the graveside service was done. Knots of people wandered like a severed worm. One slow parade marched uphill to the cemetery road, where waiting cars hugged the pavement under mist and trees. The other group meandered along an older track, cutting through oak and pine, over gravel and mud, toward the old village buildings of Paradise.

Evie and one other lonely woman walked separately from the rest. Each seemed eerily surrounded by a wall of silence, repelling intruders. The stranger, hidden in his own silent bubble, paralleled their path, but stayed well-camouflaged under trees. He shuffled his feet to the whispers of animals scurrying through fallen leaves. He kept his face buried behind his hands so he couldn't be seen.

The forest opened out onto onetime farms. The plain was patchworked with buildings now, instead of fields, but the squat, gray tower of Paradise Church still pointed prayers to the sky. Neat blocks of houses spread out from it; small family homes in tidy red divisions on the their grid of blacktopped road; larger dwellings with snaking tracks and paths; the long, low shape of the school; and, further away, lines of condos near the redbrick wall of Paradise House. People trailed like ants across the grounds of the old mansion now. A closer look would reveal old men in wheelchairs, young women pushing them, nurses' uniforms fluttering blue against green. The House was a good place for the lost. But the stranger, perhaps, might prove more lost than they.

Cars trailed along the road toward the church. Drivers from the funeral would get there first, before the walkers whose parade meandered unfocussed, unhurried, unconcerned down the path through the trees.

Someone slid into Evie's bubble of silence, invading her space. "There's food, you know. Potluck. We all brought something."

"I didn't," Evie replied, her voice as low as the gravel under her feet.

"You weren't meant to. But you should join us. We want you to."

Evie walked on, passing the entrance to the church, while the other woman reached to pull her back.

"Evie. You shouldn't be on your own."

But Evie, who'd been so long alone, didn't see why things should change, or why she should explain.

The speaker read all the words she didn't say, written clear across her face, and let her go.

Redbrick walls of the church's community room loomed over the parking lot. Playgroups and painting groups, toddler groups, youth groups, and senior citizen groups all met here in their turn, advertised with color-coded signs. Would little Amelia have played in this place, staring from her unlikely island of stillness? Would poor Evie have found relief among mothers a little less lost and hopeless than she? And the cat? Would the cat have meandered hypnotically between treading feet?

The stranger couldn't remember who the cat belonged to, but was sure the second, silently isolated woman laid some claim to it. She had some claim to this dark sorrow too, this restless parody of peace; and she was the truer stranger here, more so than he. "Poor Lydia," people muttered as they passed by her, never turning to speak to her. Because Lydia should have known and hadn't. She should have seen or guessed what her father-in-law would do. But like everyone else, she'd thought him ordinary, harmless, until Amelia died. He could be hired to mend their cars and busses, but he couldn't mend a child. So now Lydia, married to a murderer's son, walked unencumbered toward the gate, with no one invading *her* private space or inviting *her* to *join*. And the stranger hated her because he hated *him*.

That was almost the hardest part, knowing he'd met their Superman, garage-guy, with the ring of tools on his belt; and knowing he too hadn't known what Lydia's father-in-law might do. For this, the stranger also hated himself.

Evie looked back from the gate of the parking lot. She rubbed her fingers against her elbow again, like an infant sucking her thumb. Back then, her elbow had been Amelia's *thumb*, but now Evie was nothing to anyone, fading to no one again, like a ghost, while Poor Lydia walked free.

The stranger under the trees faded to shadows and couldn't be seen, while mourners slipped, one by one, into the hall. Everyone ignored the two lost women, who walked together still and so alone. Only the cat offered comfort, pausing at the gate with them. Then Evie and the man both felt oddly betrayed when their feline friend chose to follow Lydia's path along the road instead of staying. Evie clutched the gatepost harder, as if needing its support now the cat was gone. Her gaze turned hungrily back toward the church, but the man knew she wouldn't go inside. How could she share this meal with strangers who only pretended to be friends? Amelia had never liked crowds or noise or unfamiliar foods, and it wouldn't be right.

He shuffled his feet, combed black and white fingers through his ragged beard, and felt his vision dim with tears. His body hunched under its coat. The whisper of insects and birds hummed through his silence.

Suddenly the cat was back. Poor evil Lydia was gone and innocent Evie was ready to leave. The stranger glared. He didn't move though, not even when smooth-furred legs wound themselves around his frozen feet instead of Evie's. He tensed, as if to kick the cat, then stilled, afraid to be seen.

*****

When school was over, Andrew dismissed the class. Tom was first to his feet, elbowing other students out of his path. The door banged behind him then slapped to and fro as Zeke, Julie, and the rest of them passed through. Jonah the Whale waited until the tide had cleared. Meanwhile Shy Amy continued to sit, oblivious, solemnly counting buttons, ordering them by color, size and shape.

"Goodbye, Jonah," said Andrew as the last boy shuffled into the corridor.

"'Bye, Sir. Will you buy me nuggets again tomorrow?"

"Shush! It's a secret."

Of course, the secret would be all around school by tomorrow, if it wasn't already. The principal would frown disapproval at Andrew's enabling behavior. The vice-principal might call him aside to inquire whose insurance would pay if a child should choke on a chicken nugget. Other teachers might choose new names to tease him by. But he didn't care. His kids had successfully subtracted nuggets, fries, packets of food, meal tickets and more before the lesson was done. His kids weren't failures, and he knew it.

Though Shy Amy was still failing to leave her desk.

"Time to go home, Amy."

"Not yet," she answered, without raising her eyes. She spoke her words with mechanical precision. "There are three minutes left."

Andrew checked his watch and saw the school clock was wrong again. But Amy wasn't even wearing a watch and didn't carry a phone. How did she know?

Outside the window, crowds of students streamed along the road. A woman stood alone by the wall. Her coat, with red and green patterns like a Christmas tree, seemed oddly cheerful against the blacktop's gray. A white cat sat on top of red bricks, leaning lazily against her. "Is that your mom, Amy?"

Amy didn't turn her head; just answered, "She's always early."

"Well, you could go to her."

"It's not time yet."

With two minutes to go, Amy ladled her buttons into the pockets of her jeans. One minute to go, and she shrugged her arms into her coat. Zero, and she quietly stood, picked up her backpack, and left.

She was thirteen years old, the same age Amelia had been when she was murdered.

*****

The crowd had gathered inside the church hall now, institutional coffee fueling their conversation. Scents, sweet and bitter, flowed over plates of deviled eggs, ham sandwiches, and wobbling jello salads, green and red. "She's not coming," someone said, leaning out through the door to watch as Evie continued down the road. "She's heading for the park."

"Poor woman. She shouldn't go there."

"She's just going home."

Pastor Bill clapped his hands for attention and said, "Let's pray for her then." He included Evie's name in a blessing over the food. He included Lydia's name too, but breath hissed in and out through his congregation's tight-pursed lips, shuddering into that regulatory silence preceding *Amen*.

"I can't believe he prayed for Lydia," someone whispered. "Not here. I mean, he was her father-in-law. He was family." "I can't believe she dared show her face at the grave."

Busy hands, undismayed, strayed to plates, while coffee dripped from the urn into waiting cups. Conversation turned from Lydia's failures to those of the old man. "How could he have?" "What made him?" "Why didn't we know?" More importantly they asked, "How could Lydia not have known?" and, "How can she live with herself?"

Crumbs dripped from chattering lips onto paper and plastic plates, while the stranger listened outside. His ears caught words and voices flying like vultures through the door. His eyes saw figures silhouetted in window lights, while afternoon began its slide into night.

When the rattle of spurting gravel arose from the parking lot, Pastor Bill rushed to the door. It was a media van, yet another one sprouting aerials from its windows, spinning dials on its roof, and sporting stylized images of smiling faces on its side. "You can't be here," the pastor cried, as a man and woman stepped down. Their faces beamed, falsely bright as the painted cartoons.

"Why shouldn't we be here?" asked the woman, thrusting a microphone ahead of her. "We were discreet at the grave. I bet you didn't even see us."

It was true, but Pastor Bill still complained. "This is a private function. And private land."

"It's a public parking lot," the camera-man replied sullenly. "We're just following the story." But he followed too late. Amelia's mother had already moved on, taking her tale with her.

Crowds thrust around the pastor in the doorway and gathered at the van to vent their thoughts. "Bloodsuckers. Ghouls," and, "Leave the poor woman alone."

"Which woman?" asked the man, with falsely innocent aplomb. "We want to talk to both of them."

"Just leave them both alone."

"Are they here? All we need is a few words."

Some silent plot seemed to unite the sandwich eaters. They replied, deceptively, "They're not coming out, and you're not coming in."

"Aren't churches meant to welcome everyone?" The camera-man persisted, while the crowd pressed on every side. He snapped his pictures on the wide machine balanced against his arm. But the church folk held their ground, and soon the TV van rattled away.

The ghost or stranger had squatted low to the ground to watch the argument. Meanwhile the white cat leaned against his knees. Nobody noticed. When he stood again, unsteadily, and walked along the tree line toward to the street, the cat marched ahead. The stranger shuffled through the gate, touching the lamppost where Evie had leaned, ducking his head while he walked past matchbox houses and the low brick wall of the school. Poor Amelia had never attended here. Then he crossed to the park at the traffic light, following the same path Evie had trod, the same path Amelia strayed from when she died.

Don't go there. A voice spoke in his head with bell-like clarity, but no one was near. The man took one frantic glance around then jumped from the path into the trees of Paradise Park. He scrabbled through the darkness of branches and leaves, charging he knew not where. Just hide somewhere, anyplace away from human habitation, away from tended routes and play structures and duck pond's twinkling reflections; away from voices.

Then he wondered where Evie had gone. The cat nudged his knees and he turned back to find the path again.

*****

Andrew filled his arms with boxes and papers before leaving the room. His backpack hung from one shoulder, stuffed with marking and lesson plans. Car keys dangled from his hand. Stopping in the doorway, he looked back to check tables and chairs. Nobody hid on the floor; no treasures waited to be lost in the trash; no renegade jackets or scarves needed a home in lost property; no house keys; no screwdrivers or other assorted tools. It all looked okay—a little disorganized, straight lines all askew, but no more messy and disordered than you'd expect, except for the strong scent of burgers and fries, and paper packages rolled up in the trash.

Andrew set off down the corridor toward the exit, whistling softly. But tomorrow's lesson plan played behind his eyes and stopped his steps. While chattering students and teachers hurried by, the art room beckoned with a hint of visual aids and accompanying scent of dust and paint. He stepped inside.

A new teacher had been hired for arts and crafts. She was young, though gray specks sprinkled her red hair, perhaps tossed from the floor as she busily swept it. She bent her body low with fierce determination, pushing the long-handled brush under tables, out toward corners anchored by heavy metal legs.

Andrew coughed, but she didn't seem to hear.

"Hi," he whispered; then, louder, "Hi."

The young teacher wriggled around and slid to her knees; not quite the response he'd intended, so Andrew apologized then asked if he could borrow any art supplies.

"Borrow?" Her voice had an oddly innocent throatiness. "Did you plan to bring them back?"

Andrew smiled. "Well, if you think you can reuse them I suppose."

"I heard you were feeding the five-thousand today." The new teacher stood, thin hands twisting in reflection of her shyly twisting smile. She led the way to the storeroom. "I hope you don't plan to have them paint the Mona Lisa with tomato sauce tomorrow."

Andrew laughed. "Nah. Maybe we'll paint some Picasso though." He tugged at boxes of colored card while the art teacher opened them.

"Seriously though." She piled bright sheets in his arms. "Got to ask. What do you want this stuff for?"

"So we can do math?"

Amusement transformed to confusion. "Math?"

"Yeah. Subtraction."

The young teacher's smile fell into the same bemused frown all the faculty wore when they spoke of Andrew's class. It was a shame. She'd looked rather pretty when she was smiling.

Andrew staggered out from the room with his load and headed for his car.

*****

Evie staggered upright from the bench where she'd stopped to cry. The park was deserted, no children on the play structure, no tinkling voices like waterfalls of fun. An empty seat stared down over green grass and pond from its place on the hill. Even the ducks were silent.

She headed along the path into the woods again, then jumped and spun around nervously, trembling as she crouched to stare into crackling undergrowth. She'd heard something, but it was just a cat, white and fluffy, eerily similar to one she'd seen at the funeral. It wound itself around her legs, tempting her down to pet it. Then it strode beside her, small bright companion to the onrushing night.

Evie hummed the tune from a children's TV show to keep the silence at bay. She whispered its magnetic words and told herself it was truly *time to go home*. If Amelia were there, Evie would have sung louder, TV tunes being her daughter's favorite way to communicate. But the girl wasn't here. Evie's mouth pursed into silence. Trees surrounded her, hiding the dark, lonely place where her daughter had been lost. She stepped off the path, staggered, almost fell, and stopped. "Amelia."

Don't go there. A bell-like voice echoed unexpectedly, making Evie stop and stare. The sound was clear, just like Amelia's speech; as if Amelia would ever have said anything so sensible. *Don't go there*. But the voice wasn't real. Still, Evie recognized a warning not to stray—don't go to the place where her daughter died, don't wander from the path. She turned her footsteps back onto age-worn gravel and walked on.

Squirrels or birds, or rats, or cats, rustled in the undergrowth—no demons; no ghosts from the past. Evie ignored them all, kept her head down, and stared at the ground. The pathway was truly all that mattered, gravel grinding underfoot, white cat walking ahead, and everything leading her forward while the duck pond crouched behind, while the empty bench on the hill mourned Amelia's toys which had lain there at the last, and the dark trees cried.

Her child had raised her hands to catch leaves here as they fell from the sky, when she was small. So many, long years earlier, Evie and her husband played as youngsters beneath these trees, lifting their own hands too, before time tore them apart. They were children back when Paradise was a village, when Paradise Forest covered all the land which became a park. Evie had roamed this place with him. They'd danced and ridden bikes and fallen in love. But the town was younger then, and the forest deep and dark. They'd told ghost stories to each other, while stray cats wound at their feet, while Evie dreamed of Coal and the short-lived Sam. Later the land had been cleared, houses built, play structures added, and pathways drawn safe distances from streams, while innocence was lost. A human quilt replaced the slopes where once only wandering children and animals trod. Then Evie and he had gone to the bright new cinema together, celebrated progress, eaten a sacred engagement meal at Bensons on the parade. They got married and loved their lives as man and wife until all went awry. Until Amelia.

The cat deserted Evie when she reached the road. It disappeared like a ghost. When she searched the rising mist to catch a glimpse of it, all she saw was the shadowed outline of a man who maybe raised a hand above his head in greeting then disappeared. A car roared past.

"Amelia," Evie sobbed and hurried on.

*****

The engine of Andrew's ancient car shuddered to life as he turned the key. The gray school parking lot lay almost empty around him. Lines like prison bars surrounded asphalt spaces vacated by cars. He steered toward the gate, feeling oddly unsettled, his thoughts still halfway in the past while the taste of present burgers lingered on his lips. Student laughter burst like bugs on the windscreen, bringing him back. The streets were clear, so he let his gaze flash quickly from side to side, wondering which alley the shouting came from.

One lonely car slept against the school wall. Andrew recognized Shy Amy's mother beside it with her brightly checkered coat. He guessed the reason she was bent like a question mark might be Amy's little brother, owner of those diaper pins and still a babe-in-arms. He imagined the mother trying to fasten straps on the baby's seat before driving away. She had his sympathy—he remembered those days. He even slowed the car, opening the window as if to say *Hi* to her. But teachers don't greet parents on the street, especially not when children are watching them.

Andrew pressed the accelerator to pass, but his sideways glance had already been caught by Amy in the back of her car. Her eyes were clear. She almost looked at him, and maybe even responded, one hand raised in greeting in front of her face. But surely not. It must be a trick of the light.

Glass and rubber protested as Andrew tried to close the window. Duct tape around the metal handle was warm and damp against his hand. He clutched the steering wheel tighter again, then felt it jump against his wrist as the car hit a pothole head-on. The engine roared until traffic lights forced him to halt. A newer car would be nice, but this was the newest he could afford.

City streets were smoother, better maintained, and easier to drive. Downtown blocks were neat and square. But Andrew crossed the railroad tracks to the other, dark side of town. He cruised familiar lines of run-down shops in search of a treasured parking spot. His mind filled with thoughts of microwaved pizza or sandwiches if the bread in the fridge wasn't green. Then he stopped, reversed, and seated the car by the curb. Shouldering his backpack and filling his arms with those boxes and bags of art supplies from the trunk, he checked the path to make sure he wouldn't trip, then set off toward the steps to his apartment.

Once upon a time he'd had a wife to cook his meals, a child to share his table, a family; not now. *Who am I?* Andrew questioned himself. *I'm nobody.*

*****

Skies were gray. Streets were empty. And a little girl's voice would nevermore be heard.

Just past the university blocks, a ragged ghost-man hid in a low crouch behind a dumpster. Streaks in his hair, dirt in his fingernails, despair in hooded eyes, he hunched a shoulder to hide his face, in case anyone should care to look his way.

In front of the dumpster a lonely woman walked, not knowing she was watched. A white cat strode at her feet.

The woman opened the door to her home, releasing the key with careful quiet, so as not to frighten the child who wasn't there. She slipped off her shoes, so heavier footsteps wouldn't ring out to scare. She pushed the living room door in just the right place, so the hinges wouldn't creak. And she almost forgot the sofa would be empty, with no one lying there.

The white cat slipped past her and bounded onto the seat, where it posed itself and stared.

Meanwhile the woman slid down to the floor and wept.

The stranger slipped away.

*****

A white cat sat cleaning its paws at the top of the steps. It blocked the glass-framed entrance to Andrew's apartment building. It didn't belong there. Pets weren't allowed. But it yowled to be let in as Andrew struggled with the door. His arms filled with unbalanced boxes and files, he had to push with his shoulder and prop the panel open with his foot. But he managed to avoid kicking the feline, and he kept it from following behind. Then he stared back through the glass as the lock snapped closed. He wondered if the cat might see apology or annoyance in his eyes.

The elevator failed to arrive, so Andrew climbed the stairs, stomping loudly on every step and struggling not to drop his heavy load. At the top, he turned toward his apartment. A white cat sat on the mat.

"How did you get here?"

The patient creature didn't reply, but nuzzled against his feet and mewled as he patted his pockets for his key. Surely somebody else would be better equipped to feed a pet, Andrew thought. *Why's it following me?* But the cat squeezed through the doorway ahead of him, skittering with a clatter of sharp claws onto the kitchen floor. By the time Andrew had put down all his packages, one eager feline was waiting by the fridge.

Microwave pizza for dinner tonight. You can't feed half-moldy bread to someone else's cat.

Andrew slashed the top of the package with a knife. Meanwhile the cat wound itself around his feet. "You'll have to wait." His voice sounded strange. He wasn't accustomed to speaking in this place.

He switched the radio on then turned it off in favor of TV. The black screen sprang to life with a grayed-out picture of children playing, so he switched that off too. Then he carried his pieces of art-store card in from the living room. Spreading them over the tiny kitchen table, he added scissors, tape, and bags of chocolate candy bars. "Don't eat the chocolate, Cat. It's bad for you." The microwave pinged.

Since the table was covered with art supplies, Andrew sat on the floor to eat. The white cat lolled beside him, delicately nibbling bits of pizza from his hand, tonguing his fingers roughly, and batting his knees with its paws.

"You're kinda sweet, for a cat."

It purred then climbed into the hollow of his lap.

*****

The stranger sat under trees in Paradise Park, legs outstretched, knees together so the cat could recline in comfort, sharing his space. It mewled so softly and lay so soothing, so still, as his fingers kneaded their way into thick, white fur. Around him the air felt heavy, as if rich earth were falling over the coffin of his life, which seemed appropriate. It might bury him. Meanwhile thunderstorms rumbled impotent fury in his ears, but no rain fell.

She'd died here, little Amelia. Not exactly here, but near enough, in some hidden part of this forest. The trees remembered and told her tale, with watchful branches gazing down through leaves, forming circles of eyes that reflected her final gaze. Their shadows danced as she might have whirled and twirled on tip-toes here, feet unshod because she hated shoes, bare skin exposed to air. Did she undress herself that day, or did the murderer take her coverings away then hide her under leaves? Could anyone have saved her?

Trees asked their questions unceasingly, but no one answered them. Then the man, ghost, stranger, stood up again, ignoring the cat's clawing grip. He followed a narrowing path, deeper and darker into forested gloom, back down the hill toward the trickling of water, because water gives life. He stopped and crouched, bending his nose over a stream, waggling fingers in front of his twisted reflection as if to entertain a child. A guttural sob escaped from his throat, but *if nobody hears you cry, are you crying at all*? His splashing hand destroyed the image. Then he washed his face, eyes closed, heart torn, mind lost in might-have-beens.

"She's perfect." He remembered a voice, or else he heard the trees.

"She's beautiful, but she doesn't smile. Why's that?"

"She doesn't respond; slow learner I guess; there's something wrong with her."

"But she's beautiful…"

"You're beautiful," said another voice, almost real. It sounded like his own. "Come dance with me." Then dreams echoed their music through his mind. But *she* never replied. So he slammed his fists against his ears and screamed his thoughts against the night—*You could have saved her.* Could he? Or did the voices lie?

The cat kneaded his leg with sharpened claws, and the pain felt right. He stood up again, turning slowly around to observe the place where he'd stopped.

Flattened earth, near the water's edge, bore an imprint of broken walls. Perhaps some hobo had camped out here sometime. A circle of dirt might have been the place for his fire. But the grass was scarred in lines leading down and away toward a pool where water trickled, deeper than the stream, between boundaries banked with stones. The cat led the way and the man followed, finding cups and plates, cracked and broken, wedged into gaps where water washed over them. He pulled the items out, rescuing just as much as he needed then tossing back clumps of jewelry and knick-knacks that seemed to carry the tale of a woman's touch. A thieving hobo had lived here perhaps, or else a hobo's bride.

Large cardboard boxes could be used to wall his shelter, if they could be dried. Strips of corrugated roofing might lie on top. Torn tarpaulin could hold it all together and keep out the rain. There was even a wooden door lying further downstream, warped and cracked, but recognizable, with hinges of torn and sun-dried leather. The man tugged his treasures to the square of ground, flotsam and jetsam of someone else's life, and laid them on grass. Then he built a house, his own small cabin in the woods, over that dark rectangular patch where another hobo's home might once have stood. He lit a small illegal fire, using the last of his matches, and wondered if he dared hunt squirrel or birds for his meal. But no. He was a man of the forest now, one with all its creatures; he would do no harm.

Hardened strips of leather supported his door, but he wasn't sure they'd hold. Still, he swung the latch and slipped inside to crouch alone in the dark. Awkwardly ajar, the door allowed the white cat to step through in a sliver of light. A jewel in its collar reflected the red of a setting sun.

The man bent low under his corrugated roof, between his tarpaulined walls, alone no more. He stroked his hand over smooth fur, listening to purring that tried to soothe his pain.

*****

Andrew washed his mug at the sink then sat at his kitchen table to prepare the lesson. Patchwork colors, patchwork shapes, and strips of sticky tape; he patterned pieces big enough to be seen all around the class, taped candies on the back and colored paper on the front, added swathes of aluminum foil, sprinkled glitter from a jar. Weren't these the sort of games he could once have played, at a kitchen table in a family home with an excited child and wafting, happy hands: *Don't knock that over, dear*?

"Don't knock that over," he said to the cat, which sat back proudly on haunches and washed its paw, as if the thought of tipping glitter and glue had never entered its green-eyed mind.

"Yeah, I know what you're thinking." He smiled. But did he really know?

The cat stared almost as if its thoughts were deeper and broader than his.

*****

Among the patchwork houses of Paradise, Lydia Markham finally perched herself on the sofa at her husband's side. Her children were fed and in bed. The day was done.

"How did it go?" Troy asked, reaching a hand across the space where a white cat sat between them.

"How d'you think?"

"Did you speak to her? To Evie?"

"No. Why would I? How could I?" Something in the souring tone of her voice meant more than words betrayed.

"Did you speak to anyone?"

"How?" she replied, almost snarling the word. "I'm the daughter-in-law of the Paradise Murderer. Why would anyone ever want to speak to me?"

"I'm his son."

It wasn't the right answer, Troy knew. He shouldn't have made it about himself. He should have comforted Lydia with tales of kindness received, of people who'd taken them in, who'd offered food, who'd cared for their children, or those who'd kept the media away from them. Then Lydia would complain that the media were the only ones wanting to hear her voice. She'd complain even more that even they wouldn't listen; they'd distort her every word. Then she'd work herself into a frenzy again.

Troy stroked her hair and guessed he'd given the only answer after all. He *was* a murderer's son, so how could Lydia ever want to confide in him again. They sat in silence instead, hands touching, just for a moment, then sliding away, further and further apart, until a substantial ghost could have sat with the cat between them, right where it belonged.

When their smallest boy cried, Lydia jumped to her feet and ran upstairs. Troy stood more slowly, trailing fingers along the edges of furniture as if to prove he was real, not a ghost in his own home. The cat trailed after him then meowed at the door to be released.

Troy watched while his feline protector prowled away into yellow light shafting from the door. The cat snarled in fury at the shadow of a dark-furred intruder crouching on the wall. When the enemy fled, the victor, white nose dripping what must surely be a painful streak of red, made its way down the street, leapt up to another window ledge, and vanished inside. Something clattered. A crying child grew calm. And creaking floorboards upstairs bore the message that Lydia had gone to bed without telling him. Her husband keyed the lock and turned out the light, to follow silently.

~2~

Andrew held a glittery, cut-out shape, foil-covered and liberally sprinkled, at the front of the class. He hoped its shine would attract the students' attention as he asked, "What's this?"

Dull-haired Julie, who hardly ever spoke, looked up from buffing her nails. "It's a diamond, Mister." Her voice grated, and her fingertips were stained from nicotine.

Too young to smoke thought Andrew and reminded himself he wasn't here to judge them. He tipped his head to one side and agreed the card was shiny, but it wasn't diamond-shaped. "Any other suggestions? Something that's not jewelry?"

"It *is* a diamond," Julie repeated, determination strengthening her voice. "See." She held out her hand to him. "See, it's like my ring."

"Fake," shouted one of the boys from the back of class.

"Sure it's fake. So's Sir's."

Andrew tightened his grip on the cardboard and himself. "I'm asking about the shape," he said, "and this *shape* is *not* a diamond." He watched the students' faces to see who would respond, then found himself distracted by Rusty Julie's bright-ringed fingers. No one had answered, and the gleam of jewels, however fake, reminded him of diamonds in the past, all burned to dust, once given to a sweet-faced bride. "Ah, they do cut diamonds this way, don't they, Julie?" She smiled triumphantly. "They cut them into the shape of...? Anyone?"

Blank faces stared, so Andrew prompted them. "Hex...? Anyone?"

"Like witches," was a better answer than the next, which came from Angry Tom of course—"Like sex"—taking Andrew back to engagements and promises again.

Shy Amy rescued him with rainbow innocence. Her colored paper was tiled with carefully outlined shapes. She whispered, "Hexagon."

"Amy's got it," Andrew announced triumphantly. "This shape is a hexagon."

"Sex-is-gone," laughed Jonah the Whale, rocking his chair into a dangerous roil.

"Hexagon," Andrew repeated, ignoring the jibe. "Four legs on the floor please, Jonah, plus two legs of your own. And, if you take away a side…?"

"You're doing subtraction again. Boring," announced Angry Tom, though he sounded almost curious.

"I'm doing subtraction again and it's interesting," said Andrew. "Just give it a try. So…" He turned to draw a hexagon on the whiteboard, six-sided, its outline shining in bright blue. Then he colored over one of its sides in red. His neck began to ache from watching the class over his shoulder while he worked. His arm felt heavy from the strain.

"Your hexagon's bleeding, Mister," said Julie throatily.

"My hexagon's transforming."

A hum of movie music buzzed around the room while Tom sang out, "Transformers!" Meanwhile Andrew changed his picture, shifting and erasing until the red side slid away, blue edges moving closer until they met. He wielded an eraser to clean up the shape.

"What is it now?" he asked, leaving the cardboard hexagon on Amy's desk. He held a purple pentagon over his head.

Amy fumbled with the back of Andrew's card, smiling and humming to herself. A well-wrapped candy bar fell free, and she caught it nimbly before opening it to eat.

"Hey, what about me? I want one," shouted Jonah, who'd turned to watch.

"Then tell me what the shape is," Andrew replied. "We had a hexagon. We took away a side. And we've got a p…p…p?"

"Puppy," rasped Rusty Julie. Everyone laughed. "Pretty puppy, Mister!"

Even Amy managed a private smile. But Jonah complained, "You got pretties in your brain." Still, he flipped his gaze industriously from Amy's chocolate bar to the shape on the board, while Andrew held a photograph overhead. It showed a building, five-sided and famous.

Jonah shrieked in triumph. "It's the Pentagon!"

"Congratulations, Jonah. You win the next round." Andrew handed over his purple shape, with candy bar securely taped behind. "The hexagon had six sides. *Take away* one leaves five. And that makes a pentagon."

"Why not a one-a-gone, if one's gone away," asked clownish Zeke, drawing a laugh from the crowd.

"Because we're counting the sides left behind."

"Then it's a six-agon and a five-agon, ain't it?"

"Indeed it is," said Andrew, smiling, while Jonah ripped the wrapper from his treat. Amy's lips still delicately nibbled the corners of hers. "But six, in Greek, was hex, and five was pent."

"In *geek*?"

"In ancient Greek."

"Clever, those *geeks*, ain't they?"

"Oh, very clever," Andrew agreed, ignoring the jibe again. "So let's take another of those sides away."

He wiped at the board and drew with another color. The children shouted, "Square!" and finally agreed on quadrilateral, then triangle, as more candy bars and shapes were handed out.

Andrew fitted two triangles together at the close of the lesson. At last he'd made Julie's ubiquitous diamond shape. But he made the mistake of looking at her, so she yelled out, "Do I get a candy, Mister? I answered lots," though she'd answered nothing right.

Andrew smiled, placing his extra candy bars, one on each desk. *Being right's over-rated,* he thought, glancing through the window at those whispering trees and remembering when everything was wrong, when diamonds shifted, and broken lines longed desperately to be free.

*****

The town was closed and lonely and asleep. A woman who might have been Evie, short, dark-haired, and weary, walked the streets as if the world were too heavy a weight on her shoulders. It was too early for dawn and too late for night. The morning shift had only just arrived at the bus station. An old man whose beard hung down to his waist swept a corner of the sidewalk, watched only by a derelict girl whose hand reached into the waste-bin behind the café. When the woman staggered against the side of the bus, the driver proffered a businesslike hand to save her. She fumbled through her purse for a tip, but he laughed and sent her on her way.

Following the sounds of diesel engines, the woman passed a taxi-rank where drivers lounged half-asleep. She stared into the window of one, as if imagining where she might flee if she could only pay the fare. Then she walked on.

Streets awoke slowly around her. A panhandler settled into the gap between a concrete pillar and the edge of the road. He tugged his cardboard sign from a shopping cart, smoothed it carefully flat, and rested it like a kitten against his leg. Meanwhile a shop's awning opened with rattling chains. The lonely woman had timed her trip just right.

A small child kicked a can down the road until a mother's desperate voice shouted, "Get back in here." A white cat yowled and ran. Shadows whispered with secret messages to strangers, but the woman didn't care. She reached a hand from her pocket and pushed the door, where a newly hung sign swung wearily, reading *Open*. She didn't notice the ragged man peering over a fence at the edge of the park.

A notice on the wall advertised *New family homes in Paradise* and *Where's your Paradise?* The woman's gaze seemed to burn like fire as she stared at it. Then she paid for her bread and milk, waving away the grocer's muttered, "So sorry for your loss." Outside, she refused to acknowledge the street cleaner's salute. The panhandler took one look and kept his silence as she passed by. And the stranger with trailing hair and ratty beard turned away, so she wouldn't see his face. When she'd gone, he disappeared onto the pathway through Paradise Park, muttering darkly, "You shouldn't be here." His face was furrowed in a worried frown, and his hair hung gray with dirt.

The park should have been quiet, but voices suddenly clamored on the path. Students, on their way to early class, rushed forward in a cloud. The man ducked under trees while backpacks flew, coffees dripped, and bright-colored trainers with neon laces flapped against the showers of gravel and stones. He hunkered down, clutching a hand to his face to hide a sneeze.

When the students were gone, the man pulled an old burger wrapper from his pocket. He breakfasted, with quiet joy, on the remains of someone else's dinner. Being a tidy, careful person, he made sure to dump the wrapper in an appropriate trashcan afterward, before melting into mystery between tree trunks and retiring to his stream.

*****

The corridor smelled of stale coffee. Andrew tried not to run, since running was forbidden, to students at least. But he was a teacher, late to the faculty coffee-klatch, and he wanted to be there to put in a good word for his kids.

"Mister, you nearly tripped me," complained a strident student from another class. The glare she gave would wither grass, making Andrew wonder how long she'd last before she took on that magical label *reject*. But of course, calling Andrew's class *the rejects* was also forbidden, to students at least. Not *rejects*, certainly not *retards*, not *refuseniks*—one of the teachers had taken to calling them that—and not *repeat offenders* either; they were Andrew's kids and he planned on proving he could make something of them.

"Mister, you going to your meeting?" The young girl's withering glare turned to casual concern, as Andrew realized he'd stopped in the middle of the corridor. He smiled.

"Yeah, sure. Just got distracted there."

"Gotta watch that, Mister. They kicks yuz out for that."

"Thanks. I'll watch out."

He watched his feet weave a path through gray-painted, gray-floored gloom to the faculty room. He waved a hand at Jonah who was munching treats again—forbidden on the corridors, of course, to students at least. Then he arrived at the door.

The noise inside the faculty lounge was as loud and forbidding as the shouts of students with no teacher on hand. Andrew straightened his spine for courage, feeling the gentle creaks of determined joints damaged by bad behavior. He turned the knob.

"Late as usual," boomed the vice-principal, a Jonah look-alike cocooned in the most comfortable chair. The room's clamor silenced at his voice, while every face turned to glare accusingly at Andrew. He struggled not to snarl or blush.

"Find some coffee," said the dusty-haired senior teacher, sounding and looking like Julie, with cigarette-scarred voice and yellowed claws.

The coffee wasn't *lost* of course, just sitting on its shelf. It wasn't really coffee either, but it was hot and wet and had caffeine in it. Andrew poured himself a cup, adding creamer that was definitely a *repeat offender* and sugar because his diet was a lost cause. The room stayed silent, everyone waiting for him.

"Find a seat." Jonah's look-alike glared at the one remaining chair, as if considering snatching it up to break it over Andrew's head, but that would require too much effort; their honored vice-principal was far too comfortable to rise.

The hard chair, a working chair, solid and determined, was a perfect fit for Andrew's mood. He set himself down, legs splayed, coffee mug balanced on one knee, pencil in hand, and notebook pressed under his wrist. Then the young art teacher distracted him. She held out a meager plate and whispered, "Cookie?" sounding like a grownup version of Shy Amy. But Andrew had no hands to take one with, so he shook his head.

"Diet?"

"No thank you." He felt blood rush to his cheeks and his fingers trembled. He'd meant to just say no. But a loud voice boomed and the moment was gone.

"So." Jonah's look-alike vice-principal grabbed everyone's attention. He talked of schedules and targets and the importance of hitting the mark. A fist wielded with lazy imitation of boxing punctuated each point, while teachers nodded unquestioning agreement and sipped their drinks. Fixing the clock so the chimes would toll on time was a priority too.

Andrew smiled. That would please Shy Amy. Meanwhile, fixing the servers so the classrooms would all have internet "except for yours of course," was a vital task.

Andrew knew at once where the *yours* was aimed. He took a sharp breath to keep his temper down. Adding a note to his page and doodling squares and triangles around it, he muttered, "My kids could use internet too." He didn't intend to be heard; he could do without the argument. Fix windows that won't close, tighten loose handles on doors before they fall off, repaint the lines in the parking lot, and maybe find out why water was still leaking in the older boys' showers…

Andrew continued to doodle his shapes, adding a circle and two lines like the hands of a clock—triangle minus one side perhaps. *What shape is this one, class?*

"And we need to decide…"

He looked up to find the vice-principal's fierce stare boring into his eyes.

"We need to decide how long we keep the *refuseniks* on our roll."

"They're not refusing…"

"They refuse to learn. They refuse to obey. They refuse to take instruction."

"They're doing fine." Andrew sharpened his voice to their defense. "They just think in different ways."

"They don't think at all."

"Which is where you're wrong." He'd tried to stay calm, but found himself rising from his chair as his pencil rolled to the floor. The art teacher bent from her perch to hand it back. A shy smile decorated her face, distracting him, and her fingers brushed electrically against Andrew's palm.

"My kids *do* think," Andrew continued, half-embarrassed as he towered over the sea of teachers' faces glaring up at him. "They're just as capable as anyone else. They're..." He stumbled on the words, realized he was speaking out of turn, and sat himself down again. "They're good kids."

"Yes, Mr. Special Ed. And you think you're the only one capable of teaching them? Think you're so much smarter, don't you? Better than all of us, and late to every meeting, and nothing matters except the kids *you* teach. But this is a school for other kids too. Your class is just one part of the school and as such, your little *refuseniks* have to fit in."

"I *don't* think I'm better. And my kids *are* fitting in." Andrew tried to still the shaking in his hand, but it fled to his voice. "We're a *special* school..."

"School for rejects," muttered a voice further back in the room.

"...so we should take *special* effort, don't you think? We should justify our existence and prove we can make something more of *our* special kids."

The senior teacher snarled, but Andrew wouldn't be drawn back to his feet. He knew the conversation would drift again. They'd agree that as long as his class kept out of trouble, as long as Andrew didn't mind working with them, as long as somebody passed a state-mandated test sometime, and preferably soon—if only to up their numbers and avoid the school losing money—he could keep teaching *refuseniks* and keep his job.

It wasn't all about money. It never had been. Not for him. But his mind drifted back to a world of broken edges, poverty, and lost triangles.

****

A corrugated roof kept the nights' rain away, but the walls of the man's cardboard cathedral grew sodden, despite their tarpaulin cover, and the door fell off. After a few nights sleeping there, he felt hungrier and more ragged than ever, eternally worn, with dampness seeping into his bones. He wondered if his flesh would feel as spongy as the sodden cardboard. Sometimes he pressed the heel of one hand against his side and lifted his shirt to check—skin and bone, coldly white but healthy still. Would Amelia's skin have looked this way when they dug her up from beneath her bed of leaves? How long had she lain there?

The man's last bed, before coming here, had been at the homeless shelter in a nearby town. His last real meal had been bread and soup at the mission by the old white church. Not the church of Paradise—no, never there. His last home? He wouldn't think about that. Instead he filled a cracked cup with water and pondered whether he ought to risk drinking it. *Boil it first*, said the bell-like voice of silence—child or teenager, she spoke in his head almost as if she were real, as serious as Amelia might have been if she'd ever cared enough to speak.

Hearing voices might be the first sign of madness, or else the last. Still, the bell-tones soothed him, like the cat with its thick white fur. He tipped his drink into an empty soup can then remembered he'd run out of matches. He wasn't sure he knew how to start a fire without them. *You've got all the time in the world. Just try,* he told himself.

Of course you know how, was the bell-tone's confident cry.

Forest and voices listened while the ghost-man muttered to himself. *Find some wood. Collect some leaves. Mosses perhaps?* Small creatures scurried out of his path while the white cat sat, cleaning its paws, and he pondered, *soft wood or hard to start the flame*? He tugged on twigs still caught up in trees and bushes, remembering he should keep his tinder dry. Then he raised a flat plank above damp ground, slipped a leaf underneath to catch any newborn ember, and added a nest of mosses torn from a tree trunk, a home for the flame. He spun the spindle busily in its hole, but nothing came of it.

Spin it faster. It wasn't the child's voice speaking now, but his own small Boy Scout memory. Cold fingers struggled to obey. Bell-tones added, *Think of something else you can use to help it spin.*

Hunkered down on the ground, the man frowned in concentration, drawing a distant past to himself while keeping the space between invisible. He sketched careful diagrams with a twisted stick. His images were as neat and orderly as instructions in a book, parallel lines and well-constructed angles cutting through mud. A watery sun peeked over his shoulders to watch while the white cat purred at his side. "You'd know how to do it, wouldn't you?" the man said, stroking soft fur with a hand that weighed lighter than he expected. "And you'd know how to hunt. You'd not go hungry, would you?" The cat meowed.

At last the man had a small hand-bow made from threads of his shirt tied onto a strong, supple twig. He wound the string around his spindle, pressed a flat stone on top, and tried again. This time a thin trail of smoke appeared at the spindle's tip, almost invisible in the morning mist, like cotton wool caught in the air. The man set down his tools, blew on fragile embers cradled in his leaf, and started another small, illegal fire.

He heated water in the soup can, burning his fingers on hot metal sides as he tossed in sprigs of green. "It's alright," he told the cat. "I know all about these herbs. Nothing to worry about." But his brow remained furrowed as he bent to sip the brew. *Pour it in the cup, silly. And sugar would help.* The bell-like voice was sweet, and wasn't giving up on him. Where would he get sugar from?

*****

"Don't drop your cup."

Andrew jumped at the feel of someone's fingers on his hand. He'd almost dozed off, and his coffee would have spilled if the younger teacher hadn't rescued it.

"Don't want to make it too clear that you're bored," she whispered with a smile.

"Who me? But this is riveting isn't it?"

"As in *I like smashing rivets into holes*, yeah, sure it is."

The art teacher really was pretty when she smiled, but much too young for him. Andrew lifted the cup to his lips and tried not to let the bitter taste distract him from his savior's face. But the bitter fury of endless complaints bored into his brain again. Riveting; they'd drive their rivets into his kids if he'd let them.

"How did your art project go?" the young teacher whispered, drawing him back into private conversation. "You know, with all those pieces of colored card."

Andrew tried to remember what she meant, then saw a chocolate biscuit sitting uneaten on the senior teacher's plate. It reminded him of chocolate bars taped to shapes. "It went well," he said.

"But what were you doing?"

"Counting edges on shapes and then subtracting them. With chocolate bars on the back."

His savior hid a smile behind her hand. "Heresy," she whispered. "What if someone's allergic, or ADD?"

"I've got nine kids in my class. I know exactly how much sugar I can give each of them."

She turned away, and he realized he'd answered a little too forcefully. Too loudly as well. His nemesis demanded, "Did you want to enlighten us, Mr. Special Needs. Something vitally important that we've simply got to hear."

"No," he muttered, and guessed he knew exactly how his students felt when they gave the wrong answer too—overly visible then suddenly, inexorably unseen.

But unseen was okay. Unseen meant at least he was safe from getting into trouble again, until next time.

*****

Autumn's rain receded before a sudden splash of sunshine. Steam rose from the pond in Paradise Park, where fat ducks imitated small, aquatic ghosts as they squawked invisibly. Children threw scraps of bread from discarded loaves, hoping their invisible, feathered friends would reward them for the treat. Mothers complained. "Why don't you wait 'til you can see them?" Toddlers wailed and more bread was provided. Meanwhile a small group of women sat together on damp wooden benches, drinking coffee from cardboard cups, rocking smaller offspring to sleep in their strollers, and chattering as aimlessly as the ducks.

"Anyone seen Lydia lately?" someone asked, inspired by an empty space where their neighbor usually sat.

"No, I guess it's hard for her."

"She can't shut herself away forever."

"It's hard on us all."

They buried themselves in thoughts of how difficult it was, while pressure glued them down to the wooden seats. Then one tall figure pried herself free and stood decisively, causing the ghost-man to spring back further under the cover of trees. The woman leaned one arm on a stroller, while her other hand fluttered theatrically to her hip. "You know something else?" she asked, her voice as strident as a swan's. "We can't shut *ourselves* away from the forest forever either. I'm going in there." Stomping well-shod feet she demanded, "Who's gonna come with me?"

Children scrambled back from the pond, sensing a change in the mood. "Can we play on the slide? Can we swing?"

But the mothers were suddenly, stubbornly determined on a different course of action. "No. We're going for a walk in the trees."

"That's boring."

"Put your shoes on, please!"

Unseen, slinking further again into the shelter of bush and scrub, the stranger watched and listened.

Buggy wheels sank into muddy gravel and stuck as the procession embarked along its trail. Voices complained. "They should pave this over." Babies wailed while older siblings chattered happily. Then a gray cloud hid the sun, bringing silence. A twig snapped noisily.

"Did you hear that?"

"Is somebody out there? Hey!"

But, of course, he didn't reply. The cat rescued him from further investigation. Proud, feline, fluffy, and fierce, it leapt out from the trees, charging in leonine splendor toward the women, then winding its tail around their knees when it arrived. They bent to stroke it, the cat's sweet purr even louder than their children's cries. Green eyes begged hopefully for scraps of bread, and stared with haunting intensity into babies' faces. Children gathered, proffering proper adoration, until their new friend wandered away, and the women continued on the path. Through shadows, through wounded memories, through Paradise Park and Forest, they trekked up the long hill to street and sky.

"Is this where...?"

"Do you suppose...?"

"I wonder..."

"Poor little girl."

They shuddered through thoughts and sentences, all refusing completion. Meanwhile the watcher shuddered too, and the cat returned to crouch against his feet.

When the women had gone, the man searched for a clearing, a place of calm and clarity where Amelia might have danced. He lay on his back, at peace in the silence, to stare all alone at the sky—Amelia's sky. What did she think of when she lay there? What did she think of when she died?

*****

"Okay class." Andrew forced himself to shout, bringing order to the chaos of children bespattering the room. Shy Amy, as always, sat in an island of stillness, treasures laid before her, gaze fixed on a corner of the wall above Andrew's head. Jonah the Whale swam between desks with arms outstretched, reminding Andrew of childhood days when he would pretend to be a plane. Behind the Whale, a swarm of minnows giggled. But someone was bound to get hurt. These sudden rushes of energy always led to tears if they weren't stopped.

"Okay class. Sit!" Andrew shouted again, wondering if the children even grasped that he was treating them like puppies. Not that Andrew had anything against dogs. He rather liked them; their wide, bright eyes so much more comforting than the accusing stares of cats. Still, the painted *guardian angel cat*, hanging on the back wall of his class-room, watching him through every lesson with green and glorious eyes, was one of *Andrew's* treasures. Its stare a little wiser, a little more trusting, a little more secure, and its wings outspread, that feline angel promised hope and a future in spite of everything. Andrew smiled, remembering how he'd fought to be allowed to hang it there. "But surely it's got be religious or something?" He'd never yet heard of a faith that made saints from cats with wings.

Shoes scuffled and chair legs shrieked. Then, with most of the children seated appropriately, Andrew strode to the front. He'd decided to begin the lesson with a question he was sure they couldn't answer, just to get their unfocussed thoughts in tune. "Can anyone remember what we've been studying in mathematics?" *That should stump them!*

Shy Amy stared at the ceiling. Truth was, she almost certainly did remember, and equally certainly wouldn't deign to reply.

The small boy with the big stutter started to mumble, "Supper, supper, supper."

Angry Tom laughed. "You've only just had lunch, yer twat!"

Jonah the Whale leapt gracelessly to his feet with a lopsided grin. His arms moved up and down like pistons as he pushed his chair away and began to march around the room again. More plastic chairs snarled across the floor while other children prepared to join with him, and Andrew shouted, "Stop!"

Jonah stopped, one foot and one arm held theatrically in the air. The pose seemed oddly graceful.

"What are you doing, Jonah?"

"Engine," the grinning boy replied, punching his arm and adding a very creditable hoot. "Choo choo! Choo choo!"

"What sort of engine?"

"Train."

Who knew how thoughts became so tangled inside these children's brains? Andrew made the connection though, then tried to prompt another child's stroke of genius to share it around. "What sort of train engine is Jonah being?" he asked. "Can anyone remember yesterday's word? Sub-*tra*…?"

Subber-traction-subber-traction-sub…

"He's a traction engine," said the boy who drew different vehicles all over his page. "We're doing traction."

"Close," Andrew admitted with a smile. He rested his hands on Jonah's shoulders to steer the suddenly graceless child back to his seat. "Anyone else?"

"Super traction. Super traction. Super-trac…" Jonah's voice picked up volume and speed. "I'm a super super super super-traction-train…"

Other students took up the refrain, and Andrew gave them space, praising them liberally for intelligence and imagination, before telling them all to sit down again. A pity his room didn't have those chairs that stayed attached to their desks, he thought, though perhaps it was kinder to Jonah that it didn't.

"That's right, children," said Andrew. "We're doing *sub*-traction again. Now, what does it mean?"

"Can we order takeaway?" asked Class Clown Zeke.

"Have you got any candy bars?"

*****

A mystery man had been spotted under the trees in Paradise Park. A drifter. A hobo. A poor lost soul. No one would have cared except they wanted to be sure he wasn't the Paradise

Predator's ghost—Paradise Murderer's ghost after the death of the child, they all supposed. But no one dared accost him. He kept himself to himself, ignoring them.

The stranger had lost count of days as seasons changed. He snatched his food from waste bins and his water from stream and pond. He burned his carefully tended fires, as far from the tumble-down shelter as he could, so if anyone found them his hideaway might stay hid. The trees whispered Amelia's name to him, and he wondered if her ghost were trapped beneath the mud and stones. Gravel footpaths roiled under wandering feet, while councilmen declared, "We should really pave it over. Make it safer. Put up a plaque and dedicate it to her." Still, nobody ventured alone off those paths, as if they thought they might get caught as Amelia had, as if any stranger in Paradise Park could only be predator and murderer since her death.

He wasn't a predator. He wasn't even a stranger here— not really.

The shadow recognized Sundays by the ringing of bells. They tolled across the morning sky from the town-center mission where white walls anchored a steeple under their weight. A sudden rush of main road traffic announced the congregation's hurried arrival. But the stranger had no desire to attend; neither at church nor in the hall where soup still served the needs of the hungry each evening. He didn't want anyone's questions to find him out. Besides, he thought, nuts and berries were an ample diet, supplemented with dumpster-diving.

Evie had gone back to the gray Church of Paradise though. He noticed that, as he followed her footsteps tramping along the path through Paradise Park. He hid in the trees to watch her. Whenever sweet Evie turned toward him, whenever he feared she might see, then the cat strolled out, so she didn't look too far. Somehow, come rain or shine, the white cat's fur stayed white, clean, soft as a baby's head, pure as Amelia's. Sometimes it made him cry, but mostly it just comforted him when he found the cat at his side.

If Evie was really a church-going Christian believer, it didn't seem right to him. Hadn't she given up on all that faith stuff long ago? But maybe she just thought church was something to do on an empty Sunday without her child. Or maybe this gray church really was different from the white one he'd once known. Maybe that was why they'd held Amelia's funeral here. And by coming back, perhaps Evie tried to recapture the child left behind.

The man followed her, and the cat ran softly between them on padded paws. It wore the ghosts of memory like a cloak, until all three of them came, in turn, to that graveled parking lot by the stone-walled Church of Paradise. The church's redbrick hall glared out at them.

Evie pressed her hand on the old oak door. She tested its weight, knowing she was late and not caring because there was no need to be early anywhere anymore. She used to leave Amelia in the church hall during services. Not that Evie attended there. That wasn't the point. Some kind soul would care for her autistic child, while Evie rushed home to shop and clean house, without small, trailing wails and lingering tantrums distracting her. Ninety minutes later she'd be back at the same wooden door. She'd smile through her tiredness and pick up her awkward child, thanking strangers and *pray*-ers, and telling the pastor, "One day. I might join you in church one day." She hadn't meant it, but now she had no child, no hope and no purpose. *One day* had arrived.

The stranger pressed himself into the shadows, hugging trees and waiting for the cat to comfort him. It didn't have wings, but already he'd begun to think it was his guardian angel. Then he saw the murderer's daughter-in-law and felt his anger's snakelike hiss in his chest. *How dare she? How?*

The cat leapt out from its place by his feet to greet her. Lydia's three small children bent to stroke it. No husband appeared because he'd left her, or so the rumor mills claimed. "Hiding out at that garage of his," said the chattering women, which was worse than gone, since the garage was where his father, the infamous Paradise Murderer, had hidden in plain sight—except for when he was hiding out in the woods.

I'm not hiding the stranger told himself. *I live here. I belong.*

*****

"Subtraction."

The children stared at their teacher, while he stared out of the window over their heads. Shy Amy's mom stood watching from behind the wall. He could see the top of her car behind the brightness of her red and green coat. Birds watched from the trees, and inchworms lifted their heads to watch from the earth.

"Let's do some addition first shall we? Who knows this song?"

Andrew pressed a finger to his phone, making music ring out. Soon the children joined in. "Two and two are four," resounded into the corridor. *Four and four are eight. Eight and eight…* Andrew pressed *stop* and wrote a large clear *32* on the board.

"So class. If sixteen *and* sixteen are thirty-two, what is thirty-two *take away* sixteen?"

Jonah said, "Nuggets." Julie said, "Burgers." Comedian Zeke said, "Worms." Meanwhile Shy Amy ordered buttons on her desk, moving thirty-two to one side, set in two rows of sixteen. She piled the spares into a heap filling the gap between the lines.

*****

The shadow haunted gaps between trees, in the park, in the forest, along the sides of roads. He wasn't real, just a ghost left behind when a person finds he's subtracted from his world. People had become accustomed to him now. They labeled him the Paradise Prowler and didn't seem nervous anymore. He was becoming accustomed to them as well, to his slightly changed town, and all its lonely places where food could be found.

Around the back of Bensons was best, though he had to fight for his share with other derelicts and stand his ground. Bins near the diner were well supplied with uneaten ends of burgers. The park provided inexhaustible supplies of candy scraps, ice cream flavored wrappers, and half full bags of chips. Soda bottles swam with drips of discarded cola. Even the odd beer bottle could yield its brew. But best of all was the time he found a half full bottle of wine. He kept it cool in the stream's running water and drank it slowly, one cracked cup at a time, over the next few evenings. It kept the voice away.

In time, the shadow found more treasures among rocks around the stream. More cups and saucers provided replacements for mugs and plates that wore out. Bright ornaments offered a hint of life, spread out around his cardboard hole to make it look like home. A curious brooch, picked up from the path and shaped like a cat with wings, became his talisman. If the real, white cat wasn't there to comfort him, he'd finger the brooch, stroking its smooth enamel, losing himself in the red, glowing stare of a jewel on the fake cat's collar.

"Not a jewel."

"Yes, I know it's cut glass, but it's still…" He wasn't sure of the word, and he wasn't sure who he was talking to either.

"Garnet."

"Of course it's not a garnet."

"Garnet's the cat."

He hadn't thought to look before, but when the cat returned, he examined her collar. Shiny fake diamonds were strung along its length, but there, under the narrow furred chin, was one small gleam of red. Andrew checked the cat's furry shoulders then, but found no wings, so it wasn't the brooch come to life.

And he still didn't know who he'd been talking to.

~3~

Amy's mother looked as shy as her daughter. She leaned against the classroom door jamb with her red and green coat clutched over one arm and her fingers buried in its fibers. She was short and thin, just like Amy. *Like someone else's child as well,* thought Andrew. He clenched his fist under his desk, anchoring his thoughts on the present rather than the past, then he waved in welcome. The visitor took tiny, graceless steps. She seemed too nervous to meet his gaze as she pulled up a student's chair which fitted her well, her knees bending only half-way to her chin. It wasn't entirely appropriate though, since her eyes only just peered over the top of the desk. Andrew tugged an adult chair from the corner of the room. "Please, sit here," he suggested. Then Amy's mother stared through him with the same blue eyes, blank gaze, and distant disappearance her daughter displayed.

Andrew looked over her shoulder at his guardian angel painting on the back wall of the room. The feathered cat reminded him to be good. Be present and busy while ready, naturally, to listen to his guest. He loosed his fist, twined his fingers together atop the desk, and dropped his gaze to the shine of its scarred, oak surface, scratched with years of misuse. Slowly his fingernails tapped against the wood, making music as if they were boring holes in trees.

"I worry about her." The mother's fingers played the same tune in her lap. She seemed too scared to pull the chair any closer to the desk. "Are you sure main-streaming's the right way for a girl like her?"

Andrew coughed in the back of his throat, hoping his voice would come out clear as a teacher's should, instead of croaking and buried in the past. *No one main-streamed Amelia.* "I'm not sure of anything," he admitted, unclasping his hands so they could wave reassuringly. "You can never be sure. But I do know Amy's been responding really well." His voice sounded abundantly professional, which wasn't necessarily good.

"Responding how?"

Would the mother's fingers never stop moving? They threatened to hypnotize him now, just as Amy's did in class. So Andrew looked up, past an empty, worried face, to the guardian cat again. "She takes part in discussions." *At least,* he thought, *she knows what's going on.* "She answers questions," *very quietly.* "She contributes a lot. The other kids really like her." He might not quite be lying with this. *They don't really hate her anymore. They don't drive her crazy anymore.* It was better not mention how things were at first.

"I'd like to see."

Ah, thought Andrew, *but a parent never sees.* "She'll react differently if she knows you're watching her."

"I could hide."

He tried to hide a grin, imagining Amy's mother crouched under a desk, peering out between some student's knees. She returned a shy smile of her own, almost as fleeting as Amy's always were. Then she shuffled forward on her chair. Her face leaned low toward him, the ends of long hair trailing over papers and pens. "I could."

"Amy would notice." Andrew leaned forward equally earnestly to match her. One hand settled flat on the desk, balancing him, while the other brushed through his hair. "She notices everything. It really wouldn't matter where you were, she'd notice you. Can't hide from Amy."

"I guess." The mother's voice was low and resigned. Her eyes threatened to hypnotize him now, or else to see straight through to whatever he was hiding.

Who am I, again? Andrew felt warm embarrassment flood his face. He tilted his chair away from the desk and laced his arms behind his head. "Amy can't help spotting every change," he said, determined to make sure her mother understood. "It can't be done. You can't watch."

He prepared to stand, uncertain if he were trying to end the meeting, or just to prove there was nowhere to hide in here. But Amy's mother wasn't to be dissuaded. "I could hide right now, while she's out at recess perhaps. See how she reacts when she comes in. I could just stand behind you."

Not a good idea. "Recess is hard for Amy," Andrew explained. "Recess has no structure to show her what to do. She needs time to settle afterward, not more confusion."

"I know that. But I want to see if she can cope. I worry so."

Andrew sighed and walked to the window. He looked out at the students, playing whatever games belonged in this new generation. He remembered worrying about a child. He knew how the mother felt, though no one would believe it. And perhaps if he'd worried more, poor Amelia would still have been alive.

Papers rustled on Andrew's desk, like leaves, as Amy's mother brushed at them. The distant chatter of children gave way to clattering feet on the corridor. Students tramped and rattled like acorns falling down, or cabins blown away. Water gurgled through pipes along the wall, overflowing in the boys' bathroom again, reminding Andrew of a stream where he washed cups and plates and scrubbed his face.

But Amy had vanished from her hiding place at the top of the climbing frame. Recess was over. He couldn't check her now for the look on her face; couldn't tell if she'd seen her mother talking with him. Could she read lips? Did she know what they'd said?

"Come back tomorrow if you want, and I'll see what I can do," Andrew offered with a sigh.

"What time?"

"Recess is at eleven."

He ushered the mother hurriedly away, hoping against hope that she'd be gone before her daughter came into view. He didn't want Shy Amy to seem dismayed or feel betrayed.

The girl sat beside her mother, one thumb in her mouth, the other hand fondling loose skin where Evie's arm was lightly bent. She had a thing about elbows, it seemed, but her eyes were blank, and who could tell what went on behind their gaze?

He said he was leaving and his wife simply smiled and answered, "I knew you would." Was he that transparent? Was he so shiftless, so worthless? Was his presence so meaningless? The child said nothing, of course, but who could tell what went on behind her gaze. He thought they'd be better off without him anyway, and he didn't want Amelia to seem dismayed or feel betrayed.

He had to think of a way it could be done, a way to let her mother watch without scaring the child. He needed it because if Amy's mother took her daughter away, he'd feel like his class had lost its key player. Amy's success was part of his argument for keeping the class alive, and he needed not to fail Amy, because he'd failed Amelia, failed her completely. But he stared out of the window with no ideas coming to mind. The red and green figure returned to her car, scurrying on legs too short for her coat, head down, eyes glued to the ground.

*****

On a day of rare stillness and clarity, the newly named Paradise Prowler gazed at his reflection in the water of the stream. He saw his daughter's eyes in his own, her smile caught in the ragged twist of his lips. "Not a smile; it's colic," said remembered voices. Their promise had comforted him, while the child seemed devoid of emotion. Doctors told him she was autistic. "Children like her? They rarely smile." And the lie was unveiled.

He remembered the day. She sat beside her mother, fingers toying at that flap of lose skin beneath an elbow, eyes gazing into space. She looked so sweet, pure and innocent, a very different creature from the demon who shrieked and wailed when things didn't go her way, who smashed her toys and crockery and chairs, who tore the pages from books and smeared feces over carefully cleaned and papered walls. She looked like an angel—an angel with sharp claws.

"Nobody really knows the cause."

The doctors were filled with curiosity, disguised as sympathy. But they weren't all so kind. One spoke of refrigerator parents and blamed the mother, not the father, because dads have to go out to work. "If you'd held her…" But Evie had held and hugged the child, until sharp claws and elbows tore at her. "If you'd talked to her, or sung to her…" And yet, he knew, Evie had. "If you'd shown her…" Shown her what? No one showed Amelia how to wreck a home. She learned it all alone.

Of course, if it wasn't Evie's fault, and he knew it wasn't, then it had to be his—some faulty inheritance perhaps, given through his seed. So they blamed each other because they couldn't blame the child. And then, because their only words were undeserving blame, they retreated into silence.

He remembered coming home from work to a place devoid of warmth. No food on the stove because she couldn't tear herself away—but at least the stove wasn't a repository of broken pans and plates. No welcoming hug because she couldn't move away from the child. No *How was your day?* because her day was worse, and cursed, and trapped into nursing a future that would never change.

He remembered bringing home food that the child wouldn't eat. The mother would retreat into anger and claim he should have known. He remembered bringing home gifts that his hapless daughter broke. He remembered a radio shattered in scattered pieces over the floor. He remembered standing in front of a toyshop window, wishing he knew if something would please this child; jewelry stores as well. But nothing was worthwhile, and the past, its love, its laughter, all were gone.

He remembered standing outside his home, scarcely daring to enter in. He felt like a soldier outside the battle zone, like a mourner just before the funeral. It was nobody's fault that their marriage was dead. Their home was foreign soil, and the time had come to yield the battlefield to wife and child. It was nobody's fault, so why did he feel so bad?

His breath, blowing on the water now, shattered images of longed-for might-have-beens; the little girl who might have grown up; the frozen smile which could one day have warmed; the broken mind that might perhaps have hidden a loving heart, but no one would know.

"Evie," he whispered, finally shaping his lips around the word. "Amelia." And his heart was torn in two.

Father. Husband. Dismayer. Betrayer. He left his own name buried in the mire.

*****

Andrew phoned Amy's mother from the school. "Give me a few days to set something up," he said. "Things are kind of busy now. I don't want to keep her from her work when she's doing so well."

The quivering voice on the end of the line demanded more assurance. "Is she really doing well?"

"Yes." Andrew paused in automatic reply then determined to try again. "Yes, she is. She's doing great. She's my star pupil."

"Do you mean it?"

"Yes, I do."

"And you *will* call me? You *will* set something up? Just so I can see it for myself, because, you know, I do worry so."

"I know what you mean."

He almost heard her answer, "Of course you don't," but of course, he did. And nobody knew who he was, least of all he.

*****

Noise filled the forest that morning, growing louder as the day went on. It was almost like a party. Crowds, of young and old alike, thronged the paths, marched through trees, and gathered around the duck pond, the bench on the hill, and the parking lot. There was scarcely space for anyone to hide. But he knew his place. He'd watched them setting up sound systems, with amplifiers and speakers, wires like vines tangling with branches and leaves. He'd heard them testing, "One, two three," and he'd almost smiled as birds and squirrels raucously answered the sound. But he hadn't known what they were doing it for. He'd pretended not to care. He'd pretended not to hear those fate-filled words, *Memorial for Amelia,* so long after death and burial had rendered them meaningless.

A paper bag containing two whole burgers waited in the trashcan—food cast away by the murderer's daughter-in-law who didn't seem hungry, though she kept on buying more meals. The victim's mother didn't eat of course, and was quietly fading away. She stood near her nemesis now, each with that cone of silence hanging over her head, each separately alive though they seemed like they'd rather be dead. Poised by the makeshift stage, they waited ahead of the crowds while priests and pastors, imam and rabbi, passed by in robes of pomp and intensity.

Meanwhile the stranger stayed hidden under trees. The white cat twined around his feet. "Garnet," he whispered, remembering its name from long ago.

"I lost my daughter," Evie said into an ice-cream microphone, candy pink and much too cheerful for her frozen face. Her thin voice snatched at the air, while electronics caught the sound, amplifying silence to crackling booms. Confidence faded backward into the trees then reflected again. *Is she looking at me?* "I lost my daughter right over there." She pointed. He was glad he'd hidden himself this side of the pond instead. People stared. "A dog found her and dug her up. She was buried like a bone. So then we put her in a coffin. Were you there? Did you see? She was so beautiful."

He, the Prowler, had seen the coffin, but he hadn't seen the child, grown old and still. He thought she must have been beautiful; she must have looked like her mother though she'd had her father's eyes. He shuffled his feet, wondering where the dog had buried that particular, earth-shattering, beautiful feast.

The microphone fell from Evie's hands. He almost wanted to run and comfort her. But the other woman, the evil Lydia, picked it up and handed it back. She held her arms around the broken mother, for a while, then let her speak again.

"You know what I prayed sometimes?" Evie asked.

What? Evie prayed? The Prowler thought she'd given up prayer long ago, when God stopped answering, and the child's diagnosis remained unforgivably unchanged.

"For my Amelia? You know what I prayed? You know what she was like."

He had no right; he couldn't know, because he'd left her behind.

"I prayed that God would protect my little girl, because I wouldn't always be here for her, because a mother's meant to die before her children isn't she? I never expected I'd have to bury her."

A father shouldn't have to bury his children either.

Evie sobbed again. "I thought, you know, the same things you all thought—about how she'd never learn to cope on her own."

He'd thought it too. He'd known. He had to leave before his daughter's future ceased to exist, before the blame became too great for any of them to bear. But Evie always insisted on believing there'd be hope; sweet Evie, ever betrayed by his denial and her broken child. So she stood, talking now about prayer.

"I asked God to help. So I guess God must've decided she wouldn't have to cope. I guess God took her away instead of taking me. I don't like how it happened. I'm sure she didn't like it. But God took her, and now my Amelia's okay."

Evie sobbed, the sound hard and fierce, as loudspeakers turned it to shouting over the crowd. "Now she's never going to suffer anymore, and I don't need to be scared for her." It might have been a cry of triumph, but Evie's voice faded, strangling the final words. She wrung her hands and held the microphone low against her waist, a leaden weight that needed to fall to the ground.

Meanwhile the Prowler crouched over the cat, burying his face in fur. He tried not to cry, tried to make no sound, and prayed he wouldn't be heard or seen at all.

"I guess it's me who has to cope now on my own," Evie continued, "not Amelia. And I just want to ask you all to help, 'cause it's so very, very hard."

He couldn't help. His heart was stone, and he couldn't put those shattered pieces together, never again. He really was a shiftless, worthless soul.

When the Prowler looked up, the other woman had taken Evie's position on the makeshift stage. "I don't know what I lost," Lydia said, evil Lydia, unwitting daughter-in-law of a murderer. She faced the crowd's accusation with a gaze that trembled and wavered even more than her hands. She held the shivering microphone close to her nose, and clutched her stomach as if in pain. "I lost my father-in-law I suppose. And then it was like he'd never really been there for me to lose, like I'd never really known him. I feel like everything's sliding away, like it's all an illusion. Nothing's certain anymore."

Curled low to the ground, crouched like a dog beside the cat, the stranger knew what Lydia meant. Nothing was certain, and life slips away like water in the stream. He remembered where he'd heard her name, Lydia Markham, from that distant part of his life. The cat wasn't hers; it was her neighbor's, and she was married to the son from Markham's garage, just along the road. He needed to hate her, because the man from that garage was the man in the woods, the Paradise Predator turned Murderer, the man who killed the child.

Fair-haired Lydia looked around the crowd, seeing so many faces, but not the man's. She confronted their knowledge of her father-in-law and called it their mistake too. "Did you take your cars to him? Some of you did, I know. If you talked to him in the garage, if you met him on the street, aren't you wondering the same things as I am? How could we not have known? How could we *all* not have known?"

But no one had known that the man who mended cars would break the child.

—If the stranger had stayed, if he'd still been there in her life, could he have kept her from the predator in the woods? Could he have made her safe? Would he have known?

"I lost my memories of my children's grandfather, and my husband's father."

—He'd lost his child, the life he'd thrown away when he left that day.

"All the things I thought he was, the things he could have been…"

—But Amelia could never be more, would never have been anything at all. She didn't deserve what had happened to her.

"And then my little boy comes up to me and says, 'I still love him.'"

—Does Evie love me still? Did Amelia?

People in the crowd turned toward each other, anger perhaps on their faces, disgust or something else. "My son still loves him," Lydia announced firmly, sudden confidence infusing her voice. "His memories, my son's memories, he's holding onto them. They *were* real, those things he remembers; they're part of my son, part of who he is. And I'm thinking maybe that's alright, because I'm not sure how to tell him it's all wrong."

The Prowler sobbed out loud, knowing everything was wrong, everything since the day he left, since he'd thrown his own memories away. Afraid of little Amelia at three, he'd never known her at seven, at eleven, thirteen. He'd lost that right.

"Everything that's happened, all these awful things, they don't change the past."

—They don't change the fact that he wasn't there when he was needed.

"The only thing that's changing is the future."

—He had none.

Hearing nothing now but a roaring pain in his ears, the Prowler crouched to the ground. A child's high trill broke through, impossibly, but he wouldn't listen. "Daddy, it's okay.

Daddy? Daddy?" The cat clawed his knees and he was still hiding under trees.

"I wonder," evil Lydia asked, still standing in front of the crowd, still speaking into the microphone. "Is it possible for someone to *be* two people at once?"

—Could that be him? Could he be lover and betrayer, father and stranger both? Was that why he felt so torn apart?

He crouched in the shadows, waiting for the crowds to depart from the park again. He was well hidden. But then the stranger, husband, prowler, devourer, or father, felt a hand on his shoulder. He heard a once-loved, once-familiar voice whisper his name.

"Hello Andrew."

"Evie?"

Part 2

~4~

Ten-year-old Evelyn was tiny, neat, and beautiful. Long dark curls wreathed her narrow face. Small freckles played across her button nose, anchored between the shine of bright eyes and the glow of a heart-shaped smile.

She should have been playing with her neighbor, eleven-year-old Andrew, on the ground behind their homes, but instead Evelyn stood under the old oak tree and refused to move away. A neighbor's cat had climbed there in scrabbled leaps from summer's dust and debris. Sweet Evelyn pranced among twisted roots as if the ground burned her feet. "You'll have to rescue it, Andrew!" she cried. Her ballerina arms danced high while her skirt swung wide. Meanwhile Andrew thought of an un-rescued red rubber ball lost days ago in undergrowth. Finding that would be much more interesting than trying to rescue a cat. Still, Evelyn shouted again. "Andrew, you'll have to climb up there and carry it down."

Scents of green dripped around him with the sound of the girl's determined voice. Drifting leaves, sharp as summer, seemed soft as fluttering silk when they lighted on his arms. Scents of brown rose in a cloud from the dry earth around his feet. And emerald eyes stared down among the shadows of a black cat's fur.

Ever practical, Andrew measured the lack of lower branches and the width of the old oak's trunk. He angled his fingers out from his thumb, stared past them, then answered solemnly, "No way."

"But you have to, Andrew!" Evelyn's feet threw more soft puffs of dirt around her legs as she swung to face him.

Andrew asked, "How?" Then, looking for his own solution, he left his young friend bouncing, her dizzying movements almost certainly scaring the cat.

Ignoring Evelyn's protests, Andrew backed carefully toward his house. He stopped to perform a new calculation after every measured stride, pondering possibilities with wrinkled nose and eyes. Then he halted at the splintering steps and stared down at the old toy box. Its paint was cracked. Cobwebs clung to rust around its hinges. Weeds twined into chains around the box's base, anchoring it to the ground. Long scratches in the wood hid spiders, millipedes, snakes or more. But Andrew was a boy, and a girl had asked for help, so he had to try.

The box wouldn't move, not even when Andrew leaned his whole weight into it. Meanwhile Evelyn didn't move from the tree, so she'd be no help. Andrew turned from her in disgust, then tipped his head to one side so ideas might anchor more firmly in his mind; perhaps if he took all the contents out of the box, he might make it light enough to lift. *Contents, spiders, what?* His fingers trembled with mistrust, but he cracked the lid, pulling against the force of rust and time. A cloud of dust rose into his face, making him cough, but he persevered, eyes downcast and fingers reaching inside. Four broken tennis rackets were first to his grasp, their strings worn to fibers, thin as spider-webs. Next came an ancient spinning top, a hoop with a splintered edge, a worn-out rubber ball, cracked mitts, a broken bicycle pump, and a cobwebbed carton of tools. Resisting the urge to check if anything remained, Andrew slammed the lid back down and bent to pull again. The box rocked against its nest of weeds, resisted, and finally moved. Andrew wrapped his arms over the top, dug in his heels, and began to drag his treasure across the scraggy grass, edging backward toward the oak tree and the cat.

"Some help?" he asked, gasping for breath and glancing over his shoulder to his friend. That tree was an awfully long way away.

"Huh? What?"

Evelyn's dancing feet came to a stop, so Andrew dropped the box and turned to stare. "If you want me climbing up that tree for your cat, I'm going to need a boost. Will you help me or not?"

"It's not *my* cat," Evelyn snapped. But she wiped her hands against her skirt and sauntered jauntily toward him.

Andrew pointed to the far side of the box, hoping Evelyn might push while he pulled. But every time the box slid forward, she dropped in a heap behind it. "I've got splinters," she complained, holding two small white hands in front of her face. Andrew displayed his own reddened fingers and sighed. He couldn't see Evelyn's splinters, but then, what did he know? He was just a boy.

At last the box lay under the tree. Andrew jumped on top but still couldn't reach the branches. Climbing down, he tipped the chest on end, listening to the rattle of dirt and stones inside. The wooden frame rocked against the tree's gnarled trunk and threatened to fall. Andrew told Evelyn to hold onto it. She threatened to cry. Then Andrew pointed up at the cat again to persuade her. He started to climb before she could change her mind.

The lowest branch was still almost out of reach. Andrew stretched desperately, grasping for a crumbly strip of bark. If he could hold it, swing his other arm up; if it would take his weight...

Then a jet black streak of fur flew over Andrew's shoulder, past Evelyn, and down to the ground. Boy and box fell flat. Girl fell and cried. The cat was gone.

Andrew rolled onto his stomach, with ragged breath caught in his throat. Evelyn's face was streaked with tears as she lay beside him, curled on one arm, helplessly flat and trembling like a tiny kitten. But Andrew's gaze stayed just a moment too long on her, unblinking. He realized she looked oddly pretty, like a picture in a book, so he reached a hand across the space between them, then froze before he could risk touching her face or hair. His eyes were half-closed now, deep in thought or mystery. He wished he could see if Evelyn were looking at him. Then he rocked to his knees and leaned over her, smelling toothpaste and shampoo. *Yuk.*

"You okay?" he asked, wondering at how his voice growled in his throat.

Evelyn mumbled, "Sure," and Andrew scared himself even more by opening his eyes wide, bending down, and beginning to purse his lips. Was he planning to kiss her? *Did* he kiss her? *Double yuk!* Turning into your big brother is no fun!

Evelyn must have been scared as well. Like the cat, she leapt past Andrew's shoulder and ran across the grass. Her skirt swung wide as she slipped through the gap in the fence and disappeared. But Andrew's lips still quivered while he knelt unmoving on the ground. He shivered to the sweetness of her soap, frightened by the softness of the skin across her cheek, and trembling at the touch of a butterfly kiss that had maybe graced his dream.

Was this what his brother felt when he kissed that girl in the street, the night before he went away—when he thought no one was looking? He'd seemed to roll her over his arm while his head bent down to her face. He'd seemed as if he meant to break her in two.

*****

Andrew, full grown, looked back on that day and remembered he truly loved the girl he married.

*****

Andrew, still scarcely more than a child, stared out of the living room window. Bored and lonely, he almost wished there were a cat in the tree again. Then the rattling of bicycle wheels stirred him from his contemplation. The neighborhood clan of boys rode past on a mission to the local forest. He knew the routine from younger days when he'd tried and failed to be accepted as one of them. They'd follow the road's black ribbon, turn left through the fence onto the trail, then ride over ruts and around tree stumps, tangling their wheels in undergrowth, and playing until the evening's sky grew gray.

Afterward they'd return, boasting, with raucous humor, of their scabbed and bleeding knees. But Andrew had given up on their company; this wasn't his scene, and none of the boys thought to stop at his house and invite him. After all, he was just the studious, wimpy little brother of a soldier gone to Vietnam.

Sandy-haired, nose-in-a-book, lost cause—his reflection stared back from the glass in mute betrayal, while Andrew stared through and beyond. Noticing two of the cyclists were girls with their differently shaped metal frames so their skirts wouldn't tangle when they climbed aboard, he wondered if the narrower frames were as stable in a crash. Aren't triangles the ideal, unalterable shape? He felt his forehead frown and remembered, he'd meant to ask his brother one day. But Carl was gone, and Andrew had forgotten how to talk to him long ago. Still, maybe bike manufacturers didn't care so much about safety with girls' bikes, because girls don't fall off—though Andrew wondered how they'd avoid falling if they rode over twigs and stumps with the rest of the crowd.

Andrew and Evelyn both had bikes of their own; they just didn't ride them so often. In fact, Andrew hadn't ridden out to the woods with Evelyn in—well, a year at least—not since his brother left, not since they were both little kids. They'd reached that point now where spindly legs, somehow overgrown, sent knees jutting up into old metal handlebars. Those bikes were long overdue replacement, long out of style—Evelyn's, pretty pink with purple flowered vines too childishly sweet; Andrew's, with red and blue flashes of robots and explosions. Even Carl had laughed at them before he went. So Andrew and Evelyn stayed home, each pretending in silence that they didn't mind, didn't want to go out.

Of course, if Andrew's brother hadn't left, if Carl hadn't been drafted into that distant army, there would still have been someone in this house who cared about Andrew; someone who might pass his own old bike along to a needy sibling. But how do you borrow from a brother who's not there, and how can a soldier at war gift his belongings to anyone? Andrew couldn't ask his parents to buy a new bike, because they hadn't the money. Meanwhile Carl's sat unused, rusting in the shed. *Waste not want not*—Andrew wondered how long it would be until it wasted away.

Evelyn couldn't ask for a new bike either. Since her father died, she always had to *make do*. But the cycle gang and the open road beckoned. An urge to escape grew strong. Perhaps if Andrew and Evelyn rode to a different part of the woods, where the gangs didn't play, they might be safe on childish bikes with no one to betray their poverty.

Andrew thought of Evelyn's sweet smile, kitten teeth all white with tiny gaps, eyes clear as a cat's. He remembered how she'd fled from him like the cat leaping out of the tree. Had he really kissed her that day, he wondered. And was that why he never saw her playing outside anymore as the summer drew on? He wanted a reason to hang out with her now, because being alone was such a pain. Boring. Worse than cats in trees. It definitely wasn't that he wanted to kiss her again—he shook his nearly twelve-year-old head till his hair stood out from his face. Oh no; no way! *Double, triple yuk!* Though maybe, perhaps...

Back to bikes. He searched his mind for a practical suggestion.

A bike ride, even if their bikes were too small, would offer the chance for Andrew and Evelyn to get some sunshine and exercise—two things he'd learned from school are meant to be seriously good for you. And a boy should surely care about such things, not just for himself, but for those near—as in living near—to him. He should seize the day, not let a friendship end for the price of one imaginary kiss and one real cat. He should...

A boy should ask his girl out now, while she still thought him brave for climbing the tree. Wasn't that right? And maybe she would kiss him properly, perhaps, if their lips met rightly in the woods, if he bent her over his arm like Carl with the stranger out in the street? Though he'd want a nice solid tree trunk to rest her against—he didn't want to drop her. If no one was watching...?

The journey from thought into action was a little longer than Andrew might have intended, but once his mind was made up he ran with proud determination. "Going to go see if Evelyn wants to ride her bike with me," he announced as he passed the kitchen door.

"But your bike's too small," said Mom.

"Don't care. So's hers."

"But Andrew…"

He didn't wait for further complaints and counter-offers, but turned and ran. The door slammed behind him, cutting off Mom's usual question. "Got your…?"

"Yes, I've got my key."

Andrew's bike slumped on time-flattened tires behind the shed door. He tugged the rusted frame out into the light and let it sag against the fence. Then he jumped across into Evelyn's yard. *Someone* seemed to be watching from a window upstairs. He thought perhaps she waved, so he walked more slowly to the door to give her time.

His hand had scarcely touched the knob when a wide gap opened. Evelyn stood breathless in front of him. "Watcha doin'?"

"Riding my bike." Andrew stared at his feet and realized his socks had fallen down.

Meanwhile Evelyn stared past him and around her yard. "What bike?"

"I left it over the fence." He tried not to mumble. "Wanna ride with me?"

"Where?"

"To the woods."

Evelyn frowned, and Andrew realized, with a sudden sense of power, that he could probably guess what she was thinking.

"Just you and me," he said. "Not like everyone can see. And, well, both our bikes are kind of bad aren't they?"

He tried to smile then watched her walk toward the fence, all long legs and unbalanced body, her knees lifting high over waves of unkempt weeds. She wouldn't like it if anyone laughed at how she looked on a bike. But Andrew thought she looked beautiful, so differently proportioned, legs and body, though she still wasn't tall—much shorter than him in fact. His eyes wanted to measure the length of her. Then he thought of how the wind might blow her hair around her face, and how her lips would grace each passing strand. He stared at his feet under wrinkled socks again, confidence fading with the breeze, and wished he could talk to Carl.

"War has a lot to answer for," Andrew's dad would say in the evenings, watching TV. Did he know war left little brothers scared to ride out with their girls?

Andrew shuddered the thoughts away and searched for his voice. "I saw the gang head to the woods. To the top part." He tried to add some logic to the words. "We'll go the other way, not with them, down the bottom loop. Please?"

For his final plea, he reached for Evelyn's hand. His own fingers were clean, recently washed. He hoped she could smell his soap. "Please Evelyn. After all, I did try to rescue your cat."

"Not my cat," she said, but she agreed, digging down improbably at the fence's roots to drag her rusted steed from its nest of weeds.

Sandy hair blew next to dark as two heads met over matching recalcitrant tires. Evelyn's pump sang ineffectively, and Andrew tried to take over. "It's broken. I'll use mine." But his was worthless too. Back in the shed, Carl's bike stared at Andrew, abandoned. He imagined Carl staring too, as he took the stronger pump down from the shelf; thumbs up and smiling, the way he used to do before small Andrew grew too big: *Go for it kiddo.*

Andrew hoped he still knew how to ride his bike. *Do you forget? How quickly do you forget?* And did Evelyn harbor similar doubts? His feet felt more leaden than the pedals, hovering in space, trying to shape the motion expected of them. But he pressed down hard, clutched the handlebars, swung his leg, and was suddenly away. Wind sang through the spokes and into his ears, as wheels bounced over ruts and wobbled around potholes. Straightening his back with returning confidence, he steered onto the blacktop next to cars. His neck ached from holding his head up so high, and his eyes scanned for the corner into the woods. Then he risked a glance behind. Was Evelyn even there?

Dark hair streamed past her shoulders like a superhero's cape. Her face was red with exertion. And Andrew, still looking back at her when his wheel hit a bump in the road, almost fell off his bike.

He was nearly too late signaling for the turn. His muscles couldn't quite remember how to keep his arm outstretched, but the skills came back slowly. So they swung together down the path, lifted their bikes over the gate, and set off through fallen leaves toward the pond.

"This is so cool!" Andrew slid into a slalom turn and stopped just before he hit the water. Evelyn skidded to a separate halt beside him. He reached for her bike, holding it upright and keeping her close. "Look. Isn't it great?"

"And quiet." Her eyes shone bright as fireflies under the shadow of trees.

"And peaceful. Nobody's here."

"Except us."

"And…"

A bird's loud squawk disturbed them as it arrowed down for the water. The splash was like an explosion. They laughed as one.

Andrew leaned closer over the handlebars of Evelyn's bike. Close enough to kiss, if he dared, if Carl had told him how. But he probably wouldn't—didn't want to scare her. She smelled of strawberries and cream. Her hair smelled of grass and leaves as she turned her cheek. Then Andrew's mouth bounced without his volition, awkwardly snagging a mouthful of curls. She was so sweet. How could he never have noticed it before? He felt his cheeks grow warm and heard his brother's voice in his ears. "'Cause you were just a little 'un, kiddo. You're growing up now."

He hoped he wouldn't grow old enough for the draft to catch him too, as it had Carl.

*****

There were cats in the forest. At first Andrew thought they might be dangerous animals. Their shadowed bodies crept around the pond, bright eyes peeking out between grasses and leaves. Then clambering paws scrambled over the bikes Andrew and Evelyn had leaned on trees.

Evelyn told him the tribe was wild but safe, made up from strays that banded together and bred, multiplying their numbers, living in holes in the ground, and sheltering in sheds. "We had one once in our yard, a mother cat, and she had kittens, but they don't usually stray that far."

"Perhaps she was on her way to join the clan." *Or join a war,* thought Andrew, tucking stray hairs behind Evelyn's ear and wondering who wild cats fought—was the forest their equivalent of Vietnam? He shuffled to get a better angle on Evelyn's face. She leaned, propped on one elbow, awkwardly bent as if unsure whether she really wanted to lie so near a boy. Her expression seemed incongruously serious. Andrew let his gaze slip away from her eyes. He stared instead at grass strands threaded through her hair. He tried to pretend his concern was for kittens and cats, not a girl's companionship.

"They were the sweetest things."

Evelyn's hand crept over the gap between them. Soon Andrew could stroke his fingers over hers. He asked, after a pause, "What happened to them? The cats in your shed?"

"I don't know. They disappeared eventually."

"Moved on…?" as his brother had moved perhaps? Moved to fight in the forest? To die? *What sort of animal kills cats?*

He hoped nothing bad had happened to Carl since they last heard from him. Meanwhile Evelyn talked about leaving milk and food in saucers. She offered up names to identify her feline strangers, and argued the pros and cons of encouraging wildlife to be tame.

"Though cats aren't really wild are they?" Andrew asked.

"Well. Wild cats are."

And soldiers? Are they wild people? He wondered if his absent brother was wild.

Evelyn told how she'd gained the mother cat's trust, until she could approach without being hissed at. He wanted Evelyn's trust. "I even got to touch one of the babies."

Not understanding the attraction, but remembering sharp claws flying over his shoulder, Andrew let his fingers touch Evelyn's hair. It trickled through his fingers, softer than grass, and warmer. Then Evelyn told how the shed stood empty when all the cats were gone. It made Andrew think of Carl's dark hole in his life. "Not Coal though. Coal's not wild." *What coal?* He asked and she explained. "Coal. The cat you rescued."

Black *Coal* had seemed pretty wild to him, the way it leapt from the tree when he tried to save it. "So is it yours, your cat?"

"No. Someone else's. I see it around."

Andrew sighed. Maybe saving cats wasn't the way to Evelyn's heart. Perhaps he had to save Evelyn instead. If only she weren't so very self-contained. If only he could think of a time or place where she might need to be saved. Then she'd let him hold her, the way she said she'd held the cat.

He remembered his brother kissing that girl in the street. Was Carl *saving* some distant beauty in Vietnam now? Or was he shooting and dying like they showed on TV?

*****

It was only a kiss; one kiss; one miss. It wasn't even real. Andrew wondered what made it keep returning to his mind? Was Evelyn forever thinking about their fumble too? Did she hate it, love it, want to kiss him again? He didn't dare ask, and certainly didn't dare try. But he did look for any kind of chance or excuse to spend time with her.

"You're out too much," his mother complained, but he knew he'd done all his chores.

"Should stop in more, Andrew. Family needs you," said Dad, who was glued to the television, busily ignoring all family needs and desires.

But Andrew loved his parents, and had to obey, especially with his brother away. So he rationed his Evelyn-time between homework, chores, and a pretense at family life. He rationed his television time too, and his staring-out-the-window time. He measured each moment with the ticking of his watch and kept notes, just to prove no minutes went to waste. In winter he noticed the black cat stopped hanging around. He guessed it must have turned out wild after all. Then he spotted an orange colored creature that spent way too many hours next door, clearly enamored of the girl he adored. This cat vanished too, eventually. Andrew didn't ask why. Cats were just details, recorded with dates and descriptions in minimal words.

At last, Andrew decided it was time his parents gave him Carl's old bike.

"It's Carl's," Mom snapped. "You leave it alone." Wrinkles turned into a frown across her forehead and around her nose.

"But Carl's grown up."

"Wait and ask him yourself."

"He's not here to ask."

"I said wait."

His mom wasn't listening, but Andrew had to persist. "We don't know when he's coming home." He stomped his foot though it hardly made any sound on the carpeted floor. Meanwhile Dad gazed blankly at the TV news and muttered, *If he's coming home.*

Andrew stared in sudden, startled horror. He felt his mouth drop open and tasted dryness on his lips. Then Mom shoved him out of the room. He almost stopped to ask Dad what he meant, but instead he reminded himself about the bike. So he clutched the doorframe with outstretched arms and repeated, "Well, can I? Can I borrow Carl's bike?"

Mom's voice spat venom. "You do what you like." So he did.

The bike was much bigger than Andrew's, taller, stronger, with its frame covered in rust. Andrew cleaned the metal with solemn care, talking to his brother in his head. "I know you won't mind, Carl." He polished the handle-bars. "I bet you'd be real proud of me, really." He flexed thin muscles in his arms then pumped up the tires, crouching down to check the muscles again afterward for signs of growth. "I'm getting real big, Carl, aren't I? See." He squashed the saddle down to its lowest height and stared at his old, red-painted machine looking so small, like a kitten lost against the wall. It was still much bigger than Evelyn's flowered steed.

"Mom." Andrew banged the screen door aside and popped his head through to the corridor. "Mom. I'm giving my old bike to Evelyn. Is that okay?"

No one replied, though the television still muttered its muted complaint. Andrew took silence as a yes. But he couldn't ask Evelyn to ride a bike with robot stickers on the side. So he searched the shed for paint and decided on white, like their picket fence. Each stroke of his brush left streaks on the metal frame. The surface was threaded with cat-hairs and speckled with dust. It smelled of fermented fruit, stewed in glue, and dark fumes made him sneeze. But it was worth all the effort in the end, to see Evelyn smile when he gave the bike to her. At last, she'd be able to ride without banging her knees. The hard-edged triangle might be a boy's bike frame, but it looked fine.

Back by the pond, where wild cats roamed, Evelyn called her favorites to her by name. Andrew reveled in the soda-bubbles of her voice. He was growing up, and Evelyn was growing too. When she let him run his fingers through her hair—she didn't pull away!—he remembered her talking about stroking a renegade kitten. Did hair feel like fur?

Perhaps he'd try to kiss her again today.

~5~

Thin skims of snow drifted over the ground and settled like spider webs. When Andrew and Evelyn cycled back from the woods, they slowed for icy corners and stomped their feet in ruts to clear the way. Climbing the hill toward home, Andrew hoped they wouldn't stop in case they couldn't get going again. Then he saw his parents standing by the end of the drive, and knew something was wrong. He pulled on his brakes, searching his memory for what he might have done, or failed to do. What dire misdeed could have both parents on his case?

The back wheel of Carl's bike skidded and slid on the ice, while Andrew stretched his legs to the limit to keep his balance. Meanwhile Evelyn swerved past him. She waved as she turned into her drive. "See ya later, Andrew." Then he dropped his feet to the road and stared. Why wasn't his father glued to the television? Why wasn't his mother tied to the kitchen sink?

Andrew walked forward, bike clutched to his side, feet and wheels dragging noisily in half-frozen mud. Ice shards splashed to the curb. He kept his gaze mostly on his worn-out shoes, but he looked up every few steps to keep his path straight. Then he noticed his parents were smiling.

Dad's long arm draped like some kind of fox-fur around Mom's neck. His wide mouth spread in an unlikely grin as he shouted Andrew's name. Then he lifted Mom up from the ground as if to throw her in the air. *Unbelievable!*

Andrew scooted forward with the bike. "So?" he asked, halting at the gatepost, still tensing his foot to flee at a moment's disgrace. "What's up, Mom? Dad?"

Mom couldn't seem to find breath to answer him. She gasped, fish-like, then closed her mouth again while Dad took a turn. His wide smile seemed awkwardly painted on thin lips. His voice came out staccato, machine-gun style. He lifted Mom in the air again, her hair almost covering his mouth, and he snapped, "Carl's coming home, Son. Carl's coming home."

Andrew's first thought was concern that he might lose access to Carl's bicycle. Then he remembered his brother was full-grown, far more likely to demand to borrow Dad's car. So he walked toward the shed, trying to keep his footsteps slow, trying not to let his excitement grow too fast. He flung a question casually back over his shoulder. "Are you sure, Dad? 'Cause, you know, he might not… He might not even want…" *Better to expect disappointment than wait to be disappointed*; wasn't that right?

Dad's hand fell like a block of cement on the back of Andrew's neck. His voice boomed, suddenly loud and parade-ground sure. "Carl's coming home, Son."

Then Andrew swung around, dropping his cautious nature like an empty sack. His cheeks stretched so far they began to ache. "Hurray! Hurray!" He leapt helplessly into the air, landing unexpectedly into his father's frantic hug.

Mom laughed and bustled between them, then slipped away into the house, pondering aloud, "But what shall I feed him?" Her feet almost flew, dancing as lightly as Evelyn's in the woods.

Carl's coming home. Carl's coming home. Magic words whispered with every breath of air in Andrew's lungs. *Carl's not dead; Carl's not dead; he's coming home.* Hanging out with a next-door maybe-girlfriend was suddenly losing its appeal. Andrew didn't even feel tempted to dash over there with the news until his father insisted that he should. Because girls are just girls, after all, and brothers are forever.

In the days of waiting, Andrew didn't want to ride Carl's bike. He couldn't muster enthusiasm for playing in the yard. He didn't climb the tree, chase cats or even dream of rescuing anything. He just went to school, came home, and watched the road through the window above his bed, while theoretically studying.

Then Carl arrived, swinging the world's biggest bag at the end of his arm, sporting the world's biggest smile on his face, and wearing a hat that somehow meant grownup, brother, soldier, wise man and king, all rolled into one. Homework forgotten, Andrew flew downstairs to meet him, and everything changed.

*****

Carl's presence sprawled across every room of the house. He talked in a low, smoky voice of wild dances, unimaginable drinks and stores, palm trees and politicians, musicians, comedians, talk show hosts, and pranks played long ago. He filled the air with laughter and shouts of strident certainty, loud opinions, and larger than life determination to prove he was always right. Surprisingly, Dad allowed Carl to rule the television and win each argument, even politics and even religion. He, who must always be kowtowed to, never disagreed with any of his older son's opinions; just smiled that wide, eternal, painted smile, and puttered away from the eternal armchair, giving Mom a better chance to clean.

Tall and strong, Carl was everything Andrew aspired to be. Muscles rippled all along his arms, his stride could cross small canyons, and his confidence left Andrew feeling like a helpless child. Still, *helpless* was okay today; *helpless* was a great guy's shadow. *Helpless* was just a sign of growing up too, so Andrew didn't mind at all.

A different girl sat next to Carl at the dining table each night. Sometimes Andrew caught shadows of dismay in his parents' eyes, but they always vanished, like fireflies in the wind. Mom and Dad always smiled wider than a station-wagon for the favored son. They treated each of his girls as if she were *the one*, and conversed in meaningless pleasantries, no thought for the future or past. Then Carl would drive away in Dad's 'wagon, borrowed without a word from him as soon as the meal was done. He'd stay out late, dancing or watching movies with his girl, not telling, and nobody asked.

In the daytime, while Dad worked and Andrew was at school, Carl chopped firewood for the house. Andrew saw him once at the end of the day, slick with sweat, arms swinging with brutal intensity, as if he thought the logs might draw guns and shoot at him. He turned his face toward the sound of Andrew's greeting then glared, as if his younger brother had acquired a pair of horns and a tail since the last time they met. Andrew shrank back in dismay but quickly forgave his brother. Then he hid in the bushes to watch a picture of his future in the older boy's brooding eyes.

Carl's peace wasn't long, but it felt like it lasted forever until, like ice, it splintered apart.

Dad just had to know. He couldn't stay calm and compliant. He couldn't put up that perfect show forever. So he demanded to learn where Carl had been in the war and what he'd done. He asked for details, while Carl offered political debate. He insisted, "That stuff on TV, is that you? You done that stuff?" Then he looked at the screen instead of staring at his son.

A news bulletin showed soldiers bleeding on the ground, fires burning, and women and children in tears. Andrew stared at this brother's arms, wondering if bullet-holes could hide beneath the muscles there.

Carl's face twisted into a snarl, as unexpected as the glare he'd thrown at Andrew while chopping wood. "I've been there," he replied, his voice like thunder with tornados drawing near. "We take care of people, look after them as well, but that doesn't seem to matter to anyone."

For a moment the soldier-brother didn't just sound different. He exuded an alien strangeness and despair, thick as glue or white paint on Evelyn's bike, noxious above the scent of Mom's cooking. He played with his food in a way that Andrew knew was forbidden, making mountains from mashed potato, then pouring gravy from his knife like a river of blood. *Why doesn't Mom tell him not to?* Andrew quivered with the tension of the moment. Then, when everyone else had cleared their plates, Carl suddenly gobbled his whole meal up as if his mouth had turned into a vacuum cleaner.

"What do they give you to eat over there?" Mom asked with a nervous laugh. She lifted dinner out of the way to make space for dessert, while Carl's latest girl smiled empty platitudes and draped her body across his chest.

Carl stared as if he were trying to see across countries all the way to Vietnam, but he just answered, "Food."

"Do you eat what the…" Mom groped for words, and fumbled an apple pie down onto the table in front of Carl's girl. "Do you eat what the natives eat, those Vietnamese?"

"I eat food, Mom," Carl repeated.

Andrew remembered seeing soldiers on TV. They had tins on their laps and their fingers scraped something that didn't look much like food into waiting mouths. He couldn't remember when he'd seen it though. But his parent's bravery with words tonight inspired him to pursue the one question he cared about. "Have you killed anyone?"

Carl glared.

*****

There was an early Christmas dance at the local church. Mom and Dad were going, and Carl agreed to bring one of his many girlfriends—Andrew wasn't sure how he chose which one. Perhaps he rolled marbles and asked their smoked glass crystal for an answer. Evelyn's mother visited Andrew's mom to say Evelyn could come as well. Andrew, who hadn't thought to invite her, couldn't think what to make of that. He hadn't even mentioned her existence to Carl. He hadn't dared, and now he wasn't sure he wanted to share his brother with anyone else. But he had no choice.

"You'll like her," Mom told Carl. "Evelyn's nice."

Even that sounded like betrayal to Andrew's ears, though Big Brother just laughed and mussed his hair with his hand. "'Course I'll like her, little guy. She's got to be nice if she hangs out with you. Hey! Now we've both got dates." And that sounded cool; little brother Andrew included in big brother's plans.

Carl's girlfriend would surely be perfectly nice as well. But she must have lived some distance away, so Dad loaned his car to the favored son who needed to pick her up. Meanwhile Andrew's parents would walk with Andrew and Evelyn along the road. Thoroughly embarrassed by their presence, Andrew begged to be allowed to walk behind. But Dad insisted he didn't want the youngsters getting lost.

"Dad! We're just walking to church. We go there every week."

"That's not the point." And maybe *lost* wasn't what he hoped to avoid.

Andrew marched, stiff as a bulletin-board, beside his girl, until Evelyn grasped his hand. Then he jumped, zapped by unexpected electricity and suddenly scared that his dad, who couldn't see his face, might spot and criticize his goofy smile. Evelyn's fingers seemed so tiny and warm, despite the icy air. He imagined lifting her palm to his lips so he could kiss it, like in movies. But he couldn't work out how to do that without standing still, or he'd trip over his feet. And he couldn't stop walking because his parents were watching from behind. Glancing over his shoulder, he thought he saw a tear splash from his mother's eyes. Dad dabbed her face with a big white handkerchief. It was probably the light.

Loud music blared as they came close to the church. The white-painted tower seemed to sway to leaden drum-beats thundering out through aching hearts. Dancing feet and fumbling arms stretched like webs across the entrance to the hall, and the party was already in full swing. Heads leaned on shoulders as feet shuffled and kicked. Eyes gazed sleepily. Mouths sucked lips. The drinks probably hadn't been spiked, though Andrew wondered about the tiny flask Carl seemed to carry all the time. He never saw him empty or refill it. Thinking of which, was his brother here yet? He stretched his neck and turned from side to side in hopes of seeing him.

Andrew's parents pushed their way through the crowd. They sat with the older folk, gray heads refusing to bob or dance, straight backs leaning at strictly measured angles against the white wooden wall. Each held a glass of pale pink liquid, more for looking at than drinking. And each lap bore a plate of dry sandwiches balanced between the knees.

Meanwhile Andrew, having failed to find Carl, looked around for other kids from junior high and saw none. He wasn't sure if that was a good thing or bad. Perhaps they were all outside waiting to tease him afterward. Perhaps a Christmas dance at church would be considered lame by the town's thirteen-year-olds. So he stood, awkwardly balancing himself on one foot then the other, until Evelyn wrapped her arms around his waist and tugged at him. "We're supposed to dance," she whispered, her voice blowing strangely across his ear. He might have been happy to try but, right at that moment, Carl arrived. The soldier-boy ignored everyone else and marched straight onto the dance floor, promptly dominating the scene.

Andrew almost slid from Evelyn's grip. He couldn't dance. He couldn't join in and didn't dare show his weakness in front of Carl. But he couldn't face the embarrassment of offending Evelyn either—especially not here, where she could shout and Carl could hear whatever names she called him. So instead he struggled to persevere, moving his feet in scared imitation of his brother, though Carl moved legs and arms as well, smooth as a TV dancer. And Evelyn's feet seemed to follow an entirely different path.

The beat danced always a few toe-holds ahead of Andrew's legs. His arms swung out at just the wrong time, and bumped into strangers' sides while his heart began to sink.

"Hold onto me," Evelyn whispered, leaning toward him. "Look down at your feet if you need to and watch what I do. Try to follow me. No! I don't mean stand on them." She really wouldn't qualify as the world's best dance teacher.

Andrew tried, while Evelyn pulled him into an awkward semblance of musical movement. Big brother Carl flung his beautiful date to the winds, blowing everyone away. Then the music changed. Crowds parted into a ring around the dance-hall couple, cheering loudly, as if this place were Carl's own personal space, his welcome home party. Even some of the scariest adults marched up to congratulate him, while others glared. Andrew, still holding Evelyn's hand as he took his place in the ring of admirers, couldn't fathom quite which camp to belong to. These men were judging war, not dance, and his brother hadn't asked to go to over there.

"I'll teach you how it's done, little guy." Carl suddenly pulled Andrew from the safety of Evelyn's arms. "Here's what you do." He placed him, like a statue, small feet frozen to the floor. "Copy me," Carl insisted, as if he believed his brother could imitate his moves. "You can do it, little guy."

Not so little. Andrew frowned in deep concentration, watched every twist and turn and flinging limb, then felt his brother's confidence wash over his frozen fear.

"Loosen up, little guy. Feel the groove. You can do it. You're not made of stone." *But statues are.*

Notes poured down on him as he forced himself to try. The world spun around in a mist of dizzying oblivion. Nothing and no one mattered except Carl and Carl's approval. The sound of his brother's voice dictated Andrew's every move. Meanwhile his mind slid somewhere else and watched from a cobweb high on a corner of the wall. *You can do it, little guy!*

Other families arrived now at the hall. Cold air blew in with their chatter as they surged through the door. Those missing schoolmates were fashionably late and stood in a ring around the brothers. Andrew should have hidden and cried. But instead he tried to carry on, mind returning to body and heart dropping ever more stone-like with every step. He lifted his head, just for a moment, and caught a glimpse of Carl's old smile, the one he used to share when Andrew was small enough to be cute. Then his legs, re-empowered, took lives of their own again, and the dance carried on. He stopped trying to count or measure the width of his arms. He stopped wishing he could copy each design. Flinging himself into joyful, musical abandon, he suddenly knew his brother was finally, wholly, and perfectly home. And therefore all was right with Andrew's world.

Then the music stopped. Andrew found himself grasped in an unlikely, firmly-muscled hug. His feet left the floor, and Carl spun him around, just like a tiny child again. Andrew didn't mind at all.

When the world stopped spinning, he noticed Evelyn grinning happily at him.

Carl's girl went home with somebody else that night. Carl didn't seem to care, though Andrew would surely have hated it if Evelyn held some other schoolboy's hand. Still, they all climbed into Dad's car together as the night drew on and the music faded away. Dad took the keys and sat in front with Mom while Carl, Evelyn and Andrew shared the back. Evelyn took the middle seat because she was smallest, but she leaned against Andrew all the way, as if she were maybe, slightly afraid of his brother. She wouldn't speak to Carl, even when Carl asked her how much she'd enjoyed the dance.

"You're a neat little dancer, girl. Good feet."

She shuffled her knees closer to Andrew's and he didn't complain, though parts of him he'd hardly known seemed to warm at the echo of her touch.

"She's good for you, little brother. She's a keeper, your girlfriend."

Andrew smiled, while his girlfriend's—*yes! His girlfriend's*—head bounced against his chest. She defined her own beat, and he liked this dance. But all too soon it was time for him to walk her back to her door. They walked together up the drive. "Thanks for coming," he volunteered in a slightly squeaky voice, as Evelyn thanked him for the invitation he'd never extended to her, shouting thanks back to his parents for the ride. Then she left his side and vanished into the yellow light of her home.

*****

Christmas passed and ice gave way to stringy shards of grass. Andrew's end-of-term exams were coming up, distracting him from parents, girlfriend and brother. But he couldn't miss the growing arguments that filled the house; something about re-enlistment and pensions and money for college and more. Andrew planned to go to college one day. It was why he studied so hard. But it didn't seem like the arguments centered on him. He opened the front door one evening, after staying late in class, and found Carl's rigid bulk at the foot of the stairs. Sparks spat from his brother's soldier-eyes. Mom and Dad faced him from the living room sofa, spitting coal-dust out of theirs.

"I'm old enough to get shot at, Dad. I can make my own decisions." Carl shouted, as if his father were miles away instead of just across the room.

"You're not even twenty-one. You're still my son."

"Tell that to the draft." Carl turned and took the stairs three at a time, striding up to his room.

Andrew slunk quietly behind his brother's rage. The door to Carl's room was ajar, so he knocked lightly, and jumped onto his brother's bed. Sagging springs creaked complaint.

"What were they talking about?" Andrew asked, crossing his legs atop the deep green cover. "I could hear them arguing from halfway down the street. Everyone could hear."

Carl leaned back in his chair, lips tight beneath his frown. "It wasn't nothing. Change the subject."

Nothing. Nothing. Closed out and rejected again. But Andrew had a question on his mind. It had puzzled him ever since the Christmas dance. So he forced a smile back onto his face, ignored his parents' argument and his brother's dismissal, and asked, "Okay. If Evelyn's a keeper, what do I do to keep her?"

Carl tilted the chair back further, crashing its frame against the wall. His frown turned into a smile as he laced his fingers languidly behind his head. Suddenly those outstretched denim-covered legs seemed incredibly long to Andrew. They covered half the floor. Carl began to laugh. It seemed as if the windows might rattle in happy reply. "You be nice to your girlfriend, little brother," he said. "Buy her chocolates and flowers. Go to dances; go to the park; maybe sit with her in church…"

Andrew's heart thundered a soldier's drumbeat in his chest. His body trembled awkwardly, balanced between yesterday and tomorrow, childhood and the world to come. He knew this was the time he'd remember, sitting cross-legged on Carl's bed, learning important secrets of growing up, and waiting for understanding like the dawn.

In the back of his mind, he knew Carl's advice was to do all the things that war had made impossible for him. He'd been taken so suddenly from chocolate and flowers and streets of their small town and the white-walled church.

"Most of all, you don't leave her, see." Carl leaned forward, his face suddenly stern. "You don't leave her, 'cause if you do, she'll leave you for somebody else."

His voice sounded musty, heavy and hard. Perhaps there was a girl, somewhere in town, who'd left this soldier-brother when he went to war, but Andrew guessed he'd never know. He stored the lesson away and determined sweet Evelyn would be his bride when they grew up, one day.

*****

Spring brought a sprinkling of weeds over the grass. Green leaves grew on the old oak tree. Ruts in the forest turned to mud. Cats began to run again beside the sodden pond. Meanwhile Andrew and Evelyn rode their bikes, shared their dreams, and hoped for better times to come. Homework offered the promise of college and more, and both were determined to do well.

Meanwhile Carl re-upped and left and was gone.

Andrew was deep in a math calculation when he heard the car. Its engine could have halted before their yard. It might not be coming here. Or, if it had to stop at Andrew's house, it could have carried some friend from across town with a question for Mom about an obscure recipe. It was just a car, and therefore surely nothing to worry about.

The knock on the door was just an innocent rap of knuckles on wood. It sounded too sharp for a woman's hand, so Andrew guessed it was one of Dad's colleagues perhaps, come here from work with questions about his job. The knock wasn't accompanied by a neighborly "Halloo!" But it was just a knock, therefore nothing to worry about.

Low voices in the living room downstairs spoke in cultured tones, syllables carefully measured to perfect effect. This proved these visitors weren't local, so Andrew bent an ear. He worked out there were two of them, both men, but he couldn't manage to hear their words. Still, surely nothing to worry about.

Then Mom screamed.

Andrew leapt from his cross-legged seat on the bed and ran to the door. He stopped with his hand on the knob, feeling his heartbeat thunder through his shirt. He wondered what had stopped him from going further. He couldn't move.

Mom's voice continued to screech like some parody on TV. She shrieked a flurry of terrifying words; wrong time of year; wrong type of news; wrong bullets; even wrong war. The honest truth was that people make mistakes, so she might not believe what anyone said. "Never! Never!" Another wild shriek.

Andrew tried to parse the sounds and decided whatever news the strangers had brought, he wouldn't believe them either. Then Mom shouted questions as if they would somehow be heard in halls of power and debated through corridors of far-off lands. She screeched in a voice that Andrew had surely never heard before, a sound that swung around the ceiling fan , then flung itself upstairs to batter his ears like a flock of crows disturbed from a corpse. He dropped his hand from the doorknob. Frozen still, he stared emptily at the floor. Till strength came like warmth from some unknown source, and he ran out of his room.

The bedroom door slammed behind him. Andrew's legs stretched for the top of the stairs. Cold air blew from the open door in the hallway below.

"What's wrong, Mom? What's going on?"

His mother lay crumpled on the bottom step, like a wild cat wrapped around its kittens. Andrew's father leaned awkwardly over her, pressing his hand to her back. Two strangers stood in the gap between home's safety and the outside world beyond the front door.

For a moment Andrew thought he might leap down onto the family heap. But he didn't like strangers, and he didn't like fuss, so he paused for thought, shrugged his shoulders, and let his homework call him back to his room. If something momentous really had happened, if this unspeakable suspicion were really true, his parents would tell him, in due and careful course. And if it weren't momentous, he wouldn't care.

He slumped onto his bed, heart and body weighing like stone. He knew exactly what was going on. He knew the truth of what he wouldn't believe. His world was broken.

Reflections danced and sailed across his vision, sliding unwanted through the window, glinting fiercely with the falseness of an afternoon sun. He knew the wrongly directed light came not from above, but bounced from hoods and doors of shiny official cars on the driveway below. He'd seen their dark twins on TV in so many news reports. Calculating angles of reflection and refraction, he hated his thoughts. Then he dripped his own small tears onto the bed, because his own big brother might be dead. Carl, who told him never to leave sweet Evelyn, had gone and left Andrew behind instead.

Doors slammed. Wailing voices stilled into murmurs of complaint then washed into silence. The air in Andrew's room gathered ice. He shuddered and dropped his book on the bed cover. His dry throat cracked. He knew he had to get himself a drink or he'd start coughing soon. And coughing was far too close to crying again.

Avoiding the creaking step on the stairs, Andrew shuffled down toward the kitchen. He heard his mother's knife chop loudly through food then thud on wood. He saw his father in the living room, watching endless TV with unmovable gaze. So the world hadn't changed after all, and his guess might be wrong. Proud soldiers marched across the screen, and Carl was surely among them, still alive, still hopeful. But silence weighed like winter, blaring through the noise of the television, louder than the sound of meat slapped down on the board, and heavier than air. Andrew asked his mother, softly, "What were those men here for?" and nobody answered, or nobody heard.

In days that followed, the house grew quieter yet, until even the television's endless voice was stilled. Cutlery clattered to plate and table at dinner. Salt was passed in response to a nod of the head. Questions were met with puzzled stares, or hands pointed in answer to doors or cupboards or darkened corners of the room. Packed lunches came without wishes or words. The refrigerator made more noise than Andrew's parents did. And the vacuum cleaner drowned their weary breaths.

Mom hurried through a marathon of cleaning. Every picture was straightened in Carl's room; his bedcovers were washed and turned down, each corner measured precisely, each angle laid to match. Carl's curtains hung, not too closed and not too wide. His desk was polished to an oaken glow; his papers neatly stacked below the lamp. The room looked like a shrine and smelled of lavender and soap. Then Mom closed the door and insisted Andrew must never go inside, as if war and death were contagious, as if once he entered the room he might never be released.

"Mom, Carl's not a vampire. He's not a ghost."

She slapped Andrew's face. Mom *never* slapped his face; she never slapped anybody's face! She'd always taught Andrew that nobody's faces should ever, ever be hit. But perhaps, if she could slap him now, that meant that Andrew was suddenly *nobody*. Without his brother, he might as well not exist.

One day, Mom even tried to tell him he mustn't ride Carl's bike. "Everything should be waiting, just like it was."

Andrew backed away before replying. "Mom, he's not ridden his bike in years."

"But he might."

Frustration tore the cruel truth from him. "Mom, Carl's dead. He's not coming back."

"We don't know that. They could have made a mistake."

Andrew knew the truth, but he hid his tears. He knew because, if Carl ever did come back, that beautifully ordered, perfectly manicured mausoleum upstairs wouldn't be his home. He'd think his family had turned him into a ghost, instead of some distant stranger making him dead.

So Andrew dragged out the bike, his brother's bike, despite his mother's complaint. He tugged it from its corner of the shed. He flung his leg over the bar and settled himself in the seat. Too big? Too heavy? Just right? Nothing would ever be right again. He rode off down the road.

Above the rumbling wheels, the rusted chain, unoiled, clattered and groaned. It had grown too loose, but Andrew's brother would never tighten it again. The front wheel wobbled and Andrew knew he would have to straighten it himself. Later. He steered through traffic, signaled turns, maneuvered without danger, and followed the track. Then a pothole almost knocked him down. His breath was ragged and sour.

When he reached the forest pond, he lay down to cry.

The rattle of another bike, the rustle of footsteps in the grass, the sound of another person's awkward breaths—nothing distracted him. But suddenly Evelyn's slender arm was laid across his shoulders. He felt how rasping gulps of air tore through him, but she didn't move. Then he wrapped himself around his friend and sobbed into the comfort of her sweater. She smelled of lavender and lime. The scent of her made his heaving cries grow louder. But neither he nor she could let go. And he thought perhaps he'd survive.

~6~

In the mornings Andrew woke with the birds and wondered why sleep wouldn't keep him. He breakfasted on dry cereal and toast, because the last of the milk went into his mother's nighttime cup of tea. He carried a tray into the bedroom to wake his parents. They stared at him as if they wondered why sleep wouldn't keep them too. Then Andrew rode his brother's bike to school.

In the afternoons, Andrew stopped at the shops on his way home. He emptied his pockets of coins to keep the fridge stocked with food, making sure the cupboards wouldn't be totally bare. He told his mother he needed more cash when he got back, and she asked no questions, just dipped her hand in the housekeeping jar.

Mom would be sitting in the kitchen, dressed in her nightgown. She seemed to have stayed there all day long. With the radio turned low, she stared at the walls, and kept her back to the window so the world couldn't venture in. Cups and plates moldered on tables and counter tops until Andrew washed them and put them away.

He told his mother which meals to cook, then placed the meat and vegetables before her with chopping boards and tools. If her hand froze up while she held the knife, he'd take it from her, completing the task in her place. He kept watch over pans, turned down the heat, and ladled the results onto plates.

In the evenings, Andrew's father came home from work. He dumped his bag on the floor then slumped on a chair in front of the TV. Pictures moved without purpose across the screen; the sound, like Mom's radio, was turned low. Andrew's father ate from plates brought in from the kitchen and balanced on his lap. He drank only if Andrew remembered to place a cup in his hand. His body stayed glued to one spot until night, when he would follow Mom's frail form upstairs to bed.

When everyone else was gone, Andrew might wash his clothes. Sometimes he was too tired. And sometimes, if he remembered, just before they went upstairs, he'd ask his father for money.

"Why?"

"We need more groceries. There's nothing in Mom's jar."

With fingers crossed, he hoped against hope that his father would refuse. Not giving him cash might mean the beginning of thought behind dead eyes. It might mean a chance for real life to resume, with at least one parent not sleep-walking. But Mom and Dad both gave him all he asked, demanded nothing, and ignored the things he managed to give to them.

Dust thickened in layers across the floor. Cupboards grew dark with dirt. Cobwebs hung in front of the unopened door to Carl's bedroom. Windows turned opaque with mottled glass.

But on Saturdays, Andrew and Evelyn took their bikes and rode to the woods. They lay in the long grass by the pond, noses tickled by seeds and stems, ears assaulted by sounds of squirrels and wrens, and the yowling of cats. They smelled the cleanliness of water and trees, talked of school friends, TV favorites, movie stars, war, the weather, and whose team ought to win the match. Just for a while, Andrew pretended he lived in the same sweet world as everyone else. Evelyn even talked about church, that gray-white painted place where the Christmas dance had been held, where Carl told Andrew to hold onto his girl.

On Sundays, Andrew watched through his bedroom window as Evelyn and her mother set out for the weekly service. He made sandwiches while watching for their return. Then he offered one plate to Mom and one to Dad, leaving Mom's on the kitchen counter and Dad's beside his father's chair. Mom didn't watch him work or thank him for his effort. She didn't ask where his own plate was, or where he was going when he told her he'd come back later. Instead she gazed at the wall and twiddled dials on the almost silent radio.

Andrew said, "Goodbye," and, "Just heading next door," but no one replied. Then he closed the front door quietly and left for his one well-cooked meal of the week, meat and vegetables shared with Evelyn and her mother, before an afternoon cycle-ride back to the pond.

*****

"You could come to church with us as well, you know." Evelyn forked mashed potato into her mouth as she spoke.

Andrew inhaled the scent of roast beef, savoring it slowly and waiting to reply until he'd swallowed the rich, dark juices down. "No thank you. Rather not."

The craziest thing was, he didn't even know why not. Why shouldn't he still go to church? Why shouldn't he sit there with his girl? Why shouldn't he pray? After all, nothing else had seemed to work. Then he wondered if his brother's funeral had been held at the little white church? That would be reason to stay away, for sure. Was he crazy not to know?

"I'd rather not," seemed the safest answer he could give to Evelyn's request. It required the least thought, because he didn't remember the funeral, and not knowing made him feel insane, like he should be locked up. He couldn't ask, because it would sound so strange. How could anyone forget? But trying to know felt like falling off his bike, feeling his balance slip and slide, and seeing the promise of bleeding broken knees before the crash. He didn't want to pick those scabs, for all that the memories might be dear to him. And in truth, he thought perhaps he might have missed Carl's *sending off*. His parents had argued about it, he remembered. He'd pretended he wasn't listening or didn't care. They declared him too young.

That was back when they still spoke of course. Andrew had listened while they reversed the clock on his passing years, as if forgetting time might bring their best son back again.

"I'm not a kid." He remembered how he'd stomped on the kitchen floor. "I'm not. I'm not." But he wasn't sure they'd heard.

"It might be too traumatic for you," said Mom. "You're so young. You could be scarred for life."

They deprived him of hope as if false hope were anything to cling to; as if a child might not long for closure as well. As if denial wouldn't scar.

So… did he go?

He picked around the scabs anyway, while emptying his plate. He remembered wanting to see the body and stare into his brother's dead eyes. He wished he could hold Carl's frozen hand one last time. But Mom said there wasn't enough of his brother left for him to see. So Andrew imagined they might have put someone else into the casket, and Carl still lived. They might have got it wrong. "Mom, how do they know?"

She talked to him about dog tags instead of answering, as if his brother were somebody's missing pet. Andrew thought of wild cats in the woods, tamed by Evelyn's insistence on giving them names. Names make you real. Names are power. But no one, except for Evelyn and her mother, ever mentioned Carl's name now. Andrew couldn't even remember if the coffin had been sealed.

He tried to imagine it; a fancy, wooden box perhaps, six foot long, light pine, with shining copper trim. Did they bring it home and rest it in the parlor, inviting mourning visitors to come in? Or did Carl hide in some ugly funeral palace with candles all around? Perhaps they left the coffin in the white church, next to the hall where Carl taught Andrew to dance. Or was the funeral held far away, so a soldier's body could lie in a soldier's grave? Was Carl's name carved on a copper plate, or did dog tags take its place.

Did Andrew even cry, he wondered now? Did he weep, where everyone could see, or only down in the woods? Did he stay with Evelyn and her mom and answer questions about nothing while his mind was far away? Or did his parents choose to leave him home alone?

The craziest thing was, here, years later, Andrew truly didn't know, and his parents wouldn't say.

*****

How old were they then, back when Evelyn and Andrew cycled to the woods and pond, and found their pathway blocked—teenagers? Fifteen? Sixteen? How long had Carl been gone? And what had they missed?

Riots of mud-pools spread from rutted tire tracks all around the forest's edge. Exhaust's evil scents poured over them, smothering the tang of wood fibers and the sweetness of sun-drenched leaves. Engines roared, and the crack of broken branches slashed the air. Trees were falling, torn from ground churned into a battlefield. Their foliage ripped into tangled masses, they waited to decay. A dead cat lay where a vehicle's wheels had trodden. Splattered and bleeding, its furred body glommed onto stones that should have been covered with undergrowth. Were there human bodies too, or human bones?

Andrew steered Evelyn aside, taking care that she shouldn't see the pale, frail flesh. He wrapped his arm over her shoulder, guided her bike over rivers of gravel and stones toward the smooth-paved road. Then Andrew stopped to read the signs they'd ignored, small print in black on white, pinned to lampposts and flapping high and torn. He learned a new subdivision was being built, with homes drawn neatly on diagrams, clean-lined, surrounded by parks and rivers and beautifully-tended lawns. An architect's view, washed to gray in the rain, showed sunshine gleaming down. Their forest was neatly bounded by wrought-iron fences and graveyard walls. It seemed aseptically perfect; every angle just right. Even the shapes of people were rendered in swathes of idealized perfection, women slender and tall, men fair-haired, long-limbed, tending kindly to their wives, and children in strollers—like elves in Eden.

Andrew clambered onto his bike again, while Evelyn struggled to hook her skirted leg over her rusted white frame. They rode in gloomy silence along the road toward town. Construction sites loomed behind every bricked façade, blocking every dead-end street. Busses roared, and bustling shops spewed customers into the chaos. Andrew sighed. Their little town was changing. Signposts reading *Paradise* just didn't seem to give the right impression.

A cinema poster showed a tower wreathed in fire. Andrew checked his pockets for cash and guessed he couldn't buy treats but had enough to cover the tickets. He swore to himself he'd get a job soon to pay for more luxuries. Then he led sweet Evelyn past a newspaper stand with its anti-war and anti-Nixon slogans. Pretty gray pictures of political smiles disguised black lying eyes. He leaned his bike against a wall in the alley. Evelyn let him lock hers onto his, the cable as tangled and wild as a Paradise snake. Then they headed inside.

Lines of local teens waited at the kiosk. Andrew met their stares with pride, standing with his girlfriend at his side. He was real and he belonged. He started to call her Evie because it sounded like a movie-star name, which made him belong even more. It made him feel grownup, more deserving of her, while a *Towering Inferno* grew in his heart.

*****

Andrew valued the cinema's distraction as school years passed. So what if cigarette smoke stung his eyes and scratched the back of his throat? So what if cinema speakers rumbled and roared, voices muffled by too much sound and music blaring too loud? The plastic chair dug into his thighs with its back slung too low to support his broadening shoulders. But Andrew didn't care. He rested his arm behind Evie's neck, and let his hand slowly snake to the top of her blouse. He slid his fingers scant inches behind her collar to touch smooth flesh. He bent his head to Evie's herb-scented hair and let the soft strands stray over his cheeks. He dipped his other hand in popcorn, held in a tub between her knees. But sometimes he let his fingers slip from its edge, just once in a while, so they touched the silky smoothness inside her thigh. He licked salt from his fingertip and imagined sweet temptation. Then the music's final score poured sudden light. Another story drew to its magical end.

"What did you think of it?" Evie asked, holding the popcorn close to her chest while they strolled, hip to hip, out of the hall.

"Yeah. Cool," said Andrew, all thoughts of the movie and its title retreating from his mind.

"I liked how she…"

"Me too." He bent to silence her with a kiss.

"And when…"

He kissed her again.

They walked down the street toward the bus stop—no bikes these days because they were older, full-grown, too big to play. Andrew's pocket was weighted with coins, enough for popcorn and fares, and more left spare if they wanted to visit the milk bar on the way.

"Please," said Evie, tempted by sugary sweetness.

"Sure," Andrew replied, letting the bus run past without asking it to stop.

Brash lights from behind the counter lit the gray of the plastic room. Bright music clanged like tin cans pouring sounds across the way, while Andrew's pennies clattered to choose the song. He watched the disk's bright platter lift and spin. He saw reflections dance across the wall. They drank sweet soda, topped with ice cream, and stirred the sticky froth. Then Andrew checked his watch. The final bus was almost due.

"We've just got time for the store," he said, disentangling his arm from around sweet Evie's back. "I've gotta buy food." So they hurried along aisles, dashed through the checkout, threw carefully counted cash with anxious smiles, then sat with paper bags of groceries balanced across their knees while the bus took them home.

Evie's mother opened the door too fast, as if she'd waited for them.

"We shopped on our way."

Mother laughed when Evie showed her the bag. Andrew wondered if she could smell the milk bar's raspberry on her breath. But all she said was, "Thanks. You doing okay, young man?"

"Yeah, I sure am."

"Heading off to some big college soon?"

She always asked, as if she wanted him to prove he was good enough for Evie. But Andrew replied, "I think I'll just stay here. They've offered me a place, and money too."

"You could go anywhere," Evie complained from behind her mother's shoulder. "You could do great."

"Sure, and why? I want to stay with you."

Evie's mother said she admired his dedication. "I know you're really sticking around to care for your parents. You're a good man, Andrew." But Andrew's father and mother scarcely noticed when he went back home. They hadn't said a word about the college applications strewn over the table. They didn't complain that he was home early or late. They didn't thank him for the paper bag filled with food. And they hadn't washed their cups and plates or even bothered to stack them in the sink.

Andrew cleaned around them. He stared at the offer from Stanford then tossed it into the garbage. Evie's mother was right all along. His parents were here, and he really couldn't leave.

*****

Term ended. High school ended. Paradise Park was opened to visitors. Newly laid gravel crunched under Andrew's and Evie's feet on the tangling paths. Birds newly restored to their nests sang merrily. Squirrels pattered through new grown grass, and everything was neat and tidy and clean, no longer the wild, old place of childhood dreams. Even the stream and pond had been tamed by ugly concrete banks. "Stuff will grow there soon," said Evie, ever hopeful. Meanwhile wooden benches waited, smelling of workshops and soap, while plastic-tipped play structures gleamed and longed for children.

Andrew headed up the hill to sit down, but Evie slipped past him, giggling like a child. She ran to a low black swing in bright orange frame, plunking herself on the seat, pressing her feet into the ground to take the strain. Andrew slapped himself down beside her, feeling like the adult guarding a child. A gray cat ran past.

"D'you suppose the wild cats have settled in again?" Andrew mused, leaning back.

"What cats?"

He swung forward and stared at Evie in surprise. "You know. The ones that lived in the woods. You always talked about them. You even gave them names."

She swung herself high. "It was a long time ago."

"Yeah, but…"

Then Evie dug her heels in harder, swinging out of his reach. "Cats die, don't you know, Andrew?"

"Yeah, but I was wondering…"

Her voice came again from the top of the sky. "Like Coal. Like Sam."

"Like who?"

Evie crashed to a halt and jumped from her seat. Then she turned to stare accusingly, while Andrew tried to remember the names of all those wild cats and kittens. Coal? The one in the tree perhaps? A flash of black paws and tail?

Evie spoke again, hands on her hips. "Coal died on the road. A car ran over him."

"Hey, I didn't know." He shrugged his shoulders and wondered if he should go to comfort her? Should he ask how long ago?

"You didn't care. You scarcely even noticed." Accusation burned in her unexpected glare.

"But…"

Then she told him Sam had gone the same way. But who was Sam, thought Andrew, as he gave the wrong answer again: "A wild cat, like the strays?"

"Sam was mine." Evie stomped like a two-year-old. "Then they built this park on their graves. They killed off all the cats."

Andrew still couldn't fathom what it was they were arguing about.

"And now you're going away."

But he wasn't. He'd told her he was staying. She said he really ought to leave, and Andrew thought he'd never understand women.

The gray cat returned, or else another one wandering to take its place. It looped a winding tail around Evie's legs, stilling her stomping anger until she sat; then it leapt into her lap. Andrew breathed scents of fresh-mown grass. He listened to the whisper of idly flowing water, heard the chatter of children and ducks, and felt the cool breeze blow across his hair. All was right with his world, and one day soon he'd ask Evie to spend her life with him. Paradise Park just might become his Paradise after all.

*****

"I'm off to lectures, Mom." Andrew ducked his head through the kitchen door.

Mom didn't reply.

"Dad, I've got electrical engineering today. Got any questions you'd like me to ask?"

His father stared sullenly at the TV, where pictures of Jonestown flickered lifelessly.

"For heaven's sake, you guys. Carl's dead. Why can't you wake up and see?" He hated the way his words must surely hurt them. But silence drove its needles under his skin, making him cruel. He really had to leave.

Closing the door behind him, he whispered, "Don't drink the Kool-Aid folks."

"Don't drink the Kool-Aid." Students laughed along the corridors. Rumors and talk of Jonestown's disaster filled the campus halls. Lecturers bent their heads in reverence. Students raised their heads, disguising dark embarrassment. Then day's end came, and Andrew wandered home. He wondered if his father would still be watching the silent news. Would he say anything—cyanide and the People's Temple, useless faith and senseless death and cruel massacre—or would his sullen vacancy still hold sway? Would his mother care? Other people's sons had died, the news declared, so far away, drinking sugar and spice. Daughters, grandchildren too.

The door wasn't locked when Andrew got home. He touched its knob with surprise, sure he'd turned the key this morning as he went out. Then he pushed into the room, feeling the blast of dust blown into his eyes, smelling decay, and hearing a silence even thicker and grayer than before. The television wasn't switched on, and his father was gone from his chair.

Andrew dropped his backpack on the floor and strode to the kitchen. The fridge sucked air as he opened it to grab a carton of juice which he upended in his mouth. Pushing the door closed with a heel, he noticed all the pots had been washed. They stood in serried ranks, stacked neatly by the sink. They stared with some secret message just for him, in Morse code perhaps, but he couldn't read between their lines. Everywhere was tidy, as empty and clean as Carl's room. He ran upstairs.

"Mom? Mom, where are you? Mom?"

Slamming through doors he checked his own bedroom, his parents', and the bathroom too. Then he stood at Carl's door. It shone like hope in the darkness. The jamb was clean of cobwebs, brushed, as if someone had stepped through recently.

"Mom?"

Andrew turned the knob almost reverently and walked inside. But no one was there.

Sunlight sparkled through the shining window pane. Curtains hung fresh-washed with shadows of damp. A scent of pine and lavender rose from polished pools of light on the furniture. The bedspread was smooth. The floor was dust-bunny free and well-hoovered. All the patterns on Carl's old rug glowed warm in the afternoon sun.

Andrew opened the closet door and buried his nose in the scent of moldering clothes. He sensed just the faintest hint of his brother there, but nothing else. No one was home.

Outside, Andrew ran to the garage and pulled on the doors. No car and no parents waited for him. He leapt the fence and rushed to Evie's house. "Evie! Evie." He hammered on the door.

Footsteps rang on the stairs inside as Evie and her mother rushed to answer. In moments, Evie stood breathless, facing him. "What's wrong, Andrew?"

"My mom and dad. They're not there." He felt his face crumple, tears of terror pricking his eyes. "Where's my mom and dad?"

"How should I know?" Evie asked. She reached for the doorframe, and Andrew saw her hands were trembling. Why should she be afraid? He stretched his own arm to lean on the jamb. He wanted Evie to wrap him in her comfort, but she just stared. Then her mom appeared behind her. "I thought I heard the car," she said. "Earlier today. Isn't that a good thing? Like they're getting back to normal at last."

Normal would have been Mom shopping and Dad chopping wood for the fire. No one was home.

Warmth bled through the open door, bearing comfort in its wake. It wrapped itself around Andrew, like a kitten tugging at his ankles and knees. It drifted out with scents of dinner soothing the cooling air. But he couldn't care.

"Do you want to stay and eat?"

Andrew demurred. "No. I'd better be here for them when they get back."

*****

Later he wondered if his parents had planned this all along. Perhaps they'd just waited until they believed he was old enough to cope. Perhaps they'd stayed around just long enough to see him off to college. Had they believed, somehow, in their slightly deranged and broken minds, that it wouldn't hurt? So they'd left him here and gone to be with Carl.

On a corner of the winding forest road through Paradise, they'd crashed into a tree. The police ruled it an accident, but Andrew was never sure. Perhaps they'd drunk their own Kool-Aid in hopes of finding their missing son again. Because

Andrew had never been, could never have been, good enough to stand in his brother's shoes.

The funeral parlor reeked with acid flowers tinged with smoke. Evie held his hand, threading warm fingers along the sticky dampness of his palms. Visitors trailed past the open caskets with empty words. They said they were so sorry. But none of them had helped in the silent years since Carl had died. They weren't sorry enough.

The funeral was held at the little white church, that place Andrew so long refused to enter. It didn't bring back memories. He still didn't know if there were any to be brought back. *Where was Carl even buried?*

A new, young pastor spoke words that meant nothing at all. He couldn't even begin to describe those people who'd brought Andrew and Carl to life. But Andrew was old enough now to smile graciously and thank these strangers—old enough to behave like an adult it seemed.

Andrew was nineteen, and Evie was the girl next door who would one day be his wife. Sometimes he wondered did she marry him out of pity, or out of love?

Part 3

~7~

Andrew strode into the faculty room, feeling his face grow warm at the sudden silence. They'd obviously been talking about him, criticizing him, and finding him wanting. Again.

The vice-principal's voice boomed in greeting from his usual all-cocooning chair. "So, what are you teaching your *refuseniks* now, Mr. Special Ed? Can they manage two plus two?"

Andrew tried not to let it get to him. He made his way over outstretched legs toward the back of the room while muttering a stubborn reply. "They're doing good."

"One plus one?" Ripples of awkward laughter followed the question.

"They're doing addition, subtraction, and multiplication. They're doing good."

"Doing *well* then." The senior teacher's voice dripped ice.

Andrew's ears burned as well as his face, but the art teacher had saved him a chair again. She slid a paper cup of coffee into his hands as he sat down. No more pottery cups? Saving on washing up? He smiled his thanks.

"Multiplication?" Art Lady whispered, her red hair tickling his cheek.

"Well, soon. I hope." Then he leaned away from her, just a little, not enough to cause offense. He remembered when the touch of a woman's hair on his cheek meant love, love meant Evie, and life was filled with many kinds of hope.

*****

Andrew and Evie were married in the Church of Paradise, across the park, since Andrew refused to darken the doors of the old white church anymore. Afterward, they marched across that same park every Sunday to join in with worship. Andrew remarked on how their forest wilderness had changed. The lake was gone. A duck-laden pond with elegantly scattered reeds seemed a feeble substitute. Fierce ragged slopes were tamed to gentle lawns. The undergrowth was weeded into polite, well-ordered, Paradise Park-like submission.

"I think it's beautiful," said Evie.

Then Andrew, eager for any excuse, proffered a passionate kiss. "You're beautiful." He hoped against hope they might be too late for church.

*****

The faculty meeting finished. Art Lady made no further advances. Andrew's classroom waited. And there, sweet Amy's mother waited too, on a child's chair carefully placed at the far side of Andrew's desk. Andrew set his paper cup down on a piece of paper, checked there were no incriminating notes that his visitor might have read, then stared at his wristwatch while preparing to sit down. "I'm sorry," he said, shifting on the chair as guilt and annoyance warred for his attention. *There's a full-sized chair in the corner. Why doesn't she sit on that?* "Did I know you were coming?"

"You said you'd phone me." The mother's eyes challenged in a way the innocent daughter's never would.

"I don't..."

"About letting me see her in class. I want to know she's okay."

Andrew remembered it now, a promise as easily forgotten as it was hard to make. Guilt threatened to win, while childish voices rose from the playground outside, while his watch ticked inexorably, while lunch-time's recess wound to a close. *Why won't she just go home?* But that wasn't fair. Andrew would always be the guilty one, the one who'd gone away.

"I'll let you know when I come up with something," he said, shuffling to his feet, wondering if he looked as bumbling and foolish as he felt, or decisive instead. The kids would be back in the classroom soon. "Seriously though, she's good. Amy's doing really well."

"I want to see."

"I know." Andrew led the way to the door. *He* hadn't wanted to see.

*****

Andrew and Evie both wanted children. It was another of those magical things they were bound to agree on, unlike church. They wanted a host of boys and girls, a whole classroom full, a baseball team. Weekends, their family would dominate the park, smashing balls into that manicured pond, and scaring the ducks away. Their kids would split the silence apart with cries of bodacious delight.

"Saturdays," said Evie, as Andrew described his dream. She nestled her head into the crook of his arm, bouncing awkwardly at every bump in the path. "They won't play games all weekend. They'll be in the choir on Sundays."

"And everyone will follow us to church."

"Even the ducks."

"They'll quack all through the service."

"I thought that was the pastor's job."

Evie thumped him lightly on the elbow and checked the time. "Hurry up. We'll be late."

*****

"Subtraction." Andrew felt almost relieved, now the room was occupied solely by teacher and students. Their disapproval of him would flow with honest good humor, rather than dripping with anguish and guilt laid on top of failure and loss.

"We know subtraction," someone called out, while another child groaned, "Boring."

"What about subtracting *difficult* numbers; *big* numbers?"

"Like ten?" Jonah bounced too scarily on his chair, making Andrew frown. Then he smiled again.

"Oh, like lots more than ten." Andrew rapped his knuckles against the desk to attract everyone's attention. "Tell me,

Jonah," he demanded, pointing because the movement of his arm would keep the students watching. "How many chicken nuggets would you like to get in a meal?"

Everyone laughed, youthful voices half reluctant, maybe embarrassed, maybe scared he'd catch them with another question next.

"Depends," Jonah muttered lugubriously.

"Okay, how many in the meal you had in class the other day?"

Jonah frowned as if trying to remember. "Eight?"

"Would you rather eighteen?"

Everyone answered, "Yay."

"And what about twenty-nine? Is that more than eighteen?"

Small frowns replaced those wide smiles now. Andrew imagined how the students might search his question for traps, so he repeated, "Would you like twenty-nine chicken nuggets?"

"Yes, yes!"

"And how many more than eighteen is twenty-nine?"

Jonah held out plump hands and tried to count on his fingers. Angry Tom seemed to be counting on his fists and struggling as one followed the other. Julie began to recite her numbers aloud, pointing embarrassingly skyward with a single finger for emphasis. She earned a blaring laugh from Zeke who swore she'd sworn at him.

"Gave me the finger, you did. Does that mean you lo-o-o-ve me?"

Andrew walked to Shy Amy's desk and saw she'd written the numbers neatly, tens below tens, units below units, as if she'd studied and learned it all before. She probably had. She wasn't in this class because she couldn't learn, but rather because she couldn't prove she'd learned. "Nice job, Amy," Andrew whispered but didn't think she'd heard.

"Okay," he announced, bouncing on his heels as he marched back to the front. "Let's do it on the whiteboard."

He wrote the number twenty-nine in big bright figures with a marker that smelled of fruit. Meanwhile Jake shouted out, "Will you buy us some nuggets?"

Andrew ignored him, pointing to the number two and asking the students, "What does two mean?"

"More than one," Zeke laughed

"Not enough," Julie grated.

"It's less than twenty-nine," said Jonah with a sigh.

But Andrew repeated, "What does the two mean here, in this number, when it's part of twenty-nine?"

"Is it… like… like the two in twenty?" Julie swallowed the sound behind the end of her pencil.

"Yes it is." Andrew smiled to encourage her. "It's a two that means twenty." Then he asked, "But how can two mean twenty?" He wrote another two and said, "This one doesn't. So how does it work?"

When empty frowns and blank stares greeted the question, Andrew guessed more edible nuggets and tangible examples would be required. But for now he explained. "This two means two tens, which is twenty. The number after it"—someone shouted *nine—did that mean they were listening?*—"The number after it represents the ones. It means nine ones. Two tens and nine ones is twenty-nine."

"We know that," groaned Angry Tom. "Boring."

But Andrew guessed the students would survive being bored just a little bit more. He wrote the number eighteen with the one below the two on the board, eight below nine. He showed his students what they already, boringly knew, subtracting units from units and tens from tens. Then he pulled out his phone to order a giant pack of nuggets, treats for them all, if only the students would complete a worksheet first.

"Amy, would you hand this around?" He held the sheaf of white papers in front of her staring face, but she didn't respond. Julie snatched them away. "Okay. Put one on each desk, Julie. And Zeke, hand around pencils to those who need them."

Not that Amy needed a pencil. Her rainbow colors still strewed themselves in glory across her desk. She was beautiful, Andrew thought, just like Amelia. And she was peaceful, not like Amelia at all.

*****

"Evie. Evie, are you there?"

Cold evening air, crisp with late summer sunshine, blew in behind Andrew through the door. Leaves, quick-dried with the first hint of fall, crunched underfoot. Sweet tangs of distant smoke promised flower-beds reordered for spring in the still-growing patterns of Paradise Park. But Andrew cared for none of it. All that mattered was the sight of his wife on the sofa, smiling, waiting, eager to welcome him home.

A tan cat tried to slide past Andrew's feet, but he pushed it outside, refusing to trust it wouldn't harbor germs to hurt their precious, unborn child. Meanwhile Evie laughed at his contortions.

"I like cats, remember."

"Still not sure I do." Andrew left his shoes on the mat, hung his coat on the peg, and crossed the floor on quiet, sock-clad feet. "Don't get up," he insisted, as he had done every evening since they'd learned Evie was pregnant. "I'll make dinner. I'll bring it to you. Just keep watching your program while I work."

The kitchen felt like his private kingdom now. He dragged pots and pans from their hiding places, measured ingredients, ladled, and stirred. Meanwhile Evie's voice was a bubble of laughter behind the cooking sounds. The scent of her perfume wafted above and beyond the smells of food. Andrew listened to her every word, taking notice even when he was silent. He knew which TV programs she liked, what color dress she thought would suit her best, how high her heels should be. He knew which flavor of tea would send her to sleep and which would wake her. He guessed which name she hoped to give their child, though he was sure, in spite of all Evie's complaints, the baby was bound to be a boy.

"Alexis?" he suggested, adding just the right amount of salt to a pan of vegetables. Evie's comedy had ended, and the television was silent.

"Amelia."

"Adam." He stirred fresh herbs into the sauce, savoring their steam.

"Amelia."

"Aardvark." He laughed.

"You idiot!"

Andrew laughed again. "I'm surely not going to call our baby *You idiot*, my dear!"

The house was filled with the pursuit of happiness, with bubbling pans, radio bands, choices of channel, and the contented voice of the woman he loved. The silence of college days seemed so far away, when murmured conversations used to hint, "You heard what happened to his folks?" "You never know when that one's going to crack." It was all so long ago. Now Andrew's world was proud and smooth, his poise unbreakable. If the shadows crept up on him sometimes at night, while Evie slept and he slipped to the bathroom, he'd know the voices were just the settling sounds of new wood and foundations in their bright, clean, modern house. He'd return to the bedroom, draw curtains aside, and watch the silver moonlight bathe his bride. Then he'd know all was well. *You heard what happened to him? He got married. He's the happiest guy alive.*

Evie complained, once in a while, that this birthing thing took too long. Then Andrew would remind her that God—her God, not his, since he owned none now—was surely offering a rest before the storm.

* * * * *

Jake demanded nuggets before the next day's lesson even began. Andrew, who'd checked before class, was almost ready to make an order for two boxes of twenty-five. But first he insisted his students had to try some *even harder* subtraction. Everyone groaned.

"Can you subtract eighteen from twenty-five?" Andrew asked. The whiteboard still sported its numbers from yesterday, so Andrew erased one digit and started to write.

Julie almost snarled from her seat in the middle of the class. "It said twenty-nine."

"Yes, but there were only twenty-five nuggets in the box when it arrived yesterday."

"Who ate the rest?"

Andrew sighed. "No one." Distraction would always be easier than subtraction. All the same, he plowed ahead, pointing to the units on the board. "You can't take eight away from five, can you? You can't take more from less. But what about...?" He added a big bright one next to the five. "What about taking eight away from fifteen?"

Jake counted on his fingers again. Angry Tom waved his fists. Then Zeke surprised Andrew by shouting the obvious question. "Sir, Mister, it ain't really fifteen, so how's that work?"

"Ah," said Andrew, delighted at the chance to reply. "It works because I'm borrowing one of those tens from twenty five. If I borrow one ten, if I take away one ten from two tens, how many will be left?"

"If I borrow all of Amy's colored pencils she'll have none left," mumbled Zeke.

"And if you ask her nicely, she just might let you use them to help us in class. But for now, who wants nuggets?"

Someone muttered *burgers* while another child shouted *fries*. But Andrew wouldn't allow the distraction this time. He wouldn't compromise. "Nuggets," he said. "But first we have to finish this subtraction. Now look at the board."

Eight pairs of eyes looked up, while Shy Amy refused to even acknowledge his existence.

*****

One night, the shadows crept too close. Moonlight washed like ghostly fingers over Evie's face. Her features contorted, ragged with onslaughts of pain. "The baby's coming," she proclaimed, between tortured cries.

Andrew maneuvered his wounded bride downstairs and into the car. He turned the key on the engine before remembering he hadn't turned a different key in the door. So he bashed his hand in frustration on the dash while Evie cried.

Doors locked, house safe. No one could get in, and a child waited now to get out. Andrew drove along the small town's empty roads, watching streetlamps burn with mocking eyes. He shrank from puddles left by rain; they glared like threatening ice. He heard the whisper of tires and felt an ocean crest its waves of fear. But ahead, the hospital's clean, white lines were lit in diamonds and squares, a singular painting, a pattern of black and light. The parking lot had too many corners. Evie shrieked as her water broke, just as he found his space. Andrew wondered how he'd wash the seats. But Evie and his son were what mattered now, not stained upholstery.

Crossing the road with his hand at her back took forever. She could only walk five paces then lean and heave. Andrew raised her up. Evie held him back from running away. This just might be too much.

"Here are the steps." Andrew felt like a teacher guiding a nervous child. He wondered how they'd make it to the top. Should he have parked over there at the emergency doors? "Here's the entrance." He pushed the metal-framed glass, delighted to find it moved away smoothly and fast. "Here's the corridor. Here's reception. Here's where I book you in."

A woman at the desk took their names and pointed to the polished steel of elevator doors. Andrew's reflection stared back in abject fear. "Here we go then." Someone ran toward him with a wheelchair. Andrew bent to help Evie sit then gripped the handles like hope. "Sixth floor." He almost threw up as the ground began to move. Then doors sprang open. "Another corridor, love. We're almost there."

He had to keep talking, the only way to keep his terror at bay. Another desk loomed, and Evie was too busy breathing for two to make words. Andrew answered the questions quickly, for her and the child together. He talked their way into a shiny birthing room. He talked Evie out of her clothes and onto the bed. He talked to her thin legs, parting them lovingly with words. Then he leaned his beautiful, hot-flushed bride onto her side. He rubbed her back as they'd taught him to, and talked their unborn baby into his heart.

"No!" Evie shouted.

"Yes!" shouted Andrew instead.

The doctor arrived, though Andrew scarcely noticed. Lights shone on metal. Cloths were green and lay on Evie's knees. Then, finally, the nurse raised a small bundle high, proclaiming with pride, "You've got a little girl."

"Amelia."

*****

At recess, Shy Amy liked to sit atop the jungle gym. She had the same languid nonchalance as a cat trapped in a tree, the same smooth-limbed appearance of total relaxation under those oddly innocent eyes. Below her, classmates either pretended to be worried for her, or else ignored her, depending on the mood of the day. Today was a day for ignoring because they were irritated with Amy's skills; she'd done too well on those harder subtraction tests. Still, Amy's indifference depended on nothing at all; it was simply a part of her.

Andrew stood at the classroom window, eating a snack bar and keeping watch on his students from behind the glass. He hoped he might be invisible, but sometimes it looked like Amy's eyes were staring straight at him. He'd catch a tiny shake of her head, as if she almost wanted to communicate. Or perhaps she'd let herself be distracted by a fly or some passing game. Then her stillness returned.

Cat or panther, Andrew wondered, looking at her languorous pose. Was she waiting to pounce?

Behind the wall, just far enough away, perhaps, for Amy not to notice, a parked car waited for her mother to return. Just behind the tree, just still enough, perhaps, for Amy not to notice, a bundled figure watched. Andrew wished she'd go away.

Meanwhile the students' chattering voices cut through glass in a buzz of pale, white noise. Andrew might as well be out there with them, for all the peace and quiet he'd find in here. If he closed his eyes, he might remember playing games from the past, or trying to pretend he was Amy's protector. *Or Amelia's? Somebody's?* Or else he could head to the faculty room for a cup of badly-stewed coffee.

You're her teacher, not her father, he told himself. Which was just as well, given what a hopeless job he'd made of being Amelia's father. So perhaps he should be glad Amy's mother was still there. At least she cared.

*****

Andrew's family and his joy were surely complete. Tiny Amelia was as perfect in every way as any parent could hope. Ten fingers, ten toes, a beautiful smile—for all that the doctors insisted on calling it gas—hair like spun gold, eyes so wide and bright they saw straight through you; arms and legs that waved in happy delight; and a gentle nature, so quiet, so sweet, and so good. She even slept through the night.

Andrew and Evie talked to their child all the time, though she never answered back. "Just you wait," said Andrew. "One day you'll complain that she never stops talking."

Evie laughed. "I know. I can't wait." She counted fingers and toes again before heading back into the kitchen. "D'you think she'll say *Mommy* or *Daddy* first?" Then she returned, placing dinner plates side by side on the dining room table.

"Oh, *Daddy* of course." Andrew coughed and cleared space between the chairs so they could keep the cradle close while they ate. He tickled the bottom of Amelia's feet and watched her tiny face scrunch red and white, almost ready to cry.

"Don't frighten her." Evie clattered knives and forks into their places. "She doesn't like distractions."

Then Andrew leaned forward. "I'm your daddy," he said solemnly. "Daddy. Daddy." But his baby didn't reply.

Evie laughed again and carried their dinner from the kitchen. "Your favorite," she said. But every meal was Andrew's favorite now that he was a father. Every day was perfect, every dream a delight, and every cry was music to his ears.

*****

The bell's loud clang tolled through classroom and yard. Students streamed like ants to form their broken lines in front of the door. Meanwhile Amy clambered slowly down from the jungle gym. Every movement seemed so very carefully calculated. Every handhold offered just the right amount of stretch. She was a spider, descending from her web.

Andrew watched from the classroom window. *Hide away Mom,* he whispered under his breath, watching Amy's mother shrink further behind her tree. He noticed, with surprise, how the child had developed that smoothness of incipient womanhood. *Poor girl.* What would life hold for her? As mother still hid, *poor Mom,* how would she cope? Would Shy Amy, beautiful Amy, suddenly attract a boyfriend's gaze? Would she run away to marry some scary stranger? And would anyone ever love her enough to respect her?

He sighed. Did autistic children even know how to fall in love? Then he shook his head, embarrassed at his own insensitivity. If things had been different, he might have known the answers, but now he never would.

Amy turned her head sharply, as if someone nearby had caught her eye. Not her mother, it seemed. Amy was looking the other way. Andrew guessed, since she never did anything by accident, she must be looking at something or someone else, *a friend perhaps?* Did autistic children have friends?

"Of course we do."

Andrew jumped. The room was empty, the children still outside settling into their lines. The voice was an unsettling echo inside his head.

*****

Amelia didn't talk, not at one year old, not at eighteen months, not as a two-year-old either. She screamed. Like a cat stuck in a tree, except you can climb to rescue a cat, then its claws will dig in your shoulder with desperate eagerness to escape, and it will be gone. Meanwhile Amelia would still scream.

Morning, noon and night she screamed, as if with fury at ever having been born—her existence one long nightmare whose fears she was adamant must be shared. Those smiles Andrew once found endearing proved they really were only gas. They vanished all too fast in a crumpled face of furious tears.

Amelia screamed at food, at her mother, and at her father too. She screamed in bed or out of bed, in the house or out on the street. She screamed when her parents tried to dress her, then again as they took her clothing off. She screamed for the doctor, screamed for the cats in the front yard and birds in the back; she screamed at busses, screamed at cars, screamed far louder than any child before her; screamed without ceasing.

"She's okay sometimes." Evie would throw out the syllables nervously, twisting her hands together as if trying to pull off the ends of her fingers. Her skin had reddened with cleaning and wiping up tears. "It's just, sometimes, she screams herself sick."

Then Andrew would try to spoon a mouthful of food between wailing lips. Evie would declare, "She likes it sometimes," but their baby never enjoyed her food when Andrew offered it her. Was Evie lying, or saving the best for herself?

Andrew would try to dress the child on a Saturday morning, to give Evie a break. But flailing arms and legs would shred the flimsy material. Then Evie would snatch the garment back, lips pinched in a straight hard line. She'd tug another dress or skirt from the cupboard and take over the task. Life would be easier for everyone, even Evie, Andrew guessed, if his wife took over everything.

When nighttime came, when, if ever, the child was asleep, they would both be worn out. No peace, no quiet in this house that had ceased to be a home; no conversation, no comfort of lingering hugs. Carl had died in the Vietnam War. Now Andrew lived in a war zone all his own.

*****

Open mouths widened like caverns in front of the students' faces. Flapping lips seemed disconnected from the sounds these voices made. Andrew struggled to bring his thoughts to the present, while Amelia and Evie hounded the past, and Carl was caught by the draft. He wondered what these kids would have made of haunting threats back then. He remembered how boys, who weren't so much older than these, rushed off to war. Carried away on a wind of politics and good intentions, they paid in blood, obeying because their only alternative was too cruel to consider—flight, loss, a new identity? There again, if identity is what's condemned you, why not go find a new one?

And what was he running from, school teacher to a class of misfitted anti-heroes?

And why was he mourning his brother, instead of his daughter?

Andrew guessed Angry Tom had a bit of Carl in him, eager to grab the machine-gun and fire away. Carl's friends had included an older Jonah the Whale who somehow passed the fitness test. Did violence slim him down to a handsome physique before a bullet wasted it all? *Don't think about Amelia though,* he told himself. *And don't, please don't look at Amy. Don't look for her mother.* So he didn't. Too much subtraction was shredding him apart.

"Who's ready to move on to another topic?" Andrew asked, scarcely listening to answers as they came.

Some days you teach with a power that reaches into and out of you; ideas pour like water; you watch them flow. Other days you retreat into your hole while the water streams past. Those classes you forget before they're even begun; automatic pilot taking over while the teacher's dead to the world under the deadening glory of his task.

Those boys who died were only allowed to subtract, never add or multiply.

And Amelia?

And Amy?

*****

"Amelia's gone!" Evie announced one evening, as Andrew walked through the door.

He stared, uncomprehending, then realized nobody was screaming at him. Silence reigned, broken only by Evie's sobs of concern as she waved her hands before his face in helpless dismay.

"Amelia's gone! Do something!"

Then he wondered why they couldn't enjoy the moment, just draw breath, just this once. After all, here he was, returning to wife and daughter after a long, hard day at work. All he wanted was a nice cup of coffee, a sit-down with the TV before dinner, and the chance to read the headlines in the paper. When had he last had the peace and quiet to do that? *Just five minutes. Please.*

Instead Evie's voice insistently intruded, as if she didn't think he had enough things on his plate. She hadn't even made dinner. "Amelia's gone!"

So what! Gone to playgroup or school? But she was too young. Gone to church? Left behind at a friend's house perhaps? How was Andrew meant to know? He'd only just got home.

"She's gone, Andrew! Do something!"

Turning wearily, he asked his wife, "Gone where?" then walked past her into the kitchen. A mug with water, filled from the faucet, would quench his thirst. He looked around the room, once so bright and happy, now dark with disarray, dull and empty of anything but the basics, the easy, the mess.

Evie's voice sobbed. "I don't know where, Andrew. She never goes anywhere."

Andrew tossed his drink down his throat while his mind searched through distractions for a reply. "You mean you don't know where she is?" It sounded impossible. Could Evie really not know? She'd been home with the child all day.

Leaving his mug in the sink, he turned to face his wife. He needed to instill a little calm into this frantic dismay because, after all, he did love her still. "Okay, sweetheart. So where do you think she's gone?"

He stared into Evie's eyes, praying his healing balm might help, but she just screamed, "I don't know," then bent her head and quaked like a broken sparrow.

Had Andrew done this to her, he wondered? Had he turned his brave, strong wife into quivering jelly, or had their child destroyed her? He reached an arm toward her then stopped, uncertain whether to hold her hand or keep himself at bay. Choosing neither, he drew a deep breath and asked, somberly, "Where can she have gone? What do you think? Can she have left the house?"

Evie's hand crept to the kitchen door. She began to shake the knob, as if to pull it off. "No, no. I don't think she knows how. Don't think she could open it." At that moment, Evie didn't look as if *she* could open the door either.

"Okay then." Andrew took charge. "Let's search the house." He strode back into the living room, muttering *Stupid child* under his breath and hoping his wife hadn't heard. If he switched on the TV, at least he could listen to the headlines while he searched. Electronic voices might insulate him from his wife's continuing whine.

He opened cupboard doors, glanced into corners, listened to music, guessed what the next jingle might advertise on the box, and then moved on.

"Have you looked under the sofa," Evie suggested. She leaned against the wall like a ladder, her wringing hands like dishrags attached to a rung.

Andrew tried not to laugh because it would probably sound too cruel. But really, Amelia was a child, not a puppy or a cat. She was two and a half, and far too tubby to fit or crawl into such a tiny space.

"But she might!" Evie insisted and he knew, if he didn't make a show of listening, she'd check it for herself.

Evie crouched. Andrew heard the click of her knees and saw her skirt ride higher over her thighs, offering unconscious temptation. He wished her face were pressed against him instead of crushed to the rug.

Sudden guilt made Andrew crouch at her side, smelling sour scents of spilled milk and juice, feeling stale bread crumbs like splinters against his chin. But there was no danger they'd find their child down here. He stood again and pulled the sofa aside to check behind. More stains, more dust bunnies, more crumbs; no pale pink-skirted daughter with raging eyes. When he shoved the sofa back again, Evie was gone. Only the TV's empty dialog disturbed the silence.

Upstairs, floorboards creaked and furniture thudded and squeaked. Evie was searching their bedrooms one by one, crawling under metal frames, pushing boxes aside, and coughing in the layers of dust that sprang like kittens out from under them. "Amelia." Her voice echoed, but no one answered her, while Andrew sighed. "Amelia!"

In the bathroom, Evie tore the curtain back from the shower, metal rings shrieking dismay, but no child inside. She opened the toilet lid with a crash. Andrew, laboring behind her, watched with disgust. The TV was playing another tune; he almost heard the words. But he couldn't hear Amelia.

Evie ran in front of him, took to the stairs in scary leaps, and shouted again, "Amelia." She rushed back to all the places they'd already looked, checking on each, three times at least, as she must have checked before while Andrew was at work.

He left her to it and settled on the sofa to watch TV, until she came to a sudden furious halt, right in his line of sight. *What now?*

Evie reached behind herself to the switch, and electric voices fell silent. Dark daggers flew from her glare. "Your daughter's missing and you sit watching this."

"You said it yourself; she can't get out of the house. She'll turn up when she needs to."

"But she's missing."

Andrew glowered. "You lost her, not me."

"Just get up from there. She's our daughter. We've got to find her."

"Where?"

"I don't know. She must have got out."

Evie's voice dissolved like Kool-Aid in the water of her tears. She shivered, as if an icy breeze were blowing over her grave, while Andrew watched. He didn't stand to comfort her. He didn't hold her close. He didn't whisper sweet promises and lies. She stared from empty eyes and all his romantic stirrings were gone. Then she ran outside in her carpet slippers, stumbling on broken paving stones, staggering across roads, and crying to everyone she met, "Have you seen a little girl?" Andrew followed in watchful silence, standing guard at a distance, unseen, uncared for, and waiting unknowing until they found their child.

Heads shook sadly in answer to Evie's shrieks. Then someone pointed toward the park. Evie ran, not checking for traffic, not looking to see if anyone else were around. Meanwhile Andrew, who Evie thought so useless, walked steadily behind. He held a photo of their child in his hand, backed up Evie's questions with images, and made sure it really was Amelia the stranger had seen in the woods. Then he hurried after his wife.

"Amelia!" Evie dived onto the cavernous path under the forest's arch. Andrew followed at her back. And they found the child, naked in the light of a wavering lamp, dancing like a firefly, silvery bright and moonlit in the long, dark grass. Her clothes lay neatly folded on top of her shoes at the edge of the path.

"Amelia?"

Andrew's heart beat faster at the sight, as if the possibility of losing her had only just become real, as if the rest were the dream of a hungry soul.

They carried her home together, united as a family now, father and mother caring for a curiously obstinate child. But the cracks had multiplied, and the glue of love couldn't hold.

*****

Amy's mother stood outside each day, same stare, same coat, same hope, but always hiding behind a different tree. Andrew almost wanted to start a calendar and check for patterns. He might have to check for cats as well. Black, brown or white, there was always one feline companion on the wall, watching the worrying mother or else the child, or watching him.

~8~

"We're moving on to multiplication today." Andrew strode to the front to make his announcement then turned to face the class. "Who knows what multiplication means?" A sigh of hope rippled through him, knowing at last he'd prove his answer true from the faculty room. His kids could add and subtract. They could multiply too. But they couldn't seem to answer a simple question, and they stared as if zombies had suddenly conquered their souls. His sigh turned sour.

"Okay class. It's simple question time. How many nuggets are there in a regular pack?"

"Eight," said Jonah, who would probably know better than anyone else in the room.

"Okay, so if I buy two packs of nuggets?"

"Buy one jumbo. My Dad says it's better value."

"Suppose they've run out of jumbos." Andrew cast his gaze around the room, demanding their attention. "Who knows how many nuggets there would be in *two* regular packs?"

Angry Tom's sullen complaint was at least predictable. "I'd rather have burgers."

Julie's echo followed. "Two burgers."

"I want five."

Andrew focused his eyes on one child at a time, before turning back to Jonah. "I'm sure you know, Jonah. Come on now. How many nuggets in two packs?"

The boy's eyes glazed. Andrew wondered what snacks he'd indulged in outside—was this a sugar-daze? But with no replies forthcoming, Andrew tried a different tack. He grabbed an orange marker from the box and stretched to scrawl bright circles across the whiteboard. "Let's work it out." Soon his neck would ache from looking both ways at once, but it was part of the job. He drew eight irregular, orange blobs to one side of the board, following with eight on the other side. Eight voices counted and shouted out the answer, "Sixteen nuggets! Sir, will you…?"

"And…" Andrew drew the word out luxuriously, stretching his neck and listening to its quiet crack. "*And* if we buy three packs?"

"But will you, Sir? Will you buy three packs for us?"

"Get burgers too."

His hand drew pictures, as if it knew the way without his eyes, while he gazed at the students. Lines, circles, squares, and soon they were beginning to work it out. Adding multiple times takes time—yes, that was his intent. Adding multiple times is slow and, he agreed a little too promptly, it's *boring* too. Then he drew some money out from his pocket and smiled at the room's immediate intake of breath.

"I'm only a teacher," Andrew announced. "I can't afford meals for everyone, but I can afford some nuggets." Ignoring the murmur of complaint from burger eaters, he continued. "I'll buy four helpings of nuggets for you guys to share, as long as you promise to work on what's on the board."

Angry Tom leaped from up his place, but Andrew redirected his gaze at once. "If you want treats, you gotta work for them."

So Tom began to count. "That's twenty," he exclaimed, pointing at Andrew's four boxes on the board.

"No, Tom. It's more."

"It's twenty-four?"

"Thirty-two," someone shouted from the back.

"Thirty-two nuggets in four packs. That's right," Andrew said, as if deliberating on what he already knew. "And we've got nine students here. So how many nuggets do you think each one of you will get?"

They groaned again.

"Remember, you promised. You've got to work it out before the nuggets arrive, or you'll get none."

They hadn't promised of course, but they set to the task.

Andrew took out his phone to make the order, while nine young heads bent over desks. No one used calculators in here. They weren't allowed, but no one seemed to think of using them, which said something about diligence, authority, imagination even amongst his *refuseniks*. Andrew just wasn't sure quite *what* it said.

Shy Amy had the answer first of course, working it out with buttons on her desk. She looked up at Andrew—really looked at him—and he saw she seemed confused. "Don't worry," Andrew told her, waving his hand dismissively. "I'll cut the extra nuggets all in two."

Amy almost smiled at this. Her eyes seemed brightly focused and clear, making Andrew wonder if Amelia's eyes had ever looked this way. Then she answered the other question, the one he hadn't asked. "One piece left over."

"Yes, Amy. There'll be half a nugget for me." His teaching skills were worth half a nugget, surely.

*****

Andrew, Evie, and the child attended a wedding together once. It was held at that Church of Paradise where Evie still attended, though Andrew had decided a Sunday lie-in better suited his mood. They were invited, not because they knew bride or groom, but just *because*, as Evie explained. It made no sense, though everyone who was anyone was here. And Andrew was still almost, nearly, someone in this town. He lived here. He knew people. He worked with Jeremy Irons in that tall, glass building by the park. And perhaps he'd gone to school with the groom, back in their distant youth. Or with the sweet bride's brother? Had Evie known the bride? Still, he couldn't remember, and he didn't recognize the faces all around. He stared and tensed at proffered glances, while the church grounds resounded to whittling strangers whispering withering words; he would much rather have stayed at home.

Turning to Evie, Andrew asked miserably, "How long do we have to be here?" Meanwhile Evie tugged another cake wrapper from their daughter's mouth, wiping her face with her sleeve.

"As long as it's polite," she replied, with expressionless face and voice, her hand wrapped firmly around small Amelia's arm.

"Why don't we go home? Amelia's not enjoying it, is she? And neither are we."

"We can't go yet."

Drinks and cakes filled the air with sugary sweetness, while music blared from loudspeakers in the trees. Voices chattered and shrieked. Sticky grasses lay in untidy heaps around their feet. But when Andrew tried to shuffle away, Evie pulled him back. "Let's just stand. Just wait awhile. When we've paid our respects, we can go."

"You sound like you're at a funeral. *Pay our respects.*"

"You know what I mean."

Evie's words might have been decisive, but her voice was lifeless and low. Andrew heard it louder than anything else, like a gunshot in his soul. *Did* he know what she meant? Did he ever know what Evie meant anymore? And how had they come to this?

Amelia was in one of her quiet times, absent from life and silent as a ghost. How had *she* come to this?

Perfume assailed their noses first, as the bride's bright mother approached. Andrew tensed, because smells could so easily set their child into shrieks of disaster. Voices too.

"Hello there," the bright-flowered mother boomed. "How good to see you both." *Not all three of us*, thought Andrew. Which one was she leaving out? She bent to the child. "Ah, such a beauty you are. A real heartbreaker you'll be when you grow up." Amelia had broken her father's heart already.

The woman straightened, stiffly correct, to stare into Evie's face. "Is she always this quiet?"

"Sometimes," said Evie. Her cowering respect oozed thicker than the woman's perfume.

"Can't trust the quiet ones, hey?"

Andrew guessed their hostess had drunk too much. He guessed perhaps he'd drunk too little. Then he tugged on Evie's arm again and begged, could they please go home now?

Amelia, doll-like, innocent, an angel who would never scream and surely not disobey, simply stood there and stared.

*****

Questioning faces fed Andrew's sense of delight. These kids weren't just in it for the food, however much they wanted him to think so. And that was what he liked about this class. His students didn't learn by rote. They didn't believe just because a teacher told them so. They weren't in the business of buying educational approval with right answers, or earning brownie points with blind obedience, saying please and thank you, and checking the right boxes on every form. These students were real.

Jonah chewed the end of his pencil, now all the nuggets were gone. But light had begun to waken behind his eyes. "Multiply," he mused, in a voice far lower, far deeper, than his usual scornful cry. "Hey, Sir. It's just like addin' up ain't it?"

Andrew jumped proudly on the answer. "Yes Jonah, that's right. Multiplication is just like adding up, but..." He paused for emphasis, waiting until all nine pairs of eyes turned to him—even Shy Amy's. "But... multiplication lets you add up even faster."

He waited for the thought to provoke more questions. To his mind, multiplication's triumph was the way the numbers made sense, like coming home to find your dinner cooked and the dishes done. Multiplication's like realizing you don't have to work so hard. *Or like falling in love.*

Angry Tom responded first, with his usual lack of grace. "Yeah, like learning all those tables and failing the test. It's all about remembering ain't it, an' I thought you said math wasn't about 'membering."

It was true; that was exactly what Andrew had said. So now he pointed out it's the patterns that count, not the memory.

"You can remember it if you want to, Tom, and lots of people do. But then they only know what they've remembered." He smiled. "You guys are cleverer than that. You're going to learn how to work it out, so you'll know the answers even when those other kids have forgotten."

Life's like math he thought now. *Life's about patterns, not remembering,* but his pattern was broken and only the haunted fragments remained inside, invading his mind like soldiers trooping to war. He shook his head again and started writing numbers on the board, matching them in pairs like husbands and wives, fathers and daughters, ladies and tramps. "What's nine add one? And eight add two? And seven add three? And what about six add four? Yes, it really will help. Can you see the pattern there?"

*****

Evie's voice was high-pitched and sharp when Andrew got home from work, but at least Amelia wasn't screaming. "She took her clothes off again."

Andrew opened the newspaper. "Really?" He told himself he didn't care. He didn't dare to care.

"Down in the park again. Under the trees. The doctor says it's a phase."

He scanned headlines and refused to reply.

"It's a phase. He says she'll grow out of it." Evie snatched the page, its rip resounding like a gunshot. "Andrew? Are you listening to me?"

Andrew repeated dully, "She'll grow out of it. Great. I wish she'd hurry." He shuffled the torn newspaper to show the next page. "What's for dinner?"

"I wish I knew *when*." Evie had ignored his question again. Only their daughter mattered.

"Dinner?" Andrew ventured, raising his eyebrows to stare up at her. He wasn't accusing. Just a friendly request in a house that would almost be peaceful if Evie wasn't shouting.

His wife turned on her heel. "The doctor says I shouldn't tell her off or I'll frighten her."

"Good." Andrew reached for the TV remote. The scores would come up soon.

"But how do I stop her if I can't…"

"Shush a minute." He'd spotted his favorite team. He listened to the match report then turned, but Evie had gone. Four-year-old Amelia sat in the kitchen spooning something sticky onto her face. He tried to pretend he didn't see her, didn't ask what it was, didn't dare admit he cared. She wouldn't have answered anyway.

*****

Amy's mother waited on the far side of the wall. The school day ended, and students all trooped by. She glared at Andrew's classroom window, as if she thought her stare might force Amy to leave before time. Because it really wasn't time yet, and the school bell was still wrong. While everyone else was eager to be gone, Shy Amy kept to her own, internal, perfectly tuned, atomic or anatomically mystical clock. And her mother waited.

Andrew waited too, unable to tidy his room until all the students were gone. He wondered if Amy's baby brother might be crying in his seat, strapped in the car in fall's unexpected heat. He wondered if the brother was autistic too—*does it run in families? Are boys more susceptible or less?* Then he wondered if he should open the classroom window and wave, perhaps shout "Hi" and invite the mother in. But she'd ask about visiting during class, and he couldn't deal with that. So instead he turned and packed his notes into his case. He would leave when Amy left. He'd buy some food on the way home, so the white cat who'd adopted him wouldn't go hungry. He'd prepare tomorrow's lesson, and Amy would be back, same as ever, ever unchanging, tied to desk and clock when the next day began.

*****

One day Andrew came home from work to find the TV blaring in the living room. It was a change at least from coming home to Evie's or Amelia's screams. Some stupid children's program filled the screen. Amelia's blank eyes stared at it, unwavering.

He remembered his daughter had seen this program before. She'd seen it a hundred, a thousand, a million times. Variety was *not* the spice of her life.

He tried to recall how the story went. Perhaps he should throw some well-aimed quote at Amelia. Then she'd reply, and they'd call it conversation. Evie did this with their daughter all the time, but Andrew felt like an alien, not familiar enough with their language to follow the words. So he hurried past.

Following into the kitchen, his wife seemed more relaxed than usual. More TV channels must be good for the family's flawed dynamics. Andrew asked—he'd been worrying about it all day—if there was a chance she was pregnant because she'd felt so ill the last few mornings.

"I killed your son," Amelia shouted from the living room.

Meanwhile Evie answered, without even looking at him, "I'm not."

Andrew tried to ask how she could be sure, but she ignored him. Then Amelia added, "Jack in the box, go back in the Jack in the box." Andrew couldn't begin to guess her meaning.

Evie didn't seem to want or need his presence, so he slumped back into the living room and dropped himself into his chair. The TV's blare was meaningless. This place no longer even felt like home. This pale-faced, sweet-faced invader on the sofa had stolen his world, and oh, how he wanted his wife back, his dreams, his hope. He wanted someone to talk to about politics, football, sunshine, flowers in the yard; someone who'd offer him sympathy when work went badly and rejoice when it went well; someone who remembered when Paradise Park hid wild cats under its bowers; someone who knew him, and knew his wife, his life. But all Evie knew, all she ever talked about, all she cared for was the child.

"We need to see someone," said Andrew, throwing his voice over the sound of the TV and catching Evie's eye.

"I see people," Evie answered from the kitchen.

"Not people. I meant a doctor."

"I said I'm not pregnant."

"Not for you, for Amelia."

"I killed your son," Amelia repeated, rocking back and forth, zombie-like, on the sofa's sagging springs.

"It's just a phase."

*****

It was lunchtime and Andrew's half-eaten sandwich lay rejected on his desk. Its smell, of tinned ham and pickles, repelled him. But he always ate canned meat and pickle sandwiches, every day.

Perhaps it was the fact that he was eating alone, when he could have joined the others in the faculty room—could have been even more alone in the crowd. Perhaps it was the knowledge that if he looked up, his eyes would inevitably search for Amy's mother through the window. Perhaps it was that feeling of avoiding everyone, just like before. He needed his cat.

*****

Evie sat on the sofa with her daughter. Dinner hadn't been made. The floor hadn't been cleaned. Pots hadn't been washed.

Andrew strode into the kitchen and checked the fridge. The milk was old and out of date. The margarine tub was empty. Cheese was green.

In the cupboard he found stacked cans of meat and rows of pickle jars. On a shelf underneath was a lonely loaf of bread. He made his sandwiches and carried them into the living room. "Anyone hungry?"

Evie took one and ate without looking or speaking. A few moments later Amelia took one too. Had she noticed him, or just the food?

Nobody spoke. He might as well have eaten on his own.

*****

Amy's mother was back. She sat across the desk from Andrew again, pitifully grateful for nothing. "Thank you for seeing me," she said, while he kept his gaze on the unwelcome sandwich.

"Anytime," he replied, swallowing bile. It really wasn't quite what he meant, but it felt like the right thing to say.

"I'm just worried about her." The mother twisted her wedding ring around on her finger. Her hand moved slowly toward the bread, almost as if she were hungry. "You know, about Amy. I worry. I notice things."

Andrew watched her wandering hands—easier than watching her eyes—but he kept silent.

"I know. You think I shouldn't keep watching her, but I have to, you see. I have to be sure."

Twisting fingers retreated, so Andrew took another bite from his lunch and swallowed guiltily.

"She never plays with the other kids."

He didn't speak. At least she went outside with them, which was more than she'd done back when the school year began. What did her mother expect?

"She never leaves school with the other kids either. Did you know that? I think she's avoiding them."

At least Andrew had an answer to this concern. "She's just watching the clock."

"What clock?" The mother spun around, checking the walls and her wristwatch automatically.

"I think young Amy's got a clock in her head. She waits until it's *really* the right time to leave, and the school bell's always early."

"Really?" The mother's voice grew as vague as Evie's used to be. She lifted her eyebrows out of their habitual frown and spoke slowly, uncertainly, as if she wasn't sure the words were allowed. "Her dad's just like that. Like he's got the clock and the calendar programed into his brain."

Andrew wondered if *he* was like that as well. Was there some autistic gene and he'd passed it on to his child? Could being too organized mean you somehow carried an elemental risk? And was it his fault poor Amelia had been wrong in the head?

A happy female voice seemed to answer him. "It wasn't your fault."

Andrew stared at Amy's mother. "What did you say?"

"I said her dad's the same." She squeaked defensively. "Not that I blame him though." Nimble fingers twisted now around the strap of her purse. "You know, in the old days they always said autism was the mother's fault. Rigid moms. Too worried about appearances. Said we were frozen. Did you know?"

Of course Andrew knew. But he wasn't going to say why. Evie and Amelia were his secret; his alone.

"It wasn't your fault." He repeated the words the voice had said in his head.

*****

Soft sofa cushions sagged beneath mother and child. Evie's arm hung awkwardly bent on her lap, not wrapped, like a mother's arm should be, around her daughter's slim shoulders. It was a pose invented to please one person and nobody else, the child in perfect comfort while the mother contorted to agree.

Amelia's hand cupped her mother's elbow, fingers pinching and stroking at the loose flap of skin over the joint. Her eyes were glued to the TV screen, glazed with empty self-interest. She didn't turn to greet her dad, not even when she made her alien pronouncement again. "I killed your son."

Evie scarcely moved to acknowledge him either. Her face angled very slightly in the direction of the door. She pursed her lips and squeezed their pink to whiteness, pantomiming silence. So Andrew, unwelcome, unwanted, stormed from the room and crashed upstairs as noisily as he could. Rejected in his own home, unable to select what to watch on TV, unable to choose when to speak or what to say, he was always at the beck and call of this wife and child who wouldn't even acknowledge his existence.

Eventually he grew hungry. He made two plates of sandwiches, left one downstairs for Evie and Amelia, and took the other upstairs to eat alone.

*****

"The bell's going to ring for the end of lunch."

"Does she come in on time?"

"No. I told you. She works to her own schedule. When it's really time she'll come in, just like she'll leave when it's really time to go home."

Amy's mother stood, shaking her head as she pushed the chair out of the way. "You ought to fix the clock on that bell."

Andrew agreed, but this wasn't his job. He ushered the mother out his room before she could disturb his students. "I'll call you," he lied again. "I'll set something up."

*****

In the bedroom, a picture stared down from the wall; Andrew and Evie in better times, before Amelia. Light danced in their eyes, but perhaps it was just the afternoon sun through the photographer's window. Evie smiled, and Andrew remembered how she used to melt his heart. His body would feel like water. He'd just have to look, and his soul would be filled with longing, waiting to pour himself into her. He dated her, watched her childhood shyness blossom to womanhood, and then he eagerly waited to be married to her. He remembered how they'd walk, arm in arm, his long stride shortening to fit with hers until they felt as one, parading under trees that would one day be labelled Paradise Park. The scent of Evie's herbal shampoo, tingling perfume at her wrists and throat, and soap on the back of her neck all intoxicated him. He placed half-strangled kisses on her lips, until the day she opened her mouth to let him devour her whole.

Mom and Dad… No, he wouldn't think about Mom and Dad. Nor Carl.

Their wedding photo looked down from another wall; Evie crowned in white like an ice-cream cake, Andrew in his suit of featureless gray. Flashlights turned its blandness into shine. But they'd had all the world to live for then, and wedded bliss was everything they'd desired. He hugged his bride in the kitchen, made love to her before dinner, danced around the living room to the sound of birds and bees in the trees outside. Her stomach grew and he treasured the kick of tiny, unseen feet. He kissed her there and imagined their son peeking out somehow through her navel, laughing at him. He talked and sang to the baby every night, reciting football scores just in case it was a boy, and nursery rhymes for a girl. Then the great day arrived.

Another image showed Amelia, dressed in pink, hugged in the crooks of both their arms. Her tiny face peeked out from the circle of its bonnet. She was wrapped and safe in their undying love.

Andrew stood in front of this picture now, while tears rolled down his cheeks. Grown men don't cry. Grown men don't. *Don't!*

Then he tried to imagine prying the child from her grip on his wife's crooked elbow on the sofa downstairs. He couldn't kiss either wife or infant now. Neither of them was his to love or desire. They'd hidden themselves behind a shield and retired to a world of their own.

*****

When the school bell rang, too early, for the end of day, all but one of Andrew's students trooped out. Andrew glared at the watch on his wrist. Would they ever fix the time? Meanwhile Amy waited for the perfect moment to arrive.

"You could go, you know." He didn't expect a response to his suggestion, so he jumped when Amy's bright gaze locked onto his.

She stared with eyes opened just a little too far, something not quite right about their focus. Then she opened her mouth, and her voice turned husky and dark as she forced a reply. "That would be breaking the rules." She sounded almost like

Julie. She even tilted her head to one side, just a little, as Julie would, fingers closing against her lips as if they clasped a cigarette or hid a smoker's cough. She let out a rattle of rasping breath and offered a grin of parodied seduction. Then she leaned back in her chair, tilting it, all languorous body, sinuously curved like a cat's.

Andrew stuttered. "No, Amy. The bell has gone. You could go."

"I want nuggets." Suddenly the girl's small body seemed to swell. She stretched her arms out widely behind her head. Her voice turned sluggishly hard like Jonah's.

"Then go out and ask your mother." Was it best to humor her, or should he worry?

"I want them now!" Angry Tom's sharp words spat out from Amy's lips. Her eyes seemed to glower as she jumped up from her seat.

Andrew scooted behind his desk and asked, "Amy, what's going on?"

Then she sat down again. "Don't know. Don't care. You wouldn't understand." Her nasal voice carried the sting of class clown Zeke, while Andrew stood and stared. But as suddenly as she'd changed, Shy Amy was back, stacking rainbow paper and pencils into the pockets of her pack, as if nothing had happened. She gathered her buttons, and headed out the door, just the same as she had done each afternoon before.

Something surely *had* happened here Andrew thought, rubbing the nub of his thumb against his chin. He stared out of the window to make sure Amy got safely to her mother. Maybe something was just beginning to happen; some kind of crazy teenage breakthrough that he truly wouldn't understand. He'd not been there when his own daughter reached this age. He'd not been there when Amelia became a teenager, nor when she died.

Guilt set his fingers scratching the back of his ear. If he could draw blood, then pain might pay for pain. But he loosed his hand, and gathered his breath and possessions. Was Amy trying those different voices and personas for her mother now? What would the mother say?

A white cat trotted along the schoolyard wall. Its delicate steps paralleled those of Amy as she followed the path. Then it turned to stare at the classroom window with bright green eyes that bored into Andrew's mind. Surely a cat couldn't see that far. And surely Andrew shouldn't have been able to recognize its eye color from here.

A third eye gleamed, bright red, in the shining collar around its neck.

*****

The doctor finally referred them to a specialist. The specialist asked so many questions they felt their lives undone, replaced by checkmarks and crosses along the page. He asked about Amelia too, then shut her in a room where she screamed to be free. He watched through a one-way window and said they mustn't intervene. Nurses marched in like robots with food and puzzles and toys. Andrew and Evie were dismissed, sent home, while their child had to stay until the day was done. Then they returned.

"Autistic," the specialist pronounced, as he bade them sit in his study. He steepled his fingers on his desk, like a shield to protect himself. "Your daughter's autistic. No question about it. She'll never grow up to be normal."

Andrew felt the air rush out of his lungs. He shrank into the chair, wishing he had the strength or will to reach for Evie's hand. Was she flailing too?

"You've got to face facts and stop deluding yourselves I'm afraid. There's nothing to be done."

Andrew had to ask, "Why?" though he couldn't see how the answer would change anything. *Nothing to be done?*

The doctor turned to him, ignoring Evie, who sobbed at his side. It was nice to be noticed, though he didn't like the words. "It could be something to do with your wife, you know, sir. Not your fault."

Andrew's body jerked in its chair, while ice poured down his back. Was this meant to be comfort?

"We notice it a lot. Cold mothers, affect-less, no emotion toward the child."

But Evie hadn't been cold in the past, not until Amelia stole her warmth. *Nothing to be done?*

"Motherhood has that effect on some women. Nothing to be done, like I said, though I wouldn't recommend you have any more children."

Andrew shivered as winter invaded deeper into his thoughts. "I killed your son," said his daughter's voice in his head. His heart felt frozen, like lost hope, or frost growing thick and black on window glass. His thoughts stopped, eternity left over when love has died. Then he pushed his chair away from the desk and struggled to rise, gaining distance between himself and the doctor and his wife. He walked around the room, alone with its walls, while the carpet silenced his footsteps, making him feel like a shadow or a ghost.

"What if it wasn't my fault?" Evie asked, uncertainly, behind him. "I mean, I thought I'd done everything right. I talked to her, all the time."

"Well, nobody's sure." The doctor had sounded pretty sure. "Nobody really knows what causes it. Just a theory I'm afraid, and can't be helped. I'm not blaming you."

"Yes you are. Or else you're setting things up for me, so I'll blame myself."

She shouldn't take things so personally thought Andrew, who so far hadn't thought to blame *himself.*

✲✲✲✲✲

Amy seemed almost normal in school the next day, sitting peaceably in her chair, counting buttons and laying down rainbows over the desk. Andrew taught the class to multiply by patterns. He showed them how to create their tables instead of reciting them, coloring the numbers and seeing how the answers fitted the rule. "It's eight then six then four then two then zero," he said, as the students summed from two to four and beyond. Then, "seven and four and one and you take away three," as the tables continued. Candy bars helped.

Amy seemed almost normal until she shouted, in a voice as hard and furious as Angry Tom's, "I want candy, now!"

The class fell silent, students shrinking back in their chairs, amazed at their good girl gone bad. Then Amy dropped her gaze to the buttons on her desk. Shy Amy again, she whispered soundlessly, while Andrew sighed with relief. Still he wondered what she might come out with next. Quiet Amy, sweet amenable Amy, was so much easier to deal with than this mercurial stranger who glared out from her limpid eyes.

Shy Amy? Andrew shivered. Perhaps he really did need to talk with her mom.

*****

Soon Andrew felt like a ghost in his own home. An awkward emptiness had enveloped the sacred family he once had loved. Evie and Amelia sat in the living room, dead yet demanding to be fed. Meanwhile Andrew was demoted from inconvenience to annoyance. An invader to be endured in their well-ordered lives, he wondered more seriously if they'd really be better off without him—wondered, wondered, wondered until he knew. *Just send the money home, and leave us alone.*

Passing the back of a hand over stinging eyes, dashing away tears, and drying his bruising cheeks, Andrew reached up to the top shelf of the closet. He lifted down his suitcase, and opened it like possibility spread across the bed. "I love you, Evie," he muttered, squeezing underwear into shoes before stacking their shapes like plates interleaved with vests. "I love you, Amelia." He fumbled shirts into awkward folds and layered them out on top. "I love you both." He tried his best to maintain the creases in pants, then added jeans and sweaters, a jacket, some socks. He leaned hard over the case to make it close, then snapped the locks. But he had to open it up again when his eyes caught sight of Amelia's picture on the wall. A tiny baby wrapped in pink, sweet fruit of his loins before the fall. The frame fitted neatly between two layers of clothes. He pressed the snaps again. It was time to go.

Downstairs the TV show still blared. Evie still sat with Amelia clutching her arm. An empty sandwich plate lay discarded between them.

"You going out?" Evie asked but didn't ask where or why, as if she didn't care.

"I'm leaving," Andrew replied.

Evie said nothing, though he still half-hoped perhaps she'd beg him to stay. Was he so invisible? Was his suitcase invisible too? Was invisibility catching?

"We'll all be better off," he muttered. Then he paused, still wishing for more. It was almost a challenge, a final chance for Evie to change his mind. But laughter roared from the TV set. She probably hadn't heard. It didn't matter anyway.

*****

Amy multiplied her strange personas, while the class worked on calculations, questions, and tables. Despite Andrew's insistent answers to her mother that public school was the best place for the child, he found himself learning to doubt his confidence now. But he'd persuaded her, at last, not to keep calling in, not to keep spying from behind her tree, and not to keep risking being seen. So she only stood at the wall each evening, staring accusingly, and making no move. They couldn't discuss the future or Amy's changes, since they never met. He wasn't sure if this was good or bad. Did he really want her mother to know what she was saying in class? Would the mother blame him for her child's proliferating natures? This wasn't the sort of multiplication he'd planned.

"Who can tell me the pattern for five times something?"

"Patterns is for girls," shouted Amy in dark imitation of Tom's scornful voice.

"Yes Amy, and you *are* a girl. So, can you tell me?"

She began to chant in a voice like a five-year-old's, or like Zeke's acid scorn for five-year-olds. "Once five is five. Twice five is ten. Thrice five…"

"What's thrice?" Zeke shouted, leaping to his feet.

"Mice!" shouted Amy, jumping away from him. She paused, as if on the edge of collapse. Then, revitalized, she danced around her desk, singing "And mice is twice as nice," and kicking her legs twice as high in the air as Andrew had ever imagined she might dare.

Jonah the Whale squeezed out from his chair. Then Amy, suddenly silent, began to parody his waddling walk, head down, arms akimbo, body wobbling with the beat of her feet.

"Amy, sit down."

"Don't want to." She sounded like Angry Tom again. Andrew realized he'd have to raise his voice and shout louder to get her attention. It felt wrong. You can't shout at someone who doesn't understand. Shouting will just make them worse.

*****

He caught the last bus out of town, leaving the car behind for Evie to drive or to sell, not really caring where he went or how long it took to get there. He'd sleep while he rode.

Of course, choosing to leave like this was impractical. Spur of the moment decisions leave too many moments hanging; and what about his job? But Andrew hung his head as the bus bore into the night. There'd be time enough when he arrived to decide what to do next...

...except, of course, he didn't know when he'd arrive or even where.

Counting options, Andrew decided he'd have to return in the morning, just so he could hand in his notice to Mr. Jeremy Irons in his glass-walled office—make a clean break. But he wouldn't return to the house; it was broken beyond repair. The job had been the only thing keeping him going.

He told himself he'd find another job. He'd do something else. Or the open road would beckon, its route unsigned, leading him nowhere or anyplace but here.

The alternative—sleep almost fled at the thought—the alternative was he'd change his mind after all and simply go home. Go back, unpack, and pretend that nothing had changed.

Just now, that felt to him like the ultimate betrayal. He couldn't mess up their precious lives again. His wife and child needed each other, but didn't need his arguments or his helplessness anymore, butting out, butting in. He didn't need the pain of watching a precious girl fail to grow, fail to learn or belong, never make friends and never earn her own keep, never even yearn to see her dad. *Forever* stretched too far with a child who was destined only for never, who would never be free.

The engine clanked its way through gears, while the bus bore Andrew into mist and gray. Cold glass bled ice against his forehead as he leaned against the window. He felt the tremble of its frame when rumbling wheels lumbered on. Bumps in the road made the surface flicker sharply against his skin, like Amelia's heartbeat when he'd laid his hand on her chest in fatherly awe the day she was born. But the window was bright with distracting reflections, wild as the confusion of his daughter's mind. A white cat, trotting along the path, kept time with the bus's wheels. Slim paws danced high, straining against a gleaming gold leash held by an improbable teen. This could have been Amelia, fully grown with Andrew's nose, her own fair hair, and Evie's angled chin. Then Andrew saw her dressed in white for an impossible wedding, holding the cat like a gorgeously bound bouquet. The feline ghost flitted down from her arms and ran ahead of the bus, proving it was all a dream, and Andrew was truly asleep. Cold shuddered through him as he pondered, *What have I done*?

✳✳✳✳✳

Andrew found himself wondering what new change each day would bring. He tried not to let his face show surprise. He projected a carefully tended impression of knowing what would happen before it did. But Amy announced one morning, "I'm not Amy. I'm Aimée," and he couldn't help stopping to stare at her.

Really? Amy's strangeness seemed only to multiply more. But at least her voice was back to its normal squeak. Andrew guessed he could try calling her Aimée for a while, though he wasn't sure how he'd remember. The other kids looked so blank they'd probably not even noticed she was pronouncing it differently.

"Multiplication tests," Andrew said, anchoring his wandering thoughts in the need to teach.

"Boring."

It had to be done, so he gave them each white sheets of paper and read the questions from the book. Who cared what seven times six was or how fast the answer could be written? Jonah's thick fingers struggled to shape the figures quickly enough, while Andrew followed time by the ticking of his watch. Julie had mixed up her sixes and nines again. Tom simply wrote random numbers on the page—when Andrew frowned he just laughed; "You're asking random questions. What do you expect?" *Secret misfitted master of misunderstanding.* Meanwhile Amy, Aimée, strove to write down both question and answer in time that allowed only for one, unless her rainbow pencil could fly like the wind. School tests, school inspections demanded this, though Andrew knew

his class was bound to fail. Sometimes he wished he could shout and rail like Tom.

*****

A quiet town closed its eyes as the streetlights went out. Stygian dark settled over the bus station's gloom. Blackness drowned the sound of birds and insects, the rustling of creatures in night-time's undergrowth, even the steps of a few stray wanderers trekking lonely streets. An approaching bus squealed its brakes, but their echo seemed thickly muted as if scarcely daring to break the weight of silence. The town was asleep.

Mist rose thin and gray from midnight streets. A white cat yowled and curled its tail around a dark lamp's frame. Brakes squealed again. And now twin headlamps tore the gloom, bringing their threat and promise, leaving matching eyes of glowing red behind.

Time slipped. The bus had arrived and gone. The cat stayed, watching the slumping figure of a man with a case in his arms, its bulk held carefully tight as if it were a child.

Brought back to reality now, Andrew stared at empty streets leading off in every direction, cold and black. He wondered if someone had forgotten to switch on the lights. Then he saw the yellow glow of a rooming house window. A washed-out vacancies sign buzzed and hummed like an angry bee. He strode forward with false confidence, climbed the steps, then wondered why his legs felt suddenly so tired. His bag, his worldly goods, seemed very wrong and heavy and grim. He dropped it to a space on the step by his feet, looked down and up, then struggled to pull his gaze away from the greenish glow of a cat's eyes watching from a windowsill. White cat, like the one in his dream.

*****

The white cat waited for Andrew outside his apartment building. It wound its tail around his legs as he walked toward the door. It ran ahead up the steps then slipped inside onto the corridor, watching and waiting eagerly. It climbed the stairs while Andrew took the elevator. Then it leaned against the door to his apartment, ready to rush in. It slid, sharp-clawed, across the kitchen floor, as soon as the door was opened, always coming to a rest in front of his fridge.

Andrew's cat knew where the food was kept. But Andrew still hadn't quite figured out how it came to be his cat.

After eating, Andrew liked to lie back on the sofa watching TV. He kept the sound turned low and talked about Amy, as if his feline friend would understand. He asked if Amelia had ever been that way. Had she tried on different personas before she died, or changed her name, or had she died too young? Was Amelia trying a different persona that time, when the garage guy killed her? And had he maybe thought she was somebody else?

"She was okay."

Then Andrew laughed at himself. "First sign of madness, talking to yourself. Second sign, talking to the cat."

"Talking's good for you," said the voice.

The TV bored him so he picked up a book. The bump of the cat's back, carefully balanced on his lap, made a perfect place to rest his hands, though its twitching tail tickled his fingers as he turned the pages. Sometimes two green eyes stared from a twisted head as the cat arched itself, gazing lazily upward, distracting him.

*****

The alien doorbell sang like the first bird of dawn. Its call echoed into silence, while secret eyes inside checked the visitor out. Then the door swung wide, revealing a woman, dark-haired, with pointed chin and an eagle's brightness to her stare. Sharpened fingernails, red-painted, hung from her outstretched hand, making the man think of a kitten about to attack. The cat shrank back.

"Name's Tess." The woman spat her words through a dark, tobacco haze. "What's yours?"

Cold, night air stole the syllables away, while her visitor nervously replied, "An-drew?"

"Need a place to stay?"

He nodded.

"Missus kicked you out?" The woman dragged air through her words like a broken-down movie-star, clutching at fame in the smoke of her cigarette.

But no, Evie hadn't kicked Andrew out. He'd left of his own volition. So now he twisted the ring around on his finger, shook his head and muttered, "I just had to leave."

The cat almost snarled, making Andrew dance his feet away from its glare, kicking the bag against his ankles.

"Left her with the kids didja?" Noir lady sounded both sultry and viciously accusing.

Andrew bowed his head defensively. "Only one kid."

"Only one desertion then." She tossed her head, tangles of dirt-ashed curls whirling against thin shoulders.

Andrew complained, "You don't understand."

Then Tess, his maybe landlady, laughed, declaring all men are alike. "I don't need to understand you. I just need you to give me your cash, and you will 'cause I'm the only place that's open this late. Got a room, up those stairs."

Andrew widened his eyes when she told him the cost. So cheap? He said nothing and realized Tess was misinterpreting his stare. Did she think he was undressing her with his gaze? Did she think he'd care to undress anyone but his wife? Lost soul from the Paradise bus, had he become a devil escaping heaven now?

The white cat leapt from its windowsill and ran across the street with paws raised high. Its fur shone almost gold in the glow leaking widely from the door. Then Andrew laughed, relieved at the distraction.

"Cats are everywhere," he muttered, while reaching into pockets to find his cash. He could stay here perhaps, find a job in this place, and it wouldn't be too far. He could dream of going back, once in a while, to see the child, see Evie, see them happily settled without him. It wasn't desertion after all, no more than a tom-cat moving on while the kittens stayed safe at home, wild cats in a forested paradise.

Wandering thoughts glued him to the spot, while Tess's smoke-roughened laugh beckoned from the bottom of the stairs. It was done. He heaved a helpless sigh and crossed the stranger's threshold into life.

*****

The test was done. It was time for a new topic. "Today, we're going to study division, class."

"I live on Division," announced their favorite clown, Zeke.

"I live on Division." Amy's sweet voice parroted with her own unique intonation. Was that a touch of genuine personality Andrew wondered, but surely not. Then he returned to his task.

"Division is like the opposite of multiplication."

He paused, staring at his students and trying not to classify their opposites. Amy's sometime amenability would oppose

Tom's aggressive nature. Zeke's wild excitability against Jonah's placid stillness. Julie's hazy cough against... But he was meant to be teaching them.

Andrew's dream was that one day one student might recognize his meaning. *Yes Sir, just like subtraction and addition are opposites*. But no one ever would, unless Amy, through some continuing strand of uniqueness, found a way to express what she surely saw.

"Division's like where the shops are," Zeke mumbled.

"Yeah, if it's shops you're looking for," teased Tom, while Julie shrugged her tee-shirt down from her shoulder exposing bare flesh with a rainbow tattoo. Andrew didn't want to know what *she* looked for on Division. She was only a kid. And Amy, equally only a kid, stared entranced, as if bared shoulders were the height of enticement. Perhaps she was staring at the rainbow.

Andrew imagined his students divided into gangs on the notorious street. Tom would govern the thugs, for sure. Zeke would be a dancer, light on his feet, keeping the audience amused while young pickpockets divided the spoils. Julie would be the prize gangster's moll—was he showing his age? Jonah would be the one who always gets into trouble but somehow escapes—everyone would make fun of him, and no one would want to have him in their gang. And Amy—she'd be the innocent mark, unsuspecting, all unknowing of what went on around her.

Andrew suspected he'd play the innocent too. What did he really know about these students' lives?

Part 4

~9~

"Hello Andrew," said Evie. "I knew I'd find you here."

The Paradise Prowler, dark and ragged, shrank back into the trees, as if their fallen leaves and tangled branches might render him invisible. Perhaps the emptiness of his silence would swallow the woman's words, as if they'd never been. He wasn't here, and neither was she.

"Andrew, don't leave." She reached for his shoulder with a sharp-clawed hand, eagle talon outstretched to its prey, but then she almost fell on top of him. A wounded eagle perhaps. Andrew, crouching in the fabric of his own shadow, held her without holding, without believing. Meanwhile the air was filled with mourning, inspirational prayer, and song from the gathered crowds as the memorial service ground on. Meanwhile nobody noticed them. Meanwhile the man and woman stared, neither of them whole, nor free.

Andrew opened his mouth but wasn't sure his voice still knew the sound of words. He'd only spoken to the cat and the dream recently. The air on his tongue tasted thick with sorrow, dead leaves, and rotting seeds.

Evie pulled out of his grasp to fall against the stump of a tree. Her voice seemed lost in the effort to keep her body from dissolving. She'd used her last, faint breath to say his name.

Between them were fallen leaves. A child had been buried here, or somewhere else, under these or similar trees. Andrew shuffled his feet deeper into the loam. He was the one who should have died; he felt the weight of it. Love buried by betrayal, it should have been him in that shallow grave. But could love rise from a dead child's tomb?

A white cat arose, dust and leaf-mold sliding smoothly away from its pristine fur. It arched a shiny, sinuous back and swished its snake-like tail. It stared, green-eyed with jealousy or debt, and beneath its chin a small red stone shone like a drop of blood or glowing guilt. The cat twisted its head toward them, each in turn, its slitted eyes accusing, whiskers quivering disdain. Its purring voice generated a canopy over them, while hope breathed strangely in the scent of its white-washed shine.

"Sweet thing," said Evie, dropping her hand and her gaze to the feline intruder. She slumped and sat with her back against the stump. "Somebody loves you, don't they?"

Was she hoping Andrew would say he loved her still? He squatted back on his heels, watching as Evie's fingers parted fur. Then he noticed his own hand, dirty and grim, reaching out with a will of its own. He saw Evie's ring, its mirror image invisible on his finger. He heard soft memories stir behind the purring of the cat. An echo wakened in his chest, while sound bubbled into his throat, filled his mouth, and trickled out. The grating syllables surprised him.

"I loved you, Evie."

She didn't answer, accuse, or ask why he'd left. Instead she petted the cat. Her eyes turned away while Andrew shuffled, squat frog to her princess, until he was seated beside her, legs outstretched, resting his own dirt and shame on the same decrepit stump. She fell into his embrace while the cat snuffled softly and lay against their knees.

Gathered crowds meandered away from that place, as they had from the church and the grave, without seeing the stranger under the trees.

*****

Darkness was falling when Andrew awoke. Evie lay like a sparrow in his arms. He moved her fragile bones, hoping she wasn't dead. Then he soothed her feathers as she stirred. "You're cold," he said, surprised how natural it was to use his voice after all. "It's not good for you to fall asleep outside."

"Take me to your place," said Evie sleepily.

"I don't have a place. I can walk you home, if you…" He paused. "If you'd let me."

"Stay with me," she mumbled.

He knew she didn't mean what she was saying. Her mind was back in the safety of childhood days. She probably thought they'd stashed their bikes somewhere. Andrew laughed bitterly. "I'm not the staying kind. You should know by now."

"Yes you are. You just lost your way."

They rose up like a four-legged ghost out of the trees' gray fog. Andrew steered Evie toward the path, skirting the pond which steamed like a boiling kettle. Gravel crunched underfoot. Scents of fallen leaves drifted with sweeter fragrances of perfume, of crowds gone their way. Ahead Andrew spied the path to his secret cabin, but its cold and damp might make sweet Evie ill. He had to protect her. He'd promised that, once.

He'd promised to care for Amelia too, but it was too late now; too late for Carl to care for a wounded little brother; too late for Andrew's parents; too late for Evie's mother, who never did move in with them because she died just after the offer was made. Andrew knew himself, a breaker of promises, destroyer of all things good. But for now, he was the man who would try his best not to destroy what was left of Evie; at least, not today.

He wasn't sure if he pushed her, or she pulled him. They staggered together through forest and park, then stumbled on midnight streets past empty restaurants with rich warm smells. They must have looked like two drunks. Andrew resisted the urge to check dumpsters for food. Evie pulled him up the path to their house. He steadied her from falling, while she dug through pockets in search of tinkling keys. They waltzed together through the once-familiar doorway and stopped like a movie when the power goes out. Evie pointed a claw-like hand at the stairs. Andrew didn't want to head up there, but she towed him behind her and wouldn't let go of him. He was worried she'd fall if he tried to pull away. He was worried *he'd* fall if he stayed.

"It's still our room. Nothing's changed." Evie's voice croaked and giggled, as if she were stoned on misery. Perhaps she really was drunk. Did she know what she was doing?

"I can't stay," Andrew insisted, pushing her gently toward the bed so she could sleep again.

"I won't let you go." Sharp claws clutched his hand.

But Andrew was dirty and broken. He didn't belong. He would spoil every lovely thing in here. All his clothes were rags, and he smelled like an open sewer, rancid steam rising visibly from his clothes.

Evie must have known. She offered the shower, pushed him into its cavernous cleanliness, then stood outside holding a towel so he couldn't escape. Water rippled and roared over him, hiding Evie's voice while she threw the inevitable questions in his direction: "Where have you been living? Do you work? Have you got a job? How did you find out?"

Andrew heard only one word in three, even as he guessed her meaning. It provided sufficient excuse to silence any hopeless attempt at reply. But watery weariness poured up and down from the bathroom floor to ceiling, steaming like secrets as he dried his body there. Vapors spread their blanket over him. He had no clothes.

Hot, weary, and wrapped in a towel of unreal, unreasoning white, he stumbled out and staggered toward Evie's bed. He promised he'd just lie down for a minute then leave, but he didn't wake until morning. Then he saw sweet Evie lying beside him, as if he still belonged. He felt her arms tighten the moment he moved. He smelled the morning scent of life and death on her breath.

If you leave someone, if you leave your wife and child, why would she waste her time in looking for you?

"Because she loves you," said the bell-like voice of the child who had never been there.

Andrew stayed silent but questioned it in his heart. *How can she love me?* While the silent, invisible, eternally absent child offered adult condolence. "Love needs no reason, Daddy."

Do you *love me?* Andrew asked in unthinking dread, snatching his breath from the air as he spoke to a ghost, almost fearing the answer.

"You'll find out." Silence giggled in the emptiness after her reply.

*****

Evie rushed around the room, seeming to panic as she tried to gather his things—had he really left so many clothes behind, so long ago? She stuffed strange shirts and trousers onto shelves as if the doors might close and hold him. Her arms flapped fragile as naked wings, breath twittered, and unmoored flesh vibrated at her throat. Andrew wanted to tell her to relax, to stop, to let him go, but what right had he? Instead he sat on the edge of the bed, feeling the same dark tension grow in him. He longed to be free and alone under the trees, but he couldn't dare desert her, not again. He burned with an urgent desire for his cabin by the stream. For dreams, bikes, distance, memory, for the past, for a black cat leaping down a tree. He jumped to his feet.

"Evie, I've got to go."

"Don't leave. Don't disappear again." Evie rushed to his side and her arms smothered him, but she didn't seem real. Even her hugs weren't real. "I've only just found you."

"You're not thinking," Andrew muttered into her hair—so thin and graying now. "You don't really want me. It's just the pain talking." He pulled away from her, stood up, and staggered to the door, but couldn't turn the knob, his fingers all thumbs. The broken world tilted around him as he dropped to his knees then fell to the ground. She didn't need him, but perhaps he needed her.

"Andrew! What's the matter?"

He couldn't reply. His mouth couldn't find the words.

"Andrew!"

But all he could think, the only phrase he could hear in his fracturing mind, was *Amelia's gone.* While his body lay still. While his thoughts flailed far away in wild desperation.

He had to get back to the forest—this much he knew—to the trees where she'd died, to the clearing, dark shaded and calm, where her body might have lain. He had to get back to the place where her fragile soul waited—had to change things around—had to alter the past. He had to… *and follow the cat that had followed the bus and the child, and had haunted the trees.* Had he spoken aloud?

He heard Evie's voice as if from the end of a long and lengthening tunnel. "Andrew." But he couldn't stay with her, because Amelia wasn't here. Amelia was deep in the forest still, where he'd found her small voice whispering in silence. He couldn't leave her again. He had to get back.

"Don't be silly, Daddy. I'm dead, and you need to rest."

Not dead, not really, for all that he'd seen her laid into her grave. He wouldn't believe it; he'd just pretend she'd run away again. She'd be home in a minute, home in his hideaway cabin. He had to get back.

When Evie's hands touched his, Andrew pushed her away, but his arms were kitten-weak. He crawled to the door and tried for the knob again, but his fingers slipped. He couldn't get a grip. His heart beat too fast, because Amelia was leaving and only he could save her. But he was trapped in this room. He'd left her behind so he started to cry. And the world went black.

*****

"Where did you go?" Evie asked as Andrew lay, propped up on pillows, against the headboard of her bed. The mattress wobbled while she spooned thin chicken soup between his lips. He knew it was chicken soup because it was white and he was ill, but he couldn't taste it.

"I went…" He tried to tell her, his tongue as thick as a chicken-wing clogging his mouth. "Next town… On the bus… Cat… Girl…"

"What did you do?"

More soup. More drool wiped away with a warm, wet cloth. And more questions asked. Andrew tried to remember how to use his tongue, then swallowed more food. "I got a job, laboring."

"You? A laborer?"

"Helped in…" The letters wouldn't form. "Th-k." He struggled. "In school."

"You helped in schools? Like, a janitor? Why?"

"Guilt," he said, an easy word expressing a deepening truth.

Then she sat beside him on the bed, cool fingers stroking against his fevered brow. "You didn't need to feel guilty, Andrew. We did okay. You sent money. And she always did relate…" Evie gulped. "*Amelia* always did relate better to me than to you."

"My fault," Andrew whispered. "My fault." Because it had to be all his fault, from Carl who'd rather go back to war than stay home, to parents who'd rather die, to mother-in-law, to mother and child who needed something he could never give, to Amelia dying; it was all his fault. "Ever." He closed his eyes to find the words. "Ever…thing I touch." His anti-Midas touch. Medusa perhaps. "Everything turns to stone."

Eyes closed, his sight turned gray as stone as well. Life seemed wrong, but he hadn't the strength to change it. He should be down in the forest, quietly dying, not here being cared for by the wife he'd left behind.

*****

Another day. Andrew struggled to loose his legs over the side of the bed. Evie stood in front of him, holding the inevitable, steaming dish of soup while he stooped down like a recovering child. She was small and thin with her nightgown billowing around her knees. Her breath was ragged as feathers fallen to ground and rough as smoke.

His image in the mirrored wall looked back at him, equally thin. His body was a question mark glued on the flowered cover of the bed. His open eyes gazed at the woman's hands. His questing fingers trembled while hers stayed firm, pressed together around the dish, holding soup in mute supplication. He lowered his arms.

"How did you find out?" Evie asked.

Andrew lowered his face to his hands. Tears pricked his eyes. "Newspaper," he muttered, stuffing words through his fingers to feather-down and down to the bed-cover. He remembered the image on the side of a stand by the road, something half-unseen and half-ignored, like the signs that told them Paradise Forest was changing so long ago. The headline's words in letters far too tall, *Murder in Paradise*, and the touched-up photo of a fair-haired, innocent child, *his* child, *his* angel, stared at him. Names of people he remembered accompanied words of shock and horror, all of them asking, *How could we not have known?* The garage man, who'd fixed his car for him, had raped his child. *Death in Paradise. Community in mourning. Community in shock.* He was in shock.

Could he have saved his daughter if he'd stayed? Could he have spared his wife this pain? Or was his world condemned by his Midas-Medusa touch, always bound by fate turning gold into dust. He'd been ready to see his marriage die, but not his child as well. Not a child with an unlived, unlivable life. Not a child betrayed by fate and again by him.

So he'd waited at first, as if somehow pretending not to know might reverse the clock, unmaking the news. He'd gone to work each day as if it weren't true. But he couldn't wait in the end, because her picture had started a fire in his heart. Then he left, with only the clothes on his back. He walked away from his job and his rented room. He didn't even take a suitcase this time, or catch a bus. He marched in shoes that wore into holes, with blistering feet no more than he deserved. He stole into the town where once he'd lived, and begged for dinner at the church where once he'd mourned. He hid in the forest where once he'd loved, and he waited for death to claim him. But death delayed, so he watched his baby's funeral from under trees where none could see.

"I saw you," said Evie. "I was so sure I did."

Then he built himself a cabin in Paradise.

Then Evie found him, haunting the memorial service, guarded by a cat.

*****

Evie carried two plates of scrambled eggs this time. She handed one to Andrew, then knelt on audibly creaking knees at the bedside as if to pray.

"Really?" Andrew asked, but Evie didn't answer, just whispered words of grace and thanks and promise.

When she fell silent, the obligatory *Amen* stuck in Andrew's throat. He refused to utter it, asking instead, "So, can we eat? Have you finished praying now?"

"I've finished my prayers." Evie rose slowly, revealing knees roughened red by the carpet's weave. She sat beside him on the bed. The mattress dipped and swayed.

"Same thing," said Andrew, not sure why he couldn't let it go. Was he searching for something to make her throw him out? He took up his fork. "Prayers. Praying. They're the same."

"No they're not. Praying's like breathing. You do it all the time." Evie, who'd given up prayer when God didn't answer and didn't heal her child, now lifted her fork to her lips, her elbow brittle and angled sharp as stone. "God's done more than enough to save me, my love. I wouldn't be here now…"

"You didn't believe it," Andrew insisted. "Not like this. Not like it made a difference. You were angry at God back then. I know you were."

"You were angrier."

"I was honest."

Evie finished eating then stretched back, flat on the bed. She leaned her small gray head against the pillow. She smiled, so sweetly, so calmly religious, and it didn't seem possible. Andrew shivered, her *praying* dripping and steaming like dry ice, another cold reminder that she didn't need him. She'd only rescued him to save his soul. She'd only brought him here because she saw he needed her. She'd only married him for sacred pity. He really should have known.

She never loved me, he told himself. Love would have searched for him the day he left. She never loved him as deeply as she loved her child, nor as she loved her God. And *he* would never love the God who let a sweet child die.

"You don't know if I was sweet," said the bell-voice in his head.

"I know now," Andrew answered, not sure again if he'd spoken the words aloud. "And I know there is no God."

"So who do you think is letting me talk to you? The cat?"

*****

It lay beside him on Evie's bed, a very convenient, very white, very luxurious cat. It was always there when Andrew needed a friend, and always eager to please. His guardian angel, Andrew thought, not knowing yet that a girl from town had painted a cat like that, white-furred, silver-collared, red stone under its chin, with shining pale blue wings; not knowing yet that he'd find the picture one day, many years later, in a thrift store, and hang it proudly on his classroom wall—his one great personal possession to make an impersonal learning space seem real.

It was a cat like the one he'd met before in the forest. It was a cat that suddenly wasn't there at all, when Evie turned its way.

*****

Andrew had showered so many times the forest grime was almost a memory. He'd soaped his uncut hair and beard until they were kitten's fur instead of brittle like winter grass. His skin felt smooth, hanging a little too loose perhaps, like clothes a size too large, like Evie's skin. And his fingernails and toenails shone, their half-moons clean and pinker than they'd ever been before, or at least than he'd seen them in a long, long time. He wore clothes that didn't quite fit, because Evie had thrown out his rags and these were the things he'd left behind—when Amelia was small, still alive, when he deserted them.

He wanted to stay, stay for good, and make love to her, but now he'd washed for morning, and his clothes were laid on the bed. Andrew and Evie stood in their almost nakedness, like teenagers unsure if they dared take this step, instead of man and wife. Not old, they weren't, but older. So they dressed each other as if for death, each button carefully fastened, each zipper closed, each strap in just the right place. Then they said goodbye.

"Stay in touch," said Evie.

He wouldn't. He didn't. He didn't deserve that she should even care. And anyway, you can't mail letters from a broken-down cabin in the woods. She didn't need to know he was going back there.

"You're sure you'll be okay? Take care."

Then Andrew became a nobody again, undying, undead for years, until a do-gooder followed the cat and did good enough for him. He bought the thrift-store picture with his earnings from sweeping streets. Then he saved up, cleaned up, applied for a grant, and went back to college to retrain and become a teacher to failing kids.

*****

Brother, parents, family, child, house, forest and wife; he'd lost it all because of his Midas touch. So now a lost teacher taught the lost, failed father taught a failing child, and coward taught the brave. They threatened to take away this new life he'd made, these clever administrators with their need for measurable learning and superficial grades. They threatened to send his students somewhere else, and deprive sweet Amy of the chance to climb from her autism-labeled shelf.

Andrew stared out of the classroom window at clouds all gray and another wasted day. It wasn't fair! He remembered, long ago his mother used to say, "Life isn't fair." But that was before she stopped being there for him. Before he lost it all.

It wasn't fair!

~10~

"Andrew? Mr. Callaghan? Sorry."

Her name was Stella DeMaris and this art teacher wasn't so young as she looked, or so shy, for all that she was the newest member on the faculty. Her face, finely wrinkled beneath a thin layer of make-up, leaned too close over Andrew, and he blinked at her, owlishly.

"Sorry," she repeated, in a low, throaty whisper. "I thought you were falling asleep. Didn't want you dropping your coffee on the floor, not that it really deserves the name of coffee of course." She chattered quietly and smiled, while Andrew wondered if she was planning to spend all their faculty meetings rescuing his coffee. He noticed again how her small, delicate features resembled Evie's, how her hair curled in just the right way, framing her face, and how her hand cupped around his paper mug in motherly protection. Then he smiled his thanks, coughing lightly as he tried to find his voice, and wondering why the coffee hadn't succeeded in keeping him awake.

Stella whispered again. "Gets awfully boring I know, but you gotta watch out. Him over there had his eye on you." Her breath brushed Andrew's ear while herb-scented hair tickled his nose.

"Oh."

"Don't worry. I distracted him."

Stella's smile looked more dazzling than shy as she stared at Andrew now. He wondered exactly how she'd distracted their esteemed leader. Then he wondered how to extract his hand and coffee without causing offense, because she wasn't Evie and temptation only led to tribulation. Her fingers hovered dangerously close to his knee. Warmth, unrelated to coffee, spread toward his groin.

"Watch out for flying rumors."

"Huh?"

"You and me. I'm sure they think we're an item now."

But Andrew was nobody's item, for all the loneliness of an empty home. He had no desire for human connection beyond the needs of the job. He had no desire for any connections at all, and he had no explanation for a strange, white cat that had invaded his life. Or for voices from the dead.

For now, he edged his chair to one side, rocking it warily. Get rid of the cat, he thought, while Stella laughed, her voice purring low and warm.

"Don't worry. I know we're not. I'm just keeping you out of the can't-be-trusted-to-stay-awake-in-meetings book."

Andrew hid another cough, thinking there were much more important things he couldn't be trusted with. Then he heard: "What shall we do with that autistic kid?"

His heartbeat hammered in his ears.

"She should be in a different sort of school." The senior teacher announced this proud conclusion so very firmly and fairly that it could only be right. After all, the school had other children to think of, and someone had said on TV…

Andrew couldn't resist interjecting, "We're running the school by TV reports now?"

Someone said how a kid with autism had gotten a gun…

"Where would Amy do that?"

…and shot someone.

"She's not like that! And there are no guns in school."

Another autistic kid landed his care-giver in hospital. And one used a knife. "No empathy; that's what they say. They don't know what they're doing, I know, and I'm not saying it's their fault. But we're all at risk as long as she's a pupil here."

Andrew interrupted again. "You've heard all these things about other kids too." His voice surged with sudden certainty. "If it's more boys than girls that get into trouble, should we kick out the boys, make this an all-girls school? Is that what you're saying? Or maybe it's more one-parent kids, so we kick out anyone who hasn't got two to their name?"

Of course, it didn't help to argue. Tom's angry lookalike snarled pointedly. "Over-reacting's not going to get us anywhere." As if Andrew were the only one over-reacting to anything.

"We could get her tested," said someone else.

"*She* has a name, and *she* doesn't need to be tested." Andrew kicked the chair out behind him as he rose to his feet. The shriek of wood and metal on the floor matched the roar in his ears, while ripples trembled across the coffee cup. "*Amy's* in my class with me every day. *Amy's* the one who brings the other kids up to speed. *Amy's* okay."

"Yeah well. Some of those other kids shouldn't really be here either."

Andrew balanced coffee cup, voice and temper, like a juggler about to fall. "They're doing fine."

Then Stella spoke up, cool, rational, and sweet. "Don't we have an incident log? We really ought to, you know. And if those kids' names aren't in the log, then there's really no grounds for dismissal."

"Of course we have a log."

"So what does it say about Amy?"

Nobody answered, and Stella continued, forcefully, "So, what's the point of this discussion if we don't even know what the incident log says about these kids? And especially about Amy?"

The topic was swiftly dismissed, debate diverting to the next thing on authority's secret agenda. Meanwhile Andrew smiled at Stella. Their newest, youngest, shyest faculty member could certainly make herself heard. She'd be a good ally. He hid his voice behind his hand and asked her to join him in a meeting with Amy's mother, thinking a woman's touch, or words, might make all the difference there too. Warmth flooded his face when she agreed, and tension grew in his groin. That wasn't what he meant.

Heading back along the corridor, Andrew saw Amy had found another hiding place. Her fair head appeared behind the bushes outside a window. She almost looked at him, then hurried away. Andrew wondered unhappily if those bushes formed a hedge all the way to the faculty window. Could Amy have been hiding, listening in to the teachers' discussion? What might she have heard? What might she have made of it, or would it all have blown over her head?

"Strange child," said Stella, watching the girl tug spikes of leaves from her hair.

Amy frowned, deep in concentration, nimble fingers weaving like dreams into every strand.

"Indeed she is. But she's good. She'll make it, somehow."

*****

Andrew's guilty conscience pricked him now. He'd planned to phone Amy's mother—really he had—after he talked with Stella, maybe set up a time for all three of them to connect. But she called him first. "Today," she said. "I'm coming in today," which left no time to process his guilt or organize strategy. The woman was almost crying as she entered the room. She stood with hands on hips, chin jutting forward over her coat. "My Amy says you don't want her here."

"That's not true." Andrew pointed over his desk to the folding chair still leaning against the wall. "Why don't we sit and talk." But Amy's mother stood frozen to the floor.

"Why would she lie to me? My Amy doesn't lie."

Andrew had hoped to discuss Amy's behavior and ask if she was acting strangely at home. Now he had to defend the school instead. He tried to ignore the complaint, leaned back in his chair, and sighed. "Amy's a valued member of this class. Seriously. I do want her here, and I'd really hate to lose her."

Amy's mother scraped the folding chair to the desk and sat down at last, squaring her hands on her lap. "Then who doesn't want her? Why is she saying that?"

Was this another cruelty from Andrew's Midas touch? "Perhaps she heard…" He hoped she hadn't heard. "Perhaps she thought…" He hoped the mother would assume he meant some tactless remark had been made by another child. Instead she leaned forward, placing her elbows possessively on his desk, raising her face to anticipate the end of a sentence better left un-started.

The classroom door swung open, and Stella walked in. *Salvation!* "She may have heard some of the other teachers talking. They're quite keen to get rid of the whole class to be honest. But we're not going to let them. We'll stand up for all our kids." Stella settled herself on the edge of Andrew's desk. His eyes were distracted to the skirt riding up on her thighs, but he turned away. How long had she been listening outside?

"That's good to hear," Amy's mother allowed, pointedly turning her face away from Stella and toward Andrew. "But it sounded quite personal, the way my Amy said it."

Stella spoke again, her voice calm and soothing. "Her name might have been mentioned. But she wasn't the only one."

Andrew almost smiled, remembering the faculty's singular lack of calm when the topic was discussed. He wasn't sure what other names had been listed, but he'd believe anything this smooth, new teacher said.

"I don't know…"

Amy's mother might be unconvinced, but renewed decisiveness flowed through Andrew's veins. He patted the desktop. "Please don't worry."

"And I'm still not sure that this is the right place for her."

Andrew grew more sure, more convinced, the more he fought for Amy's right to stay. He'd grown to rely on her wry smiles as the math class advanced, the feeling that somewhere inside she was on his side, and the quiet responses that were always so correct, as long as he phrased his questions well. He hated to think of Amy locked away with *handicapped* kids, Amy treated as if she were wrong when she was so nearly always right. "She's coping. Seriously. She'll do fine."

"I've been told she'll never do fine."

"And I'm telling you she will."

"But how do you know?"

He knew it in his bones, and if occasionally he questioned those rose-colored, Amelia-scented spectacles, it was only for a moment. He lauded Amy's successes for Amy alone, and not because they'd been denied his child. He wasn't trying to build his student into the daughter he'd lost. Really he wasn't. But how could he reply?

She's not me said the bell-like voice in Andrew's head, the one fast becoming more strident again, after years of almost-silence while he trained for this job. The voice's persistence made him wonder if stress were driving him insane. Or insane again. Meanwhile, on the wall, that much-loved, white cat painting from a previous age seemed to flap its wings, halo slowly sliding over one ear. He almost imagined he heard it purr.

"I don't know," he replied with an attempt at honesty. "But I honestly believe that Amy's going to make it. I believe in her."

The mother buried her face in her hands. "I just wish I could see it."

Then Stella laid a hand on her frail arm, something Andrew, being male, couldn't do for fear the action would be misconstrued. "You know... if we stand outside, near the window at the back of the classroom..."

What was this? Andrew frowned, wishing he dared nudge Stella's leg under the table and change her direction. Mother and art teacher planning to hide in the bushes, just as Amy surely must have hidden outside the faculty room? But Stella continued. "If you stay down until I know all the students are facing the front, then you could look in. And if Andrew leaves the window open, you might hear what they're saying."

Andrew demurred. "Of course, Amy's quiet." *Don't do it,* he wanted to shout.

Stella smiled so sweetly. "But she'll hear you call on her, Andrew, and she'll respond. You know she will."

The mother nodded agreement, though tightly twining fingers betrayed she wasn't holding much hope.

Then Stella stood up. "Let's get out of here before recess ends. We wouldn't want her to see you invading her classroom space, would we?"

"What about your art class?" Andrew asked, wondering why Stella seemed so willing to help in so unwelcome a manner.

"I've got a student. I'll ask her to run it while I'm out."

The bell tolled loudly, still out of time, and Stella hurried out the door with Amy's mother at her side, just as the noise of students rolled and roared onto the corridor.

*****

"So, what have we been studying?" Andrew faced the class, trying hard to keep his eyes away from the open window and the figures standing behind it.

"Math-em-a-tics," they chanted, faces almost eager as they awaited whatever strange new thing would be on offer today.

"And where did we start?"

"Sub-track-shun."

The afternoon chant had wormed into their minds quite successfully. Andrew continued. "Who knows another word for subtraction?"

"Takeaway."

"Burger and fries."

"Sausages."

The chant was progressing fine, but it was time to interrupt. "Here's a new one for you to remember. Minus."

Jonah the Whale wheezed painfully, spraying donut crumbs from his mouth. "Minors, Sir? You mean like us, like not allowed to do stuff."

"He means like people in mines, when they dig stuff out. Dontcha Sir? That's what you mean?" Julie's rough voice might almost have belonged to a miner.

Andrew smiled his *not quite* smile at her then strolled to Amy's desk. She'd drawn a circular hole on her page, with a minus sign above it. *Curious.* "What is that?" he asked. But Amy was staring at a corner of the ceiling now. Andrew touched the back of her hand to attract her attention and repeated his question, watching Amy turn her gaze back toward the page

"Subtracting," she whispered, enunciating each syllable with painful persistence. "Minus is like miners subtracting the earth."

Was that a genuine, original simile? It felt like a breakthrough, as if Amy the factual had suddenly learned imagination and symbolism. "Very cool," Andrew replied, then raised his voice to address the rest of the class. "Did you all hear Amy?" He marched to the front. "Miners subtract the earth from the ground. That's subtraction, and it's really good, Amy. But what about *minus*. Not quite the same word is it? We're talking about…"

Tom broke in. "They'd like to dump us minors underground."

"Subtract us from the school," croaked Julie. Conversation began to buzz.

Andrew steadied his voice over the competition. "Relax, class, we're talking about min-us." He wrote the word on the board.

"Like mind us?" asked Jonah.

"Yeah, like don't dump us," said Julie. "Like you're minding all of us when you listen to us."

He guessed the distraction would have to run its course. But he nudged them with ideas when conversation paused. Addition is plus. "Plus sizes for Jonah," shouted Tom. Times is multiple plusses—"Jonah and the whales." Meanwhile, the students' knowledge of faculty debates had divided and conquered. But what should he say?

Amy curled her head low to the desk, covering the paper with her hair, while her shoulders seemed to heave.

Andrew stood over her again and asked, "You okay, Amy?"

"Minus Mom," came the half-sobbed reply. "Minus school. Minus Mom. Minus school."

He wasn't sure what Amy had seen, but he guessed she must have become aware of her mother, watching still from behind her, outside the window. He waved as if to shoo his visitors away. Stella pantomimed obedience. Then Andrew turned his back. Just as long as this group didn't end up minus Amy he'd be happy. And so would the bell-like voice of his dead daughter in his head.

You think one bit of imagination is a miracle, Dad? You've really got a lot to learn about us autistic kids.

*****

Amy shrank back into her shell as the class grew rowdier. Within days, she seemed as silent and still as when Andrew first met her, like silent Amelia just before a storm. He was glad her mother wasn't begging to watch anymore.

No more fanciful pictures adorned Amy's colored pages during the class. The vast array of buttons stayed in her pocket instead of raining over her desk. Her rainbow pencil was replaced with boringly simple black on white. Her pale eyes stared, as if the world held no further meaning, no promise left for her.

Andrew tried to coax her out of herself. He wheedled her for answers, endlessly asking, "What's wrong, Amy?" and receiving nothing in return. He called on her with questions, but she wouldn't look up, and the other kids took to teasing her again. "Amy's on another planet, Sir. She's a plastic doll."

Tom, always ready with the inappropriate, gave a swift wolf-whistle, pumped his hands, and declared, "Whoohooo. Think what I could do with a blowup doll."

"Can we blow her up, Sir?" Jonah's gleeful expression owed more to computer game explosions than innuendo.

Then someone else, with something sounding almost like sympathy, offered an answer that might have worked one week in four: "Amy's on her period, Sir; she's hormonal. You mustn't worry."

Sadly, the teasing went on for several weeks without release. Andrew feared it might drive his favorite pupil away. Then he reminded himself that teachers don't have favorites. Still, if Amy dared complain more loudly at home, tales of teasing might drive her parents to withdraw her. He didn't want that. He was so sure they'd made good progress together; so sure that Amy could almost, at a push, fit into regular society and take that coveted place denied Amelia. Now he had no idea what was wrong with her.

Math class passed from subtraction, via multiple addition, to multiplication, division and beyond. Fractions paved the way for percentages. Then came the much-dreaded lesson, introducing long division without calculators. The students treated it with predictable dismay, especially when Andrew threatened to confiscate any electronic assistants he found in their hands, including cellphones. His *refuseniks* were almost normal in their refusals today.

"But Sir, we can find out the answers on the phone. We need our phones."

"What if your battery runs out?" Andrew asked, amenably.

"I'll borrow someone else's, yeah."

"What if you're all on your own somewhere, and nobody knows where you are?"

"Like you're lost in a forest?" Julie suggested with a cough, while Andrew struggled not to get lost in memories.

"Wouldn't be found dead in a forest, Sir. Not me."

Sad memories, of Amelia found dead, raised their heads and snarled at him.

"There's always someone with a phone these days, Sir. Always."

Andrew thought instead, *there's always someone with a threat.* Predators and prey chased their way through fields and forests of his mind. But why did Amy stare at him that way? As if she knew the forest of his retreat, as if she knew the places where batteries die and reception disappears, as if she knew… He shook his head and simply said, "Not always," then continued the lesson.

*****

Andrew had often wondered how Amy would take to long division. Would it offend her logical sensibilities—her need for predictability and order? Or would she simply ignore the whole thing, as if the lesson had never taken place? Would she let him see the thoughts behind her eyes?

"Long division's not logical," Andrew confessed, catching the autistic girl's gaze and determined to challenge her, but getting no response. She laid her head on the table. "Long division's all about guesswork."

At least this got a reaction from the other students. Feet kicked and chairs scraped noisily back from their desks. "You can't say that. You can't guess in class, Sir. Guessing's not allowed."

Angry Tom stood up with pretended authority. He rapped his knuckles on wood. "Gotta get the right answer, answer, gotta answer, all the time." His voice quivered between high and low, breaking hormonally with lugubrious resentment. "That's what school's all about, Sir. Gotta be right."

"Or they dump you with the rejects."

"They *minus* you."

"And you get taken away."

Andrew was only teaching math, not sociology, but the kids had a point. His marker squeaked on the whiteboard as he wrote the heading there to catch their eyes. "Long division," he repeated in his most commanding voice, as bell-like as Amelia's in his head. "Long division"—even the words sounded dull—"is all about working your way *toward* the right answer from the best guess you can make. And the better you guess, the less time it will take."

Jonah asked why you couldn't know the answer from the start. The way he stored memories like food, he'd probably know half the answers to anything Andrew set, just from having seen the questions before. But, "*Not* knowing," said Andrew, "is what math is all about. Not knowing, and going ahead to figure it out. It's not magic, not memory, not lists of all the right answers and perfect formulae; it's not like history where you have to keep in mind everything you've been told. Math is methods. Math is your own ideas, worked out in your own head. It's how you bring things together in ways that work, that work for you." As speeches go, it wasn't bad.

"Ways that get you a job?" Angry Tom had seated himself again. His face wore a sullen frown, though faint hope lit his eyes.

"Ways that help you get a job, for sure," Andrew replied. "And not just a job teaching kids like you lot either."

They laughed at this and tossed their unhurried spit wads across the room. Andrew didn't complain. They were still talking, still taking notice, and that was the most he wanted.

"What jobs need math?" someone asked. So Andrew sat edgewise on a corner of the desk and regaled them with tales of shopping, washing, calculating dosages of medications for pets or the right amount of soap in a poodle-bath, high finance and low, computer games and how to get the best value for your cyber-buck. Still, division was the subject of the lesson, so he steered their conversation toward the game he'd planned for them.

As the room quieted for a moment he raised a hand, commanding their attention. "Listen. You've got fifteen soldiers in your army," he announced.

They took the bait without hesitation. "Fifteen orks or storm-troopers?"

"Orks," Andrew replied, not missing a beat. He hadn't been too sure before, but since Amy was ignoring him, he chose to flesh out his game with ideas from the guys' current green-skinned, monster-featured favorite. "You've got fifteen orks, and you've got seventy-three e-dollars between you to get them ready for battle, so what will you buy?"

"Seventy-three swords," shouted Jonah.

Andrew laughed. "Fifteen soldiers would only have thirty arms."

"That's multiplication!"

Not bad! thought Andrew, adding, "What about guns and lances and phasors and… whatever else there is."

"Fifteen cyber-lances; one for each soldier," Tom shouted.

Andrew had to ask how much a cyber-lance cost. The boys, even minus their cellphones, knew the answers and called them out, while Andrew catalogued an imaginary store on the board. Another exercise in multiplication showed there wasn't enough money. Then a mournful groan settled down like a black cloud.

"So," asked Andrew, undeterred by the misery growing around him. "How many cyber-lances *could* we afford?" He offered the fraction, seventy three divided by seventeen, smiling as the promise of long division reared its ugly head. Guesswork offered some radically wrong suggestions, all of which were given equal weight, written on the board, calculated, checked and rejected. Eventually the students settled on four cyber-lances, with money left over to split between phasors and swords.

"And that's what it's all about." Andrew clapped his hands as the last words were written on the board. "You used a bit of guesswork and multiplication and, in the end, you did some long division."

He felt proud of them, and of himself for leading them to this place. But Amy still sat, sullen, almost lifeless, never raising her eyes from the desk. What went on in that sweet mind, Andrew wondered. Could he guess and refine his estimate of her? Was she somehow dividing her attention between class and home and some secret all her own? And was nothing left over?

But perhaps, as the other students suggested, she'd simply checked out, gone to another planet in her head, and given up on them.

*****

Andrew developed another game to help his students practice all the topics they'd learned in math. He split the class into two teams. Each group had fixed amounts of imaginary cash, all listed on the board, while a corkboard he'd borrowed, or acquired, from Stella's art room was decorated with images of things they might buy. He'd printed the pictures out from an antiques website. Each piece was labeled with a price and a percentage by which its price might be expected to rise. Andrew told the students to choose what they'd like to purchase.

"You've got to stay in budget," he insisted. "No going into debt. And you've got to look for those things you can afford, whose value will give you the best return over time."

"You mean like when you give them back?" asked Jonah, flailing his arms as if to pantomime the return of unwanted gifts.

"No, like selling them at a profit, at the end of the game."

"Real profit?"

"E-profit, guys. I'm not made of money."

The teams bent their heads to the task, eagerly shouting out different ideas and calling each other names. "I'm buying… no you can't; it's mine… think you're the only financial whizz on the block." Meanwhile, Amy's team worked at a serious disadvantage since she wouldn't take part, but Andrew kept hoping something might spark her interest.

Just when he'd finally accepted that his favorite student would sleep through the whole game, Amy looked up with a beatific smile, her first smile in weeks. She pushed back her chair, moving slowly, and startling like a bird when the chair legs shrieked on the shiny floor. She made her way to the front of the room, dancing in small graceful steps while keeping her eyes fixed on the whiteboard, looking neither right nor left. Then she began to take down pictures, with no clear motive defining which she'd choose. She positioned Andrew's tacks like her endless buttons in tidy rows across his desk, then tucked her chosen images, one by one, into an opened pocket of her backpack. Closing the flap, she turned and made to walk away.

"What are you doing, Amy?" Andrew asked, while the other students groaned and prepared a spit wad arsenal.

"Packing." Her voice was clear and undismayed, as bell-like as dead Amelia's.

"Packing for what?"

"Packing so I'll have money, so I can sell things, so I'll have more."

Andrew groaned now with the rest of them. "You know those are only pictures, don't you, Amy? They're not really worth any money."

"Why not?" asked Amy. She frowned and spat the ugly word, "Pretending," in reply to her own question. Her mouth seemed to chew the syllables like a plateful of cold fries.

Pretending was meant to be difficult for autistic students. Andrew remembered that. "Yes Amy," he confessed. "It's only pretend. So please would you put the pictures back."

She hesitated, protesting mildly that she needed *real* money, while small frown lines of confusion split her brow.

"I can't help with that, I'm afraid."

Amy shook her head, almost the same small action Andrew had made. Shining hair cascaded down her back. Then she twisted her neck to stare over her shoulder, a Julie persona flowing, feature by feature, into her face. Amy's delicate, gentle frown turned to a snarl, and her small mouth stretched large, while Andrew stared. Then Amy sighed and theatrically pinned each picture back in place, precisely where he'd positioned them before. Meanwhile Andrew scribbled notes on paper and realized the items she'd chosen were exactly the ones he'd intended for the best returns. If Amy's team followed her advice, they'd get the best e-value for imaginary bucks and win the game. If only Amy could channel that genius into the real-life world.

"Amy, Amy, Amy," he sighed, as she quietly returned to her seat, head bent in defeat. "What shall I do with you?"

Amy thunked down onto her seat. "Nuffin'." She reached into her pockets and scattered buttons over the desk. Then she added, solemnly, "Thirty-four."

He guessed there must be fifty buttons there, or more, and couldn't imagine what she meant.

The class was beginning to lose its focus now. Andrew turned his attention back to the board. He called out items, describing them loudly like an auctioneer. One by one, he offered imaginary treasures to see what the teams would buy. The room filled with laughter, complaints, and roars of dismay—the school board wouldn't approve perhaps, but math was frequently hinted behind these youthful cries, so Andrew was happy. Claims of, "You twit! I'm making piles more than you," had to be backed up with calculated data, as everybody knew. Each proof was carefully examined. Well-measured profits filled the classroom's air, guaranteed to please as well as annoy.

The boys began to chant when Andrew reached a particularly gruesome item. He'd labeled it *axe-head from a medieval battle-field.*

"Blood! Blood! Blood!"

"That red stuff's blood ain't it?" Julie interjected. Her voice was gravelly and dark.

"Well, you should know, Lady Muck."

"Shut up!"

"But how much money will it make you? Work it out," Andrew demanded, distracting the Tom-and-Julie-show from their threatened fisticuffs.

He checked his own calculations too, found a missing digit, and corrected the maximum profit his students could achieve— thirty-four-thousand imaginary dollars. *Thirty-four?* Then Jonah announced, with casual flippancy, "Hey Sir, Amy's gone." And the world began to tilt. *Thirty-four?*

*****

"Amelia's gone!" Evie announced that evening as Andrew walked through the door.

He'd stared, uncomprehending, expecting screams from his daughter then realizing silence reigned. Evie's sobs of concern were the only sound, like a vinyl record that's run to its final groove. She flapped her hands like wings before his face in helpless dismay, and they made more noise than her words.

"Amelia's gone! Do something! Amelia's gone!"

Years later, after Andrew himself had gone, the newspaper proclaimed, "Dead girl's body found in park." But what chance would she ever have had, poor misfit, misbegotten child, in a world of predators and killers.

*****

Andrew opened his eyes, trying to remember where he was. Students stood on every side, eyes wide with concern, arms flapping pointlessly like flightless wings. "You okay, Sir?" asked Julie, reminding him of all the times he'd asked if Amy was okay. He wondered when he'd sat down, and how had the kids gathered around without his noticing. Then he pushed himself up from his chair, pressing his legs against the desk for security. His knees trembled, and his breath quivered like butterflies in his chest.

"Are… Is…" Andrew coughed to cover his embarrassment. "Amy… Right, did you say Amy's not here?" A cloud of hands and faces blocked his view, but the students stepped aside, clearing a path, so Andrew could look between them at Amy's empty chair.

Thirty-four. That was what she'd said. He walked along the aisle and leaned over her desk, one hand resting on its surface to balance him. A pile of buttons lay heaped into a mountain, with pencil neatly placed beside them, a graphite, straight-arrowed stream. Andrew wanted to move the buttons and count them. He guessed now that there'd be precisely thirty-four, and he wondered what Amy had done with the rest of them.

Small pieces of paper lay next to the pencil river. If Amy had any imagination, if Amy were there to imagine anything with him, what would the papers mean? But the space beneath the desk, where Amy's backpack should have waited until the real end—not the bell-tolled end—of class, was suspiciously vacant.

"Does anyone have Amy's bag?" Andrew asked because, of course, they could just be playing tricks on him and on her.

The students shook their heads. "She must have taken it with her, Sir," Julie volunteered.

"That's why she was putting those things in it, d'ya reckon?" said Jonah. "She's going somewhere and she wanted to take some money."

The students suddenly bent their heads, in unison, to an urgent task under their desks. They fumbled with clasps and straps, checking their backpacks for financial contraband, as if Amy were a thief. Perhaps they feared she might have ghosted around the room, stealing precious supplies while they worked at Andrew's game. But no one screamed the discovery of missing cash. Which was surely good. If Amy had no money, how could she go anywhere? Why wasn't she here?

*****

A rumor declared the school might be closed for investigation. But lessons began as usual after the weekend, the only interruption a long and boring time of interviews with random officials the day Amy disappeared. All Andrew's students were present on Monday, all except for Amy. But the room, usually filled with noise, seemed cruelly stagnant and still. He wondered how the most unobtrusive member of the group could generate such silence. Her empty desk crouched like a gaping hole, too wide to be contemplated, too inexplicable to be defined. Subtracted, Amy was larger and louder than she'd ever been before.

Questions went unanswered. "Who can tell me...?" Nobody could.

Andrew's eyes were drawn to the ever-vacant desk. Amy would raise her almost vacant eyes with the reply. But she wasn't there.

Around the room, arguments started and stilled, unfulfilled, as angry faces found themselves caught in Amy's empty stare. That lonely space distracted all of them, making even the loudest students wait as if their glares could somehow bring her back. They'd add and divide then suddenly lose their math in a single question, repeated over again, "Have they found her yet, Sir?"

The answer never changed. "I don't know."

Tom insisted his classmate must have been kidnapped and raped, or turned into a sex slave, sold off to some mystic chieftain far away. A dancing girl in ribbons and veils, "And if you pull the edge of her skirt just right…"

"How would you know?" asked Zeke, his clown-voice dropped, hair uncombed, eyes reddened as if he really cared.

Jonah imagined she'd wandered off, searching for burgers and fries, and somehow got lost. "They'll find her in a shop."

Meanwhile Julie declared she'd slipped through a magical wormhole; whisked away by the power of hope to some universe where she wasn't strange or different anymore. "You know, Sir." Her coughing, breathless voice almost lightened into joy. "Like, she was never quite all here, you know, but now she's okay because she's all there instead. You see what I mean?"

Zeke just complained that *he* wished *Julie* was *all there*, then he wouldn't have to listen to her smoker's cough.

Andrew stared through the window, imagining Amy's head might peak out from behind the bushes. Was she hiding like her mother? Would she smile that secret smile at him? Or would he see her walking down the path as if nothing were wrong. *She's waiting for the bell, for the right time.* He chewed his fingernails and sighed.

The police had no leads of course. Their radio alerts hadn't brought up any sightings. Nobody knew anything at all, and how could a child just vanish? Especially a child like Amy? Even Amelia had been found.

Sweet, complicated Amy with luxurious hair, shy smile, buttons and rainbows; she'd simply disappeared.

Amy's mother became a fixture in Andrew's room, visiting him at recess every day. Sometimes she arrived alone, sometimes with the baby in tow, and once even with her husband, who'd taken precious time from work to offer his support. Andrew sat safely on his own side of the desk, feeling guilty because it was his class Amy had run from. That Midas touch again. It could only be his fault.

"Not that I blame you," Amy's mother said.

"No no," her husband agreed, or was he disagreeing?

"But you know how I feel, don't you? Like you're the last person she spoke to before… Like maybe she said something… you know… or you said… someone said… Maybe it's something you've forgotten, Mr. Callaghan. Something… like you didn't realize how important… didn't know what she meant."

But no one had ever been sure what Amy meant.

Andrew tried to remember. She'd said so little in that last class, head down and staring at the desk—*I need money* perhaps and *thirty-four*. Was it the number of a bus? The number of thousands in imaginary dollars; that's what Andrew thought it meant, until he counted the buttons. Coincidence? Or just a random thought? Her thought or his? Meanwhile the other kids had talked, while Amy disappeared.

"I asked if she was okay, I guess," he conceded. "But she said nothing was wrong." It didn't help.

"Yes, she told me that too, all the time. But she mustn't have been okay or she wouldn't have gone. You could see something was wrong with her, right, couldn't you?"

But what could he have seen? What should he have seen? As Amy left the room that day, in the middle of class, at the wrong time, when the bell hadn't rung, and the clock wasn't telling her to go, which way had Andrew looked? What had he failed to see?

Amy's mother bowed her head toward her lap in helpless defeat. "I always said this wasn't the place for her."

Then Andrew, though he hadn't the words or the energy, struggled to the school's defense. "But she…" He wanted to say she was doing so well. He wanted praise for how much she'd progressed with him. But now she'd *progressed* right out of his classroom, right out of her family's life, and he surely should have known. He shook his head, shrugged helpless shoulders, and added, "She seemed worried, sad."

"I should have kept her at home."

"I don't…"

"But she wanted to come."

"She said…"

"And I knew I couldn't keep her away. You know what she was like."

Andrew repeated those last two things, which might have meant something or nothing. "She said she needed money, and she counted her buttons. Thirty-four." It *had* to be important.

Amy's father scoffed. "She never knew what she was talking about, that girl. What would a child like her want money for?" Meanwhile his wife tugged urgently on his hand, just like Evie had tugged on Andrew's hand so long ago.

A child like Amy, like Amelia, Andrew thought. Where was she now?

He stared around the classroom, sunlit and bright, but his eyes saw instead the gloom of forest and trees. He hoped and prayed they wouldn't find Amy's grave in a shallow ditch like Amelia's had been. He hoped she wasn't clothed in undergrowth. He hoped she wasn't silently dead and already fading away. Meanwhile he sipped on cooling coffee, choked on platitudes, and tried not to blame himself too much, in case he too disappeared. He'd done it before.

~11~

Andrew was late to the faculty meeting again. One of the students ran ahead of him, clearing a path through the crowds, wafting draughts of sweat, stale beer, sticky soda, chocolate and nicotine in the air over his head. The air was so thick, he imagined he could see the trails of forbidden secrets clouding over the student body. But his guardian wouldn't let him divert or delay. "This way, this way," she yelled helpfully, while Andrew, glowing with embarrassment, hoped her voice wouldn't attract wrong-doers or carry far enough to be heard inside the faculty room. As he flung open the door onto a sea of waiting faces, he knew this latter hope was vain.

"This way, this way," boomed Tom's look-alike with a smile devoid of mirth. He spun Andrew around by his shoulders, pointing him toward the table where coffee awaited.

Tiny Stella whispered, with a rather more genuine smile, "This way, this way." She filled Andrew's cup, adding milk and sugar, and leading him to the second least comfortable seat in the faculty room. He tried to switch places with her, but they nearly tripped and it all grew too embarrassing, so he stayed where he was put. Then the meeting began.

"So, Andrew, Andrew. What shall we do with you?"

"Sorry I'm late." Andrew tried not to let too much of his frustration bleed into his voice.

"Not that," came the reply. "No, what shall we do with you, entertaining that girl's mother in your school room every day."

Entertaining? He felt warmth spread from ears to nose, inducing an almost overwhelming need to reach for a handkerchief. There wasn't any entertainment going on.

"I mean," his superior continued, "she doesn't have a child here anymore, Andrew. You do realize that?"

"Amy's still enrolled."

"Amy's not here."

Did the vice-principal have to put so much glee into the announcement?

"And so, dear Andrew, Amy's mother has no reason to be here either. Amy's mother should simply stay away. And you, young man"—he pointed an accusing finger, though Andrew scarcely felt young anymore—"you should stop encouraging her."

Andrew shrugged and began to defend himself. "I'm not…"

"You tell her to go away. If you don't, I will."

"Tell a grieving mother…?"

"She's not grieving. Amy's not dead."

"You don't know that."

"But she's still enrolled, Andrew, as you so rightly said. And we don't enroll ghosts."

Andrew shuffled awkwardly on the chair, drawing angry protests from its metal legs. A defeated sigh bubbled into the coffee in his throat. But Stella's hand rested lightly on his thigh. When he turned to face her, she mouthed, "Don't worry. It'll all work out." Then Andrew smiled thanks while conversation moved briefly to budgets, past discipline and dockets, then back to police reports. Andrew's head dropped. He guessed he was beginning to snooze, reminded himself he mustn't, held tight to his cup, and tried to widen his eyes, then realized they were shut.

"She's been seen."

The words came out of nowhere. Andrew thought perhaps he'd heard Amy's name but wasn't sure. He struggled dizzily awake and swung around to find who'd spoken. His chair began a precarious wobble beneath him, before his feet could set it back in balance. "Seen by who?" His mouth burred, full of cotton wool, and he struggled to form the words.

"Hold on. I'm reading it." His colleague stared down at the glowing screen of a phone resting in his lap. "Police say a trucker came forward. He gave her a ride out of town."

The icy senior teacher banged a hand on the table, but Andrew ignored her and asked, "Why didn't the trucker speak out earlier?"

It seemed a logical question, as others agreed, their attention firmly diverted from the meeting. But apparently the trucker had been on the road, not listening to news, just getting on with the job. He saw no reason to think the *young woman* he gave a ride to was a missing girl.

"Young woman?" Andrew spluttered, trying to imagine lost Amy playing that role.

"Swears he thought she was eighteen, nineteen or more."

"But how?" She with the perpetual light of childhood and strangeness in her eyes, how could she seem so old? Then Andrew wondered what she'd done to make a trucker think… He groaned, clutching his arms around his chest. "Oh no. Did she? Did he?"

"Nothing like that. Nothing wrong, he says. She just wanted a ride. He gave her a ride. End of story."

"So where did he leave her?"

Loud rapping of knuckles intruded again, demanding an end to the talk. But another teacher leaned forward to pass the answer, like Chinese whispers, to Stella, to Andrew. "Next town. He left her in the next town along the road."

Andrew nodded his thanks and the teacher added with an almost human smile, "You really should get a decent phone."

Andrew wanted to know which town, which direction, how far, and how long ago she'd been seen. But discussion steered back to budgets and whether they could, or even should, continue to squander funds on the special needs class. Still worrying whether Amy was alive, dead, or nearly dead, Andrew battled again for the rest of his kids. He forced a reminder into his head, to watch TV and read the newspaper tonight, and check the internet. But the simplest thing might be to ask his students when he got back to class. They'd have heard it all by now.

*****

"Sir, Sir, they found Amy."

A hedgehog of teenage bodies bounced around the doorway as he returned to the room. Each voice offered a different version of the tale. "She'll be back tomorrow." "She's gone for good." "She's dead as a doornail, Sir."

Andrew marched to his desk and faced his eager, investigative team. He demanded loudly that they should all, "Sit down!" Then he picked on the student least likely to exaggerate. "So, Julie. What do you guys know that I don't?"

A roar of sound rose in reply, but Andrew raised his hand for their attention and shouted, "No!" until they quieted again. "One at a time please, class, and Julie tells me first. What do *you* know, Julie?"

The tall girl coughed, inevitably, then blushed and spluttered as she leaned over her desk before beginning to speak. It seemed a trucker had spotted Amy on a roadside, heading west. He offered a ride—"She didn't ask him for one; I guess she wouldn't know how."

Tom interjected gleefully, "I guess she'd need someone to tell her how to climb up and open the door!"

More voices joined in, until Andrew raised his hand for quiet again. "Julie?"

"The trucker said she was real *re-fined*." Julie twisted her lips around the word, more laughter trailing her. "A proper little lady, he said, and she told him she was going *wes-s-st*."

"Go West young man," someone quoted, unexpectedly.

Julie coughed then added, "He said she didn't talk much," making the room dissolve into laughter.

Andrew sighed. *Silent and refined* really did sound like Amy, so he answered, "Yeah, we all knew that. But where did he take her?"

The trucker had offered to drop his rider in the next town, or at a rest stop, or buy her a meal. But Amy still didn't say very much, so he took her to an eatery and left her at the table, studying the menu.

"Think she'll pass AP dinnertime, Sir, if she studies it enough?"

Andrew smiled at the feeble joke, while his legs grew forest-stream cold and his knees began to quiver. He asked what happened next.

"Nothing," said Julie. "Trucker said he left her at the table and didn't see her again. He paid for her meal though. Nice guy."

"Someone must have seen her." Andrew stared out of the window, dreaming perhaps he'd see her too, tired from walking back to school through endless days and nights. A white cat kept watch from the school's low wall. But lugubrious Tom brought Andrew back to earth.

"Guess that's what they pay cops the big bucks for," he announced. "Bet that's what they's trying to find out. Asking everyone. Scaring everyone like cops always do. They'll scare Amy too, if they find her."

Andrew thought they'd scare him as well, but he felt an itch in his feet and an awkward need to go out there after the child and bring her home. Bring her back before some forest carpet caught her, before some predator from Paradise took her down, before she was gone forever, like Amelia.

The bell-voice answered in his head. "I'm not gone yet."

The winged cat on the classroom wall seemed to flap its painted feathers and wink at him.

"Okay class. Let's get some work done, shall we? Amy will just have to catch up when she gets back." Andrew smiled as he spoke, sensing *when* might a stronger word than *if*. Just possibly it might prove truer in the end. If prayers could make it so, those silent words his heart kept sending skyward would surely help.

*****

They were waiting for him outside the school. He had to pass their car on his way across the parking lot, but it was just a car;

an ordinary car. He paid it no attention until one of them opened a door and stood in front of him, blocking his way. "We just need to talk, Mr. Callaghan." A dark, official voice; he wondered at once, had they found her? Was she dead?

"Why?" Andrew asked, trying to step around the man, to make this conversation go away. His car was just a few short strides ahead. He could drive home. He could bury himself in a book and refuse to switch on the TV or look at the internet. He could cuddle the cat. He didn't need to know.

"If you'd just get into the car…"

"Why?" Because whatever it was, they could surely tell him here. He was her teacher, not her father. He wasn't going to cry.

"We just need to talk."

Andrew tried to ask why again, but felt the pressure of expectations drive his feet toward that open door. Suddenly a hand pressed down on his head, gently but firmly folding him into the blackness of a cold, unpadded, unwelcoming seat. "What is this?" he cried out in sudden terror, trapped behind bars, feeling the ice of other people's fears flow through the rear of the car. "What's going on?"

He scrabbled useless fingers at scratched plastic when the door closed on him. There was no handle, none on the inside anyway. He banged on the glass, imagining his face seen from outside, mouth opened wide in a silent scream. At least there were no cameras, yet—nobody taking his photograph to fill the next front page.

One of his captors turned around from the seat in front of him. "Don't make a fuss, Mr. Callaghan. We just need to talk."

But why would they choose to talk like this? "Why not in school, in a classroom, the faculty room?" His voice squeaked, embarrassing him further. "Why here? Why the car and everything?" Then, voicing the fear he'd hoped would stay safely hidden, he asked, "Am I under arrest?"

Outside the car, student faces must surely be staring now. They'd point at him. They'd draw their own conclusions and brand him a killer. Was Amy dead?

"Tinted windows," said one of the officers, as Andrew's panting breaths grew short, and panic grew tall. "Don't worry, Mr. Callaghan. Nobody can see you."

It wasn't much comfort. "They saw me get in."

"We just need to talk."

The driver started the engine, its roar sending floods of fear through Andrew again. He stomach heaved and he wanted to scream at them to let him out. He imagined a movie scene with the car rounding a corner, door opened wide to drop him toward a cliff where he'd pay at last with his life for what he'd done, but he'd done nothing—not here, not now—nothing to harm or to heal. Whispered words resounded in his head. *We have not done those things we ought to have done; we have done those things that we ought not to have done.* Was that a prayer? Was it meant to comfort him? Its lines repeated, babbling through his mind as he opened and closed his mouth. Then the bell-voice offered comfort. "Daddy, wait." So he stilled himself for her and sat, waiting, remembering to breathe.

Outside the glass, streets drifted past as if nothing were amiss. Shoppers crossed at traffic lights. Car horns blared when someone delayed too long. Clouds scudded softly through a painted sky. All was right with the world. But Amy was surely dead, and Andrew was heading to his doom.

"Where are you taking me?" he asked eventually, forcing words through chattering teeth.

"Down to the station." So they really were the police, not imposters who'd learned too much about his past.

"Why? Is she dead?"

"We're hoping you'll tell us that, sir."

"Why? Am I under arrest?"

"You're a person of interest."

"I'm a teacher." His teeth parted at last, releasing an anguished shout. "She disappeared from my class."

"Exactly, sir."

Exactly, like exactly the right answer, found when subtractions were exactly completed, correctly. *And what are we studying today, class; does anyone remember? We're studying subtracted students... Amy.* "Why aren't you looking for her?" His voice squeaked again, while his mind processed their answer. *Exactly, sir.* Which meant losing her from his class placed him under suspicion. How did that work?

"We are looking for her, right here, right now," the cool, calm voice replied, and the car drove on.

*****

Andrew wasn't sure how he'd ended up in this room. The walls were featureless gray, school paint before the students' work gets added to spruce it up. School gray for the end of summer, but school vacations hadn't begun. Not yet. It wasn't time. He was running out of time.

There were no windows, and that frightened him. He wouldn't see Amy rushing down the path when she returned; he didn't want to miss her. So he stared around for the thirty-fourth time, checking to see if gray plaster might have changed to glass while he wasn't looking. Then he turned his attention to his coffee cup, where limpid liquid rippled, featureless gray as the rest of the room. It looked and tasted like dishwater, but he felt it might be impolite, even dangerous, for him to say so. He sipped again at the cooling plastic and imagined the cup would taste just as bland as the drink it contained.

The table, gunmetal gray like everything else, was anchored to the floor. The chair could move, but it wasn't clear where or why Andrew might move it; any space was as featureless as the next. Overhead a gray, metal cage was knitted into tiny squares over a buzzing strip light. Even the light seemed gray. Beneath it, a covered vent let air in and out near the ceiling. It was too high to reach and probably wasn't big enough to crawl through. Besides, the woman watching him, strong-armed and stolid in a second chair stationed by the door, wasn't terribly likely to let him escape.

Andrew twisted trembling lips into a smile as he faced the policewoman. He wanted to believe she was human, because that might mean he was too. But her flat, robotic features didn't change. She didn't smile. Her hair and eyes were gray.

Behind the woman the dull gray door with its mesh-entangled window stayed resolutely closed. Andrew stared at the window's square, instead of staring at the woman. He tried to hope someone might look in and notice him, walk in and explain, or his guardian might go out. But it was a pointless hope. His breaths grew short again, tightening his chest, and blackness filled the space behind his eyes. Even his darkest memories seemed just another shade of gray, unimportant strands of the strangled veins encroaching on his vision. He'd collapse, grayly, if nothing happened soon. Then the woman would pick him up and nothing would change.

"Don't worry, Daddy," said the bell-voice in his head. He shook as if to dislodge her from his ear. How could he not worry, trapped in here? And besides, Amelia couldn't talk if she was dead.

Was Amy dead as well? He wished they'd just say it and be done with it. Then he wished Amelia would let him know instead.

Shuffling his feet, Andrew made the chair legs creak on the floor. The gray women stirred. He lowered his eyes to the desk's dull metal gray, afraid to meet her eyes. He stared at the scars of myriad dents and scratches. Was his heart torn up like this? Did he look like a murderer now, locked up in this dull gray place?

When the door opened, its sudden bang snapped at him. Cool air rushed in, making Andrew realize he must have been hot, not cold, in this nothingness of gray. Then the man from the car unfolded a chair, setting it down on the opposite side of the table. His shirt sleeves were rolled above the elbow, revealing well-muscled arms on the table top. The woman moved to his side. The door closed silently.

"So," said the man. "What can you tell us, Mr. Callaghan?"

Andrew wanted to speak, but his voice coughed instead. Then he forced out words. "What do you mean?"

"We'd like you to tell us where she is."

"Where who? Where Amy?" He felt like a babbling student repeating the question. *Sub-track—a traction engine. A bird. A plane.* Who, where, what, why?

"It will make things easier."

But questions are never easy; that's why you ask them. So Andrew kicked the table, styling himself after his students still. Tom would shout. Zeke would laugh. Jonah would roll his eyes. And Julie would swing her leg back and forth, so he kicked the table again while he pondered pointlessly, *What things?*

The coffee cup rocked. Andrew rocked his chair. The world began to spin in a graying fog.

"Let's just start at the beginning."

What a good idea. Andrew slipped into teacher mode, straightening his elbows on the desk and trying his best to remember where the story began. Suddenly this dull gray room felt like the end, and he didn't dare speak, so he waited instead.

The interrogator opened a page in a fat gray file. Andrew couldn't quite see the photograph. Upside down and faded, gray like the room, it blended at its edge into scribbled words, handwriting mixed with type, scraps of newspaper covering the shape of a face perhaps.

"So." The policeman's voice was hard. "You had a daughter kind of like Amy. Isn't that right?"

He's talking about me!

Andrew breathed her name like a sigh. "Amelia."

"Autistic, yeah?"

But she was so much more than that. She was sweet, his little child. Gentle. Innocent. Except when she wasn't. The man repeated his question and Andrew answered, feeling his cheeks stretch into a smile. "Yes, she was autistic."

"And she died?"

He bent his head.

"Under suspicious circumstances?"

Breathing hurt, so Andrew coughed, the sound like thunder in his ears. "Yes, she was murdered. You know all that."

"And who...? And you...?" The man paused, never completing his questions, while gray walls loomed, closing in.

And me, Daddy? Was she really speaking to him, even here?

Andrew pushed his chair back from the table. "What are you suggesting?" he protested. "That I murdered my own daughter?"

"Did you?"

"No! You know who did it. They found the guy."

"No one was charged."

And, of course, it was true. No one was charged with Amelia's murder, because the monstrous mockery of a man who killed her shot himself rather than be caught. Surely the police had all the information in their fat gray file. Surely they knew.

Andrew stared across the desk, recognizing the picture now. Upside down, half-hidden, and faded, it was still his precious child, trapped within the words that described her death. It was a closed file, closed case, everything done.

"We know *someone* killed himself," the policeman continued. "All the evidence pointed to him. But something could have been overlooked, don't you think, Mr. Callaghan? And she was your daughter. I'd imagine you'd really want to know."

"I do know."

"Did you kill her?"

"No!" Andrew almost leapt from his chair, then saw the woman, large, gray, and threatening, reaching for him. He almost screamed, but emotions strangled him. The sound came out more like a sob.

Then Amelia, dead Amelia who he hadn't killed—surely he hadn't—whispered softly in his ear, "It's okay, Daddy. It will all be okay. You'll see." The child he'd failed to comfort was comforting him, and nobody else could hear her.

"Well," said the man with the stern, gray face, "Let's move on, Mr. Callaghan. Tell me about Amy."

Andrew watched his hands turn slowly gray as everything else. He twisted gray fingers together, wondered where the color was going, and asked wearily, "What about Amy?"

"You taught her?"

Present tense, not past. "I teach her," he squeaked.

"And she's kind of like your daughter?"

"She's autistic, yes."

"A substitute, perhaps? A stand-in, was she, for someone you lost?"

Where were they going with this?

The interrogator thumped the desk, making Andrew jump, and the chair-legs shriek again. "Did Amy remind you of your daughter?"

Andrew shouted back, "Yes. Of course she did."

"And did you want to take her away perhaps, turn her into your daughter?"

"No!" He just wanted to teach her.

"Did you kill her, Mr. Callaghan? Did she get to be too much for you, just like your daughter did?"

"I didn't kill… I didn't kill my daughter."

"Did you kill Amy?"

Andrew shrank back onto the chair, feeling cold gray metal through his shirt. He shivered, as the harsh, gray voice continued. What if his leaving really had killed Amelia? "You didn't kill me," the bell-like voice protested. But things had all been pretty crazy back then, hadn't they? Or was that afterward, after she died? He didn't remember much.

He remembered his brother, his mother, his father, his anti-Midas touch. He remembered running away, because he knew he'd destroy them if he stayed; living away, an empty, gray, gray life devoid of love; and Amelia's face in black and white on the front page of the paper. He hadn't touched his child, but Midas had, and he wasn't there. He hadn't protected her, so it was his fault.

"You acted strangely, didn't you, after she died? There are reports." The questioner shuffled pages as if he needed to check those facts so clearly memorized. "Reports of you skulking around in the woods, Mr. Callaghan, in the woods where she was killed." He looked up with eyes as gray as the gray, metal desk and asked, "Had you hidden there before, Mr. Callaghan? Did you lure Amelia there? Were you trying to get her back? Taking her away from her mother, perhaps, and she resisted. Is that how it happened?"

Andrew shook his head.

"You didn't mean to kill her, did you? But she resisted you. And then it was easy, the suicide; it was easy to pin it all on the dead guy."

Andrew shook his head again, closing his eyes to the gray, because black seemed preferable. He felt his shoulders droop. His head hung low and dipped into the hollow of his hands, where he cradled himself, lying flat across the desk.

"So what about Amy? Did you lure her away too? Did she resist you?"

Andrew looked up in slow protest. His voice was toneless, as if a computer were reciting words for him. "Amy was in my class. She disappeared from my class. My only crime is I didn't see her go, because I was teaching the other kids. I couldn't have taken her anywhere. You know that. I've got a room full of witnesses."

The gray man didn't seem dismayed. He even smiled a little. "Perhaps you told her to meet you after class."

Andrew laughed at that, a bitter sound that ached in the back of his throat. "Do you really think Amelia would do anything I told her?"

"Amelia?"

He buried his face in his hands again. "Amy, I meant. Amy. Do you think Amy would ever obey? She was autistic, for heaven's sake."

"So was Amelia."

*****

They left him with just the gray woman watching over him again. He stared at the walls and listened for Amelia's voice, but she was silent. He listened for Amy's voice too. *Come on,*

Amy. If you're dead, just tell me where you are. Tell me anything. Get me out of here. But no one replied.

He tried to remember the details of Amelia's death. It felt like pulling the scab off a doubly healed wound. She'd died in the woods. The murderer died in bed. Inextricably intertwined, they tore at him like withering vines, pulling him down into the ground. Gray vines. Gray ground. Gray earthy loam in the woods, where he'd lived in gray boxes, cooking meals in gray, rusted cans.

He'd fallen apart when he heard Amelia was dead. He remembered that now. But it didn't mean he'd killed her. He ran away and hid in the woods where she died. He'd wanted to die. But perhaps he was trying to find her, to beg forgiveness— forgiveness for what? There is no forgiveness for the Midas touch.

His brother and mother and father had left him alone to fend for himself. Then he'd left his daughter and left his wife. He hadn't been there to protect his precious child. But he hadn't killed her. So he threw back his head like a hyena and screamed at the empty, gray walls. They weren't listening. "I didn't kill my child!"

The gray woman sat on her chair and didn't reply.

*****

"Just tell us where she is. If you've hidden her away she'll need food. She'll need help, won't she? Just tell us where you've hidden her, so she won't be on your conscience."

The gray man was back, but Andrew didn't know the answer to his question. He only wished he did.

"It will go easier on you, sir. Even if she's dead. It will go easier on you, if you'll just tell us where she is."

Andrew couldn't tell what he didn't know.

"What did you do to her?"

He stared at his own gray hands on the gray, metal desk. "Nothing," he answered in a voice that had also turned gray. "I'm her teacher," he repeated. "I teach math."

"Ah, but it's more than that, sir, isn't it? You've refused every effort her parents made to get her in a special school. Determined to keep her in your class weren't you, sir? Your favorite pupil, wasn't she?"

Andrew sighed.

"So did you hear something? Her parents planning to take her away from you? Is that why you did it?"

"They weren't. We'd talked. They'd agreed…"

"But what if you'd heard they'd changed their mind? Did you take her away, because you thought you could do a better job, look after her better, teach her, make her succeed where your own daughter failed? Are you trying to turn her into your daughter now? Trying to give her the chances your daughter missed out on."

"I'm just trying to teach her." Andrew paused. "I *was* just trying to teach her." The past tense echoed like a gunshot through his brain, as if his student were already dead and gone. "She *was* doing so well."

"And she wouldn't do so well if they took her away. Isn't that what you thought?"

"No… well… maybe. I don't know. I just thought she was doing well."

"So you told her to hide away somewhere, so they couldn't take her away."

Andrew wished it were so. He wished he'd hidden her so he could bring her back, but he hadn't. There was nothing he could do; nothing useful he could say. Instead he stared around at the gray, wishing his eyes could rip its mask away. "No," he repeated, dull and fierce and miserably repetitive. "I didn't tell Amy to go anywhere, and she wouldn't have gone anywhere if I had told her to."

"I thought you said she was doing so well."

"At math!"

*****

They gave him a meal with meat and gray gravy. Gray mashed potatoes puddled on the edge of the plate. But no knife was offered—only a plastic fork to eat with. The gray woman watched, or was it a different, gray woman observing him now. He didn't know, only that her hair and hands were equally devoid of color. Then the gray man came back.

"What was your relationship with Amy?" he asked again.

Andrew felt his voice drain into the brew of his dishwater coffee. "I was her teacher."

"Surrogate father perhaps? Or lover even?"

"Her teacher." He twisted the gray paper cup between his scrabbling fingers, trying hard not to crush it.

Andrew's interrogator persisted without a pause. "You could have been her father, couldn't you? Like you were Amelia's father? Couldn't you?"

He could have been, but why would Amy have wanted a father like him? A disastrous failure whose Midas touch turned every love to stone instead of gold.

"Did you think you could do better than her father perhaps? Felt like you had something to prove with her, did you?"

"Amy had her own father." His voice had begun to crack. "She didn't need me."

"Did she have another lover perhaps?"

"She's a child. Just a beautiful child."

"And how did that make you feel?"

It wasn't a question of feelings, Andrew thought. He'd dealt with them long ago with the psychiatrist, when he clawed his way back from the dark park's bleak oblivion, when he turned into a human being again. Human beings have feelings, but they have control as well. Isn't that what he was told? And Amy was his job. So he insisted, yet again, that he was just her teacher. No, he hadn't wanted to remove her from her father. No, he hadn't wanted to prove he could do better for her. Amy's parents were doing just fine, doing perfectly fine. And he wasn't at all annoyed that they might want to take her away. He was concerned—of course he was—as any caring teacher ought to be. He thought it was better for Amy if she stayed. He wished she *had* stayed.

"You thought only you could love her?"

"No!"

"You thought only you could teach her properly?"

"No!" Why wouldn't they listen? "I just thought that she was progressing. I just wanted the best for her."

"Which only you could provide, in so many ways?"

It wasn't true. Other teachers could have taught her too, but Andrew hadn't wanted to lose the progress they'd made together. He hadn't wished to inflict the stress of change on a fragile child. He wanted the best, and nobody was willing to understand.

"So you took her away. And what happened to her then?"

He didn't take her away from anyone. He didn't subtract her.

"Just tell us where she is."

Andrew jumped as the gray man slammed his fist down on the desk. Then Andrew slammed his own fist too. "Just look for her, why don't you?"

His outburst changed nothing. His interrogator merely smiled, as if Andrew's anger was just what he'd wanted all along. Then he asked about Andrew's relationships with other teachers in school. Was Andrew the odd one out, the one with no lovers, no spouse, no social life? And him with his persistent belief there was hope for his rejects still?

"Not rejects," Andrew answered automatically, wondering which teacher the police must have gotten their information from. Then, he was asked, was he angry with the system that betrayed these kids? But he wasn't angry, just sad. He was sad that kids could get left out, that finances could take the place of care and concern, that success should be measured so very exclusively. He was sad that children could be lost and found, lost and dead, or lost and disappeared. He was sad for Amy.

"So sad that you took her out of the system?"

"No!"

"So sad that you killed her?"

"No!"

"Then, what?"

Andrew buried his face in his hands, almost tipping over the last of an endless stream of crumpled paper cups. "Just sad," he muttered. "Just sad. Why don't you go and find her?"

*****

They gave him more coffee, dishwater still, and sandwiches thinly stuffed with graying meat. Decay filled his veins, reminding him of the forest and its darkly bacterial ground. He thought of cardboard boxes turned into walls slowly dissolving in rain. But he ate the sandwiches anyway. A man who once survived by dumpster diving can eat anything.

"So what happened?" the gray man asked again. "When Amelia died?"

"I went back to my wife."

"Amelia's mother?"

"Yes."

"And stayed with her?"

They knew he hadn't. They knew he didn't live with Evie now. So, "No," he said. "I couldn't stay."

"What happened then?"

He struggled to answer, trying to make sense of his own actions long ago, of broken, meaningless events he'd filed for deletion from memory. "I went back."

"Back where?"

"To Paradise. I went... back into Paradise Park, where Amelia died." Andrew rested his hands on the desk, steepling fingers in front of his face. He could see white papers in their yellow-gray cover through the gap between his fingers. "Didn't you read the report?"

The gray man coughed and wrote another mark with his blue-gray pen. "And then?"

"I dunno." The change had been slow, but Andrew wasn't scared anymore. This place couldn't hurt him after all. So he shrugged his shoulders and leaned back in the chair, feeling its white-gray plastic bend reluctantly. "I guess I just woke up one day and didn't want to be a hobo. Someone offered me a chance, and I wanted to make up for it all I suppose... like

Amelia's memory deserved something more from me. I took a job. Saved my money. Went to college. Trained. And got my life back together. I began to teach, because I'm good at it."

His interrogator seemed hardly to be listening. "To make up for what?" he asked, holding his pen like a sword ready to stab the papers on the desk.

"Make up for letting Amelia down, and Evie too. For not being there when I was needed. For walking out."

A crumb from his sandwich lay on the table top. Andrew leaned forward and watched it quiver as he blew his breath on it, as if it might grow legs and walk away. Would the policeman reach across and squash it like a bug?

"And Amy?" the gray man asked, looking up.

"She reminds me of Amelia, yes. But she'll have a better chance. I'm teaching her. She's learning life skills too, not just math." Enthusiasm dripped its deceptive power into his veins. Light slipped into the shadows of the dull, gray room. The heating vent was painted white, and the floor was scuffed with lines of red and brown. Even the chair-legs still bore slivers of silver sheen.

"Where do you think she is, Mr. Callaghan?"

Andrew answered decisively, "I don't know."

"But if you could guess?"

He paused.

"Do you think she's dead?"

Amelia's voice answered swiftly in his brain. "No Dad, she's okay." So Andrew said no, and the policeman asked him why. "How do you know?" If he said how he knew, they'd lock him up forever and lose the key.

"I just think she's okay," Andrew answered. "She's better than they think."

"Than who thinks?"

"Than everyone who writes her off just because she's labeled autistic. It's like that truck driver said—the one who gave her a ride—she's quiet, but she's not crazy. Amy can cope."

"Do you really think that?"

The policeman leaned on the desk as he lifted himself out of his seat Andrew just sighed. Of course he didn't know for sure that Amy could cope, but it was what he wanted to think, what he desperately needed to believe, so he answered, "I hope."

*****

The room grew hot and cold, or else Andrew just felt hot and cold as fear dripped through his veins. No one would tell him when he could go. "Don't worry, Daddy," said Amelia's bell-like voice, but he was afraid to answer her in case they labeled him insane.

Eventually a different man came to question him. His voice was softer, less accusing, more like someone looking for information. He wanted to know the very last thing Andrew remembered Amy saying, her final words in class, so Andrew answered, "Thirty-four," and still didn't understand.

"Thirty-four what?"

"Just thirty-four. She was winning thirty-four thousand dollars in a game I'd set up for them. It could have been that. Or perhaps she had thirty-four buttons on her desk, and the coincidence made her speak. I don't know what she meant."

The policeman offered a smile of sympathy. "Very literal aren't they?" he said, staring up at the ceiling, shoulders back, hands loosely linked in front of him.

"Who?"

"Autistics."

Andrew wanted to explain how each child was different, how rules that might apply to one could be useless in describing another, and how even the most severely autistic might break with tradition and suddenly be hooked on symbols or fantasy or interpretation of dreams. Instead he took the easy way out and agreed.

"So she probably meant the game."

"I guess." If only he knew.

They let him go.

*****

The school board placed him on administrative leave, *just until this all boils over.* They promised to discuss his position soon, before the budget cuts came through in fall. He might still have a job—who knew—but *don't hold your breath.*

The media surrounded him with microphones and cameras, asking about his wife, his daughter, and his student. They tore the details of his life to blood-soaked rags in front of him, while a white cat watched from the curb beneath their feet.

Andrew's neighbors closed their doors to him. No one offered to help or bring groceries. No one wanted to hear his side of the story, except for the cat. Even the church's steeple stared accusingly down the length of its long stone nose. So he hid himself away. Frozen dinners, frozen juice, frozen dreams. His only warmth was the cat's soft fur, and it wasn't even his to hold and pet.

When the phone rang, he thought it might be Amy's parents calling to accuse him, or the cat-owners asking for their pet's return. Instead a voice, once-familiar, now long-forgotten, spoke his name. The tone was just like Amelia's in his head, but it was older, more real, and much less clear.

"Andrew," Evie said

Part 5

~12~

His ex-wife's kindness was almost too much to bear. Evie suggested Andrew might need a place to stay and offered the spare room in her home, in his old home, in a past from which he'd extracted himself long ago. She offered her company and the peace of a town where nobody would recognize him anymore, who he had been, who he'd lost, nor how he'd been accused. "I know you didn't do anything to that girl." Her words poured like freedom into his ears from the telephone.

Andrew thanked her while tears, unwelcome weakness, rolled down his cheeks. He felt the water prick his skin and wondered, if he looked at himself in the mirror, would he see again the hobo of Paradise Park?

"Just let me know," said Evie, her voice so calm and low, distant in space and time, and yet so near. "The offer's here for you."

She said no more into the growing pause, seemed ready to leave it at that. Then Andrew forced an answer through his lips, decision made before doubt could intervene. "I'll come... now... Please... I'd love... I need..."

"Just ring the doorbell, Andrew, whenever. You know the way."

He saved her number, one he'd never thought to ask for or need, into his phone, wondering vaguely how Evie could have found him. But his phone number wasn't a secret. He just couldn't imagine Evie searching for it. Then he scurried around the rooms of his small apartment, tossing underwear and clothes into plastic bags. Spare shoes—you never know when you might need them; his shaving gear—he decided to shave himself first, scouring the bristles of guilt away. Then he showered as well and packed his shower gel. He might want some books—after all, he was still a teacher until they took his job away.

The carrier bags bulged and bashed against Andrew's legs as he walked around, but he wouldn't pack a case. It wouldn't feel right, going back to Evie like that. The thud of shoes and books bruising his knees was apt punishment, reminding him a good husband and father doesn't leave. The checking of every window, electrical outlet and faucet was quiet compensation for departing Evie's home so long ago without any preparation at all. Nothing would drip or leak or switch on or swing open here in his absence, though a child had died in the place he left before. He watered the lonely Christmas cactus, given him by a student, so it might live. He checked for the cat, but couldn't find it. Dropping his bags on the floor in frustration, he cracked a bedroom window open after all, just in case the cat were hiding somewhere inside. Could it leap to the tree? The ground was a long way to fall. But cats, unlike humans, always land on their feet. Then he checked the street for watchers, media, police…

Armed with phone, plastic bags, and a faltering dose of hope and confidence, Andrew stepped out of the door and into the groaning confinement of the elevator. Would anyone see him walk to his car? Would they follow? Report him? Complain? He hoped not and hunched his head down into the comforting warmth of his hood as he tried to hide.

Down a few steps, up the road, and around the corner—it wasn't far to walk. The car door clunked as he opened it, but nobody seemed to hear. He tossed his bags from the front seat into the back, rested his feet by the pedals, and turned the key. The engine purred, adding to his worries for the cat.

Asphalt lay as gray as Andrew's mood, but his mirrors didn't reflect any followers when he pulled away from the curb. No cat trailed his wheels this time, not like his flight from Paradise before. But perhaps this cat was glad he was going back.

Soon shades of green and brown surrounded the car. Summer's dryness had leached the colors, as if it were August not June, as if the school's long break, not yet begun, were at its end. Andrew wondered who was teaching his class, then thrust the thought from his mind. Instead he'd watch the wide, blue sky and dream it might lighten his mood. The distant glitter of water rippling on lakes could promise hope. The cat purring in the back among the bulging plastic bags—how did the cat get in there?

Signs showed the way, and Andrew followed carefully. It was a journey he'd never ventured since changing from hobo to man. It felt like heading into the past, a thought that dampened his mood again as it surely couldn't bring Amelia back. Then he took the turnoff for the place where he'd grown up, for Paradise.

Nothing much had changed. Blacktop was scarred and scratched with age. Potholes blinked fresh water from their depths. The old church tower still loomed over its gravel parking lot. Andrew drove past the school, past houses with paint beginning to peel and roofs looking weathered and worn. He saw the garage still sported a sign with Markham Motors written in vivid red, a murderer's blood. He wondered if the son had decided to keep the place going. Might as well label it *Paradise Predator Motors, home of the Paradise Murderer.* How could anyone advertise the name of the man who had killed Amelia?

Tension tightened across Andrew's shoulders. His fingers clenched the wheel. His gaze wandered, checking for traffic and more, and his breath came in desperate gulps. He turned at the light, safely, carefully, like a child taking his first lesson, just learning to drive, then he followed the road alongside Paradise Park. Grass grayed wearily in summer heat, but ducks still swam on the pond. The hill watched over it all, perhaps with a few extra benches added on top. The children's playground showed its age, with red rubber underlay and blue play pieces scattered near the wooden climbing frame. Trees stood guard still over the place where Amelia had lain.

Dark trees. Haunting trees. Angry, daunting trees. These trees had sheltered Andrew, luring him to emptiness and death, then spat him out. These trees had watched, unmoved, while his daughter died.

Andrew reminded himself to breathe as the road snaked through forest green. He could almost smell the dampness calling him back. But then he was out among the street lights and traffic of a busy thoroughfare. Shops displayed their wares. Bright signs offered the best food in town, the greatest art to be found for miles around, and a bank's expensive trust, but Andrew's gaze didn't waver. He turned toward the road where he'd once lived, looked for a parking spot, and backed the car into its waiting space. Then he snatched his bags and walked the last few yards, through remembered scents of cooking, engine oil, and city murk.

Evie's door was still green, just like it had been before. Andrew raised his hand, as if he somehow expected to be holding the key between his fingers. Then he pressed the bell and listened for its remembered tune. Nothing had changed.

A safety chain rattled before the door swung wide. Evie smiled a wary welcome, lips wavering, eyes inclined to frown. "Come inside, Andrew. Nobody's looking. It's nice and quiet here."

Nobody's looking felt like music to his ears. He desperately hoped no one would ever look. He longed to disappear.

The plastic bags hung heavy on his arms, but Andrew's feet wouldn't move. Frozen between two different pasts and a present, unsure of who he'd become, his chest felt taught with invisible chains that bound him to the spot. Evie's hand grabbed his arm to release him. Her fingers must have held some other key. She pulled him inside. Then Andrew followed his one-time bride, soap's perfume luring him along the corridor. He looked into the living room where Evie and Amelia used to sit, and he closed his eyes against the pain. The TV was still there, still old, still dusty too, and still playing pointless programs and music-less tunes.

Evie led Andrew upstairs and pointed to the second bedroom. "Spare room," she said briefly. "You can make yourself at home." Then she turned away, her starched skirt swishing through the air.

But this was Amelia's bedroom. Andrew stood on the pale yellow carpet, staring at walls devoid of character, remembering history. A blocky red and green quilt that he'd never seen before couldn't hide the memories. *I can't sleep there.*

"Yes you can, Daddy," said the bell-like voice in his head. "I'm dead, remember. I don't need to sleep in a bed."

But...

"And you've got to sleep somewhere." She'd taken on a sing-song cadence now, directing him. "And I know you're not going to sleep in Mommy's room."

"Got the cover at a garage sale." Evie tossed the words over her shoulder. She wasn't looking Andrew's way, but she must have been watching him. Perhaps she thought he was surprised not to find Amelia's flowered quilt. But the bell-like ghost was right, of course, so Andrew dropped his bags to the floor and thought, *I can't go putting my clothes in her closet.*

"Dead, remember?" Amelia spoke again. "I don't need closet space, unless I'm the monster in the closet."

Andrew sighed and unpacked.

*****

It was comfortable here. Andrew ate freezer meals prepared by hands that weren't his own. He ate alone in his room, unable to cope with company. But no one complained. And he didn't need to wonder if he'd be recognized in the supermarket, since he never went out. Evie invited him to church, of course, but he wasn't going to risk being recognized on a church aisle either. Besides, Andrew no longer believed in God. Evie should have known that.

"Of course you believe," Evie protested, as she strolled past the guest room, not trying to enter, not risking invading his space.

"How can I?" Andrew asked. "I mean. Come on. Why would I believe in a God who lets all this happen? What's the point of him?"

He'd walked to the door of the bedroom, the nearest he came to admitting a real world still existed beyond this space. Evie pressed her hand on his arm. "All this?" She waved at the hallway and the stairs, then back at Amelia's room. "All what?"

"Us, Amelia, Amy." Andrew stared at the carpet's fake yellow sun. "I've failed them, every one."

"No you haven't."

He looked up. "I failed my brother. I failed my mom and dad."

Evie clutched her church purse to her chest. "You didn't fail them."

"I should have known. I should have done something. I should have been…"

"You didn't fail them." She crossed her arms like a prayer.

"I should have been someone worth living for."

"You were. I lived for you." Evie's free hand strayed to his arm again.

"And I left you. I failed you, too."

Then Evie did invade his private space. She wrapped him in her arms. Her bag crunched behind him. "You came back," she said, "for the funeral, and the memorial. You didn't fail me."

Andrew's gaze crossed the hallway and the years. He remembered hiding in the trees at Amelia's funeral. He remembered Evie staring at the ground, ignoring the world around her, as dirt fell dark and unfeeling on a small girl's coffin. He remembered how she'd seemed absorbed and lost in emptiness, while small stones rained down.

"I saw you," Evie said, as she'd said before, "with the cat. You were under the trees. Nobody knew."

With the cat. A cat—or *the* cat—had traveled in the back of his car, but Andrew had never seen it since he arrived. Was it real? Where was the cat? *The cat's alright.*

Stumbling like children, Andrew and Evie crossed the bedroom and sat together on the red and green quilt. Its smooth shapes crumpled under them. Well-ordered, well-embroidered lines shifted to awkward chaos. But Andrew's mind was still miles away, drifting under the trees again to that later day, Amelia's memorial, where he heard the sounds of strangers gathered in the park. Birds were silent, honoring the dead. People coughed with muttered cries. Microphones hummed. Loudspeakers crackled and clicked. He remembered Evie's voice swiftly changing from proud and strong to broken then back again. And the other woman, Lydia the garage man's daughter, what had she said?

"His daughter-in-law." Evie corrected him, so Andrew realized he'd been voicing his memories aloud. The daughter-in-law had talked about forgiveness, but it didn't make sense because no one forgives a murderer.

Evie corrected him again. "Not forgiveness. She talked about love."

"And where was God in all of that?"

"God was the love that brought us together again."

He coughed. It sounded too trite.

"God didn't take our child, Andrew. Peter Markham took our child. And God gave us back her memory."

The bell-voice awoke in Andrew's mind again. "See, Daddy. I'm my memory." He preferred to think of her as a ghost, and he preferred not thinking at all about his wife's capricious God.

Evie picked up her purse again and turned toward the door. She stopped with her hand on the knob. "The church will still be there tomorrow, Andrew, and next Sunday, and the next. When you're ready, I mean."

"I'll never be ready," he answered, as her steps resounded on the stairs.

"I'll pray for you."

*****

Andrew had finally left Amelia's room. He was making an effort now to eat his meals with Evie, to pretend he was real and had a life beyond being the media's suspect of choice. They sat together on the sofa. Indian spices scented the air, rising in the steam from plastic trays. They forked food to their mouths in time with each other, like robots pretending to be human.

Suddenly Amy's face was there again, staring out from the TV screen. It was one of those bland, school photographer's photos where she looked serene and beautiful and normal, and at least eighteen. Andrew guessed this was why the trucker hadn't realized she was a child. Then he looked at Amelia's photograph on the wall. How would she look now if she were still alive?

"I'd be all grown up, Daddy. I'd be all grown by now."

Amy's parents were interviewed with the same empty questions and answers. They'd graduated from, "Please return our child," to, "Please, if you've seen her, please let us know." The police chief reported how they'd heard of sightings all across the country. Andrew looked into the officer's weary eyes and imagined he wasn't thrilled at this follow-up interview. But who would phone in sightings to the police? Andrew sighed. After all, the truth is everyone has a thousand look-alikes. If he wrote down the population of a town, he could almost guess the probability that Amy's twin might be found. Was there one in Paradise?

"There's only one of me," Amelia answered in his head.

"Yes, dear." Had he really spoken out loud? "But it's Amy they're looking for."

"There's none of *her* over here 'cause she's not dead."

Did that make *any* sense? Andrew wondered where *over here* might be but didn't dare ask. Instead he clung to Amelia's promise, that Amy wasn't dead. If she wasn't dead, perhaps he could find her.

Snatching paper and pencils from Evie's cluttered tabletop, Andrew started writing notes, adding numbers and words in urgent columns and lines then crossing them out. *Thirty-four buttons. Thirty-four-thousand dollars. "I need money."* Wasn't that what Amy had said, before she counted the buttons and announced the number to him? Or did she announce the number because it agreed with the money she'd counted in her head. Was she pleased because of its serendipity? Did she speak because she'd always planned this day to run away, or was she seized by something magical about a meaningless number, thirty-four?

Stella DeMaris, the pretty young art teacher, phoned him. He almost missed her call, hearing the noise of his cellphone like just another tune in a house full of ghosts. She filled his ears with eager news of the faculty and school. She was the one who'd taken on Andrew's class, she assured him. She was almost as excited as he about the students' end-of-term progress. "Even Tom's calmed down," she said, "and Jonah's sticking to his diet, and…" Was it all because Amy disappeared? "They're going to keep the class in the fall, I think. I keep speaking up for it, for you, and they've not said they're closing it yet, and school's out next week."

He felt like he heard only one word in thirty-four, but *School's out* stuck in his mind. He'd almost forgotten the daily routine and the pattern of the year. But what was Amy's pattern in all of this?

Thirty-four, and *I need money.*

Had she spoken to anyone else besides him, to the students perhaps? Had they been interviewed? Was there some precious clue still missing because nobody had asked?

"Stella," he begged, thrusting his voice into half a space of silence. "Stella, please ask the kids if Amy said anything to them."

"But I thought…"

"She didn't talk?" His voice rushed in, squeezed out by the weight of fears. "I know she didn't talk much, Stella. But if she said something, anything, it just might be important. Just ask them, please."

Phone in hand, he fell to his knees, pleading with the living room window or the sky outside. He imagined Amy sitting atop the climbing frame. If someone asked could they could climb it too, did she ignore them or answer *Thirty-four?* When she stood in the corridor, waiting to enter the room, if somebody stood on her toe perhaps, did she say *ouch*, or did she give some secret message, revealing where she'd gone?

Stella promised to ask, and Andrew allowed himself, just for a moment, to bask in a ray of sunshine as if it were hope. Then he heard Evie's cough at his side, so he finished quickly. "I've got to go."

"We're praying, Andrew." Which one of them said that? Did Evie think he was on his knees in prayer? But the phone disconnected and he staggered to his feet. Stella and Evie might rest their hope in dreams and speculation, but Andrew needed more solid reality.

Or symbols? Or thirty-four?

*****

Evie asked who *she* was on the phone, so Andrew replied, "Just a friend, a coworker." How had Evie known it was a woman?

They sat together again on the sofa, leaving their empty food trays on the floor. Andrew struggled to decide what to do with his arms. Wouldn't he have hugged Evie to himself once? But she leaned forward, hands on her knees, prim and proper as a church mouse, staring at the TV.

"You know, I don't want to take anyone's place," she said, her voice like ice poured on his hurts. After all, he was the betrayer, the bringer of ills. But Evie went on. "You're just here because you need a place to stay." He coughed at that, grateful and confused that she understood. "And we're old friends," Evie added, with no whimpering of pain, almost with friendly warmth. "That's all it is. You do understand, don't you Andrew? I'm just helping out. I don't want anything from you. We're just old friends."

Warmth washed over him as Andrew replied, "Not so old."

"I saw how you looked at your phone when you answered it. She means something to you, that colleague of yours."

"No," said Andrew, because surely she didn't. He wouldn't let anyone become important in his life. He wouldn't dare, not he with his Midas touch.

Amelia's bell-voice laughed at him. "Not even me?" But she was dead. She proved his point. "Not even Amy?"

He didn't know how to answer a ghost, so he swallowed his voice in his throat. Then Evie spoke again. "Stella, you said? She will mean something to you. You mark my words."

Andrew frowned.

"I know you, Andrew Callaghan."

Sure Evie knew him, but she didn't love him. And nobody else would ever love him again. He wouldn't let them in.

"Except for me. I love you, Daddy."

Amelia was surely just his imagination, no more real than the angel cat with wings that hung on his classroom wall.

"No, Daddy. You're not imagining me."

He groaned. She couldn't be real.

Then Evie said Andrew should invite Stella to visit when the schools shut down, and he agreed.

*****

They crowded into the little living room, Stella and Evie on the sofa together and Andrew on the chair, pictures and notes scattered across the coffee table, and a white cat proudly situated on the floor—not Andrew's cat. This one was fluffier, wasn't it?

Stella produced a map from her bag and drew a line along the trucker's route. "That's where he says he took her."

Go West young man thought Andrew, remembering what the students said in class.

Stella agreed. "It goes straight West, and… oh." The cat jumped onto her lap, and she looked up in surprise. As her eyes caught Andrew's she added, "I forgot to tell you. You know you asked about what Amy said to the kids before she disappeared. Well, they told me. All of them. She'd said it lots of times."

"Said what?" Andrew asked, watching her slender fingers bury themselves in the cat's thick fur.

"She said, *Go West young man.*"

Andrew's heart skipped a beat, and Amelia laughed in his head. "You never listen, do you, Daddy? You heard her. Why didn't you know?"

He reached for the map that Stella had dropped on the floor. Coffee smells drifted, brown coffee, not gray, with steam gathered under the map's wide wings and watery coils like smoke rising from its edges. Evie's soft-soap cleanliness cleared the air. Stella's flowery perfume hung like a memory of springtime, and dust-mites floated like gold. The map's lines were bright as student light-sabers. Its numbers glowed with vivid neon hues. Andrew started to laugh.

"What is it, Andrew?" Stella, Evie, and the cat all stared at him.

He spluttered. "*Go West young man.* Look at this. She was telling us where she was going all along." He pointed to the line of a road on the map. "Look which road goes West near here. It's obvious! Our Amy's heading West on Route 34!"

The map was passed from hand to hand, three sets of fingers tracing the jagged line while the cat looked on. Stella protested, "But why?" and Andrew sipped his coffee again. It would all come clear soon—he was sure of that—if he could just think, just remember; if he could just somehow work it out. The cat's loud purr was a soothing symphony.

That time when the faculty talked about closing Andrew's class—he remembered it now; remembered seeing Amy appear from the bushes as he headed back to the other students. If she'd been listening outside, hidden under the faculty window, could that be what had set this whole thing off? Was that when she started acting so strange? When she regressed and wouldn't talk in class again, and Andrew thought he'd lost her? Then she tried that *different persona* trick and almost drove him crazy. Could she have been thinking *If they're kicking me out, I'll leave on my own terms*?

"You think she planned it?" Stella asked, while the cat arched, comfortably purring under her hand.

"No." He didn't, because she wasn't the planning kind. But she might have kept the thought there in her head, waiting for some mysterious impetus. She probably checked her routes out on the map. Maybe she listened to the lyrics of a song, or watched a movie, or heard someone say *Go West* for some strange reason. Then she looked for the road, looked West, remembered the number. And one day she counted her buttons.

"Didn't you say she counted them *after* your game?"

But perhaps she'd counted the cash in the game, and it matched the buttons and matched the route, and that was her call to act.

Stella frowned. "I thought autistic kids were into reality, not symbols and coincidence."

"Who says the symbols wouldn't seem real to her? Three *thirty-fours* was just the right answer, the one she'd been waiting for."

It made such perfect sense now he thought of it. He remembered Amy wanted to pack up the treasures from the wall, asking for money for her trip. He remembered her showing her buttons, and then she left, without any money after all.

"How on earth would she cope?" Evie asked, refilling their mugs and offering sugary cookies that made Andrew sneeze. His eyes slipped to the picture of Amelia on the wall. Poor, dead Amelia.

Andrew had no answers, but he knew that Amy must have gone West because the trucker said so. Now he was sure she'd continued going West. "If we could follow her..." he whispered, excitement thrilling through his veins. The cat agreed, leaping down with pointed tail, equally ready for the chase.

"Or we could tell the police," said Stella, carefully placing her mug down on the table.

Andrew shook his head and laughed bitterly. "Do you think they'd listen to me? They'd just lock me up again."

Meanwhile Evie stirred more sugar into her cup. "You could do both. Stella could tell the police. And you could look for her."

The white cat jumped to the edge of the open window and was gone.

*****

Stella told the police when she returned home from Paradise. They agreed that there'd been sightings in the West. They agreed they'd continued to look. But they weren't interested. Then Andrew and Stella agreed on a different plan.

They would take Andrew's car because it was marginally newer. He was afraid it might be recognized, but Stella, back at school and arguing with him over the phone, said he was just being neurotic. "No one's even interested in you now. You were five-minute news. They've almost forgotten poor Amy ever existed."

"Surely not." But her name hadn't appeared again on the news, nor in Evie's newspaper.

"Not in mine either," Stella replied. "She's yesterday. Which movie star said what about whom's far more interesting to the media."

After Stella's call, Andrew discussed their ideas with Evie. It seemed like the right thing, talking with her. After all, he couldn't exactly discuss what they were planning with Amy's parents, and Evie was a mother who'd lost her child.

She agreed. "You take your car and you go find that girl, before anything happens to her. And you take your Stella with you too."

So they planned a date and arranged how they would meet. Andrew drove back from Evie's house, retracing his steps on a route he was coming to know only too well. As he passed through Paradise Park, he ignored the siren call of haunted trees, refused to look at children playing on swings and slides, and pretended all was right and well with the world outside. He even tried to whistle. He was doing something right.

But the road back to Stella was filled with empty spaces. Andrew's mood turned gray, though the sky stayed blue and bright. He knew in his heart, in his broken soul, that he had no hope. He didn't deserve to find Amy. It was all a waste of time.

"No it's not, Daddy," said the voice in his head, but Andrew wasn't in a mood to listen to ghosts or cats, so he drove on in silence. His sunlight whistle had turned to a sigh of despair.

Stella waited by her window and rushed out the house when Andrew's car approached. She flung her backpack into his trunk, while he struggled to find that positive mood he'd started out with. "You travel light," he said, swallowing darker words in his throat. Stella agreed. But Andrew knew he was traveling heavy with regret.

They weren't on Route 34 yet of course. It didn't go through their town. But they drove on the road the trucker had taken, going nowhere, wasting dreams. Andrew smelled Stella's perfume and hated it. It made him think of flowers and funerals. He slumped lower down in the driving seat while the engine slowed. His foot rose from the pedal, admitting defeat, and he hadn't the energy for speed. What was the point?

Beside him, Stella gazed at newspaper clippings and maps. She hadn't even noticed that he'd lost the plot. "The trucker said they took this road," she announced lightly, red hair bouncing around her face. "And he left her at a roadside café, somewhere around here. Do you suppose we'll find it?"

Misery rumbled through Andrew's throat and stung behind his eyes. It wasn't the café he expected to find, but rather a body buried in shadows and leaves.

He sensed Stella turning to face him, clothes rustling on the seat. He felt her fingers rest so warm on his arm they burned through his shirt. "It really bothers you, doesn't it?" she said, her voice like warm, sweet milk. "You're really worried what someone might have done to her. But she's not your daughter. It doesn't have to happen again."

Andrew kept his gaze firmly forward, listening to rumbling wheels on the road and refusing to acknowledge his colleague's concern. "The world's full of rapists and murderers," he replied, hearing the snarl in his voice. He gripped the wheel like a lifeline out of hell.

"It's full of good people too." Stella's voice lilted with good vibrations though they died in the space between them. "Good people like you."

"In that case everything's hopeless." Andrew almost laughed and cried. "'Cause I'm not good." He turned his attention to straightening the wheel in a sudden gust of wind, wondering how Stella kept her voice so light. "I left my wife and child, and look what happened to them."

"It wasn't your fault."

Stella and Amelia seemed to answer him both at once, but Andrew still didn't want to listen to ghosts, even if Amelia's touch on his shoulder was ice to Stella's fire. He imagined his daughter sitting in the back seat, watching him, her and Amy together, two teenaged daughters on a road trip to Route 34.

"I should have been there."

"It wouldn't have made any difference. She'd still have died."

"You don't know that."

"It really wasn't your fault."

Ghost and woman agreed again. But Andrew wouldn't give in. "I lost my brother. I lost my father and mother. I lost my wife and daughter. I lost Amy right out of my own class." He strangled the words as they strangled him, as his clasped hands strangled the wheel.

"And it wasn't your fault," said Amelia, while Stella replied. "And now you're going to find her."

"How?"

"We'll find her because you're a good man, Andrew Callaghan. I know we will."

It wasn't enough, but Amelia added an irresistible promise. "I'll help too, Daddy."

So he asked her, "Is she still alive?" unsure if his voice was silent or speaking out loud.

"Of course she is," both women promptly replied.

*****

So the man who might be bad drove with the woman who was sure he was good. A wraith reclined unseen in the back seat of the car. And all of them hoped to find a girl who'd gone missing and might be a ghost.

~13~

The trucker's town was both too big and too small when they finally reached it. Andrew followed the main street first then doubled back along the old city road, through and out of town. Afterward he switched his attention to manicured subdivisions, dusty squares laid out with houses and yards, all clinging tight to space behind lines of stores. He followed back alleys where wild cats roamed. If any child were dumpster diving here, he'd surely find her. No forest to hide in. No wealth of different places to sneak away when you're nearly discovered. It wouldn't be like Andrew's hobo days, nor like Amelia dancing in the woods. Amy would have to be visible, and soon he knew she couldn't be hiding here.

"We need to find the diner where she ate," said Stella, her eyebrows scrunched into a frown, as if she didn't understand why Andrew was cruising around back streets. She probably didn't, but his throat was too tight to offer an explanation. Stella had never dumpster dived. She'd never given up on life and crouched like a wild thing in the woods. But Andrew was searching for the diner too, the place where the trucker left young Amy, buying her one last meal. It felt like a lost cause though, leaving a bitter taste in his mouth. Too many eateries lay scattered on the main road and street corners. Even more of them hunched in dark disguises, pretending to be parking lots or warehouses, ensconced outside of town.

He coughed then moaned the truth—his truth anyway. "We'll never find her." His balled fist struck the steering wheel and the car swerved awkwardly in its approach to another traffic light. Stella seemed to ignore him and the traffic, her fingers fumbling with maps and a folder of cuttings from newspapers. Pictures and articles shared space with town plans on her lap, slipping and sliding precariously; but the light was changing, and he had to glance away.

At last Stella spoke. "It's got to be a diner on the main road, or at least near to it."

"So?" There were still too many to contemplate.

"On Route 34, don't you think?"

"Who knows?"

"And maybe somewhere with a motel attached, I'd guess. After all, the driver said he left her and paid for her meal. He said she hadn't even chosen what to eat, so he must have put it on his bill to pay in the morning."

Stella sounded so confident and practical. Andrew didn't want to pierce her hopes but felt he had to complain. "He ought to have paid for *her* room."

"Perhaps she didn't want a room."

So they drove back along the way they'd come and stopped at a motel just a few miles before town. Stella showed a photo of Amy—an artfully clipped school picture from the yearbook. The lost child looked so gentle and sweet, but the waitress swore she hadn't seen her. Then Stella pulled out another image, the one the newspapers ran. The waitress laughed, almost spilling the coffee she'd been about to pour.

"You two more of those newspaper types?" Her chortles turned to coughing, a stark reminder of Julie in Andrew's class. He wondered how many cigarettes the waitress smoked per day.

"No," said Stella.

"Are you...?"

Suddenly Andrew was scared she might recognize him from his photo in the paper. He tried to hide behind a menu, but Stella placed a hand on his knee to calm him.

"We're family friends," Stella lied. "You know. Just trying to keep the story alive. If we keep asking, keep showing her picture, maybe somebody will remember."

"Family friends?" The waitress didn't seem to believe it.

"I'm a friend of her mother." Stella smiled, that wide, sweet, guileless, loving smile, and the waitress backed away, the danger gone.

Andrew whispered his thanks, bending his head toward Stella's ear, while trails of gray steam rose from weak-brewed coffee. "Good move, that."

"Well, I am friends with her mom; I sat across that desk from her often enough." Stella squeezed his knee again and added, "Besides, that evil teacher in the paper's a single guy, and we're a *couple*. At least, we should pretend to be."

There was a warmth and wonder in that word. He'd like to be half of a *couple*, part of a family again, maybe one that had never lost a child. As Stella leaned closer, he thought how he'd like to bury his nose in her hair and breathe the scent of her shampoo. He could place his own hand on her knee and touch her warming flesh. He could make their coupling real, but he knew it couldn't happen. He hardly knew this colleague beyond the school's gray walls. They weren't a couple at all, except for this smiling pretense. They couldn't be because Stella was sweet, and everyone Andrew cared for ended up hurt.

Frowning now, he lifted Stella's fingers from his leg, holding them just long enough to make the gesture seem appreciated. Then he set her hand beside her mug and drank another slug of gray-brown caffeine.

"So, anyway," said Stella when the waitress reappeared. Andrew placed his hand over the coffee mug—*no refills please*—while she continued. "About young Amy. Is this where she was seen? Did *you* see her?"

The waitress shook her head and flounced away, muttering something over her shoulder; it might have been the name of another diner. But Andrew saw her chatting and pointing from the counter. He was suddenly afraid she really did know who he was.

"Let's move on," he whispered to Stella. "I'll just pay cash."

Stella pulled his face toward hers. "We're not scared of them," she insisted, her voice low and hoarse. "Kiss me. Prove you're not him."

The words made it even more like pretense—how could he prove he really wasn't himself. But Evie's quiet voice piped up in memory: "She'll mean something to you soon." Then Amelia's bell-like silence chimed as well. "I like her, Dad."

****

Andrew was losing hope as they trailed through diners, drinking sodas, coffees and teas, eating cheese on toast, and wondering how much more their stomachs could hold. Chili fries was the menu item of choice at this place while evening drew on, so they called it dinner.

"Yeah," said the waitress when they showed the picture of Amy. "We're the place. But really, there's nothing to tell. Cops have asked us, newspapers asked, even the tourists have asked us; you wouldn't believe it. Everyone."

Andrew thought she'd walk away at that, but instead the waitress pulled up a chair and nibbled on a fry from Stella's plate. She pointed to a table in the corner, tucked beneath a shelf of plastic statues with blind and deaf monkeys and a wandering cat. "The trucker, he sat over there with her and ordered a meal. Then he ate his and left and said we should bill his room."

That table thought Andrew. He tried to imagine Amy tucking into her own chili fries while the plastic cat kept watch over her shoulder; would she have counted every bean?

"Took forever eating, she did."

So perhaps she did count them.

"And then she went out. Just upped and left and didn't even ask us for the bill. Just as well the guy'd dealt with it."

Andrew choked on his water in dismay. They'd watched a thirteen-year-old girl walk out of a diner, on her own, and nobody stopped her?

"Why would we?" said the waitress when he queried her. She seemed offended at his tone, and scraped her chair back from the table. But Stella took over the conversation, smiling her thanks, and volunteering that Andrew was just a bit upset.

"We're friends of the family," Stella explained, yet again, and the waitress said, "Sorry for your loss," as though Amy was bound to be dead. Then Stella returned her hand to Andrew's knee, to keep him calm. He could get used to this.

She pulled him closer when the waitress left. He breathed her hair.

"Don't get so uptight," whispered Stella, as he pulled away. She leaned closer. "Seriously," she added. "You mustn't. You don't want to draw any attention to yourself." Then she leaned back in her chair, as a child might do, and added with a smile, "Once up on a time, we used to play this game."

"What game?" Andrew asked, "and when?" just for something to say.

"When we were kids. We used to look around a diner when we were out for a meal. We'd try to guess who all the people were. How old, you know. What they were called. What they did with their lives. Why they were here."

Andrew couldn't see the point but Stella urged him to try. Reminding himself that she'd given up her summer vacation for this, he felt a duty to humor her.

Movement outside the diner's plate glass window caught his eye, and he pointed to a fluffy white cat. "Moggy. Nine lives but he's used up eight. He lives with a nice little girl in a really very ordinary, ordinary, ordinary, little home."

Stella pointed a forkful of fries toward an elderly couple at *Amy's* table. She looked quizzically at Andrew, begging him to try another guess.

"He's a farmer," Andrew offered obediently after a short pause for thought. "She's his wife."

Stella added details with a smile, still nibbling delicately at the fries. "They're here to celebrate a wedding anniversary," she surmised. "How many though? Twenty-fifth?"

"Isn't that something special?" Andrew leaned back. "They'd go somewhere better than this, wouldn't they?" Then he added, "I think it's their twenty-fourth. They're trying to decide where they want to go next year."

"Seriously," said Stella, "they might be a little bit old for twenty-five. Perhaps they're approaching their fiftieth."

Andrew tried to count how many years he'd stayed with Evie.

But now Stella pointed her menu toward another table. "What about him?"

"Businessman," Andrew replied. "Driving through, on his way to an important meeting."

"And her?"

They worked their gazes around the room, identifying truckers, traveling salesman, shopkeepers and more. Then Stella pointed to a purple-haired teenager sitting all alone. "What about her?"

Andrew's mood darkened with the thought that the girl might be a runaway, abused maybe, and needing help. She had a silver ring through her nose. When she spoke to the waitress, Andrew was sure he saw the shine of a stud glinting in her tongue.

Stella's hand had strayed back to his knee, while the white cat watched, green-eyed, from the window near purple-girl's table. "So what would you do, if she got up to leave?" Stella asked.

Andrew shrugged, trying to pretend he didn't care.

"Would you stand in her way? Would you call the cops? Get up and follow her? That would be seriously creepy."

He shook his head, realizing this was where Stella had been leading all along. She was teasing him. Had it ever really been a game? But laughter played behind her eyes and convinced him she'd enjoyed their chatter too. "She could be Amy," Andrew rasped.

"She could, but you couldn't challenge her, and neither could anyone else. She might be somebody's daughter with a perfectly good reason to be here. She might be older than she looks."

He watched the purple-haired girl shift in her seat. He couldn't believe she was anything more than thirteen. But would he call the cops, if she walked off alone? Could he? Could he insist that Stella should?

A gust of wind blew cold around Andrew's ankles as the bell jangled over the door. Its sound drew Andrew's gaze to a gray-haired woman who walked slowly, sallow-cheeked, narrow-waisted, weighed down with plastic shopping sacks. Purple-hair jumped to her feet, scraping chair legs across the floor.

"Mom!" The girl shrieked. She hugged the woman and pulled out an extra chair at her tiny table, stacking shopping bags by the table leg. "So how did you do? Did you find it?"

Find what? Andrew wondered, but guessed he'd never know. The girl's strident voice had lowered to a gentle hum. And in truth, how much can we know about any of the strangers we meet on any given day? Maybe *that* was the point of Stella's game.

*****

They left, along Route 34 of course. Andrew drove slowly, imagining every moment that he might see her. She'd raise an improbable thumb in the air to beg a ride, smiling that secret smile at him, or else she'd sit in the long grass counting cars. Flat ground stretched green in every direction, with hummocks of emerald trees adding shape and texture. Scrubby undergrowth edged the road, grayed by exhaust fumes. Andrew, in his darkening mood, wondered if he might spy Amy's tennis shoe poking up over weeds. He'd spot her body, broken, bleeding and lost. If he looked hard enough, he'd see what all the others had failed to find, because that was his fate, to learn that another life he'd cared for was gone and swept away; always, evermore, forever his fault.

The engine sputtered as gears tried to find their hold. His foot had left the accelerator again.

"Andrew, we're holding people up," said Stella, as the thirty-fourth car shrieked past them with horn loudly blaring. Grass seemed to sway in the rush of its wind, tires swooshing on blacktop with the sound of Amy's name. But Andrew didn't care. Behind him, bell-like Amelia was silent, a ghost lying invisible in the back seat. He kept checking the mirror, wondering if he might finally see her face, and if Amy might appear beside her. Then he shook his head. Perhaps he wasn't fit to drive.

"She's not dead yet." Amelia's bell-tone rang in his head while cold fingers massaged the back of his neck.

Andrew wondered what Amelia meant by *yet*. Ice shuddered through him, dripping sharper than tears behind his eyes. Then another car, tailgating him, blared its horn and flashed its lights. Andrew clung to the wheel like a lifebelt.

"Andrew, you're going to cause an accident." Stella's knuckles were white in her lap, while more cars approached ahead, lights flashing yellow in the gathering gloom. "We need to go faster."

"But I'll miss something."

"Or hit something. Please Andrew." Her voice was tight.

"Please, Daddy," came the bell-like cry in his head. "She's not dead yet, but we have to get there safely."

He wanted to ask "Get where?" and must have spoken aloud. He heard Stella shuffling in her seat as he pressed the accelerator. Turning slightly, he saw puzzlement on her face, but he didn't know how to answer.

Stella's voice was subdued, as if she weren't quite sure where the question came from, or why Andrew cared. "Getting to the next town before nightfall would be best. Getting there in one piece."

"Get there in peace, Daddy, and we'll rest in peace."

Not at all sure he liked the sound of that, or the sight of a white cat staring out from the trees, green-eyed, red jewel winking on its collar, Andrew searched the road ahead for signs and promised to stop soon.

*****

They booked one room at the motel, to save precious cash. But they asked for separate beds and carried their bags, eyeing each other warily, each uncertain of what the other might presume.

Stella asked to the use the bathroom first. She exited, seemingly hours later, wreathed in steam, scented with oils, dusty with powders, and wrapped in a sweatshirt worn over quarter-length bottoms with printed flowers. Andrew eyed her wet hair, surprised because he'd somehow imagined all women washed their hair in the morning. Underneath, her face was cloudy, older somehow, and less threatening.

"I like to let my hair dry while I read," Stella explained, leaning back on the pillow and pulling bed covers up toward her shoulders. She placed the folder of photos and newspaper cuttings on her tented knees, instead of a book.

Andrew left her to it, carrying his toiletries past her into the bathroom. There he drank in memories with the steam's warm perfume: Evie with her childish love of flowers; Amelia with her need for clean, fresh herbs, always the same, and woe betide if the shampoo ran out and they hadn't got more *right now*. The mirror's clouds revealed a gently shaded image of his face, age washed away so he could pretend at youth. But his body sagged around the waist and couldn't keep up the illusion.

He'd packed sweatpants just in case they had to end up sharing a room—he didn't dare show his knobbled, hairy knees to an almost-stranger. But he felt cluttered and bulky when he came to his bed, climbing under the covers with soft felt clinging, and an ancient tee-shirt smothering his chest.

The light over Stella's bed was too bright and wouldn't let him sleep. But he couldn't ask her to switch it off, so he turned to look at her. She held a picture out to him—Amy in the retouched, thoroughly grownup, newspaper image.

"It's no surprise people thought she was an adult," she said.

"You should look at last year's photo though," Andrew replied. "She looks more like eight than eighteen." He felt angry at others' presumption of Amy's age.

"Yeah, but you never can tell."

An image of the purple-haired girl came back into his mind, the older woman looking so harassed and gray, the waitresses and their chattered tales; so many people and so little anyone could know. Then Andrew smiled.

Stella smiled back, placed the pictures down on her knee, and asked him, "What?"

"Just that I thought you were in your early twenties when I first saw you. There in the faculty room, fresh out of college, full of bright ideas." He knew now he was wrong, but hoped the comment hadn't come out like an insult. *Never ask a woman her age.*

Gray roots showed in the thin orange curls still drying around Stella's face. But her broadening smile turned wrinkles into laughter. "Fresh out of college? That was a while ago. I'm fully qualified you know."

Andrew nodded, still smiling.

"Over qualified too, if you must know. And I've had eleven jobs."

"Eleven?" He raised his eyebrows in surprise.

"Yeah. Cutbacks, politics, last in first out. You know the drill. Spend a few years on supply and then you move on." She tossed her head, the curls stuck tight to her skull suddenly making her look like a teenager. "Footloose and fancy free, that's me. And what about you? What's your story?"

But everyone already knew all about him. Andrew shook his head, unable to reply.

"I only know what was in the papers," Stella insisted, "and they only tell what they want you to read." She rested her hands on her knees, covering the pictures. "What about the real you? How did you meet Evie?"

Her question took Andrew off guard. It carried him back to an age when he too was footloose-*ish* and fancy free, at least as much as he'd ever been. But did he want to confess?

He closed his eyes. "We were neighbors," he began. Perhaps he was asleep and dreaming this. "Grew up together, almost. Evie and her mom. Me and my folks and my..." He couldn't mention Carl. "And then, when my folks... well..."

couldn't mention the car crash, "when they died, well, we kind of got together. We just clicked."

"Grew up together?" said Stella, picking up on the safe part of the tale. "Like the kid next door?"

Andrew's cheeks tightened into a smile as Stella's words sent him to a happier, carefree place. He remembered how Evie would bound and bounce with life when they were kids. He remembered her begging him to rescue a cat, then teaching him all about strays. They sat by the water's edge in the forest. They'd ridden bikes—Carl's bike; he tried to push *that* memory away. They'd gone to movies, maybe, or soda fountains, or ridden busses to and fro from town—he wasn't sure.

Wind whispered outside the motel room door. Rustling leaves reminded him of how they used to climb trees, scrambling high in the overgrowth while imagined tigers lurked and hunted below. Armies of trucks had arrived at their forest one day. Their playground was walled off with orange tape, and soon those metal machines cut everything down, raining sawdust and leaves on the ground. Evie had cried for squirrels and birds, though Andrew tried to remind her that cats would have eaten them had they survived.

Carl died, or was that earlier? His parents? Andrew's eyebrows wrinkled wearily into a frown. "We were very… proper… courting," he said, hearing a very proper tightness strangling his voice. "It's how things were in those days."

"I'm not that young!" Stella laughed, throwing her head back with a loud crack against the wall.

"Yeah, well. We were." He wouldn't—should he ask if it hurt? "Then we married and bought our own little house. You've seen it. She still lives there." The truth was, they married and their house was knocked down to make way for a roadway expansion. The compensation bought that new little house. Andrew couldn't even keep his family home intact.

Stella asked if he'd been a teacher back then, but no; he'd worked in finance, using his numbers in another, more lucrative way. Then the baby came, much longed-for, and she'd seemed so perfect; she'd made their lives complete. *Amelia.*

Breath hissed in and out through Stella's lips before she asked the next question. "When did you know something was wrong with her?"

"Me? I didn't believe it until the doctors said so. But Evie knew." He remembered how Evie would complain, when he came home, wearied by work. *Their baby* still hadn't learned to smile. *Their baby* still wouldn't speak. But Andrew leaned over the crib and insisted he'd seen a perfect, bubbling look of joy.

"That's wind," Evie answered.

Andrew didn't listen, assuming she was just looking for reasons to complain.

"I should have listened," he told Stella now. "I should have paid more attention."

But Stella excused him too easily. "You were distracted. Work takes a lot out of you."

Her words brought comfort, but they weren't enough. Andrew had failed his new family just as he'd failed his old. He rolled over awkwardly in the bed, wrenching his face toward the door, so he wouldn't have to see when Stella's pleasant nature turned against him. Then he continued to speak, forcing the words through clenched lips, trying to get his story straight.

"She wasn't just *easy*, Amelia, she was *barely there*. I had to admit it in the end. At church, even at a wedding, she stood with Evie, all wide eyed and vacant; took no notice of anything, and then…" But that wasn't all of it. With no explanation, sweet Amelia could explode into furious sound. It was like flipping a switch, he remembered, though Evie had always said she had her *moments*. Soon those *moments* stretched into hours, days, even weeks. Screaming, banging her head on the floor, scratching her fingers into the carpet until her broken nails bled, she was a dangerous dynamo. No one could guess what would turn their tiny angel into a demon. No one could protect her.

Then came the doctors. A phase, they said. She'll grow out of it, they said.

Later they told the grieving parents Amelia was developmentally delayed. *Subnormal*, thought Andrew. *Retarded*. Their perfect baby girl.

And finally came those whispered words, not really a diagnosis; autism; *refrigerator mom*.

Stella interjected, "What on earth is one of those?"

Andrew explained how the doctor had seemed to blame Evie for being too cold or too distant with their child. "She was never cold," he said. But he'd tried to be warmer, just in case it might be true. He'd struggled to smother Amelia with unwanted affection, until her rejection weighed him into submission. Until, that final day, he saw the two of them sitting together on the sofa, Evie staring at the TV show as if she'd been hypnotized, Amelia rubbing her finger on loose skin at her mother's elbow. The room looked like a volcano had gone off, no dinner, no coffee even, and nobody turning their eyes to welcome him home. Andrew felt like an invader in a stranger's house, unwanted, unneeded, un-everything, and it all got too much for him.

"But I really should have stayed. I should have understood."

"Perhaps you were meant to move on," Stella whispered. "Perhaps it was for the best. She needed all her mom's attention, and there wasn't any left over."

"No." Andrew sighed, denying good intent. "I was selfish. I left, and I wasn't there to help. If I'd stayed perhaps… if I'd stayed she might not… If I'd stayed…" The words ran out until he tried again. "And then she was dead, and I'd ruined her as well. I ruin everyone I touch. So I ran away."

"That's when you lived in the woods?" Stella asked. Andrew nodded, still not facing her, and she continued. "It was after Amelia died then, not before, so the papers got it wrong. You weren't in the forest before, and you couldn't have been the predator, whatever they say."

"The papers get everything wrong." He almost spat the words.

"But we'll get this right, Andrew. We'll find Amy, or else we'll both die trying."

He stared at Stella's shadow on the wall, afraid to turn his gaze toward her face. He watched the rippling gray of her shape, graceful, dancing. He wanted to guess if she meant *die trying* as a joke. But Stella was already turning on her side to switch off the light, so he risked facing her. The curls on the back of her head still looked damp, frail even. He felt an urge to touch them or smooth them straight, but her separate bed was too far away.

"There is good in the world, Andrew—good people, not all bad. Not like in the news. And there's good in you." Her voice was muffled by the pillow as she finished. "You have to see that."

With no lights, Andrew didn't have to see anything.

"Good night, sweet prince." Her last words made him laugh, which was comfort and peace. She was good at that.

"Good night, Stella, star of the sea."

****

"Do you suppose she kept going on 34?" Andrew asked, as they came to the junction with Interstate 80. "I mean, it's not as if it's still going West."

"But it does go West eventually, and she's one determined child. Do you think she'd change her mind?"

Andrew struggled to choose. "It depends if she was fixed on Route 34, or on going West." Which depended on which came first, the magic number, or some reason to leave. Where did she hope to end up? Had anyone thought to ask if she had relatives out West, or friends of the family?

"Friends like us?" Stella smiled. She'd grown into the habit of saying they were *friends of the family* whenever they showed their photographs. But they were fake friends, and the junction drew too close. "Going west is much bigger," Stella mused. "She told the kids *go West* before she ever said *thirty-four*. So maybe the number was just a means to an end."

"Should we take the interstate?"

Stella didn't answer, but Andrew swerved the car into the exit lane. "I just wish we knew *how* she was going, not where." White lines flashed, marking the way. "She couldn't have walked this far. She couldn't. Someone's bound to have picked her up. Someone should have come forward." The junction signs loomed overhead, and his hands clenched on the wheel.

Suddenly Amelia stirred in the back of Andrew's mind, or the back of the car. "Take the interstate," she demanded in tones of youthful authority. "It's faster. I like fast."

At the same time, Stella looked up from her map. "This is Princeton, sweet prince," she said. "D'you suppose they'll have someplace for food."

Somehow he missed the junction anyway. Was there another lane? Did he drift the wrong way? So now they drove through town instead, blue skies overhead, traffic lights and railroad lines, with wide gravel spaces watched over by warehouses, almost painted blue as the sky. They stopped for coffee, ate pie, passed a school, and decided a burger place was most likely where Amy might have eaten. But nobody knew her there, so they strolled out to check the map. Stella still had the picture in her hand.

"You looking for that girl?" asked a stranger. He jumped down from a pick-up across the parking lot. White-bearded and loose-limbed, garbed in faded jeans and a gray tee-shirt, he wiped his brow with a ragged handkerchief and spat a tobacco line as he approached. "Heard she was some kind of runaway."

Andrew shrank back warily. *Friend or foe?* And how could the stranger have seen the photo in their hands? What was his game?

But Stella, always more relaxed, piped up her regular refrain. "We're family friends." The lie sounded almost natural now on her lips. "Have you seen her?"

"Sure," said the stranger.

Really? Andrew tensed.

"Like I told the cops. She was heading West." The old man pointed to the freeway entrance ahead.

"Who with?" Andrew asked, fear tightening his voice. She couldn't have headed West alone.

"With a nice young man, nice car." The stranger smiled. "She was hitchhiking and he picked her up, right about here."

Andrew struggled as images of rape and murder filled his head. "But what was he… what might he…?"

"You're the teacher guy aren't you?" the stranger announced. "And you?" He turned to Stella. "You a teacher too?"

She nodded, while Andrew tried to back away.

"Don't mean no harm," said the man, spreading his hands before him like some elaborate surrender. White hair shone like a halo in the sun, or like a white cat's fur. Andrew almost expected the man's eyes to flash green—was he even real— was he real as the cat, which probably wasn't real either? "You're good people, and she's with good people, that girl. She'll be okay."

Andrew stood frozen, but Stella asked for him, "How can you tell?"

"What? That she's okay? That you're okay?" White hair bobbed into the clouds behind the man's head, then his face turned to Andrew, while a white cat—*oh, of course a white cat*—wound around his legs. "She's got her guardian angel with her, that girl, just like you has."

"Who?" Andrew felt his voice fade into dreams and sleep. "What angel?"

"Your daughter of course. You've got yer guardian angel riding wi' you, and the girl's got her cat."

Amelia's bell-like voice laughed in Andrew's head. "Really, Dad, didn't you know?"

****

Stella was silent as they drove on. Instead of fumbling with papers in her lap, she stared at the road ahead, as if accusing it of some dire misdeed. Meanwhile Andrew, though driving faster than before, looked warily at every tree they passed, watching for what he dreaded most to see. When he chanced to glance at his passenger, he felt indicted along with the road and quickly turned away.

Eventually Stella spoke. "You're not one of those New Age pagan types are you, Andrew?"

He realized how rarely she used his name and felt a vague regret at how sharp it sounded on her lips. *Mr. Callaghan*, though formal, seemed far less threatening, and out of school he'd been comfortable to embrace his namelessness. But he wasn't New Age—not old aged either—so he muttered, confused, "What do you mean?"

Stella wound her fingers in the air. "You don't really believe dead people turn into guardian angels like that guy said?"

Andrew registered wing-flapping fingertips at the edge of his vision. He'd never really given the question much thought. Angels, ghosts, illusions, they were all the same to him, no more real than the painted guardian angel cat on his classroom wall.

"Because angels and people are different, you know," Stella continued, as if it were somehow vitally important that he hear.

Andrew answered, "Yeah, they are, I guess," just for something to say. The concept took him back to younger, more innocent times, when faith was everyday, church was Sunday, and angels were valiant messengers sent down by a Biblical God. Sometimes they had swords.

"So your daughter can't be an angel can she?"

He didn't answer, not wanting to share the presence of the voice in his head or, worse still, analyze it away.

"Even though she's dead."

A cruel blow. Amelia had been dead for years, but the word still stung like bullets, even more while he imagined he could still hear her voice. Andrew buried his secret behind a complaint that maybe dead people *can* be ghosts, to which Stella protested, "But ghosts aren't real."

"And angels are?"

"Maybe."

And cats? He thought of the painting again. Was it a flying cat on his classroom wall, or an angel disguised as a cat? He remembered buying it and thinking it might bring good luck, or even blessings. The woman in the art store hadn't seemed to care—she just wanted to make a sale. But the picture was painted by some girl who'd made a poster for the memorial for *that girl,* for Amelia. Andrew hadn't dared confess, *that girl* was his daughter.

All those years ago… His hobo existence after Amelia died; how he'd longed to join her then. Even after Evie brought him back to life, he'd returned to the forest, hoping to die again. Loving and living hurt too much. Until one day… he'd opened his eyes to the sun through a hole in his wretched cabin's roof. He'd heated water for tea in a can and added dodgy roots and leaves and berries. That should do it. Then the cat wound its sinuous body around his legs, clawing his ankle until it bled, nipping with dagger teeth at the holes in his knees when he sat to comfort it. He'd stood to chase the cat away at that, then found himself following instead, through the trees, along the path, and out toward the old white church and its generous free meals for those in need. Some stranger took him under her wing, gave him clean clothes, told him to bathe, and pushed his life toward the straight and narrow, back to hope.

"You feel guilty?" the woman had asked, once they got to know each other, once he was settled in his one-month-only-room, and another free meal slipped so sweetly down his throat.

"Yeah," he mumbled around dry bread.

"Then do something. Help other kids like her."

He'd asked her how, and his savior leaned back in her chair, scraping its legs so they squeaked on the linoleum floor. Then she asked in turn, "What can you do?"

"Math," Andrew had answered. It seemed a pretty useless skill.

"So teach. They're always in need of math teachers."

"Not people like me. Not…"

"Get a job. Save some money. Then go to college and train."

She brought an extra cookie for him from the counter so he couldn't run away. Her urgent offerings of advice made it sound so easy; just apply, just fill in these forms, just get these references. This stranger, who almost seemed familiar, guided his hand until he remembered, days later, and promptly forgot, *she* was Lydia Markham, *she* was the daughter-in-law of the murderer. Was *she* feeling guilty and doing something about it herself? Had she recognized him?

After he trained, when he graduated and felt like he'd finally made it and was human and whole again, he went to Paradise for one last look around and bought the painting. He wanted something to remind him of the white cat he supposed, to prove that hope hurts and scratches and bites your ankles once in a while, but hope's still worth following out of the woods. He was following it now.

"Where did you go?" Stella asked.

"Huh?"

"Just then, like you were miles away."

"I don't know." He didn't want to explain, not just now.

So Stella explained instead. "I just didn't want that farmer's angels to turn you all pagan-spirit-ish."

He remembered what they'd been talking about now and answered, "Don't worry. They won't."

Soon it was time to switch drivers again. Stella assured Andrew she'd take care of his car. She promised they'd stop when she was tired and stay the night in a motel. She even agreed to keep an eye on the gas and the temperature, and not let the engine overheat, as if it would at this time of the evening.

Andrew leaned back in the passenger seat, closed his eyes, and pretended to sleep.

*****

Miles flew by, or crawled, depending on your point of view. Half the time Andrew wanted to arrive; the other half he didn't even know where he was going. Had Amy really traveled this path before? Was there any hope they'd find her, with so many motels and rest stops unseen on a road that traveled between here and there—between here and where?—so many places to lose her trail.

At first they pulled off every time they saw signs for lodging or food. But miles crawled slower than dead ants across Stella's map with nothing achieved. No one had seen the girl in the photograph. Nobody even knew why they were asking. One long-lost child was long-dead news and their task had no ending in sight.

Another motel room offered shelter, another pair of beds, again and again, like the ones that went before. Flat plains of green were punctuated with smooth-skinned black of rivers. Banks of trees matched ranks of armored trucks in parking lots. Unchanging sky was blue till the clouds washed in, then gray, then blue again, flat and blank as Andrew's heart.

Stella kept a firm hand on the map when Andrew drove. She counted off the junctions and miles. Then she swapped places and complained at how Andrew just let the map lie as it was. Didn't he care, or did he already know every stop on the freeway by heart?

They'd passed into Nebraska now. The horizon was still bland and straight as the road. Occasional farm buildings or colored banks of trailers broke its line. Occasional trees tried to rear their heads but gave up and lay too low, too close to the ground. Gray chain links enclosed green fields. Red roofs and blue were almost as flat as the sky that loomed over them. And power poles stood proudly arrayed to measure the passage of time.

For a while, they let the Lincoln Beltway distract their thoughts to history and politics—a teacher thing Andrew guessed, always looking for reason to educate. But then their conversation drifted again to the media, to the relative unimportance of missing persons in the news when movie stars might suffer clothing catastrophes any day.

Clouds threatened rain then changed their minds again. Meanwhile Stella drove, then Andrew, then Stella, their stops growing fewer, as if the Beltway miles were honor bound to stretch to infinity. Still they turned on and off the freeway, following stray cats' leads or mild inclination to motels or restaurants. Still those concrete bridges to nowhere brooked no answers between them and offered no hope.

For all her anti-spiritual rants, Stella was the first one to point out the surprising frequency of those fluffy, white cats. Andrew opened a lazy eye and grunted at the presence of the first, the second and the third, then chose to ignore them. After all, he'd been ignoring cats now for half his life. Wild cats at the roadside were hardly something to change the face of the world.

"But there's another one."

He pretended to snore.

"And there. Why are they all so white?"

All cats look white in the dark. Or was that meant to be black?

"And another. Look at its eyes."

Andrew didn't need to see the eyes. Cats' eyes were bound to be green and meaningless, so he pretended to snooze.

Somewhere along the way he must have fallen properly asleep. Suddenly he noticed the sound of the wheels had changed. He opened his eyes and wondered where he was, why the world around him had somehow disappeared. Who was in the driver's seat next to him? Then it all came back. Concrete barriers gleamed white in the headlamp beams. Trees and scrubby bushes dared a closer approach, like shadowed ghosts. And silver stars looked down.

"Where are we?" Andrew asked, trying to stretch in his seat.

"I dunno. Somewhere near somewhere. Lincoln perhaps."

When the wheel noise changed again, Andrew glimpsed moonlight glinting on a short wash of water. Rustling trees shrank back against the shadows while cloudy, artificial light washed pale against the sky. Stella pulled on the wheel, veering the car to the side.

"Where are you going?"

"I dunno. Somewhere near Lincoln, I guess."

"But why are you turning off?"

"Because of the cats."

"Huh?"

"Because all the cats were heading this way, every last one of them, so I thought I'd follow them."

And Stella had worried that Andrew might be weird? For all her denials of angel interventions and daughterly ghosts, she seemed oddly content to let felines determine their route. But what if cats were angels in disguise? Andrew listened to gravel rattling against the car. He imagined the scrabbling of cats' claws and thought of his painting of the guardian angel cat again—not that its guardianship amounted to much, but he'd been willing enough to let a cat lead him out of destruction in Paradise Park, when his knees and ankles bled. That dangerous brew could have been his end—he'd planned it to be his end. Instead, just now, in this one moment, he felt glad to be alive with Stella at his side. Glad for the present. Don't think about anything more. Don't think about Amy. Don't think about the troubles that lay behind or those that might come next.

A white cat paralleled the car's bumpy route. A cat tethered to emptiness. A cat that ran too fast for any feline, and one that reminded Andrew of the bus—of running away so long ago, where now he felt more like he was running home. That cat hadn't been real, he remembered, and neither was this, though its fur was white, and a red eye winked from its collar.

"What now?" he complained into sudden smothering light. This wasn't a town, but reds and whites and streetlamps flared ahead. Brake lights, truck lights, the price of gas…? Stella said the cat would show the way. Then she turned across the traffic to enter a parking lot.

"See," she said.

"See what?"

"The cat. It's led us to a motel."

Stella's night vision must be better than Andrew's, or else her optimism. But there really was a vacancies sign at least. They staggered wearily out of the car, weighed down under travel's long night. Andrew knocked where the doorbell said press, and they leaned against each other as if drunk when lights came on. Andrew flashed a credit card, signed a book, and thanked a stranger for the key.

The white cat, waiting at the door to their room, refused to move away. When Andrew pushed on the door, the cat ran inside. Not a New Age pagan angel or ghost; it was just a cat, he told himself.

Amelia laughed.

*****

The cat strode in as if it owned the room, then jumped onto Stella's bed. It was Stella's bed, because she always chose the one further from the door. She wanted to ensure Andrew knew she wasn't trying to entrap him. She always left the bathroom clean, always made sure she was clothed from head to toe, and always left that escape route clear to the open road outside. Stella was proud of her self-control and her fierce integrity. But now a white cat lay in the middle of her bed. She didn't want to disturb it. But she had no intention of sharing her sleeping space with fur.

Andrew dumped his case next to the bed by the door. He unpacked the sweats that he'd worn each night, laying them neatly on the pillow closest to the door. A double bed. Two pillows. He faced the entrance—the exit—then sat down with his back to Stella, slowly removing his shoes and socks. "You going to use the bathroom first?" he asked over his shoulder.

She always did, so Stella left her pack judiciously placed between the two beds. She took her purple, flowered pajamas and sweatshirt out, then retired with her toiletries bag to the over-bright bathroom, with its over-bright lights and hissing pipes. The door clicked firmly closed behind her and she turned the lock. Then she stood and listened as bedsprings protested Andrew's every move. She wondered what the cat was doing.

Standing by the mirror, Stella held her toothbrush in hand, and froze. There was something vaguely wrong about making the noise of cleaning teeth while somebody listened. It hadn't mattered before. They'd had their own halves of motel rooms mapped and planned. Somehow those certainties made the bathroom's emptiness more secure. But now she imagined Andrew listening to every stroke of the brush. Would he be disgusted to hear her spit? Would he be aroused by the sound of water splashing when the shower ran? Would he…? She drove the thoughts away, imagined cursing the cat, and got on with the job.

When she left the bathroom, Andrew lay on the far side of his bed, face to the door, clearly ready to escape. He had those ratty sweatpants on again and his threadbare shirt. The covers were bunched beneath bare feet, tugged over to one side, exposing the pillow where she would lie if they chose to share the bed. He swung himself upright, grabbed his own toiletries bag, and walked past her, gazing through her, on his way to the bathroom. Then Stella lay on his bed instead, and wondered what to do, while the white cat looked on.

"I can sleep on the sofa," Andrew announced when he came back, smelling of toothpaste and soap.

"No," said Stella. "The cat's on my bed. I should take the sofa."

"Technically"—Andrew laughed—"I think the cat should take the sofa. And this bed might just as well be yours."

"Or we could share. It wouldn't have to mean anything."

"Of course…"

"But if you wanted…"

"We *would* sleep better in a bed. And sleeping better's good if we're going to drive."

Somehow they, neither of them, dared disturb the cat, which continued to watch, unperturbed. They struggled to slide into the one bed, side by side, one head on each pillow, arms carefully straight, and legs, so neither would touch the other's body by moving in the night. The cat meowed and some unspoken agreement turned them as one, fingers fumbling, eyes unable to look, until they found their comfort with bodies together, still ramrod stiff and straight, still not... until they were wrapped together in each other's arms.

Slowly, surely, Stella's hands slipped down. Andrew's need pressed against her legs. She molded her fingers smoothly, ready to hold. Andrew cupped his hands over Stella's breast, feeling the hardening response of loneliness. His breaths grew faster. Hers as well. Need grew stronger. Desire, intent and more. Andrew bent his head under the covers, as if the dark might hide him. Then he wrapped his lips around sweet Stella's spark and sucked hard, drinking her sighs. She pressed her body closer to guide him in. She gasped. He cried.

Slowly, surely, strangers no more, they learned the comfort of others, while a child was still lost. Somehow their lovemaking sealed a sacred covenant to find her.

"I like her," Amelia whispered in the back of Andrew's mind.

"She'll mean something to you," said Evie in memory.

By morning the cat had disappeared.

*****

"Where to now?" Andrew asked as they breakfasted among vacationing crowds, chowing down stacks of pancakes with butter and bacon on everything. He was surprised how good it all tasted, and wondered if last night's lovemaking had caused the world's explosion of light and flavor. He didn't dare ask if Stella felt the same, so he stuck to the mundane.

"Who knows?" she replied. "Doesn't your guardian angel tell you?"

"I'm not sure she works like that," Andrew answered, unguardedly.

Stella jumped on his words. "She? You really think you have an angel?"

Andrew wondered whether confessing to love, or to hearing voices in his head, would be the harder task. Fearing both, he filled his mouth with a forkful of food, while Stella waited and stared. At last he ventured, around a few last scraps of salty savor, "Last night was good."

"And your *female* guardian angel?"

"She…"

Stella was clearly patient. At least Stella, with a full mug of coffee to stare into, was clearly patient.

"She talks to me sometimes…" Andrew groped for words. "My daughter, I mean… I'm sure it's just imagination, but ever since she died… Just sometimes… She…"

Stella's hand shook slightly, sending ripples wide across the dark brown surface of her drink. "The ghost of your dead daughter talks to you?" she clarified.

"Only sometimes."

"And what does she say?"

Andrew looked down at toast crumbs on his plate, unsure how to reply. After all, Amelia said whatever she wanted, whenever she wanted, it seemed. If he wanted her to talk to him, to advise him which way to go for example, she was never there.

"Yes I am." Her bell-voice sounded clear and loud. "Go to Denver," she added.

So he answered, "Denver," in tones of shock and awe.

"Oh…kay…" Stella shuffled maps from her pack onto the table and opened them out. She shifted salt and pepper aside, then used the three-creased advert for Omaha Premium Beef Nebraska Steaks to hold the page where she wanted. Tracing a line from Lincoln, I-80 to North Platte then, somewhere afterward, to 76, to Denver, she proclaimed, "Denver it is."

Andrew stared at an empty third chair at their table. He wished he could conjure an image sitting there, a teenaged Amelia to laugh and smile at him. But she wouldn't even be a teenager now. If she'd lived, she'd be as adult as he, probably driving her own car, making her own wild road trip across the States.

"Dad!" He heard her laugh. "If I'd lived I'd be in an institution by now, or else I'd of driven poor Mom insane."

Her words poured salt into old wounds. "I should have stayed."

"Then I'd have been in an institution even sooner."

"But you might be alive."

"What's so good about being alive? This way I get to be me."

He hadn't realized he was crying. He had no idea how much of their conversation had taken place out loud. All he knew was Stella stroking the back of his head. His face lay flat on the white tablecloth, tears staining it gray, while savors of spilled salt and bacon fat assaulted his nose.

His hands shook when he tried to sit upright again, but Stella grasped them in hers, smoothed them, soothed him with her voice. She told him it was okay to cry, and he wondered when he'd last allowed his feelings such free reign. Grown men don't cry, not when their daughters are murdered, not when their mothers and fathers and brothers have died, not when school children disappear and the world is filled with anger, murder and fear; grown men don't cry.

"Yes they do," said Stella, as if he were a pupil standing at her desk. "Yes they do. And they do just what we did last night. And they like it. And they're not afraid to say so."

"So there," Amelia echoed, her voice disappearing in the distance.

"Could we do it again before we leave?"

*****

The door to the motel room was closed when the maid wheeled her cart that way. The *Do not disturb* sign hung on the knob, so she checked her watch, tutted quietly, and moved on. Meanwhile a while cat lay on the window ledge, its smooth back covering the gap between the curtains, its quiet purring as gentle as the wind in the trees.

Inside the room, suitcase and backpack guarded the door. Man and woman stood beside the rumpled bed. The man fingered the woman's cheek and neck, tussling strands of curly red hair, smoothing pale pink skin. He slipped his hands under the top of her shirt so the fabric rippled and rose over her shoulder. Then fingers slid lower.

The woman unbuttoned her collar. She rested her hand on the man's, pressed closer, moved his fingers downward until, together, their warmed palms cupped her breast. The man urged his attention to her sleeves, tugged them from her arms, she moving, he maneuvering, still holding each other tight. She unbuttoned his shirt and rested her head among the hairs of his chest. Her fingers fumbled with his belt where his arousal welcomed them. Then he pushed away. She stepped back, a puzzled frown on her face, and stopped as her legs touched the bed.

Andrew undressed her slowly, first with his eyes, then his hands. He removed each item of clothing and underwear as if it were gold, running his fingers along her flesh as she were made of finest, sheerest silk. Then Stella set to undressing him. His pants and underclothes fell in a tangled heap at his ankles. She kissed and caressed where none but Evie had touched his flesh before. He pulsed with longing, but waited, giving her time.

The cat purred even louder now, as bedsprings creaked, as the two tense, eager humans fell on the covers. Nobody heard but the maid in the room next door, tut tutting again, while Stella and Andrew purred their own soft language of sweetness and light.

Stella's warmth was damp as a river in the sun. Andrew entered her like a battered branch grown whole, pulsating with life. They held each other, life-rafts both on a stormy linen sea, and waves that might have battered, soothed, till thrashing limbs were one long languid form.

The cat's tail flapped, and flapped again.

*****

Andrew almost slept when his body was spent. He saw himself walking in woods, gray-shrouded with gloom. Then sunshine broke through. A white cat lay all languid on a branch beside his hand. He stroked its fur and told it, softly, improbably of his daughter and how he loved her. "She's disappeared."

"She's here." The cat transformed. White fur reappeared as silken hair flowing smooth on a beautiful head. The young woman, who looked so much like Evie and yet so different, smiled at him.

"I don't…"

"She's here." A child now held his hand instead. They stood below the hanging branch, she staring up at leaves, he down at the crown of her perfect head.

"She's here." He thought a patch of rumpled ground might be her grave. But instead a teenager laughed and pulled him away. "Come on, Daddy. She's not *there*. We've got to find her."

Then he awoke.

Part 6

~14~

Destination and relationship bound them together now. Andrew and Evie's journey almost made sense, laying itself out like some long-planned vacation with routes drawn on a map. They'd head for Denver, forgetting conveniently that a ghost or guardian angel had told them the way. Maybe they'd take in Lexington—"They named a ship after it…" Amy would surely be found on some wide street-corner, waiting for them, with traveler's thumb upraised. Andrew's guardian angel would lead her, or lead them, to ensure the meeting took place, and their journey would be done.

"I always fancied going to Colorado," Stella announced, while wheels hummed softly below them.

"Huh? Why?"

"The skiing of course."

Andrew continued to drive, his hands loosely in control as the car bounced gently along the wide, straight road. "I'd guess the ski resorts are closed in summer," he replied, all practical.

"But we'll see the mountains! It will be glorious."

"Is Denver even in the mountains?"

"Must be, or how could there be skiing?"

Wide acres of flat, green plains filled the windscreen's view, belying the prospect of any change. Not that Andrew shared Stella's mountainous dreams. "Give me a beach, sweet waves and sunshine," he said, watching waves of distant clouds scud in the ocean of sky.

Stella laughed, throwing back her head and seeming so relaxed, as if they were planning a second honeymoon, not hunting a missing child. Her hand slid across the seat to Andrew's thigh. He jumped in surprise, jerking the wheel aside, then regretted his apparent rejection. But how could thoughts of acceptance and love belong in his life? Could he love Stella? Could he risk it? Could love dawn so fast?

"Dad, you've loved her for ages," said the bell-like voice residing in the back of the car.

"None of your business."

"What?" asked Stella.

He hadn't meant to speak aloud, so now he swiftly demurred. "Nothing." But his eyes strayed again to his companion. Trim, delicate, red-haired with fire in her heart; was this a real relationship or just a continuing dream, as false as the child who wasn't traveling with them? If he dared to love Stella, wasn't she bound to get hurt? Could he do that to her? Then he watched a narrowing line tighten her lips and wondered if his unconscious rejection already caused her pain.

"I'm sorry," he whispered.

Stella's voice was sharp as she answered him. "Are you talking to me this time, or the voices in your head?"

All Andrew could do was say sorry again and hope the moment would pass.

In the back of the car, Amelia seemed more real than this fragile not-quite-relationship. He glimpsed her narrow face when he checked in the mirror, lanky, silken-haired like the teenager of his dream, though she was gone when he looked over his shoulder. Was she really trying to mend his life, or did the voices in his head mean he'd finally gone insane? And where was Amy in all this? Would they ever find her?

Trees grew darker, taller, and more proud, punctuating fields and sky with hints of hope. Silence drifted into music from the radio, then static. Stella pulled some CDs from her purse and different sounds ensued, though Amelia's frown suggested she didn't approve. Clouds grew more ominous, threatening a storm, before they turned empty and gray. This wide sky left too much space for uncertain moods to switch and change.

Meanwhile the freeway sped across ribboning streams. Dark gray, white-striped and yellow, concrete edged, it crunched the miles through banks of occasional bushes and repeated songs. When the horizon tilted it might have been the first faint shadow of hills. But then the plains were blank again, empty as Andrew's long-dead hopes for the future. He couldn't love. He couldn't risk loving again. He glued his lips to silence.

"You can't risk *not* loving, Dad." *Does she read minds?* Bright eyes smiled encouragement from behind, in the mirror's harsh reflection. But she was a child, wasn't she, though she grew to adulthood faster than the miles?

Stella took her turn at the wheel. When they reached the junction for Denver and Cheyenne, Andrew almost asked her to simply go West. After all, it was how their journey began. *Go West young man.* But Amelia had mentioned Denver, or else he'd imagined it. Was that worth turning for? He sighed, reminding himself the cops hadn't found the child when they searched much smaller towns. Denver was huge and he knew they wouldn't find her here. Failure loomed.

Stella's breathy voice hummed an old folk song, where *sisters* were gone in both directions. But where were the daughters, Andrew wanted to ask? Meanwhile the road still promised to split, and choices had to be made. Amelia, dead Amelia who should be gone, filled his head with words, while innocent Amy was silent.

"Denver," said Amelia's determined voice. "Denver, Denver, Denver." No one sat behind Andrew, but the mirror reflected her smile, so he smiled back. Then Stella, almost as if she'd heard, pulled out into the empty lane marked for the exit. South it was, and Denver became their deliberate destination. The junction's maze and signage fell into the past. The city, unseen, promised to wait more than a hundred miles away. It beckoned like hope in sunset's deadening gloom. And the bell-voice was stilled. Perhaps the teenager had fallen asleep.

"I'm tired," said Stella, still driving, still staring straight ahead. Buildings and signs, like a child's scattered blocks, began to dot the fields as the sky grew dark. "Should we stop for the night?"

Andrew nodded agreement, though stopping felt like betrayal. This wasn't a journey for comfort, rather for loss and failing to find. Still, driving on risked their entering town in the middle of the night, with nowhere to stay. Or else it risked Stella's falling asleep at the wheel. Andrew, in no state to take her place, felt his fogged head rock against his chest. Then he found himself jerked into wakefulness, as their wheels rumbled and slowed on the exit ramp. Down into darkness, following an unlit road, down, down, and down, they finally approached the lonely lights of food and motels in an endless sea of night. Another anonymous room beckoned them, with its one wide bed, no question now of whether they were together in this or apart.

Togetherness, followed by food, then followed by sleep.

*****

Their morning street, as they left, was a desert of dry slopes, so dead and empty even the lines of approaching traffic disappeared. No mountains though, despite the promised skiing. Far in the distance, on a foreign planet, it looked like life could maybe be sustained, but never here. So the car ate miles, and its occupants sang together to the radio. Sometimes Andrew was sure he heard a younger woman's voice, sweet Amelia's perhaps. But Stella's tones were just as sweet as he could need them to be. He let her hand rest on his thigh, head on his shoulder while he drove. He let himself believe, just for a while, that maybe he could find true love again—even find a missing child. Cracked pavements rattled the wheels of the car, while skies as endless as desert plains were wracked with raven calls.

Stella raided the cooler for drinks, then laughed as foam spilled wetly over her jeans. She passed the opened can to Andrew. He took it in his hand and prayed for smooth driving. A lonely lake drew a line of silver in the scene behind Stella's face, making him think of flattened halos and saints. A stand of hardy trees made him almost believe there was life on Mars.

Had Amy slept in some trucker's cab as she traveled along this road? Had she counted clumps of grass? Had she seen the one red tractor and asked her driver why it wasn't blue? Had she even known what she was doing?

"Of course she knew, Dad."

They passed another junction, roads to nowhere intersecting, patterns laid in blacktop over sand. Sentinel columns carried electrical wires. Silence hummed and Stella put another CD in the slot.

"Are those airplanes?" she asked, when ranks of white appeared in the gray-green blur.

"Dunno," said Andrew, his hands tightening on the wheel. Meanwhile lines on the ground resolved into buildings together with a wealth of black-and-white cows.

The pavement was cracked again. Wheels juddered and jumped. Green fields with darker trees drew close as they came to another junction. "Straight on for Denver," said Stella. Andrew already knew. Coffee and bathrooms beckoned him. Houses lurked. And the startling jade of watered fields contrasted with cerulean signs under an empty sky.

"You'd never believe it thundered so much last night."

Andrew's heart thundered more with every mile. He eyed each truck stop, wondering if here was the place where they'd learn Amy's fate. But the voice in his head, Amelia's voice, declared she had no fate and, "Stop being so miserable, Dad. I'll take you to her. I will." Could he really trust a ghost?

"Grand Army of the Republic Highway?" Stella read the sign in ringing tones then checked her maps again. Andrew imagined a host of soldiers seeking the missing child, or of soldier ants. Roads and fields still flickered past, deserted, while music sang of days in the desert sun. He'd imagined Colorado very differently.

"There's a lake over there."

"There are hills over there."

But they were so very far away and so gray. Could they really be mountains?

Wooden poles bearing electrical wires gave way to metal towers. Desert grass was replaced with scrubby trees. Empty spaces filled with cars and buildings, low-slung warehouses, and ranks of bright-colored trailers all awaiting destination and purpose. The watching hills gained definition and peaks, maybe even glints of snow. Bold Denver approached. But how could they possibly know where Amy's latest driver had stayed? Which motel or diner shimmered with unheard news of the missing child? Andrew longed for a sign with her name on it, but instead the banners just proclaimed prices of rooms and numbers of channels on TV. Would television have reports of her?

"It's hopeless," Andrew muttered, while roads and junctions conspired to confuse, while Stella tried to soothe.

"It's not hopeless, Dad. Just do it," Amelia replied, her voice as clear as if she really were sitting behind him in the car. Still, he wished he knew what he was meant to do next. "Go to Denver, of course, like I told you."

Stella shrieked. "We've missed our turnoff!" So Andrew took the next exit and wondered where they were.

*****

Without even a diner or coffee bar to guide them, Andrew pulled off the road and offered Stella the wheel. "I'll navigate," he suggested, then realized he must have insulted her skills. "I didn't mean…"

"It's you that missed the turn," she accused. "If you'd have looked at the signs…"

"I know." She was right, so he simply confessed he thought she'd be better suited to reading the road. "I'm too easily distracted." He opened the map, and Stella promised to drive where *the Spirit* led her.

"What spirit?" Andrew asked.

She laughed. "Hey, you're the one that's talking to ghosts."

Somehow they ended up on a narrow, dry lane, bouncing over potholes, while Andrew begged, "Take care of my car," until they drew to a halt at the gate to a farm.

"Now what?"

They climbed wearily from the car and stretched their legs, walking with long grass tickling to their knees, while lost bees buzzed in their ears. The hum grew louder. Weeds swayed. Then they ducked in fear of a plane swooping low overhead. Stella asked where it had come from. Andrew struggled to answer while trying to catch his breath. And Amelia laughed. Meanwhile the plane coasted forward along its runway and drew to a halt.

"Help you?" asked the pilot, marching slowly across the field, leather boots squeaking, hands held loosely near the grips of fine-handled pistols swinging low at his waist.

Stella held up a picture of Amy, though obviously he wouldn't have heard of her. Why should he? Except he had.

"Yeah, I remember her."

Andrew staggered against the fence, asking nervously, "You do?" Was this man her savior or her killer, he wondered, and why would they dare talk to him, a gun-toting stranger in the middle of nowhere?

"Sure thing." The pilot swaggered close and climbed on the wooden posts. "Yeah. She liked the look of my beauty there." He pointed to the plane. "So I flew her around."

Andrew spaced the words out with stumbling breaths. "You… flew… Amy… around?"

"Sure. Why not? Sweet little lady. She really loved her flight. A pleasure to be with her."

Andrew struggled to imagine his student even understanding what an airplane could do. "She wasn't scared?"

"That little lady? Nah, no way. She was content as the cows, a natural upstairs."

Andrew's imagination now in total overdrive, he found his vision filled with images of cows jumping high over moons that wore Amy's face. It was beyond comprehension. But Stella—ever cool and calm and collected—kept the conversation going. She wondered how Amy could have found her way to this place. "Walked," said the man, but from where?

"From the road, I reckon." And why? "To see things fly." It made a kind of bumbling, uncoordinated sense.

After a while, the man asked why they were looking for Amy. He sounded almost protective, as if he feared he might have said too much, and they meant her harm. Andrew still feared the pilot might have harmed her himself. He could have left her buried, her body, like Amelia's, lying in a ditch somewhere that no one would find. But Stella was more trusting than he. Soon they'd been invited to the pilot's hut, where the stranger brewed strong coffee and shared his memories of a girl with angel eyes, a five-year-old's joy, and an adult's comprehension of aviation. "Strange mix," the pilot said. "Strange girl, that little angel. She didn't talk much."

Andrew guessed the man would have talked more than enough for both of them, while the plane flew high. Then he asked again, "Are you sure she wasn't scared?"

"That little angel? Been flying on her own sweet wings all her live-long life. She's a natural, I say."

Somehow it seemed almost blessed to hear that Amy, the strange, un-belonging, broken, never-grown-up, was a *natural*. It was a much more beautiful word than *autistic*.

"See, Dad. See why you had to come here?" said Amelia's bell-like voice.

Andrew held himself back from answering aloud—*You were sending us to Denver, not here*—and simply thought, *See what?*

"See, I wasn't weird and wrong and broken after all. I was natural."

So now his naturally dead daughter insisted Andrew ask where Amy had gone. It turned out her pilot had told her the Grand Canyon was the best place to fly, so she'd walked back along the unmade road to the freeway, happily announcing that she was headed there.

"You let a kid just walk away?" Andrew complained.

"An angel. A woman," the pilot replied. "That one could look after herself." Then he added, "How old is she anyway?"

Meanwhile Stella opened maps on the hood, whispering softly, "The Grand Canyon? Whatever's she going to think of next?"

*****

Andrew wanted to head back into Denver. It was where they'd been going, where dead Amelia had insisted they ought to go. But Stella preferred to press along Route 70. That, of course, begged the unanswerable question: which side of the Grand Canyon might Amy be found on? North Rim, South Rim? Andrew felt sure she'd be floating, like an *angel,* someplace in between, and no decision would be right. Stella insisted *no decision* was the same as wasting time. So they argued—their first real argument as a couple. Was the honeymoon over? But Andrew reminded himself they couldn't be a couple because, if they were, he would surely cause Stella too much pain. He saw the hurt build now in Stella's eyes, as he refused to listen to her.

Sitting together in the car, with the pilot long retired alone to his cabin, they opened the map on Andrew's lap and studied routes to find the fastest one. Andrew studied a guide book as well. Stella studied the sky. But no answer sufficed. It all depended on traffic, while Denver's roads beckoned, notoriously crowded.

"We'll just carry on along here." Stella started the engine.

"But Denver…"

"But nothing. We headed for Denver and ended up here by missing it. We've found her trail, Andrew. We're following Amy. Why would she turn back?"

Since Amy, like Amelia, was determination personified, Andrew had to agree she wasn't likely to backtrack anywhere. But then he thought, as Stella warily steered around potholes to the freeway, none of this was likely. Amy crossing half the country; Amy riding in cars and planes with strangers; Amy somehow finding food and lodging on the way; none of it made sense.

Amy *not* raped, *not* killed, *not* dead in a ditch; Amy *not* picked up by someone who'd abuse her; *not* thrown out of a speeding plane, Amy…

"Andrew," said Stella, as Andrew's angry gaze became glued to the grass beside the road. "Andrew, you're not going to find her in a ditch. Amy's okay. You've got to trust."

"Yeah, like Amelia and Evie trusted me. Like my brother could be trusted. Like my mom and dad." His voice dripped scorn.

But the bell-voice of Amelia demanded to be heard from the back seat of the car. "I'm trusting you now, Daddy. I'm trusting you to find her."

Stella, sweet, persistent and determined, added her own trustful smile.

Flat plains yielded to hills. Day changed to night. Freeway released them to side roads, to canyon drive, to brightly red motel. Andrew yielded to food and pretended to please. But in their tidy room with its one double bed, one bathroom, one hanger for all their clothes, one table and one chair, pretense fell away. He repeated the sordid details of his life to Stella, begging her to leave him and save herself. Instead she sat on the floor at his feet, rested her hand on his knee, and told him what matters is not who you've been, but who you're going to be.

"I don't know who I'm going to be," said Andrew. He didn't even know which route would help them chase the child.

"But I know who you can be."

Andrew sighed. "You can't know that. I don't even know who I am."

"I know," said Stella, beginning, sensuously, to undress him. "I know this bit, and this."

He closed his eyes, accepting her ministrations. But his mind still filled with questions. Was he a failed dad trying to make up for his sins? Failed husband, would he break another heart? Failed teacher, how had he lost a child from the middle of his own classroom? He'd even failed at hiding in the forest as a hobo. Who was he?

Stella repeated, her lips pressed now to the heaving wall of his chest, "I know who you are Andrew. I teach with you. I save you a place at meetings. I drink coffee. And I…" She leaned away and undressed herself as well, no shyness, no awkwardness between them. "I know you Andrew, and I want to know you more, in the Biblical sense."

He lay flat on the bed and smiled up at her.

*****

They woke in their tiny, alien room to blinds wide open, revealing impossible views. Foothills rolled in grays, browns, and greens. Horizons bubbled with purple hills. Coffee came with real mugs instead of paper, and almost real milk in its flimsy foil-topped carton instead of powder. The shower flowed with hot water foaming as two bodies crushed into one. Breakfast could have been lunch and dinner as well.

Stella showed Amy's photos to their waitress. It was second nature now, the thing you do first before getting the credit card out.

The waitress said, "Yeah, sure. I seen the little one. She's a right pretty thing."

Andrew recovered first from the surprise. "You've *seen* her? When? How?"

But the waitress was backing away from them, gesturing with hands held out in front to defend. "Hey, are you some deadbeat ex-husband or something?"

Stella waved her concerns away. "No, of course he's not."

"Then what's she to you? What's with the questions?"

Andrew froze, afraid any moment now he'd be accused of worse. But Stella continued fearlessly. "We're her teachers. She went missing from school. Didn't you see the police reports?"

The waitress' frown of confusion said it all. With tables suddenly turned, she'd become the guilty one for not recognizing her customer's status. But of course she hadn't seen the reports. Who would care about a girl from Illinois out here?

263

Sharp-lipped Stella pushed her advantage. "Who was she traveling with? Did you notice that, at least?"

"Her mom, I thought." The waitress stuttered, feet dancing as if she couldn't wait to escape. "She looked like a little kid with her mom, she did. The kid picture; that's who you're looking for, right? Not the teen? I ain't seen her."

But both were one, and Amy's identity was as mixed as Andrew's. Good little child. Stray teenager. Confident adult. Who was she?

"She was real sweet with her mom, you know. Please and thank you and all that. She can't be missing."

Please and thank you surely sounded like Amy.

"So how old is she? You gonna tell me that? I guessed around ten."

Andrew sighed. The trucker's teen had slipped through time again. Did it all depend on what Amy was wearing, or on who she wanted to be? Had their missing schoolgirl become a chameleon now?

"Dad." Amelia's ringing voice broke through his reverie. "Dad, she's autistic, right. You put your own pictures on her, and decide who you think she is. But inside she's herself."

"Like you are?" He remembered to answer in silence this time, just closing his eyes.

"Yeah. Just like me."

But whoever Amy was traveling with, the waitress assured them she'd seemed happy and safe. So now they knew, she'd gone this way, and it was time to move on.

They paid the check then entered the freeway again. Blacktop hugged low mountainsides, twisting and turning over tree-filled valleys below. Soon shining boulders decked the rising slopes to either side, forming islands of hope. Small streams shone in the blinding sun, while strangled trees grasped onto soil too thin to nourish them. *Go West. Move on.*

Canyons narrowed, hillsides flattened into planar sheets of rock, split and layered like wood. Tunnels beckoned. It was all so beautiful and oddly well-inhabited, with small towns offering more diners where Amy might have stopped, where coffee was drunk, but nobody knew her.

"A sweet girl, very quiet; are you sure you haven't seen her?"

Sympathetic glances made Andrew wonder if people thought the child was Stella's and his, which made him feel scared and guilty again. *Everything I touch, I hurt. My fault. My fault.* Would Amy be dead as the child who really was his?

He prayed fervently that Amy might live—prayed as fervently as anyone who doesn't believe can pray. After all, she was traveling with a mom, whereas Amelia had been in the forest alone. Alone in Paradise, in the park, with busy streets scant yards away, a duck-pond, children's playground, moms, her own mom, coffee, fat man sitting on a hill, and nobody saw her. Just like nobody here had seen Amy.

Amelia had been all alone while her mother called her name, and no one answered. Alone while a man had his evil way with her and disposed of her. Alone and buried under leaves. Andrew's head hung low while mountain peaks rose high around the road, white and triangular, like illustrations in a children's picture book. Mountain passes boasted dangerous corners and ragged cliffs. Mountain snowdrifts slipped to the edge of the road. A child would jump with glee on seeing this; and still they drove. All that mattered now was to safely descend back to the plains, to finish this passage and pick up Amy's wandering trail again.

An airplane crossed the sky above, leaving its white line scratched across the blue. Andrew wondered if Angel Amy might be up there already. But *please, let her not be an angel or a ghost; please let her live.*

*****

Utah's deserts were dead and gray when they crossed the bland State line. Rocks like jagged monsters hunkered down with tangled trees. Red statues masqueraded among the hillocks while the sun beat down. Strange sentinels watched, and distant shadows took shape to form another mountain range.

In the back of the car, Amelia dozed invisibly. Andrew glanced over his shoulder to see her then checked in the mirror instead. He restrained himself from checking his sanity. Who drives halfway across the country with a sleeping ghost for a passenger?

"Would you rather I stay awake?"

She gazed at him now, through the mirror, from clear, bright eyes, suddenly purple hair framing her face in a glorious cloud, and she was beautiful. She was also totally invisible to his real-life passenger. She was also long years dead.

"Do you think she'd have gone all the way?" Stella asked from the passenger seat.

Andrew jumped. "All the way where?"

Stella pointed to billboards flashing past, with pictures of planes and bright words advertising *Scenic Flights*. "Do you think she had the patience to go as far as the canyon to fly? She could have taken a plane from anywhere."

It depended on her driver of course, the mythical mom of Amy's last real sighting, unless she'd switched again. Was Amy still a child or a young woman now, teen or adult? But Andrew agreed they should probably stop and see. Perhaps Amelia would tell them which road to take, though he wouldn't let Stella know who guided his eyes. Meanwhile Amelia nodded happily behind him. He almost smiled, then worried if dead ghosts could really track the living?

"She's fine, Dad. Stop worrying. I wanna see the planes."

They followed a dusty road that seemed scarcely more than a farm track. Its surface was drawn with the same red crayon as the rocks. Stella closed her window against granular inroads of air. Andrew breathed its dirt like penance.

Soon the track wound through pines with picnic tables and scary views over wide open spaces. "Almost like we're flying in the car," said Amelia. She didn't sound thrilled.

"I take it *you* don't plan to fly," Andrew answered.

Stella turned, confused. "We're not here on vacation, Andrew. What do you mean?"

It was hard to explain. *Just talking to my dead daughter again?* New Age and pagan for sure.

Luckily a run-down office shack distracted everyone. Andrew swung the car into something that might have been a parking space and they went inside. Andrew and Stella went inside, that is, while Andrew kept turning back to look at the car, wondering if Amelia would wave to him through the window. Instead he found her waiting on a bench in the office. He crooked Stella's elbow in his hand, steering her to an emptier seat.

"Help ya?" asked a greasy-haired woman, bobbing up from behind the counter.

Andrew said he hoped so. "We're looking for a missing girl."

Stella took the pictures from her purse and the woman laughed. "Oh sure. She came in here okay. All on her own, she was. A runaway?"

Stella answered, "Sort of. She ran off from school."

"Really? Like one of those special schools, ya mean? Schools for the disturbed, like? She a wrong'un?"

Andrew struggled for words, but the woman's voice ran on. "Knew there was something bad about that girl. Could see it in her eyes."

Something bad about Amy? No way.

"She's autistic," Stella explained.

"Ought-istic, right. That's a new 'un on me. Ought to do as they're told, these kids these days. Ought-istic, I'll remember that one." She slapped her thigh and laughed.

"No," said Stella. "Autistic's, like, an illness. I expect that's what you saw, that she's not quite like other folk. But she's sweet as they come."

Amelia made a gagging sound and threatened to strangle herself. *Okay, not that sweet,* thought Andrew. But the woman was speaking again, insistently. "Nah, nah, too soft on 'em they are. She's bad to the bone, that girl, if she's the one we saw."

Perhaps she was thinking of someone else. Andrew asked what Amy had done.

"Threatened me, she did. Picked up a knife and threatened me."

Amy with a knife? Amelia gestured a gun against her head and pretended to die, flopping sideways on the bench.

"Said she wanted to fly, and I was going to take her, as if I would."

The woman didn't look much like a pilot to Andrew, but would Amy know the difference?

"Kept saying it. No stopping her, and she were gonna kill me, for sure, she were."

Stella's fingers closed around a decorated letter-opener, blunt and shiny, lying on the counter. She asked, all innocence, rolling the blade across her hand, "What was she going to kill you with?"

"Now, don't you start, you madam…"

"Start what?"

"No need to threaten…"

Amelia rolled on the floor now, clutching her sides with teenage mirth. Even Andrew felt a smile twitch over his lips. But Stella, ever cool and calm, held the letter opener out, almost a knife, like Amy's knife, and asked, "So, did your pilot take her up?"

"Sure he did. Can't resist the sight of a bad girl, him."

She's not a bad girl! Andrew held his tongue while Stella continued, all silkily calm, "And did he bring her down again."

"Of course."

"So do you know where she is now?"

It was too much to hope. Amy had arrived here all alone— *How*, Andrew wondered? Did her fake mommy not want to drive her down the dusty track? Or did Amy demand to be left behind somewhere? He tried to imagine the scene: a worried driver, an innocent child, pretending to be all grown up, an argument, a tantrum perhaps, and the driver speeding away, afraid she might have done something wrong in offering the ride. Then sweet, shy Amy would beg for a flight, would tour the canyon's glory, and be left alone on foot while the pilot, who could have driven her, stayed to clean his plane. At least that's what the pilot's associate claimed.

Andrew clenched his fists with familiar fear. Had the pilot really let her go? And had she really been safe, walking all alone, back down the track, all the way to the busy road? They'd missed her, just by days. They'd missed her again.

"Did she say where she was going?" Andrew asked over his shoulder as they left the office.

"Just West. That's all she said. Just going West. Wrong 'un, that girl."

*****

West takes the traveler from airports of scenic flights to Bryce and Zion, and the Canyon's North Rim. Had Amy flown over them all? Would she have taken a detour, still silent Amy, to see the still, silent statues of Bryce, all arrayed in red rock, capped in white, all looking up through the forests of the night? Would she have demanded a side trip to Zion, to splash in clear, running water and let the green grass grow between her toes? Amelia didn't say no, but their detours yielded no clues, just more days gone by. The world's most glorious scenery hardly broke into Andrew's mood. He couldn't get bad-girl Amy out of his mind. What was happening to her?

Amelia mimed smoking, mimed drinking, mimed injecting something into her arm, then laughed when Andrew drew in furious breath. "Cool it, Dad. She's okay. I'm teasing you." But how could anyone know? Meanwhile his dead teen daughter grew older every day. Where was the innocent, invisible one? This almost-woman sat proud in the back seat for everyone to see, except that Stella still couldn't see her. "Chill Dad. You gotta let go." Then Stella asked why he was holding the steering wheel so tight.

"What about the Grand Canyon. Would she have tried to get there?"

Too many detours wore him down, but Amelia demanded to see. "Come on, Dad. I didn't live long enough. You have to take me."

"We're looking for Amy."

"Yes, I know," said Stella.

A white cat strolled from the undergrowth, causing Andrew to stomp on the brakes. He and Stella jerked forward in their seats. Amelia simply lay back luxuriously, because she wasn't really there. The cat walked along the center line to the junction, turned right, and followed signs to *Grand Canyon North Rim*; so Andrew sighed and signaled, following it.

"They're ice bowls," Stella read from a guide book while Andrew drove through unlikely forests into circles of green. "The lumps of ice melted, and left dish-shaped depressions in the ground. Lots of good minerals to feed the soil, so they turn into circular pastures."

Andrew didn't like forests. They reminded him too much of life and death—Amelia's death and his half-life of hiding when he thought he couldn't go on. But Evie had found him. And Evie had let him go. Evie had handed him to Stella.

Surely Stella's days of happiness must be numbered, Andrew thought, because he loved her. He loved the sound of her voice; he loved to hear her reciting natural history from the book; he loved the feel of her hand, cool and gentle on his arm; he loved her scent filling the car.

"And don't you love me?" Amelia asked.

"I love you," said Andrew.

Stella smiled. "I love you too."

Blue skies misted over to gray. Stella slept, while Andrew drove on. "You see, Dad," Amelia explained lugubriously, "I'm a woman now and I know what a woman wants, so I'm helping you out. She needs to hear you say you love her, not just guess it from tiny hints that you think are so obvious, 'cause you're just a man. She needs to be sure."

"Everyone who loves me dies," Andrew replied.

"Oh sure. Make me worry about my Mom. She loved you Dad, and she's very much alive."

He nodded. True.

"And Amy kind of likes you, in her own way. And she's not dead."

"Glad to hear it." Andrew choked on a laugh. "Did you ever kind of like me?"

"I never even knew you, Dad. What do you think this is all about?"

"Finding Amy?" What else could it be?

"Finding me as well, you dunce. And finding you."

"What's that meant to mean?"

He steered them carefully through the barrier to the park while Amelia replied. "You have to love yourself, Dad. You have to stop pretending you can't be trusted because of me. You have to let go."

"What if I don't want to let go of you?"

She leaned forward, dead breath cold as ice on the back of his neck. "You will, Dad. You will. When the time is right."

The canyon opened out—a glimpse at the side, through trees; an impossible expanse; then wider, wider; then more. He turned the car around at the lodge and drove down a narrow road between the trees, looking for hope. At last he stopped. Staring. The ground dropped away in a long winding scar. The far side hid and blinked in mist, painted landscape of death, the other edge of a massive hole in the ground. His mind absorbed a jagged tear, a child ripped from reality, a woman torn in two, and a gaping emptiness where a life was meant to be lived. He imagined Amy's wounded brain this way, messages unable to bridge the gap; no wonder she was strange. Then he looked at Amelia's ghost, quite normal now. Had time or death healed her?

*****

At the lodge, they said a girl like Amy had ridden with her family down the slope. "Is there a problem?" they asked, when Andrew jumped back with a cry. But Amelia was smiling and whispered under her breath, "Lucky Amy, don't you think?" so Andrew almost accepted that she was maybe okay, that the family she'd adopted would care for her, and he'd see her soon again.

"When do they get back?" he asked.

"Oh no," said the assistant. "They booked to cross the river and climb up the other side."

So they'd missed her, again.

Andrew pulled away from the desk, compelled by an urgent need to return to the car and drive on. But Amelia, carrying her backpack and looking, for all her invisibility, like just another student tourist, stood behind him and made him halt. Stella tightened her vice-like grip on his arm. "We'll need a place to stay for the night," she said to the smiling attendant. "Do you have any vacancies?"

"Have you booked?"

Andrew almost stomped his foot. Of course they hadn't booked. But Stella's voice stayed calm and collected, while she asked if there'd been any cancellations. She agreed to return later.

"It's Sunday, isn't it?" she added. "Do you have any services?"

Andrew groaned. Was she suggesting they drive to a church, instead of driving on to the South Rim?

"Do you have any idea how far that is to drive?" Amelia asked, rolling her eyes.

Meanwhile the attendant pointed to a room just beyond the lobby. "You're just in time," he said. "Starts in ten minutes."

Andrew wanted to leave and start that endless loop to the South side of the canyon. But Stella said it was too late for them to drive anywhere. "We'd end up stuck with nowhere to stay for the night, Andrew." Though they were already stuck in the middle of nowhere. She told him to look around and let the scenery calm him. He looked around. He saw a massive hole. She told him to witness the glory of God's creation, but all he felt was the terror of Amy falling, falling, falling, and moving ever further and further away. Stella said they should go in to worship, as if he wasn't an unbeliever after all.

The room was laid out with lightly upholstered chairs in long, straight rows. Andrew and Stella sat together with an empty seat beside them. Sometimes Andrew saw Amelia sitting there; sometimes no one. He wondered what other people saw, but everyone's eyes were glued to the vista beyond the plate glass window; wide open skies with wisps of cloud or smoke; brave survivalist trees, unless their twisted limbs were dead; rock walls all striped and colored with metals and age, or else decay; and behind them, through the other window, the lonely painted desert, smooth as a palette swirled with colors still waiting to be used—smooth as the palette of Amy's unfinished life.

Canned music played, but all Andrew heard were the memories of students saying, "I bet she's dead." The pastor prayed with cannily musical words, but Andrew's head was filled with accusations and despair. Stella held his hand and gazed in awe. Andrew held hers and tried not to scream. None of this was real. Then everyone jumped at the sound an animal's squeal.

Andrew turned. The door behind them, plate glass like everything else, hung open. In the lobby, figures backed away from the desk. A white cat, large and fluffy and bold, had its small mouth wrapped tightly around a massive snake. Limbs thrashed and whirled. The snake's strong body sinuously twined and turned, but the cat held on. Drips of blood splashed outward from the alien dance. Cries and gasps resounded all around. Chairs squeaked, pushed back by panicked occupants retreating on the polished floor.

Stella stayed still, but Andrew pushed forward, afraid for himself, for Amy, Amelia and the cat. But the battle was suddenly over. One final shake. A thud. And the snake lay dead. It seemed to shrivel straight away, smaller in its lifeless state, as if it could never really have been a threat. Andrew turned to smile at Stella. Then the doors were closed, and the creatures were gone away.

Outside, through the plate glass window, a great hole loomed, cutting today from tomorrow, cutting Andrew from his anchors, forward and back. He felt himself falling, but Stella wrapped her arms around him, while Amelia whispered softly, "Dad, it's okay. She's going to be okay."

*****

In the morning, Andrew woke with the sun. The air was scented with smoke and pine. The cabin was cold. And the white cat sitting on the doormat looked like perhaps it belonged to the lodge. Stella bent to pet it. Andrew smiled and turned to ask Amelia if this was the same white cat that had brought them together, invading their motel room. But Amelia wasn't there.

Of course, he thought. Amelia was never really there. Amelia was dead; a ghost; a figment of an overactive, overly guilty imagination. Amelia wasn't real, neither child, teen, nor student. Amelia was a dream.

"I am so, real," said the voice in his head, and he almost fell as the cat launched its furry body against his bare ankles. Perhaps he should get dressed.

"Breakfast?" Stella suggested, lifting her clothes from the chair where she'd left them last night. "If we eat a good meal at the lodge, we'll be fine to drive on."

Andrew pulled on clothes then pulled out the maps. He wondered what was fine about their route. Backtracking, all of it. They should have come via Moab and Bluff and Kayenta. Or they should never have tried.

The cat followed them to the lodge then sat outside. When they checked out they found it waiting still, and when they opened the car it jumped into the back.

*****

Stella drove. She said she felt more awake, revived by their rest, while Andrew's eyes and body felt heavy, as if his hopes had fallen into the hole along with Amy. He imagined her riding her donkey, falling, falling, falling, while Stella said they'd know if anything happened. "We'd see the helicopters, the rescue and all that." Or they'd miss them because they were driving back toward Utah, back to the junction where they could choose another path.

The journey was too long of course. Andrew knew they'd miss her again but said nothing. Meanwhile Amelia sat with the cat in the back of the car. It seemed this cat, at least, was real; Stella could see it. Which meant they had to feed it, so Stella stopped to fill the car and bought cat food in the supermarket. Meanwhile Andrew sat and tried to believe he wasn't lost or insane.

Amelia had grown up now. She didn't lay or slouch. She sat with the strap neatly fastened over her legs, safe and sound, and still singularly dead. When Andrew counted the years, he knew her ghost was approaching the age his daughter would have been if she hadn't died. It made him feel old. She told him, "That's because you are old, Dad." It didn't help.

The South Rim village was dusty and dry. The South Rim road was a track to nowhere. The four hour drive had led them to emptiness, and still a great hole loomed in the ground ahead and the life behind.

*****

"Yes, I remember her," said the man in the gift shop. "Bought a picture for her mom, but then she didn't have any money so the mother paid for her."

"I remember her," said the woman, standing guard over the donkeys. "Looked like death warmed up, but you should have seen her face, so filled with life. She was petrified, but she'd really enjoyed that ride."

"I remember her," said the attendant in the parking lot. "Thought she was with her mom, but she was just a hitchhiker. Went off with some guy."

"Did nobody stop her?" Andrew asked, his voice tight in his throat.

"No. Why?"

He closed his eyes and saw her body again, covered in a dusting of sand because there were no leaves. Stella held his hand to keep him calm. The cat yowled from the car. And Amelia's voice demanded, "We need to go."

Was this it, Andrew wondered. Had Amy found her final guide at last? Was this the guy who would kill her?

"No," said Amelia. "But we do need to go."

"Go where?"

Stella answered him. "Go West, I guess."

*****

Andrew drove now but hardly saw their route. They stopped at every rest stop, drank too much coffee, and asked too many questions. Amy had ridden with this man and that, on a bike, in a sports car, in the cab with a truck driver. She'd looked okay. She'd looked old. She hadn't looked like a runaway. Didn't the pictures on her backpack give her away? But it was scuffed and gray.

Where was she going? "West."

But where? "LA?"

"Nah, not LA," said the men in Barstow, sitting at a table near the bar. The sound of the train still rattled the windows—Andrew felt like he'd followed it for years, while tracks trailed the road. The mournful hoot was the pall over Amy's grave.

"Not LA?" Andrew turned, two coffees held in hand. He'd just been showing Amy's picture to the guy behind the bar. Now he set the coffees in front of Stella and showed it to other locals. "You sure it's her?"

"Sure we are. We told her LA's too big and scary for the likes of her, so she went with Jake."

"Went where?"

"San Francisco of course. Leastaways, that's where our Jake's headed. She's riding in his cab."

Would San Francisco be any less big and scary for the likes of an autistic runaway? And what would *our Jake* do to her?

*****

Andrew wanted to drive on, and on, and on. "We're on her tail. We're close. We have to go."

But Stella demanded they wait for another day. Barstow was a big enough place. There were plenty of motels where they could stay, and they'd get an early start.

"But what if…?"

"Andrew, why do you keep imagining the worst?"

"Because…"

"Because of me," said Amelia, "but there's lots of good people in the world as well. You have to learn to trust them."

Stella continued. "I know what happened to your daughter, but there are lots of good people in the world as well. You have to learn to trust them."

He trusted no one but Stella, and Amelia perhaps, but his daughter had disappeared again, and so had the cat.

*****

"We'll stop at every rest area, every restaurant, everywhere," Andrew insisted as he handed the car keys over to Stella. The Mojave's white sand burned his eyes. Its blue skies weighed as heavy as the grave. Houses hunkered flat to the ground as if they were trying to hide. Even the hotels here hadn't dared stand tall, painted red and cream against the desert's white and gray. Now Barstow disappeared behind, and there was nothing, the world like a canvas waiting to be colored, or one washed clean.

"It's green," said Stella. "The plants are green. It's not all white and gray."

The plants were almost non-existent and the wide, fast road had shrunk to a two-lane highway from nowhere to forever.

Rumbling wheels, softly snoring cat—but hadn't it disappeared just hours ago?—Stella's music, played too low, all lulled him to sleep. He woke briefly in a forest of metal pylons then closed his eyes again. Air-breaks shrieking brought him back to awareness, and a sign read *Coyotes, Turtles* and *Donkeys*. Trucks were stopped all around. Stella was filling the car with gas. A small market beckoned with food and conversation. They'd seen Amy. She was with *some guy*. Andrew wanted to cry.

*****

Stella claimed the hills were beautiful. She thought the Joshua trees were amazing—"Like bonsais all grown up." She loved the wind farms—"So elegant." And the train reminded her of a train set her brother used to play with. "He made these hills from blankets over polystyrene," she explained. "He built these little houses and things." But there were no houses here, and no trees until Bakersfield, where they stopped again, and nobody had seen her.

Andrew drove for a while. Could North for Sacramento really be right? Had he lost his way as well as losing the child? But traffic lights beckoned; restaurants too many to check; signposts showed the way. "Will we ever get out of here?" he complained.

Suddenly the road was wide, and the desert was empty again. Stella took the keys. "You could sleep in the back seat," she offered, when Andrew's head nodded heavily against his chest. But he couldn't. The back seat was occupied by Amelia and the cat.

~15~

Andrew's stomach floundered with the falling and flying of sleep. He opened his eyes, suddenly awake and afraid, when the car leapt over a hill, leaving his last meal far behind. Vistas of buildings towered over deep blue waters ahead and below. But the road fell into a hole, water vanished, and he shook lank hair out from his eyes. *Asleep? Awake?* He wasn't quite sure which he was.

"San Francisco?" he asked, gasping as breath and memory shifted into focus. "Is this San Francisco?" His ears pounded, and his throat felt like sandpaper, scraping the meaning from words. Ahead he spotted the Bay Bridge shining in glory, or was it the other one? He couldn't find the syllables to inquire. Wondering when his eyesight had grown so dim, he decided he was old.

"You are old, Dad." Amelia confirmed his verdict. "I told you that."

Andrew laughed. All teachers are old. He looked at his hands and wondered when those veins would start poking out, true signs of decrepitude. Then he glanced across the car at Stella, driving, not a wrinkle in sight. But why was she in the driver's seat, not him? And how had they come so far?

The road dropped into a slow, well-managed dip, then lifted up in a climb. Andrew clutched the door handle for safety and stared at colors, shapes and sizes. San Francisco, painted like modern art! He'd gone West—*old man*—for sure. But the cause of finding Amy seemed even more hopeless than before. How would you find a missing adult-child in these leaping avenues? Lose one more likely. He shook his head under the weight of scudding gray clouds. Maybe it was time to admit young Amy was lost and dead after all.

"But she's not."

Meanwhile, "You're awake," said Stella, her gaze still fastened to the road, her wrists tight bound to the steering wheel.

Andrew shrugged his shoulders. "Sure, but why?"

"Why what?"

"Why are we here? Why did we try? Why everything?" When Stella didn't answer, he continued. "Why didn't we stop along the way? Rest area or something. How did we get here?" He ran out of breath.

"We did stop." Stella's voice was patient, kind even, as if she thought he were a child.

"When? Where?"

Instead of answering, Stella pulled on the steering wheel to wend their path around another corner. Andrew resisted the urge to slam his foot down onto non-existent brakes. He wasn't the driver. He was meant to trust the driver, and he did trust her. But he also knew she hated driving in towns. Why hadn't she stopped to change over?

"Did someone say something, back when we stopped?" His head pounded. He couldn't remember. Why were they hurrying?

"No."

"So why? Why the rush?" They pushed the speed limit with every turn.

Stella's eyes flicked briefly toward him, then back to the road again. She pulled out sharply to pass a stationary truck, slipped around, and neatly paralleled the rough edge of the curb. "It's where we were going, Andrew." Her voice was achingly sweet. "It's San Francisco, where Amy was going. It's the end of the trail. It's the coast. It's what *you* said: *Go West*."

But it wasn't *he* that said it. *Amy* had said *Go West*, and he'd never even heard her. Bleak Julia's smoky cough had repeated the words like rusted iron grafted onto her throat. So Andrew and Stella had set off on this trip; they'd driven across the country, West, through so many different places, meeting and talking with strangers, showing Amy's photo and hoping and praying. Okay, perhaps he hadn't prayed so much, but Stella had. The car rushed on.

"It's hopeless, isn't it?" Andrew muttered now. "We'll never find her. No matter how soon we get there."

"Not hopeless." Stella veered around another corner, the motion flinging Andrew against the door again.

"Someone's taken her. Bound to have. She hasn't a hope in this place. She's better off dead."

Stella swerved again before answering. "People are good, Andrew. They're not all bad; you've got to know that by now. Someone will have helped her out again, just like everywhere else."

So why were they rushing? He couldn't—he wouldn't—believe in goodness though. The road's roller-coaster would lead like Amy's trail, inevitably down; hills to nowhere; conversations to silence; ocean depths tending only to despair.

Then the white cat purred. Andrew turned to look over his shoulder. He'd forgotten it was there, but now it lay on its blanket across the back seat, white fur against dark weave, slipping and sliding as the car continued its tangled, swerving route. Andrew half-thought Amelia would be seated beside it. He couldn't remember when he'd last seen her now. Had she spoken recently? But she was dead too, as Amy would surely prove to be.

Perhaps the cat had guided them at the last rest stop, dancing across white, stony ground, selecting another stranger for Stella to question about Amy, another man with a message from a missing child? "Sweet girl. Yeah. Quiet. On the back of some guy's motorbike." Some guy. Some other guy... Had there been danger then?

Andrew remembered strangers, all along the way, who'd claimed they might have seen the missing child. It seemed the cat might have guided them, so perhaps its purring now was a hopeful sign.

"Cat's happy at least," he said, smiling cautiously at Stella.

"The cat?" She barely turned her head. Her hands still gripped the wheel like they were trapped in a vice. "The cat disappeared ages ago. Don't you remember?" Her voice seemed tight, so Andrew glanced back again, and it was gone.

*****

With no cat, the purring seeming wrongly loud and intrusive. Was somebody's motorbike revving for the road? Andrew grabbed the door handle again as Stella swung around another corner, unexpectedly. "What was that?"

She shook loose strands of hair from her eyes. "Gah," she muttered. "Some stupid, suicidal, white cat in the road."

But now a shiny, red bike rode in front of them, with billowing exhaust and violently purple trim. A halo of white hair ringed the rider's helmet. Andrew asked if Stella was following him.

"Dunno. Maybe." Stella shook her head again. "I think it's what the cat wants me to do." *The cat again.*

Andrew sighed. Perhaps they were both of them crazy now, or else all three of them if you counted the feline, four with the ghost. They'd crossed the country in search of a missing child who couldn't possibly have done all the things claimed of her; an autistic who seemed like an adult; a girl with her mother; a teenager in a plane? A mysterious feline had hitchhiked with them, slept in their motel room, stolen their bed, and drawn them both together. Insanity rules—Andrew laughed out loud—and they claimed Shy Amy was the one whose brain didn't work. So now…

The white cat yowled—*outside or in?*

Stella pulled on the wheel again while Andrew grabbed at the dash. "What?" he shrieked.

"Gotta follow the cat."

The back of the car was empty, with just a few stray hairs shining white as sunshine on the blanket's weave. But sudden light glowed outside the car, warm as amber, pouring through glass, glistening with silver crystals of wildly shifting salt. "Where are we?" Andrew asked. He gazed ahead again.

"At the coast," said Stella, unhelpfully. The bike still roared, while ocean's blue lit up under cobwebbed sky, while seagulls streaked and cried. Andrew tried to ask which part of the coast, but Stella didn't know. She'd seen no signs, too busy chasing the cat, but she thought there might be piers. "There are meant to be some piers, aren't there, in San Francisco?"

The cat had somehow returned to the back of the car. It announced its presence by scrambling with sharpened claws over Andrew's shoulder and into his lap. It spat and snarled, drew droplets of red that blossomed on Andrew's leg, then swished its hair-covered tail across his mouth before slamming its arched back under his chin.

Andrew shrieked in surprise. Stella swore beside him, stomping on the brake just as Andrew's foot slammed down in helpless frustration. The car jerked to a halt and Andrew snatched the door handle, pushing it wide so he could stagger out. The curb tripped him forward. A pier's long wooden planks stretched widely ahead, providing a curious racetrack for the flying cat which fled, while Andrew pressed hands down on bleeding thighs.

"Andrew," Stella cried.

He tried to turn, intending to answer her, but his feet had leapt into motion before his mind. Legs shrieking with pain, though his mouth was silent now, he followed the cat.

Wooden planks rang to the thud of Andrew's shoes. Behind him, car horns blared on the road. Voices shouted. Angry strangers might possibly come to blows, all because Stella had stopped on the wrong part of the road. He knew it, felt distantly sorry, but all that mattered now lay ahead, the cat's swift motion demanding his fullest attention. Andrew watched it leap over ropes and tackle. He jumped and tripped and staggered upright again. The cat swung wide around a broken-down shack, paws snick-snacking as they skidded on standing water, till they found their grip and hurried on again. Meanwhile Andrew slammed his hand against the wall, drawing blood from knuckles to match the drops on his knees. Fur flew out in a ball of fury from the cat's arched back. Black doors beckoned.

Andrew swung his gaze from side to side. They were over the water now, waves bawling below as seagulls swooped and cried, as the cat ran on. Breathlessness bellowed in his ears. Forget the car and Stella. Forget the journey. Forget it all, it seemed. Just follow the cat, whoever, whatever, wherever it happened to be; the cat whose yowl of rage and despair had finally finished him. Unhinged, he felt his arms and legs like rubber. The fur ball fled.

"Run, Daddy!" Bell-tones sounded again in his ear, dead Amelia driving him on. "Now, Daddy. Run. You're nearly there." He ran.

It didn't seem strange anymore to hear his daughter's voice. But Andrew flailed to a halt, because he'd lost sight of the cat. Then he saw its white flash skitter beside a door.

"Daddy. Save her!"

The door was closed. Andrew body-slammed against it, pressing his arm on the handle, but it was locked. Where was the cat?

"Daddy! Now!"

So he stepped back, theatrically swinging his leg, feeling as false as a movie character fallen from the screen. This surely wouldn't work, but he kicked as hard as he could with the side of his heel. He rammed his shoulder into wood again. Still the door didn't move.

"Daddy, please!"

Distant voices, even the cries of seagulls, receded. The world shrank down to a single, wooden door filling its splintered frame. Andrew heard a muffled squeak behind the door's still planks; a man's sharp retort. He stepped back again and charged furiously. The cat charged too. Fur flew between Andrew's ankles as wooden planks splintered apart. He hoped he wouldn't trip over the cat. Then he was inside.

Darkness flowed around him, holding him still. A sour smell poured like old water tipped from a jar. A figure, giant-like, loomed from shadows and gloom. But Andrew knew what to do. He rammed his body into the giant, knocking him over in the gap between a wooden table and ragged wall. A child lay on the table, her form just beginning to appear as sunlight dripped in. Half-unclothed, she whimpered helplessly. The man stormed to his feet.

Andrew tightened his fist. He'd set himself up for a curious fight and had no idea how to proceed. But he placed his body between the man and child and prepared to stand his ground. Then the cat slipped between his feet, flashed upward, and slashed its claws at the man's bearded face.

Monster Man rushed forward. Andrew felt his body flail, pushed by a battering ram that threatened to topple him. He slipped, staggered, stood, and wondered why his blooded body wasn't hurting more. He heard voices then footsteps outside and felt the movement of people beginning to fill the dark shack's gloom, the presence of strangers arriving to help as he firmly stood his ground. Then a hand on his shoulder drew him back and set him against a wall. Someone said, "Sir," while other words drifted past, unheard. He noticed distant action, and couldn't tell if it was close to him. Silence roared through his head until nothing made sense. He couldn't see. The light was wrong, as if it were painted in gray with rainbows behind. Shadows, patterns, times, places and people all intertwined, with nothing solid, except the weight of the white cat leaning on his leg, purring, constantly purring, its engine soothingly calm and smoothly content. He bent down to stroke it.

"Are you okay sir?" said a stranger's voice, more clearly now as Andrew straightened to see.

"Yes, I'm fine."

"Your leg okay?"

Andrew watched the cat as its image faded. Was it ever really there? Then he nodded. "Yeah, I'm fine."

In front of him, Amy heaved herself awkwardly upright on the makeshift bed. The strange man gave her a blanket for her nakedness. She seemed uncertain what to do with it. She didn't thank him. She didn't look at him. Then Andrew coughed— dust from the cloth or from the room he supposed. Amy's eyes became fixed on him, focused and clear, while Amelia's bell-like voice spoke softly from somewhere behind her left ear.

"Thank you, Dad. You did it. She's okay now."

Was Amy okay, Andrew wondered. Would she ever be okay, or was she forever scarred by sudden abuse, by terror at the end of her glorious road? The kindness of strangers had followed her all this way, but not far enough. His shoulders heaved.

"She's okay, Dad. So am I."

Just for a moment it seemed as if two girls sat together on the wooden table, one wrapped in a blanket, the other dressed in an elegant robe of leaves. The cat jumped up and sat itself between them.

"Dad?"

"Yes."

"It's time for me to go now."

"Time?" He wasn't sure he recalled the meaning of the word.

"It's time to say goodbye, Dad. Now. Goodbye."

Bright light burst into flowers behind Amelia. Her figure, so small and sweet, so well-remembered and so recently forgotten, started to fade. One childish, white hand raised to wave one sweet, final farewell. Her lips curled in a contented smile.

When Andrew reached out to grasp her, he touched only air. No one was there; just Amy stroking a fat, white cat, which wriggled onto her lap. She smiled as well. Then Andrew stumbled and fell onto the table beside her. He sat down awkwardly, hoping his sudden move hadn't frightened her. "Are you alright, Amy?" he asked.

The policeman answered, "I think you got to her in time." Then Stella slipped through the doorway into Andrew's line of sight. She crouched in front of him, wrapped her arms around his waist, rested her head on the red-stained fabric of his jeans, and sighed. "We found her Andrew."

"Yes, we did."

He wasn't sure why, but he started to cry.

Part 7

~16~

Another year. Another classroom. The tables and the students stayed the same.

Andrew walked to the front warily, unsure how they would greet him after summer's break—as enemy or friend.

"Good morning, class." It was better than calling them children. "We've got lots of exciting topics on our schedule this year."

"Yeah, sure," said Jonah the Whale, who had lost so much weight he looked almost healthy now.

"Well, we have."

"We're glad you're back," croaked Julie, her voice still throaty, her fingers still stained with nicotine.

"Yeah, sorta," confessed Angry Tom. "Where's Amy gone."

Tom pointed to Amy's empty desk, and Andrew felt his chest puff out with pride. He'd seen Amy in the corridor outside just moments before—Amy with notebook and pencil in hand, backpack swinging merrily from her arm; Amy strolling with every semblance of student confidence. A *higher math* student now, grown out of Andrew's care, she shared just the faintest smile of recognition as she passed.

Andrew told them where she was and class clown Zeke pumped a triumphant arm in the air. "Good for her, Sir. Good for her."

Andrew nodded. "Work hard at it, and you guys could move up into higher math too. You're clever enough."

"But would anyone else cope with us, Sir? What do you think?"

The door rattled as a second teacher walked in and pronounced, "Good morning, class."

The students chanted back to her. "Good morning, Mrs. Callaghan."

Then Clown Zeke bowed down on his knees in front of Julie's desk. "Marry me!" he declaimed, while Julie tapped the top of his head with a pencil.

"Calm down, class," said Andrew and Stella together, their voices musically one.

Andrew's phone beeped a message, and he hoped the students hadn't heard its illegal sound. Under cover of his desk he read Evie's note: "Good luck to you both." He almost heard Amelia laughing again, and life was good.

I hope you've enjoyed your visit to Paradise and beyond.
If you want to learn more…

discover the neighborhood in **Divide by Zero**
and meet Sylvia, who struggled to forgive herself in
Infinite Sum.

If you want to help the author, please recommend this novel to
your friends and leave a book review.

And thank you for reading **Subtraction**.